PRAISE FOR JOEL C. ROSENBERG

"Rosenberg's imagination is a tumultuous place where Middle Eastern geopolitics combine with devious minds. Authentic, fast-paced, and totally engrossing."

KYLE MILLS, #1 *New York Times* bestselling author of *Total Power*

"Rosenberg once again proves to be at the top of his game. . . . The plot is all too possible. Marcus Ryker is a perfect hero, right where we need him, at just the right time. *The Beirut Protocol* will take your breath away as Rosenberg marches to the brink of a war only Ryker can stop—if he can save himself first!"

ANDREWS & WILSON, bestselling authors of the Tier One, Sons of Valor, and Shepherds series

"Nobody builds tension and suspense like Rosenberg, who has quickly developed his hero Marcus Ryker into one of the most formidable action stars the genre has to offer. . . . Fast, twist-filled, and ripped-from-the-headlines, *The Beirut Protocol* soars with authenticity and will leave readers breathless. At this point, Rosenberg's stuff is pretty much mandatory reading for all lovers of high-octane thrillers."

RYAN STECK, *The Real Book Spy*

"A taut, brilliant thriller ripped right from today's headlines. Joel Rosenberg is masterful! *The Jerusalem Assassin* is an absolute home run."

BRAD THOR, #1 *New York Times* bestselling author of *Backlash*

"Gripping. . . . Readers will tear through the final pages to see whether Marcus can once again triumph over evil."

PUBLISHERS WEEKLY on *The Jerusalem Assassin*

"Joel C. Rosenberg continues to mix his unique blend of prophetic fiction and nonstop action unlike anyone else working t

THE REAL BOOK SPY on *The Persian Gamble*

"Joel C. Rosenberg writes taut, intelligent thrillers that are as timely as they are well-written. Pairing a fast-paced plot with an impressive understanding of the inner workings in the corridors of power of the Russian government, *The Kremlin Conspiracy* is a stellar novel of riveting action and political intrigue."

MARK GREANEY, #1 *New York Times* bestselling author of *Agent in Place*

"*The Kremlin Conspiracy* is my first Joel C. Rosenberg novel, and I am absolutely blown away by how good this guy is. The story moves at a blistering pace, it's crackling with tension, and you won't put it down until you reach the end. Guaranteed. Simply masterful."

SEAN PARNELL, *New York Times* bestselling author of *Outlaw Platoon*

"Rosenberg cranks up the suspense, delivering his most stunning, high-stakes thriller yet."

PUBLISHERS WEEKLY on *The Kremlin Conspiracy*

"Joel Rosenberg has an uncanny talent for focusing his storytelling on real-world hot spots just as they are heating up. He has done it again in *The Kremlin Conspiracy*."

PORTER GOSS, former director of the Central Intelligence Agency

"Marcus Ryker rocks! Breakneck action, political brinksmanship, authentic scenarios, and sharply defined characters make Joel C. Rosenberg's *Kremlin Conspiracy* a full-throttle and frightening ride through tomorrow's headlines."

BRIGADIER GENERAL (U.S. ARMY, RETIRED) A. J. TATA, national bestselling author of *Direct Fire*

"If you love the ABC drama *Designated Survivor* or are always looking for the next well-written novel about America and her fight against terrorism, you'll definitely want to pick up *Without Warning*."

BOOK REPORTER

"A compelling and complicated political thriller that includes an edge-of-your-seat climax—impossible to put down."

MIDWEST BOOK REVIEW on *The First Hostage*

THE LIBYAN DIVERSION

"Rosenberg has ripped a page from current headlines with a heart-stopping plot about the Islamic State."

PUBLISHERS WEEKLY on *The Third Target*

"If there were a *Forbes* 400 list of great current novelists, Joel Rosenberg would be among the top ten. . . . One of the most entertaining and intriguing authors of international political thrillers in the country. . . . His novels are un-put-downable."

STEVE FORBES, editor in chief, *Forbes* magazine

"[Joel Rosenberg] understands the grave dangers posed by Iran and Syria, and he's been a bold and courageous voice for true peace and security in the Middle East."

DANNY AYALON, former Israeli deputy foreign minister

"Joel has a particularly clear understanding of what is going on in today's Iran and Syria and the grave threat these two countries pose to the rest of the world."

REZA KAHLILI, former CIA operative in Iran and bestselling author of *A Time to Betray: The Astonishing Double Life of a CIA Agent inside the Revolutionary Guards of Iran*

"His novels seem to be ripped from the headlines—next year's headlines."

WASHINGTON TIMES

"Rip-roaring, heart-pounding, page-turning, high-octane, geopolitical thriller."

FORBES on *The Last Days*

"An action-packed, Clancyesque political thriller."

PUBLISHERS WEEKLY on *The Last Days*

"A wild, rocketing read. *The Last Jihad* is Tom Clancy writ large."

VINCE FLYNN, *New York Times* bestselling author of *Consent to Kill*

JOEL C.
ROSENBERG

THE LIBYAN DIVERSION

Tyndale House Publishers
Carol Stream, Illinois

Visit Tyndale online at tyndale.com.

Visit Joel C. Rosenberg's website at joelrosenberg.com.

Tyndale and Tyndale's quill logo are registered trademarks of Tyndale House Ministries.

The Libyan Diversion

Designed by Dean H. Renninger

For information about special discounts for bulk purchases, please contact Tyndale House Publishers at csresponse@tyndale.com or call 1-855-277-9400.

Library of Congress Cataloging-in-Publication Data

A catalog record for this book is available from the Library of Congress.

ISBN 978-1-4964-3794-5 (hardcover)
ISBN 978-1-4964-7897-9 (International Trade Paper Edition)
ISBN 978-1-4964-3795-2 (softcover)

Printed in the United States of America

30 29 28 27 26 25 24
7 6 5 4 3 2 1

To my dear son Noah—one of the most creative people I know and admire. Your mom and I are so excited to see where God is going to take you in the years ahead.

CAST OF CHARACTERS

Americans

Marcus Ryker—special operative, Central Intelligence Agency
Peter Hwang—special operative, Central Intelligence Agency
Geoff Stone—special agent in charge, Diplomatic Security Service
Kailea Curtis—special agent, Diplomatic Security Service
Jennifer Morris—officer, Central Intelligence Agency
Noah Daniels—officer, Central Intelligence Agency
Donny Callaghan—special operative, Central Intelligence Agency; former commander, SEAL Team Six
Miguel Navarro—officer, Central Intelligence Agency
Richard Stephens—director of the Central Intelligence Agency
Martha Dell—deputy director of intelligence (DDI), Central Intelligence Agency
Andrew Clarke—president of the United States
Carlos Hernandez—vice president of the United States
William McDermott—national security advisor
Margaret "Meg" Whitney—secretary of state
Cal Foster—secretary of defense
James Meyers—chairman of the Joint Chiefs of Staff
Catherine Blackburn—attorney general
Carl Roseboro—deputy director, U.S. Secret Service
Robert Dayton—U.S. senator (D-Iowa)
Annie Stewart—senior foreign policy advisor to Senator Robert Dayton
Marjorie Ryker—Marcus's mother
Carolyn Tam—CNN anchor
Tanya Brighton—humanitarian aid worker in Yemen

Hannah Weiss—humanitarian aid worker in Yemen
Mia Minetti—humanitarian aid worker in Yemen

Saudis

Abdulaziz bin Faisal—crown prince and minister of defense
Abdullah bin Rashid—director of the General Intelligence Directorate
Abdul-Malik al-Hakim—intelligence officer

Kairos

Abu Nakba—commander of the Kairos terror organization
Hamdi Yaşar—senior advisor to Abu Nakba
Badr Hassan al-Ruzami—deputy commander, chief of operations
Tariq Youssef—deputy commander, chief of security
Zaid Farooq—deputy commander, chief of intelligence
Jibril bin Badr—terrorist
Ali bin Badr—terrorist
Mansour bin Badr—terrorist
Nasir Bhati—terrorist

Iranians

Yadollah Afshar—president of the Islamic Republic of Iran
Mahmoud Entezam—commander of the Iranian Revolutionary Guard Corps

Russians

Mikhail Borisovich Petrovsky—president of the Russian Federation
Nikolay Vladimirovich Kropatkin—head of the FSB
Oleg Stefanovich Kraskin—son-in-law to the late President Aleksandr Luganov

Others

Pope Pius XIII—head of the Roman Catholic Church
Alphonso Gianetti—head of the Vatican security services
Khalid bin Ibrahim (KBI)—chief of intelligence, United Arab Emirates

Tarabulus
(Tripoli)
Tripolitania
Ghadames
Suknah
Zellah
LIBIYA
(LIBYA)
Sebkha
Zighan
El Juf
Ghat

PRELUDE

"A ship in harbor is safe,

but that is not what ships are built for."

JOHN A. SHEDD

OPERATION DESERT STORM—16 JANUARY 1991

The inky-black skies over southern Iraq suddenly erupted with sound and fury.

It was as if the slumbering Babylonian gods had awoken from beneath the desert sands and begun hurling their javelins up, up, up into the heavens. The Basra skyline was filled with crisscrossing streaks of fire. All across the city, antiaircraft batteries were active. Air-raid sirens blared. A million residents were now awake and scrambling for basements and bomb shelters. They couldn't see the pair of F-16s scorching over their heads at the speed of sound. But they could hear the sonic booms. They could feel their apartments shaking, see their windows shattering. And in that moment, they knew Saddam Hussein had lied to them.

The Americans had come after all, and the war was on.

With triple-A fire exploding all around him, Captain Lars Ryker streaked toward his target. Upon reaching the Republican Guard base located on the city's north side, he found the massive weapons depot and fired his missiles. An instant later, Ryker felt his entire jet shudder from the subsequent shock wave.

He could sense the magnitude of the destruction he had just wrought. But there was no time to marvel at his handiwork—the night was young, and there were hundreds more targets to take down.

Ryker banked his Fighting Falcon hard to the left, then leveled out, gained altitude, and increased speed. An instant later, his wingman—right behind him—fired his missiles at a series of fuel tanks. He scored direct hits, and the fireworks were spectacular.

For Ryker, it was surreal to think that he was back in combat. In July, he had put in his paperwork to end a twenty-year career in the U.S. Air Force. It was enough already. It was time to retire, to go back to the Front Range of Colorado, back to his wife and three children, back to his golf game. Time to find a job that operated at far lower speeds and with far less danger. But Saddam Hussein had changed everything. The Butcher of Baghdad invaded Kuwait on August 2. A half-million American troops and thousands of American fighter pilots were deployed to the Persian Gulf. And Ryker had been asked to stay a little longer. He had more enemy kills and had logged more hours in battle conditions than anyone else on active duty. How could he abandon his squadron in the biggest military buildup since D-Day?

Amped up on the thrill of the hunt, adrenaline coursing through his system, Ryker turned south, veering away from the city to race back across the desert for their base in Saudi Arabia to rearm. His wingman followed.

"Stroke Five, Stroke Six, this is Manila Hotel—climb to 15,000 and turn right heading zero-three-zero—now."

The urgency in the voice of the combat air controller—forty miles away on a U.S. Air Force AWACs jet—was unmistakable. Ryker responded instantly, but the controller wasn't done.

"You've got two bandits at your eleven o'clock—five miles out—southwest bound, ascending from 3,500."

Ryker—call sign "Stroke Five"—pulled the yoke back and punched it.

5,000 feet.

6,000.

7,000.

The threat of antiaircraft fire was soon behind him, but two Soviet-built MiG-29s, the fastest and most maneuverable fighters in the Iraqi arsenal, were coming up fast. A moment later, Ryker could see them on his radar. He could hear his wingman shouting in his headset for him to get out of there as Ryker kept climbing.

8,000 feet.

9,000 feet.

10,000.

But it was becoming clear they weren't going to be able to outrun these guys.

"Stroke Six, break right, break right," Ryker suddenly ordered.

Captain Mike Merkle didn't question the order. He just obeyed it, breaking right the instant he was told. But Ryker was still climbing.

11,000 feet.

12,000.

13,000.

Suddenly new warning sirens sounded in his headset. One of the MiGs had just fired on him. With only a split second to decide, Ryker broke left, forced his yoke down, and began diving for the deck.

12,000 feet.

11,000.

10,000.

9,000.

And now Merkle was in trouble.

"Stroke Five, Stroke Five, this guy is right on my tail."

But Ryker was in no position to help. A Soviet-made R-73 guided missile had locked onto his jet and was coming in red-hot. Sweat was pouring down the inside of his flight suit. He was sucking in oxygen as fast as it entered his helmet. The g-forces were rising fast. He was in danger of blacking out. Yet Ryker kept diving.

8,000 feet.

7,000.

"Stroke Five, Stroke Five, where are you?" Merkle shouted. *"Get back here. I need you now."*

But there was nothing Ryker could do. Not yet. Not unless he found a way to break free of this missile and the MiG-29 getting ready to fire another. What's more, there was no time to think. No time for calculations. No time to ask the controller for guidance. Ryker was flying purely by instinct now, and he understood the stakes.

Hurtling toward the ground, he knew full well that if he waited too long, he wouldn't have enough time to pull out of the dive. But if he pulled out too quickly, the missile would catch him and blow him to kingdom come. And he didn't want to die. Not here. Not yet. Not on the first night of air operations.

"Pull up! Pull up!" he could hear the controller screaming in his headset.

But Ryker still kept diving.

6,000 feet.

5,000.

4,000.

Just then, he broke through the cloud cover. He was no longer over the desert. With all his high-speed zigzagging, he was now back over Basra. That was a critical mistake. One that could cost him. He could see triple-A contrails all around him. Even if he did shake the missile, he could still get shot down by artillery fire. But one battle at a time.

It was now or never. Ryker quickly throttled back his engines, reduced speed, and pulled back on the yoke with every ounce of strength he had. He could see the Shatt al-Arab River rushing up at him. He was certain this was going to be the end. The faces of his wife and three kids flashed before him just as he was about to—

But then the nose of the F-16 began to rise. The trajectory of the world's most advanced fighter jet finally began to correct. With no time left and no margin for error, Ryker pulled out of the dive, leveled, and found himself skimming over the banks of the river. That's when he felt the shock wave of the R-73 detonating behind him. Once again the entire cockpit shuddered. So did the wings and fuselage. It had been close—too close—but the F-16 held together. Ryker was alive. And he was itching to get back on offense.

He hit the afterburner and felt his body jolt back in his seat. His Fighting Falcon now had an instant 50 percent boost in speed, though it was also burning eight times as much fuel. But fuel wasn't his concern. Saving Merkle was.

Ryker radioed the AWACs, received Merkle's coordinates, and raced to catch up.

Stroke Six was in an epic aerial battle. He now had both of the original MiGs on his tail. But that wasn't all. The controller said two more MiGs were readying for takeoff from a nearby enemy airfield that was under allied bombardment at that very moment but not yet out of commission.

Seconds later, Ryker spotted the two bandits directly above him, three miles out and closing fast on Merkle.

"Stroke Six, Stroke Six—when I count to three, break right and dive. I'm coming up underneath these guys and I don't think they see me yet."

Merkle confirmed, and Ryker began the count.

But just at that moment, Ryker saw the lead MiG fire. Merkle couldn't wait. For some reason he broke left instead of right, then went into a spiraling nosedive. The Iraqis followed suit. Ryker had no shot to light up the lead bandit, but the second MiG was in perfect position.

"I have tone—I have a lock—Fox Two," Ryker shouted.

The AIM-9 Sidewinder exploded from under Ryker's right wing. Banking left and following the three jets into another suicidal dive, Ryker watched the missile home in on the closest Iraqi fighter. An instant later a blinding explosion filled the night sky.

"Splash one, splash one," Ryker erupted.

But there was no time to celebrate. Merkle radioed that he had just successfully eluded the first missile, which had slammed into an office building. But no matter what he did, he couldn't shake the remaining MiG. The Iraqi was hot on his tail as Merkle streaked down city streets, under bridges, and dangerously close to power lines. Merkle was doing exactly what the controller was telling him to do—stay low and hug the terrain as best he could until Ryker could take this guy out.

But Ryker now told his wingman to do exactly the opposite.

"Stroke Six, I'm right behind you guys," he said, his voice calm and steady. "Pull up—shoot for the sky at maximum speed—that's when I'll take him out."

"What? No. Are you crazy, Stroke Five?" the controller shot back. *"Negative, Stroke Six, negative. Stay low. I'm scrambling more jets to your position."*

"This guy's got tone," Merkle shouted. *"He's locked on. He's going to fire."*

"Pull up, Stroke Six," Ryker ordered. *"I've got him. Trust me, I've got him. Pull up."*

The controller was countermanding the order. But just as the MiG fired,

Merkle pulled up and hit his afterburner. The instant the Iraqi followed suit, Ryker's radar locked on. He fired two Sidewinders, just to be sure. The first one went wide, but the second hit its mark. The explosion could be seen and heard by everyone in Basra. Simultaneously, Merkle pulled his F-16 into a death-defying loop, dove back toward the deck, leveled out, and banked hard to the right, skimming just above the rooftops. The missile trailing him plowed into a skyscraper and detonated on impact.

Ryker's headset erupted with the sounds of whoops and hollers. Everyone on the AWACs was cheering, including Merkle. But not for long.

New warning sirens suddenly began screaming in both their cockpits. Two Soviet-made surface-to-air missiles—and then two more—exploded from batteries no one had told them were there. Merkle immediately took evasive action. So did Ryker, but it was too late. His F-16 was blown out of the sky at twenty-seven minutes after 4 a.m., the first night of air operations in the battle to liberate Kuwait.

MONUMENT, COLORADO

Marcus Ryker forced open the window and crawled out onto the ice-crusted roof.

Making his way to the edge, he stared the twenty-odd feet to the ground . . .

And jumped.

Everything that happened next seemed to be in slow motion. All he could hear was the bitter winter wind howling down the Rocky Mountains and surging across the Front Range. All he could see were flakes swirling around his head, the early signs of a January squall. And the ground and the sky. And the ground and the sky. And tree branches and snowdrifts and clouds and boot prints and then—

He hit the ground hard, his legs collapsing beneath him. He crumpled to his back. Then all was quiet. He was not dead. He hadn't broken a leg or his neck. The wind had been knocked out of him, but he was fine.

And then he heard the back door flying open.

"Marcus Johannes Ryker, I am not going to say this again," his mother shouted. "Knock it off—no more backflips off the roof or you're grounded. Do you hear me? Grounded for a month. Are you listening to me?"

Marcus didn't get up. Didn't roll over. Didn't move at all. But as soon as he could catch his breath—still staring up into the gray winter sky—the eleven-year-old promised his mother he wouldn't jump off the roof again.

"Now get a move on and shovel the driveway like I told you—and put your coat on, for crying out loud."

Marcus grunted something, but the moment the back door shut, a new plan began to form. Wearing only a ratty U2 concert T-shirt, ripped blue jeans, and an old pair of pac boots, Marcus raced for the garage. His mother had just given him a magnificent loophole. She'd made him promise not to jump off the roof. She'd said nothing about the family's Dodge Grand Caravan. So scrambling to the top of the rusting green minivan, Marcus once again began doing backflips.

When he noticed two black government-issue sedans turning onto their street, he paid little attention to them at first. It was another blustery gray and far-too-quiet Wednesday morning in the smallest and most boring town on the Front Range. Mickey Reese, his best friend since the age of five, was in bed with chicken pox. His sisters, Marta and Nicole, had already left for school.

Suddenly both cars pulled to a stop in front of their house. Having just climbed again to the roof of the minivan, Marcus stared down as two men in black suits and long black winter coats emerged from the first sedan. An Air Force officer in full uniform got out of the second sedan, along with a pastor or priest or somebody wearing one of those weird white collars. The officer came up the not-yet-shoveled driveway and asked the boy if his mother was home.

Marcus nodded.

"Would you let her know we're here?"

The man was a stranger, but he was a military man and polite enough, so Marcus nodded again, did another backflip, perfectly stuck the landing, and ran inside. He found his mother in the kitchen making homemade vegetable soup as she watched CNN coverage of the war on a small black-and-white TV that sat on the counter.

"Mom, there's some men here for you," he said.

"Marcus, how many times have I told you to take off your boots in the vestibule and not to track snow through the living room and kitchen?"

Marcus shrugged.

"What kind of men?" his mother now asked.

When Marcus shrugged again, she shook her head as she tried to hide a smile, then wiped her hands on her apron, headed to the door, and told him to clean up the snow. Curious, Marcus ignored the order and followed her to the door instead. That's when he saw her freeze in her tracks.

"Excuse me, ma'am, are you Marjorie Ryker?"

Marcus noticed that his mother didn't speak, didn't even nod. Yet the officer kept talking.

"Mrs. Ryker, I'm afraid we have some difficult news. Perhaps it would be best if you sat down."

Marcus would never remember the words that followed. But he would never forget the image of his mother stumbling back several steps, her trembling hands moving to her mouth.

ARLINGTON CEMETERY

No snow had yet fallen in the nation's capital.

The temperature was hovering around forty degrees, and it was pouring rain.

Thunder crackled to the east. Marcus—wearing a borrowed black suit, hand-me-down shoes that were too tight, mismatched socks, a bedraggled old coat from Sears, and mittens his mother had knit for him—stood soaked to the bone. Shivering, he nevertheless bravely tried to hold a golf umbrella steady over his mother's head and clung to her gloved hand as tightly as he had ever done.

Standing beside him, Marta and Nicole huddled together under their own umbrella, though in the crosswinds and driving rain, they were having no more success than he was. Their matching black wool coats were also drenched. Yet they didn't complain or even cough or shift from foot to foot as the brief ceremony commenced. Instead, as a chaplain spoke, Marta put her arm around Marcus and gently squeezed his shoulder.

"Today we have gathered to remember, to mourn, but also to honor and celebrate the life of Captain Lars Johannes Ryker," the clergyman said in a rich baritone. "A faithful and loving husband, the father of these three beautiful children, and a devoted follower of our Lord and Savior Jesus Christ, Captain Ryker will always be remembered as one of the most courageous and most decorated fighter pilots ever to serve this nation. In his storied career that spanned two decades, he shot down thirteen enemy planes—more than any of his contemporaries—the last of which saved the life of his wingman and best friend."

Marcus stood ramrod straight. He couldn't bear to look at the flag-draped casket or the freshly dug grave. Instead, he stared at his exhaled breath condensing in the morning chill.

"Captain Ryker believed what the Bible teaches, that 'to be absent from the body is to be present with the Lord.' By faith, he had come to believe that Christ had forgiven all of his sins—past, present, and future—that he had been 'born again' according to John chapter 3, that he had been adopted into the royal family of God and thus had been assured a place in heaven for all eternity. I know he believed these things because we talked about them many times. At the academy where we first met. On the many bases where we served together. And even at the Dhahran air base in Saudi Arabia just before Christmas."

Marcus began scanning the southern sky, sure that he had heard a roar in the distance but seeing nothing yet. The clergyman kept speaking, but Marcus couldn't listen. He had promised himself he would not cry. He was the man of the family now. It was his responsibility to protect his mother and his sisters. The last thing he could afford to do was show weakness. He had to be strong. He refused to watch as four officers from his father's squadron crisply and methodically folded the American flag and handed it to his mother. He refused to watch as his father's casket was lowered into the ground. He looked away but found himself flinching when the seven-man honor guard wearing white gloves fired their rifles in unison. Then again. Then a third time. The echoes of those gunshots seemed to hang in the air forever.

A solitary bugler played taps, as haunting a sound as Marcus had ever heard. Still, he kept his attention riveted on the southern skies. He saw nothing. Nothing. Nothing. The ceremony was almost over. He feared it wasn't going to happen. Had there been a malfunction? Was it the weather? Perhaps someone at the Pentagon thought his father didn't merit the missing-man formation. But if his father didn't, who did?

Then as the bugler continued to play, Marcus saw them. They were microscopic at first, four gleaming dots against a dark-gray sky. Soon enough, however, the missing-man formation was surging toward them—four F-16C Fighting Falcons flying in a V formation. As they approached the burial site, the third fighter jet from the left abruptly broke formation, flying straight up into the heavens as the other three jets remained level and roared over their heads.

As the breakaway jet shot higher and higher into the morning sky, Marcus strained his neck to follow its path until it disappeared into the clouds. His mother squeezed his hand. His sister tightened her grip on his shoulder. But the little boy couldn't restrain himself any longer, and the tears began to flow.

PART ONE

Three Decades Later

CAMP DAVID, THURMONT, MARYLAND—9 MAY

"Marcus? *Marcus?* Hey, buddy, wake up—we're here."

He could barely hear Jenny Morris's voice over the sound of the helicopter rotors. But her quick jab to his ribs got the point across. Marcus Ryker tried to rub the exhaustion out of his bloodshot eyes. Everything in his body and soul wanted to pull the weathered Washington Nationals cap down over his face, turn over, and go back to sleep. But he had a job to do and not much time to do it.

He felt the struts touch down. The side door of the chopper slid open. Daylight surged into the cabin. He could see Jenny tossing their duffel bags out onto the helipad and scrambling after them. Marcus followed her, but a bit slower. His wounds were too fresh, his joints and muscles in too much pain to move as sprightly as his colleague from Langley.

"Agent Morris, welcome to Camp David," said a Secret Service agent too young to remember Marcus's time on the force, shaking the woman's hand. "Agent Ryker, welcome back. And I brought a wheelchair along in case . . ."

Marcus shook the kid's hand and brushed off the zinger, certain some of the veterans had put him up to it. The agent smiled. Jenny stifled a laugh. Marcus ignored them both. Sure, he'd been beaten within an inch of his life in Lebanon. But there was no way he was going to give these idiots the satisfaction of seeing him wheeled in to see the president of the United States. Grabbing his duffel bag away from the agent, who couldn't have been more than mid- to late twenties, Marcus hobbled up to Laurel Lodge, where the meeting of the National Security Council was about to begin.

The first twenty minutes were a blur. Mind-numbing chitchat. Updates on matters Marcus considered unimportant and a complete waste of time given the urgency of the hour. Finally it was his turn to address the august body.

Wincing as he rose to his feet, Marcus moved to the podium. He knew that every eye was staring at him, not just because of the scars and burns all over his face, neck, and hands, but because of the gravity of what he had come to say.

He was, after all, about to ask them to kill a man.

Halfway around the world.

On precious little notice.

With very little debate.

And in direct opposition to the recommendation of one of the most respected and valued members of the cabinet, not to mention Marcus's ostensible boss.

In later conversations with his closest friends, at least those with top secret clearance, Marcus couldn't recall precisely how he had been introduced to or received by the commander in chief and his war cabinet that humid Saturday morning. Nor could he even remember thanking President Andrew Clarke or the rest of the NSC for all they had done to rescue him and his colleagues from deep behind enemy lines in Lebanon. All he remembered was the immense physical discomfort he was trying to mask from those in the room. And the immense personal revulsion he felt coming from the man who sat directly across from him.

Marcus picked up the remote from the podium and forced himself to focus. The moment was surreal. He had awoken 1,400 miles away in the barracks of a U.S. Navy facility at Guantanamo Bay in Cuba. Now, after three turbulence-racked flights—first to Miami, the second to Joint Base Andrews, and then the Marine chopper ride—he found himself in the main wood-paneled conference room on the grounds of the sprawling presidential retreat in the lush Catoctin Mountains of Maryland.

Looking at the distinguished men and women sitting in blue upholstered chairs around the polished oak table, Marcus felt as if he were facing a jury. He had been given a mere fifteen minutes to make the most important case of his lifetime.

In theory, William "Bill" McDermott—the U.S. national security advisor—should have been his closest ally in the room. The two men had known each other for nearly twenty years. Yet reality was more complicated. After finishing at Yale, McDermott had become an officer in the Marines, serving three combat tours in Afghanistan and two in Iraq. That's where they had met. For several years, McDermott had commanded Marcus's unit. They had gotten along well enough, but upon returning to civilian life, though they had stayed in touch, they weren't especially close.

McDermott had gone on to earn an MBA from Wharton, then a master's in national security studies from Georgetown, after which he made a fortune on Wall Street before reentering government service. Now forty-seven, McDermott had risen to become one of President Clarke's closest and most trusted aides.

More than five years McDermott's junior, Marcus had married his high school sweetheart, joined the Secret Service, and worked night and day to earn a spot on the elite White House detail before tragedy struck—the murder of his wife and only child during a convenience store robbery gone bad—sending him into a deep depression that scuttled his career. How Marcus had been dragged back into government service against his will was a story unto itself, though highly classified and not even known to everyone around this table. Yet here he was, one of the Central Intelligence Agency's most effective, if controversial, operatives. And who had most fiercely opposed his recruitment into the Agency? Bill McDermott. In recent years, the two had reconciled. Yet there lingered within Marcus unspoken seeds of doubt about how much he could truly trust McDermott when the chips were down.

Carlos Hernandez was another one Marcus had a hard time reading. A retired three-star vice admiral, Hernandez had been one of the highest-ranking Latinos ever to serve in the U.S. military. Then Clarke had chosen him as his running mate, and Hernandez had become the first Cuban American ever elected vice president of the United States. Born in Miami to first-generation immigrants from Havana, Hernandez was only fifty-seven. Since taking the oath of office, he had suffered two heart attacks and been forced by his doctors to undergo a triple bypass surgery followed by months of bed rest and rehab. The vice president's health problems had been all the more shocking since in his younger years in the Navy, he had been an undefeated boxer, a scrappy street fighter from the barrios who never stayed down long and loved to deliver the knockout blow his opponents couldn't see coming. Now he was back in the ring and pushing hard to make up for lost time. Because of the vice president's health issues, Marcus had had very little personal interaction with the man. They were strangers, not kindred spirits, and the vice president's eyes now betrayed no hint of where he was going to come down on this ever-critical vote.

Defense Secretary Cal Foster and General James Meyers, the stoic chairman of the Joint Chiefs of Staff, were different stories. Marcus had worked closely with each man and believed he could count on both. Yet that was not necessarily the case with Margaret "Meg" Whitney. The sixty-one-year-old secretary of state was known by her colleagues as the "Silver Fox," as much because she was a brilliant negotiator and a killer poker player as because she refused to dye her once-auburn hair. A two-term governor of New Mexico and former ambassador to Great Britain, Whitney was a rising star in the administration, especially now that her tireless shuttle diplomacy had concluded the most unexpected deal of the century: the historic peace treaty between Israel and the Kingdom of Saudi Arabia. Marcus had played a back-channel role in initiating the negotiations. He had even served on Whitney's DSS advance team on several trips, including the one to the Israeli-Lebanese border that had ended in a brutal firefight and his own captivity. Yet he had never spent a great deal of time with the secretary. For all he knew, she blamed him for the missile war that had erupted between Hezbollah and the Israelis, a war that had almost destroyed her shot at the Nobel Prize. Which side she would wind up on when all the dust settled was anyone's guess.

In the end, however, there was only one person on this jury whose vote really mattered—the president of the United States—and he could go either way.

Andrew Hartford Clarke was a riddle, wrapped in a mystery, inside an enigma.

Now in the second term of the Clarke administration, Marcus found the line from Winston Churchill describing how difficult it was to understand, much less predict, the actions of the Kremlin apropos in trying to forecast the moves of his commander in chief.

The self-made, blunt-talking, hard-charging former CEO had spent two decades on Wall Street making stunning sums of money before shocking the political establishment by ditching it all and running for governor of New Jersey. Defying literally every political pundit and prognosticator, Clarke not only won—however narrowly—but served two full terms in Trenton, slashing taxes and spending, balancing the budget, and radically reducing the state's heretofore mushrooming crime rate, before setting his sights on the big prize. No one thought Clarke could reach the White House, yet he won the presidency in an electoral landslide. To be sure, he entered the office with no foreign policy or national security experience. Nor had he ever served in the military. That had worried Marcus. Yet to his credit, Clarke had successfully navigated one international crisis after another far more adroitly than Marcus had feared he might.

Clarke's greatest strength, however, was also his most serious weakness. Rather than being guided by a set of fixed ideological principles, the man prided himself on being unpredictable. True, this had kept America's enemies off guard, continually unsure of what they could get away with and what might set Clarke off. But for America's allies, Clarke's lack of predictability was both nerve-racking and infuriating. The Israelis had come to believe he genuinely had their backs. So did the moderates in the Arab world. But the leaders of NATO? Not so much. And the leaders of South Korea, Japan, Taiwan, and other Pacific powers felt ever less secure, even as they faced an increasingly belligerent Beijing.

When Clarke first took office, Marcus was still in the Secret Service, a decorated member of the presidential protection detail for his role in thwarting a terrorist attack on the White House years earlier. But Clarke and Marcus had never been close. They had even had some serious blowups over the years, though the more results Marcus delivered in the field, the more Clarke had warmed to him. Whether any of that was going to help him today, Marcus had no idea.

In the end, the most important voice influencing Clarke was going to be Richard Stephens, the director of the Central Intelligence Agency.

Now sixty-six, Stephens was widely considered the dean of the intelligence community. Known by friends and foes alike as "the Bulldog," the brandy-swilling chain-smoker was barely five feet, five inches tall, over two hundred pounds, balding, and in possession of an explosive temper. A three-term senior senator from Arizona, he had long served as chairman of the Senate's Select Committee on Intelligence before being tapped by Clarke as CIA director on day one of Clarke's first term. The reason was clear enough. The two men were longtime golfing buddies and the closest of political allies. Behind closed doors they loved their Cuban cigars and off-color stories to boot.

For reasons Marcus could only guess at, Stephens hated him with a vengeance. He had tried relentlessly to block Marcus from working for the Agency in the first place, and when Clarke had overruled him, Stephens had worked hard to drive Marcus out.

Complicating matters was that Marcus was not the most effective public speaker. His career had been conducted in the shadows, not the spotlight.

Taking a sip of water and wondering why the painkillers were not doing their job, he drew a deep breath, gripped the remote a little tighter, and began the PowerPoint presentation he had hastily assembled en route from Gitmo.

A grainy black-and-white photo came up on the large flat-panel screens on the walls around him. As it did, Marcus realized he had left his notes at his seat at the conference table. Unwilling to look like the moron he now felt like by going back and retrieving them, he chose to press on, giving his presentation from memory.

"Mr. President, this is the most wanted man in the world," Marcus began. "To his family, he's known by his given name, Walid Abdel-Shafi. To his disciples, he's known as 'Father.' To the jihadi community, he's known as 'the Libyan.' To you, he's best known as Abu Nakba, the 'Father of the Disaster.'"

Marcus played a short video of Abu Nakba, now in his eighties, walking through a park, surrounded by little children cheering him and giving him kisses and freshly cut flowers. The man's long, flowing hair was entirely gray, as was his unkempt beard. He was stooped, walking with a wooden cane, and wore leather sandals and a white tunic covered by the classic Libyan robe known as the *jard*.

"Let's be clear," Marcus said as the video ran. "As the founder of the terrorist network we've come to know as Kairos, this man has been responsible for the murder of more Americans than anyone since Osama bin Laden. That's why, Mr. President, you ordered the most extensive, expensive, and exhaustive manhunt in American history, second only to the hunt for bin Laden. It's been my honor to be part of this manhunt, and I'm here today to tell you that we now know where Abu Nakba is hiding and to assure you that we have the opportunity to eliminate this major threat to U.S. and global security, but only if we move fast."

Jenny Morris watched her colleague operating in the lion's den.

She could see he was in severe pain. She knew the immense pressure he was under. Stephens wanted him gone. Whitney was a lukewarm ally at best. Hernandez barely knew him. That was true of most of the other officials around the table as well. In theory, McDermott should have his back, but that relationship was complicated for reasons she had never quite figured out. The president? Well, Clarke was a tough man to read on the best of days.

Yet as sorry as Jenny felt for Marcus—for the torture he'd endured at the hands of Hezbollah and Kairos operatives in Lebanon and for the horrific personal losses he had suffered over the years—she also knew that this room was severely underestimating him. In all her years in the Central Intelligence Agency, Jenny had never met anyone like Marcus Ryker. He just might be the smartest and gutsiest operative she had ever met in her own government or anyone else's, and the more time she spent with him, the more she liked and trusted him.

Getting a nod from Marcus, Jenny rose quickly and handed out black binders marked *TOP SECRET* to everyone present. Each was numbered. Each would have to be returned to her at the end of the meeting. For each contained the highly classified evidence backing up everything that she and Marcus were about to say. There were gaps in the presentation, she conceded—if only to herself—gaps that Stephens was going to try his best to exploit. But it was solid work, and she stood by it.

"To date," Marcus continued, "we've captured and analyzed 6.2 million emails, sifted through 4.37 million text messages, intercepted 12,109 phone calls, interviewed 343 witnesses, and interrogated 93 enemy combatants. But the critical breakthrough came four days ago when my team and I captured this man in Doha, Qatar."

Marcus put another photo on the screen. Though a bit faded, this one was in color. Abu Nakba could be seen on the left. Marcus identified the man on the right—at least a half-century younger—as Hamdi Yaşar.

"Hamdi Yaşar recently turned thirty-one years old. Turkish national. Born and raised in Istanbul. Moved to Doha a decade ago. Became a journalist for a Turkish daily. Then was hired as a field producer for the Al-Sawt satellite news network, where he won multiple awards and acclaim. But all the while he was a Kairos operative, loyal first and foremost to Abu Nakba. Indeed, this is the Libyan's most senior and trusted consigliere. This is the man who plotted at least a dozen major terrorist attacks from London to Lisbon, from Warsaw to Washington, and from Johannesburg to Jerusalem."

Marcus now displayed a series of photos of Hamdi Yaşar. Some showed him in custody and wearing an orange jumpsuit. Others showed him meeting with various world leaders, from the presidents of Russia and Turkey to the Supreme Leader of Iran and a group of generals in Communist China. Then came images of Yaşar's apartment, safe, and the weapons, files, and electronic devices that Marcus and his team had seized.

"Hamdi Yaşar may not be talking to us—yet—but believe me, his hard drives are," Marcus said, explaining the week he and his team had just spent at Gitmo. "His phones are. His files are. The videos of each attack we found in his possession certainly are."

Marcus turned the floor over to Jenny.

Though younger than him, Jenny had been with the Agency for more than ten years. She had been the youngest employee ever to be promoted to station chief, and in Moscow of all places. That's where the two had met. That's where the two had encountered each other's skills and grit. Jenny had narrowly saved Marcus's life. He had even more narrowly saved hers. What started as a rivalry had morphed into grudging respect, and Jenny knew Marcus counted her as one of the most trusted members of his team and a personal friend.

He asked her to walk the room through a series of drone and satellite photos, explaining why everything they had uncovered pointed to one particular facility.

"This," she said, "is Abu Nakba's home. This compound is located in the western deserts of Libya, just outside a town called Ghat, not far from the Algerian border. This is the base of operations for Kairos. And we believe that Abu Nakba and most of his senior leadership are in this compound at this very moment."

Jenny then proceeded through a series of slides provided by the NSA identifying a satellite phone purchased by Hamdi Yaşar in Doha six months earlier.

"Now that we have all of Hamdi Yaşar's phones," Jenny continued, "we know that this senior Kairos operative called one particular satphone more than any other single number. Forty-two times in the past 180 days. These calls were typically longer than almost any other calls that Yaşar made, often lasting an hour or more. And the NSA confirmed to me yet again—right before this meeting began—that the satphone Yaşar called so often is still active and located on the top floor of the main building inside the Libyan compound."

Jenny turned the presentation back over to Marcus.

"That's him, Mr. President. That's Abu Nakba," Marcus said. "That's who Hamdi Yaşar has been calling every four days, often for hours on end. And to be clear, Mr. President, this is the first time that we have ever positively identified exactly where Abu Nakba is in real time."

At that, Stephens went full Vesuvius.

"No, no, and hell no," Stephens shouted, slamming his fist on the table. *"This is not the view of the Central Intelligence Agency—not at all—not even close."*

Everyone in the room jumped, except Marcus, who had seen the eruption coming. He was surprised only that it had taken this long.

"And with all due respect, Mr. President, I must repeat the objections I made to you in private last night and again this morning," Stephens quickly added, red-faced and practically coming out of his chair. "I know you have appreciated some of the work that Mr. Ryker has done in the past, even the recent past. But I must remind you: He is not an Agency man. Wasn't trained at the Farm. Didn't pay his dues. Refuses to operate by our playbook. And need I remind everyone how many times he has brought this Agency—indeed, this administration—to the brink of international calamity and humiliation?"

The room was silent until Clarke finally spoke. "Richard, I'm well aware of your history with Agent Ryker here, but—"

"It's not that, sir—this isn't personal," Stephens broke in. "It's the fact that—"

But Clarke cut him off. "I'm not interested in the past, Richard. I just want to know one thing. Is Abu Nakba in that compound, or isn't he?"

"No, Mr. President," Stephens replied, dialing down the intensity. "I'm not convinced of that, nor are my top analysts, Agent Morris notwithstanding."

"Why not?"

"Everything you just heard, sir, was circumstantial, at best. Hamdi Yaşar bought a satellite phone in Doha—so what? And he's speaking on it a lot—so what? That doesn't prove Abu Nakba is the man he's speaking to. Have we seen photos of Abu Nakba walking around the courtyard of that compound or sipping tea on the balcony? No. Have we heard intercepts of actual telephone calls in which we can hear Abu Nakba's voice? No. We only got a drone over the site late last night. We only received satellite imagery a few hours ago. Now, could the Libyan be in there? Yes, that's possible. Anything is possible. But we simply don't know for certain one way or the other. Things are moving too fast. And key witnesses aren't talking."

"Like who?" Clarke asked.

"Hamdi Yaşar for one," Stephens replied.

"What do you mean?"

"We've had Hamdi Yaşar in custody for four days. Has he told us he gave the phone to Abu Nakba? No. Has he told us Abu Nakba is in that compound? No. Why not? Because Hamdi Yaşar isn't talking—not about this, not about anything. And why not? Because Mr. Ryker here doesn't have the stomach to interrogate him properly. As I said, Mr. Ryker is not one of us, sir. He wasn't trained for interrogations. He wasn't trained to be a field operative. He wasn't trained for *any* of this. But allowing him to lead this investigation—against my strenuous objections—is setting this administration up for disaster."

Stephens scanned the faces of his colleagues, then turned back to Clarke.

"Look, I realize there's a strong degree of sympathy for Mr. Ryker in this room, especially after all that he has suffered of late. But honestly, is a man who has been subjected to such torture and degradation—with no time to recover, much less gain some distance, some perspective—really in a position to lead us into battle? Even if he was qualified to do so, I remind you that Mr. Ryker is the victim of a crime. This has become personal for him, and it is clouding his judgment."

All eyes shifted back to Clarke, who was rubbing his temples.

It was obvious the president was seriously weighing Stephens's case. What wasn't clear was which way he was leaning. "Agent Ryker, would you care to respond?" Clarke asked.

This was it. Closing arguments. The burns on Marcus's chest and the bruises covering his back and torso were distracting him. Though he had no intention of admitting it, the painkillers had finally kicked in and were fogging his thinking. And he found himself struck by how pale the president looked and how much weight the man had lost since the last time they had seen each other. That Clarke's hair was grayer and the bags under his eyes more pronounced since taking office was no surprise. The accelerated aging process was par for the course for every commander in chief. But this was different. Something wasn't right, and Marcus felt a genuine pang of worry for him.

Forcing himself to refocus, Marcus took a sip of water and then began to speak. "Yes, it's personal," he began. "Should it not be personal to each of us in this room after all the friends and colleagues who have been murdered on the orders of Abu Nakba?"

It had been Jenny on the flight from Miami who had anticipated Stephens's line of attack. She had suggested he prepare PowerPoint slides for rebuttal, and Marcus, grateful, now used them.

He reminded them of the man who used to sit at this very table, General Barry Evans, the previous national security advisor, as he presented photos of Evans with Clarke, Evans with Hernandez, Evans with the entire NSC team, and then select images of the Kairos-planned suicide bombing at 10 Downing Street in London that had killed the man. None of the photos were macabre, just enough to make the point.

Then Marcus showed them images of a car bombing in downtown Washington, D.C., that had also been ordered by Abu Nakba, the one that had killed Tyler Reed, the U.S. ambassador to Moscow whom Clarke had intended to appoint as a new deputy secretary of state. Every eye in the room was riveted on the screens as Marcus then posted photos of Reed with Clarke, Reed with Secretary Whitney, and Reed with his wife and daughters.

Then came photos of Clarke and Whitney with Janelle Thomas, the deputy secretary of state. This was followed by images of Thomas's bullet-riddled body on the bloody floor of Lincoln Park Baptist Church, another Kairos attack in downtown D.C.

The list went on, but Marcus felt he had made his point.

"Agent Ryker, we mourn them—all of us do," Clarke said when the lights came back up. "But the question isn't whether we want to bring Abu Nakba to justice. The question on the table right now is whether Abu Nakba is in that compound or not."

"I have no doubt Abu Nakba is in that compound, sir," Marcus said, looking the president in the eye. "You have the brief. It's all there. The evidence may be circumstantial, but it is overwhelming. And I would remind you all that the Agency never had photos or phone intercepts of Osama bin Laden in that compound in Abbottabad. But he was there. And your predecessors made the right call sending in U.S. forces to take him down."

Clarke opened the binder and began to leaf through it.

"That said, Mr. President, I must add one question. Can you imagine the political firestorm that would have resulted if your predecessors had not acted to take out bin Laden—had followed the counsel of the naysayers—and then the nation learned they had just sat on their hands rather than doing everything possible to keep the country safe?"

Marcus returned to his seat, satisfied that he had made the most effective case possible.

But Stephens was ready with his own rebuttal. "Mr. President, before you make a final decision, remember May 7, 1999," the director of Central Intelligence said, his tone calmer now and more confident.

"What happened on May 7?" Clarke asked.

"That was the day during the war in Serbia that the U.S. bombed a building in Belgrade, certain it was an enemy target, only to discover they had just bombed the Chinese embassy. Three dead. Nearly two dozen wounded. And a crisis with Beijing that rages to this day."

Marcus tensed.

"And what about April 7, 2003?" Stephens continued. "That was the night an American B-1 bomber dropped a cluster of two-thousand-pound bunker-buster bombs on the Al Sa'ah Restaurant in the Mansour district of Baghdad. Why? Because the men and women sitting around this very table thought that Saddam Hussein and his two sons were there. Except they weren't. And the bombs missed the target anyway, landing on nearby homes and killing twelve innocent Iraqis instead."

Stephens paused for effect, then offered one more.

"Then there's July 6, 2008. Why is that date important? Because that's the day the White House was convinced it had a group of al Qaeda and Taliban terrorists in their sights in an Afghan town called Haska Meyna. There was precious little time to make a decision. So the president gave the order. And what happened? We ended up bombing a group of civilians heading to a wedding. Forty-seven dead, including thirty-nine women and children. Nine more were wounded. It wasn't simply a humanitarian tragedy. It was an unmitigated political and public relations disaster."

Stephens leaned back in his seat.

"Look, I've been in this game a long, long time," he said. "I've seen the price of a hasty mistake. And I, for one, don't ever want to pay that price again. Maybe

Ryker's right. *Maybe.* But what if he's wrong? Imagine the global firestorm that will engulf this administration. How will the Saudis react if we kill a bunch of innocent Muslims on the eve of the peace signing on Tuesday? How will the U.N. react? How will the pope react? You think he will still come to the U.S. on his peace tour next month? I cannot even imagine."

Now Stephens looked directly across the table at Marcus.

"Mr. Ryker, earlier you cited the case of this body deciding to send special forces into Pakistan to take down Osama bin Laden. You're right, of course—that was a decision based on circumstantial evidence. But you failed to mention that the CIA had been monitoring that house in Abbottabad for months. Following leads. Gathering evidence. Ruling out other scenarios. And pushing detainees at Gitmo hard—*very hard*, far harder than you're willing to push—to get every scrap of intel we possibly could before we took such risks. Not you. You're asking the president to make a split-second decision to send our fighter pilots—the bravest and best-trained men and women in the world—into harm's way on conjecture, against an unknown target, with unknown occupants, for an unknown outcome. That's a risky bet with the cards you're holding, young man. Too risky."

With all eyes on him, Marcus felt his face and neck flush with anger. The arrogance of this guy was off the charts.

"Mr. President, you know my family history, and you know my service record," he began, his voice quiet but firm. "I am well aware of the risks you would be putting our pilots in, sir, and I do not believe I'm asking you to act recklessly. I'm following the evidence. Not my whims. Not my passions. But carefully gathered evidence. Evidence that leads to that building in Libya. A massive and sophisticated compound in the middle of nowhere. With cinder block walls twenty feet high. No telephone wires. Not one but two satellite dishes. Towers in all four corners. A steel-reinforced front gate. And a pinging satphone repeatedly called by Abu Nakba's most trusted advisor. Is that advisor talking? No. I concede he is not. But not because I didn't push him and push him hard."

Only then did Marcus turn back to look Stephens in the eye.

"Now, is the director of Central Intelligence really asking whether I followed his explicit orders to torture Hamdi Yaşar? Is he really asking me on the record, in the presence of the National Security Council, whether I obeyed orders that Mr. Stephens issued to me verbally by phone on two separate occasions, and in writing in a classified cable that I received at Gitmo the day that Agent Morris and I arrived—orders that I regard as illegal? Let me be clear, Mr. President: No, I did not."

The nation would be told the NSC vote was unanimous in favor of the strike.

Technically, there had been one "no" vote. But since the director of the CIA was barred by law from providing policy recommendations—he was restricted to intelligence and analysis—Clarke insisted that Stephens's vote against didn't count and that it was vital they not allow the media to pick up any whiff of dissension.

Clarke signed the written order Defense Secretary Foster had prepared in advance. Foster, in turn, notified the National Military Command Center, deep beneath the Pentagon. From there, the order flashed to the combat information center of the USS *Nimitz*, steaming across sparkling blue waters of the Mediterranean, just south of Italy.

The first of four stealth fighter jets shot off the deck of the nuclear-powered aircraft carrier under a bright afternoon sun. Without radio chatter, they were effectively invisible and undetectable even in broad daylight. Powered by two Pratt & Whitney turbofan engines, the F-35C Lightning—the Navy's version of the joint strike fighter—quickly reached its service ceiling of fifty thousand feet, then banked hard to the south, streaking toward its target at twice the speed of sound.

At twenty-nine, Commander Bobby "Wolf" Mitchell was one of the most experienced F-35 pilots in the American military. He was certainly the most experienced aviator on the *Nimitz*. True, he had never conducted a bombing raid in North Africa. Nor had any of his three younger colleagues. But the mission was a dream: vaporize the headquarters of Kairos.

Mitchell reveled at the chance. Barely a week earlier, Abu Nakba had ordered his loyalists to launch a brazen raid on the Israeli-Lebanese border. After a brutal firefight, the jihadist cell had captured two Americans—one of them a highly valued CIA operative—as well as the nephew of the Israeli prime minister. That, in turn, had triggered what had already been dubbed the "Third Lebanon War," a massive missile and ground battle that had wreaked havoc on both sides of the border.

Somehow—and no one seemed to know for sure, though all manner of rumors were buzzing about—the CIA officer had escaped and organized the rescue of his colleagues. A cease-fire was now in place. The missiles were no longer in the air. The tanks were retreating back to their bases. Still, Mitchell was stunned by the scale of destruction in so short a time. Hundreds of Israelis and Lebanese were dead. Thousands more were wounded. Scores of homes, hospitals, factories, farms, synagogues, and mosques had been damaged or destroyed.

But now Abu Nakba and his senior commanders, the men responsible for all the carnage, were going to pay, and they would not even see it coming.

The complicator—and to Mitchell it was not insignificant—was a massive sandstorm consuming the airspace over their target and for thousands of miles in every direction. Brewing for days in the Bodélé Depression, a bone-dry lake bed in the Republic of Chad, the storm was now surging westward across the Sahara, through Libya and Algeria, headed at high speeds for Mauritania and Morocco. Burying everything in its path, it was also reducing visibility on the ground to nothing at all.

Mitchell scanned his instruments, triple-checking that his craft was still invisible to all possible enemies and that his weapons were cocked, locked, and ready to drop. It was. And they were. Yet he could feel his heart beating in his chest and the perspiration forming inside his Nomex flight gloves. He was, after all, responsible for an aircraft that cost the American taxpayers a cool $110 million to buy and a blistering $36,000 an hour to fly. The Pentagon was touting the plane to the public as the most advanced strike fighter ever built and deployed, and it was. But Mitchell knew every bug the engineers had found in the avionics software, every flaw they had found in the tailhooks, every detail of every F-35 that had crashed, and the name of every pilot who had died, as well as those who had ejected just in time.

He also knew that no F-35 had ever been sent into combat in a sandstorm, and he knew why. The plane's designers worried its engines could flame out—that is, stall with no recourse—if they became choked with particles of phosphorous, iron, silica, and more. They worried, too, that the supersecret coating that helped make the plane invisible to enemy radar could be effectively sandblasted off. What's more, they worried that the weapons bay doors could jam, making it impossible for a pilot to complete his mission even if he made it safely to the target.

Mitchell forced aside such thoughts. He had a job to do. Making a wide berth around Tripoli, the Libyan capital, with all of its civilian and military air traffic, he banked east, still over the Med. Two minutes later, he banked south again, aiming for a point almost equidistant between the cities of Misrata to the west and Benghazi to the east.

Slipping successfully into Libyan airspace undetected, Mitchell remained on a southward trajectory. Flying over a barren swath of no-man's-land that was largely uninhabited and nearly uninhabitable, he soon entered the sandstorm. This was it, he reckoned. If he crashed and lived, it could be days—even weeks—before anyone would come rescue him. If an F-35 couldn't make it through this beast, a Navy Seahawk helicopter certainly had no chance.

For the first several minutes, everything seemed fine. But about a hundred miles out from the Chad border, as Mitchell banked westward, his plane began to shimmy. It was almost imperceptible at first, but as he hugged the border with Niger, the plane began to shudder. Mitchell scanned his instruments. He was only sixteen minutes out. But his fears of not making it to the target, much less back to the carrier, were growing. This was not a test of the plane, he told himself. It was a test of his character, courage, training, and resolve.

Approaching the southwestern corner of Libya—close to the borders of Niger to his left and Algeria directly ahead, Mitchell and his wingman broke to the north, approaching Abu Nakba's lair from the south. The already-wicked shudder he was experiencing now worsened. But so far, both planes were still in the air, still hurtling over an empty expanse of desert, without a single city, town, or village anywhere on their scopes. And coming in behind them were the other two F-35s ready to finish whatever they failed to do themselves.

Suddenly Mitchell saw the city of Ghat light up on his radar. He wasn't worried that the airport was open or that he might be detected. That was impossible in this weather. Still, he made a slight course correction, moving now on a north-northwesterly heading, just fifteen miles out.

Then fourteen miles.

Then thirteen.

Twelve.

At ten miles out, Mitchell fired off his thousand-pound GPS-guided JDAM smart bombs. Banking eastward and flooring it, the commander watched the video feeds from the nose cones of the two missiles until they both scored direct hits, obliterating the main complex of buildings in the center of the compound. That was it. He had done it. He had accomplished his mission. The plane had survived. And so had he.

SOMEWHERE IN THE MOUNTAINS OF NORTHEASTERN YEMEN—12 MAY

Yaqoub al-Hamzi peered through his reticle down the winding dirt road.

He saw nothing yet but still made an adjustment on his Russian sniper rifle. "Anything?" he whispered to his spotter.

"Nothing," the spotter said.

"Check behind us."

"Again?"

"Yes, again."

The spotter did as he was told.

"All clear," he whispered back.

Suddenly the sniper spotted a plume of dust. It was small at first but grew quickly.

"They're coming," he said in Arabic over his wrist-mounted mic.

"Roger that," replied the voice in his ear.

Soon he could hear the roar of the powerful diesel engines. Finally he saw the two filthy, beat-up Range Rovers approaching from the south. Al-Hamzi felt sweat trickling down his back. He tried to steady his breathing, but he knew the stakes and the consequences if something went wrong.

Shifting away from the vehicles, he scanned the ridges of the nearby mountain range. He did a quick pass at first, then doubled back and took his time. He had already studied every square inch of the ridges and caves and outcroppings that cast such jagged shadows over their base camp. But one could never be too careful. If there were enemy forces lurking, al-Hamzi knew there were only a few places they could hide.

"Clear?" asked the voice in his ear.

"All clear," he replied, shifting his attention back to the Range Rovers.

Sixty seconds later, both SUVs pulled up in front of the largest of three adjacent buildings and came to a halt, their engines idling. The main house was a simple two-level structure built out of cinder blocks, with a satellite dish mounted on the roof among rusted strands of rebar sticking out of the concrete, evidence that someone had once hoped to build a third level. To the left, running perpendicular to the house, was a long, squat, single-story rectangular building that held offices and bunkrooms. It was also built of cinder blocks but had no rebar on its roof. The final building, the one on which al-Hamzi was perched, was a weathered wooden structure that had once been a cattle barn but now served as a garage and workshop and armory. In the center of the courtyard formed by the three buildings was a metal flagpole, though no flag had been raised. Ten heavily armed guards were stationed around the main house, and more men now poured out of the other two buildings.

Out of the first vehicle emerged six massive, bearded men. Al-Hamzi studied the faces of each one carefully, looking for anything out of place, any reason for alarm. He saw none. Each was dressed in local tribal garb. Each carried a fully loaded AK-47 Kalashnikov assault rifle. The men took up positions around the second Range Rover as five more similarly dressed and armed men exited. Together they formed a cordon around one more man.

It was to him that al-Hamzi now directed his full attention. Like the gunmen, this man had a full black beard, though his had flecks of gray. He was built similarly to the others as well—muscular, broad-chested, clearly a warrior—but he had to be at least twice their age. In contrast to the others, this one was dressed in a black leather jacket, black T-shirt, black jeans, combat boots, and sunglasses. The entire look was out of place, most of all the jacket, since the temperature was hovering in the upper nineties and the motionless air was thick with humidity. Al-Hamzi couldn't help but notice that as the man stepped up on the porch and disappeared into the house with three of his aides, he walked with a strut that was supremely self-confident and almost regal in its bearing.

A shiver ran down al-Hamzi's spine.

It was hard to believe the man had really come here of all places.

Badr Hassan al-Ruzami entered the conference room on the top floor.

He took off the leather jacket, tossed it onto a small desk in the corner, nodded to his colleagues, and motioned for the three younger men with him to take a seat at the table while he remained standing in the doorway, away from the windows and in full view of the others.

"Father is dead," he began.

"We've been watching the coverage," replied Zaid Farooq, the bespectacled and somewhat-diminutive deputy commander and chief of intelligence for Kairos, wearing not linen robes but an old suit he'd bought in Istanbul. "And we're in mourning."

"As am I—we have lost a great warrior." Ruzami spoke for several minutes about the virtues of Abu Nakba, all that they had accomplished together, and what a crushing blow his death was to the Kairos movement.

"It is more than devastating," said a tall, lanky man sitting in the back corner, dressed in tan-and-brown combat fatigues, a pistol strapped to his side. "It is an act of war and a call to vengeance."

Head of internal security and the third member of the senior Kairos leadership Tariq Youssef lit up a cigarette.

"With all respect, Brother Badr," Youssef said, "we expected you to arrive several days ago."

"It couldn't be helped," Ruzami said. "I had to make sure I was not being tailed. As you know, Brother Tariq, there are many foreign spies in Aden."

"Tell us you used your time judiciously," Youssef pressed. "Tell me the plan is still in play."

"We know what happened in Libya," Farooq interjected. "And we know what the Americans say happened. But the sandstorm is still in progress, is it not?"

"Yes."

"So the Americans cannot send anyone to Ghat to assess the situation."

"True."

"Then *now* is the time to make those infidels pay."

"*Patience,*" Ruzami said. "Patience. The strike happened, and Father is dead. That much is true. Let us not kid ourselves. We all knew there was a risk. Father certainly did. That's why he put me in charge in case anything ever happened to him. And that's why we developed this contingency plan to flip the tables on our enemies while they're still basking in their glory."

"If not now, then when?" Youssef asked.

"Get out your notebooks," Ruzami replied. "And I'll tell you."

WASHINGTON, D.C.—13 MAY

Annie Stewart awoke in the darkness.

Alone in her town house.

In a damp T-shirt. Her hair matted. Her hands trembling.

It had been a long time since she'd let herself think about the day she'd first met Marcus Ryker. Then again, did a nightmare qualify as *letting herself* think about it now? It was certainly a day she would never forget. But it was also so tangled up in such primal and unresolved emotions she wasn't sure it was one she wanted to remember.

Annie slipped out of bed and headed into the bathroom. She splashed water on her face and pulled her hair back in a scrunchie, then threw on running shorts and a fresh T-shirt and a new pair of trainers and headed out for her morning run. It was earlier than usual. The sun was not yet up, but she knew she'd never get back to sleep.

As she hit the pavement, she decided to rewind the tape in her head. There were, after all, good parts to that day. She remembered arriving in Kabul with her new boss, Senator Robert Dayton. It was her first overseas trip with the ranking member of the Senate Intelligence Committee, and as a deputy press secretary, Annie was excited to be on the front lines in America's war on terror. Climbing into the Sikorsky CH-53E Super Stallion, she was struck by the friendliness of the young Marines assigned to protect the senator. Pete Hwang had certainly been a gentleman, as had Nick Vinetti, God rest his soul. Bill McDermott had been a little too friendly, shamelessly flirting nonstop on their flight to Kandahar. But she had to give him credit for one good deed—introducing her to a shy but ruggedly handsome young man showing her no interest whatsoever.

"Now, the guy you really want to stick close to, Miss Stewart, is Lance Corporal Ryker here," she recalled McDermott saying.

"Really, and why's that?"

"Because Vinnie and I are notorious bachelors," McDermott said, grinning. "And St. Pete—well, don't be fooled by his cherubic face. But Ryker here, he's a good Christian and a real family man. When the chips are down, you can count on this guy."

No sooner had the words come out of McDermott's mouth than they all heard and felt the explosion. Annie could still see the lead chopper erupting in a ball of fire. The antiaircraft fire erupting below them. The pilots taking evasive action. Marcus tightening his own shoulder harness, then reaching over and tightening hers as their Super Stallion dove for the deck and finally slammed down on the side of the mountain.

So much of what happened next was a blur. Billowing smoke. Raging fires. Gunfire erupting. McDermott shouting orders. Vinetti, a sniper, taking out enemy forces approaching them. Marcus scrambling down the mountainside to reach the senator in the other chopper. Pete, a medic, attending Dayton, whose leg was badly wounded. Marcus carrying Dayton up the mountain to a cave that would serve as their temporary shelter.

She remembered Taliban and al Qaeda fighters approaching in a caravan of pickup trucks. Vinetti picking off one fighter after another and taking out several of the lead vehicles. And Marcus racing down the mountain, darting around burning vehicles, dodging bullets, heading for a rocket-propelled grenade launcher lying on the side of the road.

Annie slowed her running pace and shook her head, trying to forestall the mental image of Marcus, hit by an enemy bullet, writhing on the ground yet still trying to reload the RPG launcher. All too vividly, she remembered Marcus struggling to get the launcher to his shoulder and steady his aim. Yet just then he was hit again by incoming rounds. Lurching back, he dropped the grenade launcher. She recalled watching in horror as he collapsed just inches from a burning truck. He pulled a sidearm from its holster and fired again and again as one Taliban fighter after another came around the back of the truck. She saw two fighters go down. But then the pistol was empty and five more pickups filled with at least thirty more men were heading straight for him.

The last thing Annie remembered was the deafening roar of an A-10 Thunderbolt. It swooped down from the sky out of nowhere and lit up the road with 30mm shells, annihilating everyone and everything in its path.

The good guys had finally arrived, and not a moment too soon.

11

SOUTHEAST D.C.

Marcus watched the two teenagers enter the store dressed in hoodies and wearing sunglasses.

He couldn't see their faces, but he immediately knew something was wrong. In an instant, the two drew handguns and demanded the man behind the counter open the register.

Marcus saw fear grip the handful of customers standing in line. He watched Elena slowly take Lars's hand and pull him behind her. He saw the clerk's trembling hands fumbling to open the register but taking too long.

He tried to run but couldn't move, tried to shout but couldn't scream. He reached for his sidearm, but it wasn't there.

Marcus saw Elena glance at the door, just a couple of yards away from where she and Lars were standing. He saw the look in her eyes, saw the calculations. He knew what she was thinking. He knew they would never make it.

Suddenly the silence was broken. Marcus heard the gunshots. Three of them in rapid succession. Marcus couldn't see the shooter. But he saw the results. One round blew out the glass of the door. The next struck one of the hoodlums in the chest. The third hit him in the throat. The kid flew backward through the shattered glass and landed on the pavement with a thud.

Unable to move, Marcus watched helplessly as the other gunman wheeled around and returned fire. People dropped to the ground, Lars and Elena among them. Marcus screamed but no one could hear his cry.

Suddenly it was nighttime.

And now Marcus was able to move. He crossed the street. He heard the crunch of shattered glass beneath his shoes. He saw the flashing red and blue lights of police cars and ambulances all around him. He could see a woman's hand, cold and stiff, poking out from beneath a blood-soaked sheet. He knew that diamond ring and that gold band. He forced himself to kneel beside the body. His hands shaking, he slowly pulled back the sheet. It was Elena. Her eyes were closed. She looked like she was sleeping, so peaceful, so beautiful. Then he pulled the sheet back farther and saw the damage. She'd been hit once in the chest and again in the stomach. Blood was everywhere. His bottom lip quivered. He wanted to look away, but he could not.

Marcus leaned down and kissed his wife on her forehead, then pulled the sheet up over her face and turned to the body next to her. Again, he slowly pulled back the sheet. His son was lying facedown. But Marcus could see the bullet holes in his back, his clothing soaked in crimson. Slowly, carefully, he turned the boy over. Lars's eyes were still open. They looked so scared—haunted and alone. Marcus gently shut Lars's eyes, cradled him in his arms, and wept.

Marcus sat bolt upright.

Alone in his bed.

Drenched in sweat.

In the darkness and stillness of his apartment.

At 4:52 in the morning.

He forced himself out of bed and went into the bathroom wearing nothing but a pair of black Jockey shorts. Switching on the light, he winced as his eyes adjusted. He splashed water on his face and neck and stared at himself in the mirror. The bruises. Scars. Contusions. Burn marks. He was a mess. And racked with nightmares for the eleventh night in a row.

Throwing on a pair of gym shorts and a T-shirt, Marcus went to the living room of his modest apartment. He flipped on the television, careful to keep the volume low, and slumped down on the couch, trying to think of something, anything, besides the memories of Lars's and Elena's murders. The top story on cable news, of course, was the signing of the Israeli-Saudi peace accord on the South Lawn of the White House. The Vatican was announcing that the pope was coming to the U.S. for a four-city "peace tour," followed by a visit to Jerusalem and the first papal visit to Riyadh. When the story shifted to some boy band Marcus had never heard of breaking up, he hit Mute and padded to the kitchen.

He stuck a pod of some Brazilian blend in his Keurig machine and waited for the coffee to brew. Staring back at him from a frame on the kitchen counter were Elena, little Lars, and himself. The photo had been taken on their only trip to the Magic Kingdom. They were standing in front of Cinderella's castle. Lars, only four or five years old, sat on his father's shoulders, eating cotton candy, grinning from ear to ear, his chocolate-brown eyes wide and filled with wonder. Elena was nestled close to him, her arm around his waist, her beautiful black hair pulled back in a ponytail, her mocha-brown eyes shimmering and bright. Their happiest day at the happiest place on Earth.

Marcus bolted out of the kitchen and back to his bedroom. He fished out some clean socks from the top drawer of his dresser and threw on a pair of old running shoes. Taking his Sig Sauer and extra clips from the top drawer of the nightstand beside the bed, he chambered a round and put everything in a fanny pack he kept in the closet. Then he grabbed his iPhone, put in his earbuds, cranked up some Jackson Browne, and headed outside. Coffee wasn't what he needed just now. It was time to start running again. Given all that he had been through, he had little confidence he could make it five miles. The soles of his feet burned. So did every joint and muscle in his legs and chest. But he had to try. He couldn't go back to sleep. There was nothing to do in his apartment. It wouldn't be fair to call Pete, much less Annie. So running on empty it was.

The streets of southeast D.C. were quiet at this hour. A few cabs. A *Washington Post* truck dropping off the morning edition. A Metro Police car keeping watch near Lincoln Park Baptist Church. Marcus ran past the Supreme Court and the

Capitol, then down Pennsylvania Avenue. The pain was immense, but he refused to stop. When he rounded the White House, he nodded to the uniformed Secret Service agents he passed and headed back toward the Capitol. A car horn was sounding. He could hear a siren in the distance. American, Israeli, and Saudi flags still adorning the lampposts flapped in the light spring breeze coming off the Potomac. A few minutes later, a Marine helicopter roared overhead.

Back home, he dead bolted the door, tossed his keys on the counter, and took a long, hot shower. As he brushed his teeth and trimmed his beard and mustache, he could swear he was smelling bacon and freshly brewed coffee. Brushing it off as wishful thinking, he dressed in a suit and tie. He put on his shoulder holster, transferred his Sig Sauer into it, clipped his spare magazines to his belt, fished his DSS badge and CIA credentials out of his wall safe, and headed back to the kitchen.

Only to find his mother waiting for him.

12

"Let me guess," Marjorie Ryker said. "Couldn't sleep again?"

Marcus was amazed to see that she was awake, showered, dressed, and had made a big breakfast for them both and that her suitcase was already packed and by the door.

"You didn't have to do all this," he said, coming into the kitchen and giving her a kiss on the forehead.

"How often do I get to stay with you, much less dote on you a little?"

"You shouldn't have."

"Nonsense," she scoffed, pouring him a DSS mug of black coffee. "Now, go sit down."

She served him a Denver omelet, homemade hash browns, asparagus, several strips of bacon—crispy, just the way he liked—and a glass of orange juice.

"You made all this while I was in the shower? When did you even go shopping?"

"After the ceremony when you went back to work," she said as she served herself.

"I thought you went to visit Dad's grave," he said, sitting at the head of the table.

"I did," she replied, sitting beside him. "After that."

Marcus thanked the Lord for the food and for his mother's tireless love and kindness toward him. Before he could say *amen*, she added her own word of thanks that the Lord had rescued Marcus and his team out of Lebanon, that he was finally safe and beginning to heal, and that those responsible for these wicked attacks had been brought to justice.

"So tell me—why in the world are you wearing a suit?"

Marcus looked up at her. "Because after I take you to the airport, I'm going to work."

"They don't give you time off after being kidnapped and tortured?"

Marcus laughed. "That's why they pay me the big bucks."

"You need to rest, Marcus. You need to give your body time to heal. And not just your body."

"What can I say, Mom? There's just a mountain of work on my plate."

"Like what? Abu Nakba is dead. Kairos has been decimated. The Supreme Leader of Iran just died. Moscow is quiet. So are the North Koreans. The Chinese are a problem, I grant you. But they're not about to assassinate anybody in the State Department. The world is quiet, Marcus. Isn't it enough already? Maybe it's time to come back to Colorado. Spend time with your family. Hike some fourteeners again. Clear your head and start thinking about your future."

"Eat your breakfast, Mom," he said, taking a swig of coffee. "It's getting cold."

For the moment, she let it go. They talked for a while about how the Nationals were doing so much better than the Rockies. As they cleared the table, she told him how she'd run into Elena's mother in the supermarket a few weeks back and been invited over to the Garcias' for dinner.

"Wow, it's been so long."

"You're telling me—years."

"So how's Louisa doing?"

"Pretty well, actually. She said she's volunteering a lot more at their parish these days. And they're raising money for a scholarship fund named after Elena, for at-risk kids to come to their high school."

"And Javier?" he asked.

"Well, you know, good days and bad," she said as they loaded the dishwasher.

"And did I come up at all?" he asked tentatively.

"One step at a time, sweetheart, one step at a time."

"So what did you talk about?"

"Mostly their vacation in Rome last summer and the Vatican—and the pope's upcoming visit, of course. They're excited about that."

Religion had always been a touchy subject between Elena and her parents. They were devout Catholics. She had not only become a Protestant in high school but an evangelical of all things. That hadn't exactly gone over well, especially with her father, but during their marriage they had done their best not to let it be a point of friction. Marcus hadn't seen his in-laws since the funeral, having been effectively declared persona non grata. Maybe now things were beginning to thaw. He certainly hoped so.

Twenty minutes later, they were in the car headed to Reagan National Airport.

"So listen, I have to ask you," his mother began. "Why wouldn't you come with me to Arlington yesterday, after the peace signing?"

"Mom, we covered this already. Debriefings at the Pentagon. After-action reports to write. The papal visit is coming up. Four cities. It's a logistical nightmare."

"You can't take an hour off to pay respects to your father?"

"Not right now. Not this week."

"How often do I come to Washington?"

"You should come more often."

"You should invite me more often."

"I should, but . . ."

"But what?"

"Look, I'm just not a fan of cemeteries, okay?" he told her. "Too many friends there. Too many ghosts."

For several blocks, his mother said nothing.

As they passed the Capitol on their right, however, she spoke again.

"You know I couldn't be more proud of you, right?"

"Thanks, Mom."

"Your dad would have been proud of you too."

Marcus was quiet as he threaded through traffic.

"You've proven yourself a warrior. You've given your all toward serving and protecting your country. But now . . . well . . ."

"What, Mom? What are you saying?"

"I'm saying you're at halftime. The first half was about taking risks, doing your part. The Marines. The Secret Service. What you're doing now. Believe me, I get it."

"But . . . ?"

"Don't miss your chance to play the second half."

"Meaning what?"

"Meaning maybe it's time to make a change. Do what your father never got a chance to do—enjoy the rest of this precious life God has given you."

"But you're the one who told me I was made for this, that I should do it and not feel guilty about it."

"And I meant it. But you almost died in Lebanon. So I'm telling you now what I wish I could have told your father: Eject while you still can."

Marcus was quiet as he turned off Independence Avenue. "I'll think about it," he said finally. "Now, can we change the subject?"

"Okay, fine," she said. "Pick a topic, any topic."

He didn't have a topic. His mind was reeling from the topics they'd already covered. So she picked her own.

"I really enjoyed dinner with your friends last night," she said, her tone brighter.

In a rare move on his part, Marcus had made reservations at the Chart House, an upscale seafood place in Old Town, Alexandria, to celebrate their successful operation in Lebanon, the end of the Hezbollah war with Israel, and the peace treaty they had all played a part in bringing to pass. Senator Dayton and his wife, Esther, were there, as were Bill McDermott and his wife, Allison. Jenny Morris was there. So were Geoff Stone, Donny Callaghan, Noah Daniels, and Pete Hwang. And for the first time in this intimate group of friends, so was Annie Stewart.

"That was fun, wasn't it?" Marcus replied, grateful his mother was choosing to wind up these few days together on a more fun and lighthearted subject.

"It was good to see Pete."

Marcus nodded.

"And it was fun catching up with Annie."

"I'm glad."

"I even woke up to a lovely email from her saying how much she enjoyed seeing me and it's been too long."

"Really? Annie emailed you?"

"She most certainly did."

"Well, she's a class act."

"Are you seeing her tonight?"

"She's having dinner with her boss and some muckety-mucks from Riyadh."

"What about tomorrow night?"

"Don't start with me, Mom. We're just friends."

"Right."

"What's that supposed to mean?"

"I saw you two holding hands during the ceremony. The way you two talked and laughed all night."

"Mom, seriously, we've gone out on one date. That's it."

"So what? There's obviously chemistry between you two. That's nice. I'm happy for you. Why deny it?"

Marcus considered the question as he pulled onto the grounds of Reagan National, heading for the main terminal. "Sure, Mom, I like Annie."

"Good—so do I."

"But it's not serious. Not yet. And I don't know if it ever will be or even whether I want it to be. We're just . . ."

"What?"

"Hanging out."

"Why?"

"Mom, please, it was one date."

A moment later, he pulled up to the curb in front of the doors marked American Airlines and put the car in park. Grabbing her luggage out of the trunk, he opened the door for her and helped her out.

"Honey, listen to me," she said gently as he hugged her goodbye. "Annie is an amazing woman. And you're not married anymore. Elena is gone. I know you still love her, and I'm glad you do. I love her, too, and I miss her every day. But the Lord took her. I don't know why, but he did. You don't have to feel guilty about moving on. It's time, Marcus. It's time to take your foot off the gas, retire, and marry that girl before it's too late."

14

HART SENATE OFFICE BUILDING

Annie pulled her Fiat 500L up to the steel barrier and stopped.

"Morning, Charlie, how are you today?" she asked the uniformed Capitol police officer as she lowered the driver's-side window, flashed her Senate ID badge, and handed over the man's usual, a Venti caramel macchiato from Starbucks.

"Better now," he replied, smiling broadly as he took his first sip. "Hey, I saw you on TV yesterday at the big shindig at the White House."

"Please tell me you're pulling my leg," she replied, wincing.

"Nope," he replied as the gate rose and the steel barrier began to lower. "During the speeches, C-SPAN kept cutting to various people in the audience, and suddenly there you were. They were focused on your boss, but you were right there—you and some guy you were holding hands with. Anything you'd like to tell me, young lady?"

Fortunately, there were now six cars behind her. One was laying on the horn.

"No comment," she said, hitting the accelerator the moment the barrier was fully down.

Inside the building, she boarded a packed elevator, avoiding eye contact with everyone and trying to make sense of what Charlie had just said. If he had seen her holding hands with Marcus, who else had? She was a high-level staffer on the Senate Intelligence Committee, for crying out loud. She'd spent her entire professional life in the shadows, carefully maintaining a low profile, determined never to take the spotlight off her boss.

It wasn't that she was embarrassed to be seen with Marcus, she told herself as the elevator began to rise. To the contrary. She had always had enormous respect for him, even if he lived a life far too dangerous for her taste. She was an intelligence analyst, not an operative. She knew the nation had to be guarded by people with guns and the will to use them. But it would never be her.

Annie would always be grateful for all that Marcus had done to protect her in Afghanistan. More than grateful. She was pretty sure she had fallen in love with Marcus on that dreadful day. She had never told a soul, of course. Not her closest girlfriends. Not Senator Dayton. And certainly not Marcus. He had been engaged, after all, or nearly so.

Upon returning to Washington from Afghanistan, Annie had entered years of counseling. Not to process her feelings toward Marcus but to deal with everything else that had happened on that mountainside in Kandahar. That experience was stirred up again several years later when her own parents died in a private plane crash. All of it had given rise to nightmares and panic attacks and prescription narcotics and, for a time, an addiction to the very drugs that were supposed to help.

By the grace of God and the patience of dear friends, she had come through it all. Miraculously, she hadn't lost her job. Hadn't lost her security clearance. She'd gotten help. Gotten clean. And remained so for eight years, four months, and nine days.

Now Marcus Ryker was threatening all the progress she had made.

He didn't know how intensely he was rattling her. How could he? They had only been out on one date, intending to go to the White House correspondents' dinner but bailing on that at the last minute and going to dinner by themselves instead. Then Marcus had headed to Lebanon and all hell had broken loose.

Dinner after the peace signing with Marcus and his team and even his mother might have counted as a second date, but the truth was Annie had no idea what

Marcus was really thinking or where any of this was leading. All she knew for certain was that she was far more interested in Marcus than he was in her, and that frightened her.

There was something else Annie knew for certain—three things, actually.

The first was that Marcus was far too busy for a serious relationship.

The second was that the life Marcus lived was not one she wanted to be part of. She understood what he did, and she knew how good he was at it, but it simply wasn't for her.

The third truth was that she cherished Marcus's friendship too much to play games. If they were really meant to be together, good. She would like nothing better. But she was going to hold this thing loosely, make her own choices, and just see where the road led.

That said, she had certainly been pleasantly surprised when Marcus had taken her hand during the peace ceremony. She just never imagined being outed on national television.

The elevator door opened.

They had reached the main floor. Annie kept her head down as she made her way to the security checkpoint. There she was warmly greeted by all of the officers, each of whom knew her by name. They checked her driver's license and Senate ID. They looked through her purse, asked her to walk through the magnetometer, and wished her a good day. None said anything. But they knew. She could see it in their impish grins.

As she walked across the atrium, took the stairs to the second floor, and entered the senator's offices, Annie tried to shake it off. She had too much on her plate to let herself get distracted, much less embarrassed. Not today.

Greeting the receptionist and the few other staffers who were in that early, she poured herself a cup of coffee in the utility kitchen and headed back to her cramped cubicle. The usual stack of newspapers was piled on her chair—the *New York Times*, *Washington Post*, *Washington Times*, *Wall Street Journal*, *USA Today*, *The Hill*, and *Politico*. The historic signing of the Israeli-Saudi peace treaty was the lead story in every one of them, complete with full-color photos of the White House ceremony. Fortunately, Annie found none that included her and Marcus.

The other big story, of course, was the "Saturday Night Strike"—the bombing of the compound in Libya several days earlier and the killing of the world's most-feared terrorist. The Kairos terror network was effectively out of business. Annie was eager to see how each paper was covering the historic events, but there was no time for that now.

Senator Robert Dayton was meeting with the Saudi crown prince in less than forty-five minutes. Followed by lunch with the Israeli prime minister. Followed by the signing of a $250 billion bilateral trade and investment deal between the U.S. and the Saudis at the Commerce Department that afternoon. Followed by an intimate dinner on the seventh floor of the State Department with Secretary Whitney, the Israeli and Saudi foreign ministers, and a small bipartisan group of House and Senate members. And then a late-evening round of drinks with the Saudi intelligence chief.

Tossing the papers aside and locking her purse in a bottom drawer, Annie sat down and began leafing through the stack of pink message slips waiting for her, but she found herself distracted by the two framed pictures on her desk. They weren't "power photos" of her with various world leaders. That wasn't her style. The first one was of her in her freshman dorm room, sporting a brand-new American University sweatshirt, her arms around her parents, her big green eyes filled with so much anticipation about the coming year. The photo was faded and worn—a frozen glimpse into another time. It made her wistful, but she loved it all the same. She missed them so much.

The second was taken at that air base in Kabul, standing on the tarmac in front of that Super Stallion, just before the fateful flight. She cringed at the ridiculous pin-striped business suit she'd been wearing, not to mention the outdated shag haircut. She could hardly remember her hair quite that blonde and without a trace of gray. Next to her was Senator Dayton. Around them were the Marines assigned to protect them, all decked out in full combat gear.

On the far right, almost out of the frame, was Marcus. Six-foot-one, 190 pounds. In peak physical condition. Burnished by the blazing desert sun. That rugged, chiseled face, the heritage of his Dutch roots. And those blue eyes. How often in life did one actually possess a photograph taken in the very first moments of meeting a person who would—or at least could—so alter your future?

A great deal of time had passed since that fateful day, of course. Over the course of nearly two decades, much had transpired in both of their lives. Annie still ran five miles every morning except Sundays, though her pace was a little slower now. Her hair was a little longer. Her eyes were a little weaker—thus the black, narrow, flattop Ray-Ban glasses she'd bought in a ridiculously vain effort to feel a little hipper than she knew she really was. She was making a little more money today than all those years before. She even had some savings stashed away.

Yet all that was so superficial. The things she'd thought would never change somehow had. Washington no longer held the same mystique. The buildings and monuments were still so rich in history and grandeur. And she would never tire of the Potomac River's beauty. But Annie was no longer the starry-eyed ingenue who had come to Washington at the tender age of eighteen to study and stayed to play the Big Game. She had seen too much since then. Knew too much. The game had taken too much out of her. And now . . .

The phone rang.

Annie picked it up immediately, hoping it was Marcus.

It was not.

"Miss Stewart, the senator's ready for you."

"Of course," she said. "I'll be right there."

"What's on the crown prince's wish list today?" Dayton asked.

No *hello*.

No *good morning*.

No *my, what a lovely spring outfit*.

They were speed-walking to the U.S. Capitol subway system, and the senior senator from Iowa was all business.

"Did you talk to his people?" he pressed as they stepped into one of the small compartments and shut the door behind them, preventing anyone else from joining them. "What is the ambassador telling you? It's the trade deal, right? He wants to adjust the wheat and corn provisions again. Well, the answer's no. I'm not going to keep—"

"Senator, the crown prince has no interest in relitigating the ag provisions," Annie replied, lowering her voice as she sat down across from him and handed him a leather binder.

"Then what?" Dayton asked, flipping open the briefing book and trying to digest it as the subway began moving. "I have no interest in listening to more of his kvetching about not being able to build the interceptor missiles on Saudi soil. They'll be built here in the good ole U.S.-of-A. by hardworking Americans, or they can kiss the deal—"

"Senator, His Royal Highness doesn't want to talk about Iowa corn or Patriot missile interceptors," Annie said quietly, adjusting her glasses. "He's fine with the trade deal. It's Yemen he wants to talk about."

"Yemen?" Dayton asked, looking up. "What for? I thought—"

"It's not the Houthis or the Iranians that have got him worried, sir."

"Then what?"

"It's Kairos."

"Kairos?"

"Yes, sir."

"I don't understand," Dayton said. "Doesn't he read his cables? The president of the United States just bombed Kairos and its leadership to kingdom come."

"Maybe so, Senator, but the GID says at least a half-dozen senior Kairos operatives and more than two dozen Kairos fighters were spotted ten days ago—some in Sana'a, the others in Aden."

"And?"

"They were under Saudi surveillance for the better part of a week, then vanished."

"Vanished," Dayton repeated.

"Yes, sir."

"And that rises to the level of the crown prince's attention, much less mine, because why?"

"It's all in the briefing book," Annie replied. "But there is another matter I need to discuss with you before we—"

The senator's phone rang.

"It's the *Times*," he whispered. "I have to take this."

Of course he did. Annie sighed. She checked her watch, then sat back and took in the rest of the ride. And what a ride it had been.

After graduating from AU with a bachelor's degree in history, she'd earned her master's in international relations from Georgetown University's School of Foreign Service, graduating summa cum laude. Then Dayton had hired her. The Iowa Democrat's progressive views on economic and domestic policy she could do without. Yet his old-fashioned love of country, his nostalgia for small-town America, and his passion for what he called "the forgotten family farmers" endeared him to her. More importantly, his outspoken advocacy for a muscular military and a forward-leaning, bipartisan approach to foreign policy had intrigued her. Back then, such traits made him a rare breed in the Democratic caucus. More than fifteen years later, he had become an endangered species.

Over the years, Annie had found Dayton to be a kind and decent man. A loving husband. A devoted dad. And a generous boss. Dayton promoted her first to press secretary and later to legislative director before transferring her to the Intelligence Committee, where he had elevated her to his most senior advisor, making this conversation all the more difficult.

"Senator, there's something I need to tell you," Annie said when he hung up the phone.

"Sure, but take this number down," Dayton replied, patting himself down for a pen that wasn't there.

Annie scrawled the number on her notepad, then tore out the page and handed it and the pen to her boss. She had no idea whose number it was. Nor did she care. "Sir, this is important."

But Dayton had other things on his mind. "When we get back to the office, we need to call Dell at Langley and Hutchinson at the Pentagon. And double-check to see if the Ukrainian foreign minister is still on for breakfast tomorrow and find out what he really wants. I was told that—"

Annie was not about to be derailed. "Senator?" she interrupted, but Dayton kept speed-talking as he scribbled notes in the margin of the briefing book. "*Senator.*"

Dayton finally looked up.

"There's something I need to tell you."

"Fine. What? Spit it out. We're almost there."

Annie sat back and raised her right eyebrow. Dayton got the message. He closed the binder.

"Okay, sorry—what've you got?" he asked, remembering his Midwestern manners just as they reached the Capitol.

"I'm giving you my notice, Senator. It's been a wonderful ride. And I'm grateful to you and Esther for everything. Really. But I'm done, sir. It's time to get off."

LANGLEY, VIRGINIA

Marcus exited the G.W. Parkway onto Route 123.

Three minutes later, he was pulling into the George Bush Center for Intelligence. Showing his badge, he drove onto the campus, parked his ugly brown '86 Nissan Stanza, and entered CIA headquarters. Clearing through security, he stepped onto an empty elevator, swiped his ID, and hit the button. On the way up, his phone vibrated. It was a text from Annie.

You awake? she asked.

Marcus smiled.

Of course. Just took Mom to airport.

Good son.

Heading into a meeting, he wrote. **Can I call you later?**

Do you one better. I'm free for dinner.

See you tonight, then? he asked.

The bell dinged. The elevator door opened. Marcus stepped off onto the seventh floor and checked in at the security desk.

"Good morning, Agent Ryker," a uniformed officer said.

"Morning, Tony."

"Ryker, you look like crap."

"You should see the other guy," Marcus deadpanned. "The boss in?"

"Breakfast at the Pentagon."

"Dell?"

"Conference room," the officer replied. "Is she expecting you?"

"I sure hope so," Marcus laughed, handing over his mobile phone and weapon.

Passing through another magnetometer, he headed down the hall, grateful to learn Stephens wasn't in the building. He was greeted by officers and administrative staff who congratulated him and asked him how he was doing. One even whispered that she'd been praying for him.

Knocking twice, he entered the conference room and found Dr. Martha Dell chairing a meeting already in progress. At fifty-seven, Dell was the Agency's highest-ranking African American officer. Far more important to Marcus, she was the smartest person he had met, inside the CIA or out. The woman had graduated first in her class from Georgetown University in national security studies. She had a master's degree in Russian-Sino relations from Oxford. What's more, she'd earned not one but two PhDs from Stanford, both dealing with aspects of Chinese foreign and military policy. Fluent in Russian, Mandarin, and Arabic, she'd been a field officer in the National Clandestine Service. She'd successfully recruited and run agents, been an instructor at the Farm, and worked in a wide range of increasingly sensitive management positions over her thirty-plus years before being named the Agency's deputy director. There was no one in the building that Marcus liked or trusted more, but the shocked look on her face just then was trouble.

"Ryker, what are you doing here?" she demanded.

Everyone turned, and Marcus found himself staring at an equally shocked Pete Hwang, Jenny Morris, Geoff Stone, Donny Callaghan, and Noah Daniels.

"Good to see you, too, Doc," Marcus quipped and quickly took his usual seat.

"No, seriously, what are you doing?" Dell shot back. "You're supposed to be home. You're supposed to be recovering."

"I'm fine."

"You're not."

"Where are we with the compound?" Marcus asked, seeing satellite images of western Libya on the flat-screen monitors all around them. Clearly the sandstorm wasn't yet over. A brown haze was covering the entire border region with Algeria.

"Go home, Marcus," Dell finally said.

"I don't want to go home."

"Then take your mom for a walk around the Tidal Basin."

"I just took her to the airport."

"Then take Annie for a walk around the Tidal Basin."

"Very funny, and besides, she and Dayton are meeting with the crown prince."

"Then buy a dog. Play Nintendo. Take up scrapbooking. I don't care what you do. Just go. Now. That's an order."

Marcus sat there for a moment, incredulous. Dell was serious. And he wasn't getting any sympathy from his team. They were *his* team, after all. But that didn't seem to matter at the moment. So he took a deep breath, forced himself to his feet, and left.

Soon he was driving back down the G.W. Parkway without the foggiest notion of where he was supposed to go. Yes, his body needed sleep. Obviously he needed time to recover and lots of it. But there was no way he was going back to his apartment. Not now. There was too much to do, too many loose strings to tie up.

His phone rang, and McDermott's number flashed on the screen. Marcus tensed. Given how his morning was going so far, that couldn't be good news.

"Hey, you home?" McDermott asked.

"No."

"Why not?"

"What do you care?"

"You're supposed to be in bed."

"What do you need, Bill?"

"It's not me. It's the president."

"What about him?"

"He wants to see you."

"When?" Marcus asked, surprised.

"*Now*—how quickly can you get your butt in here?"

THE WHITE HOUSE

"Agent Ryker, thanks for coming in on such short notice."

The president shook Marcus's hand, as did Vice President Hernandez. Then Clarke asked Marcus and McDermott to take a seat on the couch across from his armchair.

"I apologize for all the secrecy," he continued. "You probably haven't come through that tunnel from Treasury since your days in the Secret Service."

"It has been a while."

"And I don't believe you've been upstairs here to the Residence since you brought me word the Saudis were interested in a peace summit in Jerusalem. But like last time, Bill suggested it might not be a good idea for you to be seen by the staff and certainly not by the press."

"How can I be of service, Mr. President—have you received the BDA yet?" Marcus asked, referring to the bomb damage assessment from Libya.

The VP took that one. "Not yet. The sandstorm is weakening, fortunately, but it's not over. Until it is, NSA can't get us any good images of the compound. Nor can we send anyone in on the ground."

Marcus was disappointed but certainly understood the impossibility of sending helicopters filled with U.S. special forces into such a mess.

"That said, Kairos is the reason I asked you to come over," the president said, motioning to McDermott, who quickly opened his laptop and pulled up three black-and-white photographs displayed side by side. "Recognize these men?"

"Of course, the Troika," Marcus replied.

"The *what*?"

"Sorry, sir—that's what my team and I have dubbed them. The Troika. They're all deputy commanders of Kairos, and with Abu Nakba eliminated, we believe these three clowns are now running the circus."

"What can you tell me about them?"

"Well, the psycho on the left is Tariq Youssef—he's their head of internal security. The thug in the center, with the glasses, that's Zaid Farooq—we believe he's their intelligence czar."

"And the one on the right with the cigarette dangling from his lips?"

"That's Badr Hassan al-Ruzami."

"What do we know about him?"

"Head of operations. Almost certainly chief among equals. Late forties, maybe early fifties. Born in Libya but grew up in the mountains of Kandahar. Joined ISIS but had a falling-out with the leadership after the fall of the Caliphate. Recruited by Abu Nakba about three years ago. Three wives, though the Saudis think at least one was killed in an air strike. A mess of daughters. Three grown sons, all of whom now work for Kairos."

"Why do you call him 'chief among equals'?"

"'Cause he's wicked smart—way smarter than Youssef and Farooq. He's also a cold-blooded killer. And impossible to find."

"You don't think they were all killed Saturday near Ghat?"

"I hope they were, Mr. President. But it's unlikely that they were all there in the same place with Abu Nakba."

At this point, the VP weighed in again.

"But, Agent Ryker, you told us most of the senior Kairos leadership was there."

"Senior commandos, communications specialists, finance experts, logisticians—sure, Mr. Vice President," Marcus replied. "But the Troika? I'd be surprised if they ever set foot in that compound, much less together."

When Marcus saw Hernandez glance at the president, then at the national security advisor, he suddenly became suspicious. There was no way that these three didn't already know everything he'd just told them. So why was he here? Was it a test? Was he in trouble?

Wincing, Clarke reached over to a side table, opened a small pillbox, took out several tablets, and popped them in his mouth, washing them down with a sip of water. Then he turned to Marcus and spoke again.

"Look, Ryker, last night, while you and Bill and Miss Stewart and your buddies were all having a victory party at the Chart House, whooping it up into the wee hours of the morning, the VP and I had a late-night meeting with Crown Prince Abdulaziz bin Faisal Al Saud and his chief of intelligence," the president explained. "I believe you know the man."

"Prince Abdullah bin Rashid, head of the General Intelligence Directorate," Marcus said. "Yes, sir, I know him well."

"Yes, well, the two brought me some very disturbing photos," Clarke said, again motioning to McDermott, who began scrolling through more black-and-white images of the three Kairos deputy commanders separately getting in and out of various vehicles and going in and out of various buildings. "It appears that all three members of the Troika, as you call them, arrived in Yemen last week. Some of these photos were taken in Sana'a. Some were taken in Aden. Others were taken in Al Mukalla."

"All port cities," Marcus observed.

"Exactly," Clarke said. "What's more, the Saudis say better than two dozen Kairos fighters were spotted entering the country as well."

"So the Saudis know where they all are," Marcus said, leaning forward. "That's great. And you asked them to capture or kill them?"

"I wish, but it's too late," Clarke replied.

"Why?"

"All of them disappeared in the early hours of Sunday morning."

"After we bombed the compound."

"Exactly—and now the Saudis have no idea where they are," the president said. "But they came to me with this information because they've also picked up an increasing amount of chatter that these guys are cooking up a series of major revenge attacks against American citizens and interests, and they're going to strike soon."

"Where?"

"They have no idea, but they suspect in various Gulf States and then in Israel."

The room was silent, but for the ticking of a grandfather clock in the corner, as Marcus contemplated the seriousness of what Clarke was telling him.

"That's why I've asked you here, Agent Ryker," the president finally continued. "The crown prince personally asked me to appoint you as head of a new joint operations task force to hunt down and destroy what's left of Kairos, and do it fast, before they can strike us."

"That's very kind, sir," Marcus replied. "But why—?"

Clarke cut him off.

"There's nothing kind about it, Ryker. The crown prince knows you're the guy who tracked down Abu Nakba when so many others have tried and failed over the years. He knows you're badly wounded and that this has got to be the last thing you'd want to do after all you've been through. Carlos here agreed, saying he was pretty sure you were inclined to step down and move on. I had to concur. I told him you would almost certainly be moving on once the BDA was in. But they were insistent, especially His Royal Highness. He said this isn't over, that America and her allies are still in grave danger, and you can't stop until Kairos is 100 percent dead and buried."

Marcus exhaled and leaned back into the couch.

"I don't know what to say, Mr. President."

"Say yes."

"But I can't, sir."

"Because you're going to run off with Annie Stewart, get married, have babies, and live happily ever after," Clarke said.

It wasn't a question. It was a statement of fact.

Marcus had to smile. "Well, that may be a bit premature, sir. As I told you at Camp David when you started ribbing me, Annie and I have only been on one date."

"Then what's the problem?"

"It's not *what*, sir; it's *who*."

"Meaning Annie."

"No, sir, I'm not worried about Annie," Marcus replied, not entirely sure that was true—in fact, suddenly quite certain that wasn't true—but Annie wasn't the person he had in mind just then.

"Then who is the problem?"

"With respect, sir, it's Director Stephens."

"Because he despises every bone in your body, especially now that I've overruled him in favor of your recommendation to take action in Libya."

"For which I'm very grateful, sir, but yes, Stephens is livid."

"Let me worry about Stephens."

"But, sir, there's no way he's going to let me head up some CIA task force to take down the Troika. That's just never going to happen."

"Then forget Langley. This will be an NSC operation," Clarke replied. "Choose your own team. Your budget will be classified and unlimited. Bill here will set you up in the EEOB. And you'll report directly to me."

Marcus couldn't believe what he was hearing. Still, things were moving too fast.

"I'm wondering if I could have twenty-four hours to think about it, sir," he said.

"Absolutely not, Ryker. I told the crown prince I'd give him an answer before his plane took off back to Riyadh," Clarke said, glancing at his watch. "So I'd say you've got about two minutes."

Marcus knew that wasn't true. The crown prince was still scheduled to have dinner at the Capitol with members of the House and Senate Intelligence Committees, including Senator Dayton. Only then would he be flying out. But he accepted the essential point that the commander in chief was anxious to get moving.

"Very well, Mr. President," Marcus replied. "I'm in."

19

The first call Marcus made after leaving the White House was not to Annie.

It was to Pete.

The fact that Pete answered immediately meant he was no longer in the meeting with Dell.

"Something's come up," Marcus began.

"Good or bad?" Pete asked.

"Not over the phone. Can you meet at that place next to the thing?"

"Sure—how soon?"

"Thirty minutes."

"Done."

"And don't tell anyone," Marcus said.

"Got it—see you soon."

It was just before 11 a.m. when Marcus entered the worst Thai restaurant he and Pete had ever been to. The spring rolls were inedible. The panang beef was worse. The tea was always lukewarm. And the prices were outrageous. Still, it was located in Georgetown with a beautiful view of the Potomac River, and for the last few years it had been their go-to meeting place when they didn't want to say on an open phone line where they were going.

Pete arrived moments later. Though the lunch crowd had yet to arrive, Marcus asked for a quiet table in the back where they couldn't be seen by any passersby.

"So what's got your knickers in a twist?" Pete asked the moment he took his seat.

Marcus lowered his voice and summarized his meeting at the White House.

"Whoa, whoa, wait a minute, champ," Pete said the moment he heard the scheme. "You didn't actually say yes, did you?"

"I did."

"Are you insane?"

"What else was I going to say?"

"How 'bout, *'Hell no, I won't go!'*"

"Pete, come on, it was the president asking."

"Marcus, have you actually looked in a mirror anytime in the last ten days? I mean, you're a freak show. You should be home in bed popping Percocet like M&M'S, not gallivanting across the globe trolling for the Troika. You've completely lost it."

"The mission isn't done."

"Mine is," Pete replied.

"What's that supposed to mean?"

"Let's just say while you were humiliating Stephens in front of the entire NSC, I was negotiating a generous severance package with him. We wrapped things up yesterday before the ceremony began. I leave the Agency on June 12."

Marcus was stunned. "And you didn't say anything?"

"I'm saying something now."

"What about last night at dinner?"

"That was hardly the time or place."

"And now is? Pete, I need you."

"Marcus, we didn't join the Agency as lifers. You did it to keep your tail out of prison. And you dragged me into it because you have no other friends. But come on. We've done our duty. Abu Nakba is dead. I'm out of here and you should leave too."

20

EISENHOWER EXECUTIVE OFFICE BUILDING

Marcus returned to the White House complex.

His first stop was the personnel office, where a clerk, alerted by McDermott's office, was expecting him. He filled out a stack of paperwork, had his picture taken, and was given a temporary set of credentials until a permanent set could be made, as well as keys to an office in the Eisenhower Executive Office Building. His next stop was to catch up with his old Secret Service colleagues, fill out more paperwork, and pick up his temporary White House hard pass.

All of it was necessary, of course, but none of it helped him actually advance the mission for which the president had appointed him, and the clock was ticking. Heading up to the fifth floor, he found and unlocked the vacant suite of offices he'd been assigned, dusted off a desk and chair, and spent the next hour working the phones.

He had a team to recruit, but that could wait. The first call he made was to Prince Abdullah bin Rashid, director of the Saudi General Intelligence Directorate, who had become a friend over the past year and a half.

"Prince Abdullah, it's Marcus Ryker; you got a moment?"

"Yes, yes, Agent Ryker—so good to hear from you. The crown prince told me the good news. You're truly on board?"

"I am, and I'm honored by his confidence. It's very kind."

"It is not kind at all, Marcus. You've earned his trust and clearly the president's as well. We should meet."

"When?"

"My day is packed. And I head home first thing in the morning. Could you meet me tonight for coffee, say ten o'clock?"

"Sure. Where?"

"The Four Seasons. I'll meet you in the lounge."

"See you then—thanks."

Marcus hung up and called Asher Gilad, head of the Mossad, and Tomer Ben Ami, who after the Lebanon operation had been promoted to director of the Shin Bet. Though it was late in the evening in Israel, both men took his call and, after being briefed on Marcus's new assignment and the seriousness of the Saudi warnings, promised to pull together whatever new intel they had on Kairos and get it to him as quickly as possible.

After them, Marcus checked in with the spy chiefs in Jordan, Egypt, Oman, and Morocco. Then he called Khalid bin Ibrahim—more commonly known by his initials, KBI—the chief of intelligence for the United Arab Emirates. Unlike the others, KBI almost seemed to be expecting his call.

"Take these names down," he said immediately.

Marcus pulled out a pen from his jacket pocket and a notepad from his briefcase.

"Okay, go."

"Jibril bin Badr."

"Right."

"Ali bin Badr."

"Got it."

"And Mansour bin Badr."

"Brothers? The sons of Badr Hassan al-Ruzami? The Kairos chief of operations?" Marcus asked.

"Exactly. We've been building dossiers on all three of his boys. I'll send you everything, but you have to understand these are sick bastards. They range in age from twenty-one to twenty-seven, with Jibril the oldest and Mansour the youngest. They're known within Kairos as 'the Enforcers.' Remember Uday and Qusay, Saddam Hussein's boys?"

"Sure."

"These guys are worse."

"Worse?"

"Much worse," KBI said. "Their father trusts them implicitly and thus gives them the most dangerous and deadly assignments. We know Jibril, for example, loves the Godfather movies. Watches them all the time. Imagines himself a New York gangster. Lived in Cairo for the last decade or so, until last year."

"What happened last year?"

"He thought some Egyptian cop was flirting with his girlfriend. So he invited the guy to an Italian restaurant, you know, 'just to clear the air.' Ends up shooting the cop in the face, just like Michael Corleone. Then saunters out of the place with blood and brain matter all over him. After that, he fled to Libya and disappeared."

"Any leads?"

"No. Now that the Saudis have spotted his father in Yemen, it's likely he's there too. But not for long. The crown prince is right. After you guys took out Abu Nakba and his boys in Libya—and brilliant work, by the way, really sharp . . ."

"Thanks."

". . . Kairos is without question planning to retaliate in some spectacular fashion, and probably with several major operations, not just one."

With those calls done, Marcus now turned to recruiting his team: Jenny Morris, Geoff Stone, Donny Callaghan, and Noah Daniels, in that order. Fortunately, unlike Pete, they all said yes.

21

Marcus was twenty minutes late.

As he drove past the Kennedy Center on his way to meet Annie for dinner, Marcus began having second thoughts. The last time he'd had plans to come to the Kennedy Center had been the night Elena and Lars were murdered. But Annie didn't know that, and the restaurant she'd chosen had a spectacular view of the theater along the Potomac River.

Marcus parked his car, got out, and brushed some lint off his suit. Reaching the Sequoia restaurant, he found Annie sitting alone at their reserved table, sipping a glass of merlot, and decked out in an absolutely stunning emerald dress that matched her eyes.

"I'm so, so sorry," Marcus said, breathless, as he took his seat across from her.

"Long day?"

"No comment."

She smiled in the candlelight. "I went ahead and ordered for us both. Should be here soon. Wine?"

"Wow—sure, thanks. You look—"

When he stopped himself midsentence, she waited, then raised an eyebrow. "Ravishing? Spectacular? To die for?" She laughed.

"All of the above," he said. "I guess I'm a smidge out of practice giving a beautiful woman a compliment."

"Yeah, you might want to work on that, Ryker," she teased as she poured him a glass of the merlot.

"I will," he said. "I promise."

"Fair enough. So, hey, that was so fun last night. Thanks for including me."

"Of course."

"I loved seeing your mom again."

"She's a big fan of yours."

"She seemed a little surprised to see us together."

"Yeah, well, right—I guess I hadn't really said anything to her yet."

"Apparently not."

"But she was so happy to see you. She talked all about you this morning over breakfast and on the way to the airport."

"Did she now?" Annie smiled.

"Scout's honor."

"Well, it was fun to catch up with her. She gave me a very detailed update on your sisters and their husbands and all your nieces."

"I should have warned you. You get my mom talking and . . ."

"To be honest, I was a little jealous."

"Of what?"

"You know, having family to visit and dote on and think about the sweetness and craziness and messiness of real life rather than all the darkness we deal with inside the Beltway, day in and day out. It's nice. I miss that."

Marcus was a little surprised to see her flush with embarrassment. He shouldn't have been. He knew her story. Some of it, anyway. But it still caught him off guard.

"Yeah, I know. I'm sorry."

Annie changed the subject. "I'm guessing your long day means you went to the office," she said. "Don't you need to recover, recuperate?"

"How can I with all the threats out there?"

"Good grief, Marcus, haven't you earned a little R and R? I mean, look at you. You're . . ."

"Frankenstein?"

"Well, I was going to say the creature from the black lagoon, but sure, go with that."

Marcus took a sip of wine. "That's not the way I'm wired," he told her. "I can't just lounge around when our enemies are on the move."

"Marcus, you were captured by a Hezbollah special forces unit led by a commander loyal to Abu Nakba. You were drugged, knocked unconscious, dragged deep behind enemy lines, and tortured. Beaten. Burned. Electrocuted. No one would call taking the time to recover from all that 'lounging around.' You're amazing at what you do. It's one of the things that drew me to you. You have convictions. You have a deep sense of purpose and mission. But that's not what this is. Something's driving you. Something's pushing you to keep going and going and going when you should rest, or better yet, stop."

"You sound like Pete."

"What's that supposed to mean?"

"Stephens offered him a severance package, and he's taking it."

"Well, good for him."

"Annie, this threat isn't over. You know that."

Just then, their waiter came back to the table, bringing Annie a Caesar salad and Marcus a bowl of clam chowder.

Marcus waited until he left, then continued. "I can't just quit and ride off into the sunset when there are new threats—serious threats—forming against the country and friends I love."

"Even after all that you've accomplished?" she pressed. "After all you've just been through?"

"Especially because of all I've just been through. You know what I saw in Lebanon? Monsters, Annie. I saw their rage. I saw the demons in their eyes. I saw how determined they are to rob, kill, and destroy everything you and I hold dear. And don't forget something that almost no one else in the world knows—certainly not my mom or my sisters or their families. Tehran has put a $10 million bounty on my head. And you can be certain that Kairos wants that money. Especially now that I've captured their bagman in Doha and persuaded the president to take out their founder and dear leader. So even if I stop—even if I decide to hand in my notice and take a Disney cruise to Never-Never Land—that doesn't mean it's over. It just means I'm alone in the world as these monsters come to kill me."

22

"So look, Annie, there's something else you need to know."

Annie could see the sudden change in his tone and body language. "What is it?"

"The president asked me to meet with him today."

"Okay."

"The VP and Mac were there too."

"And?"

"You know about the new Saudi intel, right?"

"The crown prince briefed the senator and me this morning."

"Right, so the president is keyed up about the possibility of a retaliatory strike or series of strikes by what remains of Kairos."

"And?"

"And he asked me to head up a new task force to hunt down the Troika and take them out before they can hit us."

"You?"

"I know—Stephens will go ballistic. That's what I said. But Clarke said to leave that to him."

"But I don't understand. How can—?"

"Listen, I get it—it's all happening so fast. There are lots of details still to hammer out. But it'll be run out of the NSC, not Langley. I'll report directly to the president, not to Stephens. And it's super classified. I'm sure your boss will get a briefing soon, but only as a courtesy. The Senate Intelligence Committee won't be read in on any of this. Not yet, anyway."

"And you said yes?" she asked.

Marcus nodded.

"No discussion? No time to talk about it? Just, boom, you're all in?"

"The president said the crown prince specifically asked me to run it and wanted an answer before he flew home."

Annie said nothing for a moment. Then she asked, "And when would you start?"

"I already have."

Again, Annie said nothing.

"You're angry with me," Marcus said.

"No."

"You think I'm making a huge mistake."

"Look, Marcus, it's your life. I have no right to tell you what to do."

"But you absolutely have the right to tell me your opinion," Marcus insisted.

"What do you want me to say, that I'm thrilled for you?"

Marcus knew that was neither true nor possible. So he made a counter-proposal. "How about that you'll come with me," he said, leaning forward.

"What?"

"Seriously, Annie, be our chief intel analyst. You could be our liaison to all the other intelligence services, foreign and domestic. It could be amazing."

"I don't think—"

"We'd be together every day. We could work side by side. We'd know exactly what's happening in each other's lives. And when we're not in the office, we'll never have to talk about work. And when we get these guys—when it's really done—then, well, who knows?"

"I can't, Marcus."

"Can't or won't?"

"Marcus, I've given Senator Dayton my notice."

"What? You resigned?"

"I did."

"When?"

"This morning."

"No discussion?" he asked. "No time to talk it over? Just, boom, you're out? Are you and Pete running off together?"

"Don't be ridiculous."

"You both quit on the same day—two of my closest friends in the world—and neither of you even mention it to me, much less discuss it, ahead of time?"

Annie didn't know what to say. It was the first time Marcus had ever told her she was one of his closest friends in the world, and she suddenly felt guilty for not discussing it with him.

"Annie, this is crazy. Kairos is plotting something—something big—and we need to stop them before they can execute their plan."

"*We?*" she asked softly, almost in a whisper. "No, Marcus. *We* don't have to go back into battle. *We* have paid our dues. *We* have done our job. And now it's time to hand off the baton and move on with our lives."

The waiter returned. He set a plate of seared salmon with basmati rice and asparagus in front of Annie. For Marcus he brought a ten-ounce filet mignon, mashed potatoes, and a side of carrots. Marcus thanked the man and waited while he refilled their wineglasses. When he was gone, Marcus looked back at Annie.

"So what are you going to do?"

"I don't know," she conceded, picking at her salmon. "Go back to South Carolina, I guess. Maybe teach. Maybe write a little. I haven't really gotten that far. All I know is that this town and this job and this life don't exactly afford me time to think, time to dream, time to . . ."

"To what?" he pressed. "What do you wish you were doing that you're not?"

Annie looked up from the plate and stared deep into his eyes. "It's just time, Marcus. I need to go home."

"What about us?" he asked.

"What *about* us?" she replied. "Am I wrong, or didn't you tell the president up at Camp David that *this* isn't serious, that we've only been out on one date? Isn't that what you're telling Pete and Jenny? Isn't that what you told your mom? I mean, that's fine. And it's true. But let's be honest, it doesn't exactly signal you want to take this further, does it?"

"What do you want me to say, Annie? Yes, I've been a little distracted of late, a bit 'tied up,' as it were. The last few weeks haven't exactly been ideal conditions to start a relationship. I admit that. But I'm back. I'm home. Date number two. Three, if you count dinner in Old Town. And believe me, I want there to be more."

"Me, too. I love being here with you tonight. It means a lot to me."

"But?"

"But the president of the United States has just asked you to go back into battle, and you said yes."

"Then say yes to me—say yes to this team, and when we're done, we're done."

"I can't. Look, I wish you all success, Marcus, I really do. But this isn't something I want to do anymore. I'm finished. I guess I just hoped you were too."

THE FOUR SEASONS HOTEL, GEORGETOWN, D.C.

Marcus, still in his suit from dinner with Annie, had decided to bring Jenny.

She was, after all, fluent in Arabic.

They passed through the lobby and headed to the lounge straight ahead. They saw no one. They quickly searched the main floor but still didn't find the Saudi spy chief. Then a single-word text came into Marcus's phone.

Downstairs.

Heading down one level, they still found no one. It made little sense to head down farther, for the basement level was only ballrooms. Out of options, however, they went anyway and finally found Prince Abdullah bin Rashid pacing the floor of one of the empty and darkened halls, smoking a cigarette and nursing a tumbler of what looked like bourbon.

"Hey, this is Washington, not Riyadh," Marcus teased. "I'm pretty sure you're not supposed to smoke in here."

"It's been a long day, Mr. Ryker." The prince sighed, raising his glass as if making a toast.

"Tell me about it," Marcus replied. "But thanks for making time. You remember Agent Morris."

"Yes, of course, the brilliant and beautiful Jennifer." He smiled, kissing her hand in a gesture not exactly characteristic of an Arab Muslim man.

"Cunning and crafty as always." She smiled back, surprising him by snatching the tumbler out of his hand, turning it around to face the side he had not sipped from, and downing the rest of his drink.

The prince's eyes went wide. "This one I like, Ryker. Don't let her get away."

Marcus shook his head. He was more than familiar with the spy chief's aversion to religion, piety, rules, and customs. "You said you have something for us," he said, in no mood for banter.

Rashid took a final drag on his cigarette, dropped the butt to the floor, stamped it out, and kicked it aside. Then he pulled out his phone, entered his password, and brought up an audio file.

"Yesterday, my guys back in Riyadh intercepted a phone call that originated in Bandar Abbas from what we believe is a senior IRGC operative," he explained. "We don't know the recipient of the call, but we know it was to a satellite account in Yemen."

"Where exactly?" Jenny asked.

"A suburb of Sana'a," the prince replied, referring to the Yemeni capital.

"Let's hear it," Marcus said.

They listened to the brief call, and Jenny translated it.

CALLER: Tell me you're ready to hit back.
RECEIVER: We are putting pieces into place.
CALLER: You must strike hard and fast.
RECEIVER: This one is complicated. It will take time.
CALLER: How much time?
RECEIVER: I cannot say. There are many variables.
CALLER: Do you need cash?
RECEIVER: Always, but mostly logistical assistance.
CALLER: Anything you need, but there can be no fingerprints.
RECEIVER: I understand.
CALLER: I cannot overemphasize this point.

RECEIVER: I told you I understand.

CALLER: I need a time frame.

RECEIVER: The first operation is almost ready.

CALLER: That one is easy. What about the second?

RECEIVER: I don't know.

CALLER: Give me your best guess.

RECEIVER: Not yet.

CALLER: Time is short. It must be soon.

RECEIVER: Of course.

CALLER: I can move the first tranche now.

RECEIVER: And I can report that to my superiors?

CALLER: You can.

RECEIVER: Good. Two days?

CALLER: That works. In the place we last agreed upon?

RECEIVER: Yes, I can do that.

CALLER: Until then.

RECEIVER: Allah be with you.

CALLER: And with you.

"Did Jenny get it right?" Marcus asked when his partner had finished translating.

"Very impressive, Agent Morris," the prince replied, giving her a nod.

"So the Iranians want to hit us—presumably for the humiliation in Lebanon, not to mention in the East China Sea—but they want to use Kairos operatives as their proxies, to give Tehran plausible deniability," Marcus said.

The prince nodded.

"And they want to use our strike in Libya as a pretext," Jenny added.

"It's a pretty good one, too," the prince said. "Unfortunately, as I said, we can't say who precisely received the call. And both phones were turned off immediately following the call, so we were not able to track them. But if nothing else, this certainly underscores the crown prince's growing concerns that the sudden convergence of senior level Kairos operatives in Yemen—now in direct contact with the Iranians—means that a major attack or series of attacks on the U.S. is coming."

Lighting up another cigarette and offering ones to Marcus and Jenny, both of whom declined, Prince Abdullah bin Rashid glanced around the ballroom to make sure they were still alone, then lowered his voice as he stepped closer to them. "I don't have to recount for you two my country's history in Yemen," he said. "Long. Bitter. Messy. And plenty of mistakes. But you also know that we did what we came to do. Decimate the Houthis, who were fast becoming Tehran's proxy of choice and who were attacking our airports and cities and civilian populations week after week with Iranian-built missiles and drones. Now, I'm not saying there is no Houthi presence left in that pitiful country whom Allah has clearly forsaken. But they are no longer a strategic threat to us and no longer much use to the IRGC. The problem is that, like Afghanistan and Libya before it, Yemen is becoming a haunt of jackals. If Abu Nakba were still alive, I guarantee you, Yemen would be his home base. But even with him gone—and for this we cannot thank you enough—but even now, his lieutenants are still out there, planning, plotting, preparing, with Tehran's help, no less. I fear a great disaster is coming. You had better get ready."

24

THE OVAL OFFICE

"Are you insane? Seriously, Andy, have you completely lost your mind?"

No one called the president by his first name.

No one but Richard Stephens.

But Clarke and his CIA director were alone. It was late. A lone Secret Service agent stood post outside the door. And nearly all the staff had gone home for the day.

"Richard, this isn't your call," Clarke said as he sat behind the *Resolute* desk signing a stack of executive orders.

"Oh yes it is. Ryker works for me. And I don't want him anywhere near this."

"No, Ryker works for me," Clarke shot back. "And so do you. Don't push me on this thing, Richard. Face it, you're in a tizzy 'cause he was right about the Libyan, and you got it wrong."

"We don't know that," Stephens responded. "Until that storm finally blows over, we don't know who or what was in that compound."

"Let it go. You're embarrassing yourself. I'm putting Ryker in charge of this task force. We're running it out of the NSC. And that's final. Do you understand me?"

"No, Mr. President. I do not understand you. You hired me to run intelligence operations. *Me.* Not him. And as I keep telling you, Ryker is not one of us. Doesn't think like an Agency man. Doesn't work like one."

"That's exactly why I like him."

"And that's exactly why I don't. He's rash, he's reckless, and his profile is way too high. For crying out loud, he's supposed to be invisible. Instead, the Russians know who he is and they want him dead or alive. The Iranians know who he is, and that's why they've slapped a $10 million bounty on his head. Kairos knows who he is, and that's why they targeted him, grabbed him on the Israeli border, and beat the crap out of him. He winds up on worldwide television thwarting a suicide bombing on the Temple Mount, and now the entire world knows who he is. And rather than watching yesterday's ceremony from the privacy of his cubicle at Langley or DSS, he stupidly comes to the White House, sits right next to a prominent senator, and gets caught on camera holding hands with a professional staffer from the Senate Intelligence Committee. Mr. President, this is not exactly standard operating procedure for a member of the Clandestine Service."

"First of all, I personally invited Ryker and his mom to the White House because they deserved to see the fruit of his labors. Second, Ryker's not only a war hero but a widower, and he's got every right to hold hands with anyone he pleases, and you might want to cut him a break and show him a shred of sympathy once in a while. And third, and probably most important, Ryker's the best operative the Agency has seen in a decade, maybe ever, and you know it."

"How can you say that? Ryker's gotten lucky. That's it. That's all."

"*Lucky?* You cannot be serious."

"I'm dead serious."

"All the points he's put on the board? You're saying that's all luck."

"Ryker's had a few successes, I grant you that," Stephens admitted. "But those were highly complicated operations, and you're giving him credit for the work of hundreds of Agency staff whose names you will never know. And do I even need to state the obvious?"

"Be my guest."

"This administration cannot afford the media taking a closer look at this guy."

"Why not?"

"You know why."

"The Russia thing?" Clarke asked.

"Yes, the Russia thing," Stephens confirmed. "Marcus Ryker is an assassin, plain and simple, responsible for the murders of not one, not two, but three of the highest-ranking Russian officials in the Kremlin."

"Which prevented a war with NATO that could have gone nuclear."

"You think that's going to matter when *The Guardian* breaks the story of Ryker's real record? Or the *New York Times*? Or better yet, the Al-Sawt satellite TV network?"

At that, the president stopped signing papers and looked up at his longtime friend. "Richard, are you threatening me?"

"Of course not. I'm just saying it wouldn't be good for you or this administration if the truth about what Ryker's done—much less your pardon—came to light."

"It hasn't yet," Clarke said.

"No, it hasn't," Stephens agreed, his expression cold. "But imagine if it did."

"I don't think I like your tone."

Stephens abruptly rose to his feet and picked up his briefcase off the floor. "My tone, Mr. President, is going to be the least of your worries."

Stephens stalked out, and Clarke suddenly found himself alone. Standing, he strode to the door to the right of his desk, exited, and took a walk down the colonnade and into the Rose Garden. Was this really happening? Was his closest political ally threatening to leak the story of Marcus Ryker's past, just to block him from heading up this new task force? On the face of it, it didn't seem possible. But the more Clarke thought about it, the more worried he became. And the more worried he became, the more his temples began to throb.

Neither he nor his senior team had had any advance warning that Ryker was helping the mole known as the Raven to assassinate the Russian president, prime minister, and head of the FSB. Ryker had only been authorized to get the Raven—and a thumb drive of highly classified Kremlin secrets—out of Moscow and out of Russia to someplace safe, someplace the Russians could never find them. If Clarke had had any inkling that Ryker and the Raven were planning to take matters into their own hands, he never would have authorized the CIA to use their resources to get them out, even if their actions did stop the Russians from invading the Baltic states and triggering the next world war.

Only the smallest handful of people knew any of this. Less than a dozen in the entire federal government. Yet the sudden exposure of such information would trigger a media firestorm, congressional investigations, possibly the appointment of an independent counsel and almost certainly calls for impeachment. Ryker would be forced to testify. The Raven's real identity—and real location inside the continental United States—might be revealed. And all hell would break loose with the Russians, the North Koreans, the Iranians, and whatever was left of Kairos.

Maybe he had acted in haste, Clarke realized. Maybe he was going to have to sacrifice Ryker for the good of the country.

THE VATICAN—14 MAY

"Your Holiness, it's time," said the voice behind the door.

"Come," the old man said, his throat sore, his voice frail.

The large oak door opened, and in walked a man half the pontiff's age carrying a small leather case.

"Commander Gianetti, how good to see you, as always."

"How are you feeling, Your Holiness?" the Vatican's chief of security asked.

"Not so good today, my friend," came the reply. "But the Lord is my Shepherd, yes? What shall I want?"

"Perhaps a cure for diabetes," the commander said with a gentle smile.

Pope Pius XIII laughed and then began to cough violently. Alphonso Gianetti stepped into the adjacent washroom, poured a glass of water, and brought it to him. The old man nodded his thanks, caught his breath, and took a sip.

"I'm getting too old for this, my friend," he sighed. "It's time for the Lord to let me rest with my fathers."

"Well, my job is to make sure that doesn't happen on my watch, Your Holiness," Gianetti replied. "So you'll forgive me if I don't give up on you yet."

"Perhaps, but ten Hail Marys first, Gianetti."

The old man laughed at his own joke as the commander went to the washroom to clean his hands with soap and water. When he returned, as per their typical morning ritual, Gianetti unzipped the case and withdrew a blood glucose meter. After inserting a fresh test strip into the meter, he lanced the pope's finger and positioned the edge of the test strip to take a drop of blood. A moment later, the glucose level appeared on the digital display.

"A little high today, Your Holiness," the commander said as he put away the meter and drew a syringe and bottle of insulin from the leather case and prepared to give the pope his morning injection.

"That's the least of my worries, young man, believe me."

"Actually, that's what I wanted to talk to you about."

"All the cardinals angling to be my successor?"

"Not exactly, sir."

"What then?"

"This trip you want to make to the States."

"I trust all the planning is going well."

"It is, Your Holiness, but one of the local papers is suggesting that the bombing in Libya means you will be canceling your tour."

"And you would like me to say the report is true?"

"Yes."

"You're afraid a papal visit so soon after such a high-profile military attack will reflect poorly on my office and my mission of peace."

"I wouldn't presume to counsel you on matters of theology, Your Holiness," Gianetti demurred, as the pope opened his robe and exposed his gray and wrinkled stomach. "I restrict myself to matters of your security and your health, and thus I'm concerned about a possible retaliatory action by the Kairos organization."

Gianetti pinched his subject's skin at a forty-five-degree angle, plunged the needle all the way in, released the skin, and slowly injected one hundred units of insulin.

"A retaliatory action?" the pope asked. "At the White House?"

"It's not the White House that I'm concerned about, Your Holiness," Gianetti said as he waited five seconds and then withdrew the needle. "The Secret Service is the best in the world at protecting the president and his guests. No, my concern is that you will be holding Mass in four enormous stadiums, in four very large metropolitan areas, all of which would be tempting targets for any terrorist organization, especially one whose leader has just been, well, taken off the board."

"You don't trust the Americans to keep me safe wherever I go?" the pontiff asked as he buttoned up his robe again.

"Trust is not exactly the defining feature of my job, sir," Gianetti said with a smile.

"But it is the defining feature of mine," the pope said. "That's what faith is, Commander—it's putting your trust in another. I have happily placed my faith in you, my friend, and you've never let me down. More importantly, I have placed my faith in the Great Shepherd of my soul. When my time has come, I am ready to go peacefully into the night. But more than that, the world has just witnessed a modern miracle. The Saudis and the Israelis signing a peace treaty. Few thought it was possible, but it has happened in our lifetime. And isn't this my message—calling the Catholic world to pray for peace in our time and to celebrate it when our prayers are answered?"

26

EISENHOWER EXECUTIVE OFFICE BUILDING

Marcus took an elevator to the fifth floor.

Walking down a long marble-tiled hallway, he arrived at the unmarked suite of offices in the northwest corner. It was only six in the morning, yet the entire team was already in, at their computers, working the phones. The place was humming. And Jenny Morris was waiting for him.

"Overnight the Egyptians captured a cell of Yemeni jihadists at a training camp in northern Sinai, close to Gaza," she said as she handed him a sheaf of classified cable traffic and a mug of freshly brewed coffee and followed him into his office.

Marcus had no idea where they had gotten the coffee maker from, nor how they had outfitted the office so quickly. When he had left to meet Annie for dinner, none of the team had even arrived yet. Now they were in full motion.

"How many?" he asked.

"Nine men, eighteen to twenty-six years old. All training with brand-new equipment, including Russian-made RPGs and surface-to-air missiles."

"Houthis or Kairos?" he asked, hanging his suit coat on the back of his door, tossing his briefcase onto a chair in the corner, and walking behind his desk.

"Don't know; they're not talking."

"Is this public?" Marcus asked as he took a seat and rolled up the sleeves of his white dress shirt.

"Not yet," Jenny replied. "Egyptian GID says it all went down less than two hours ago. They want to better understand what they have before they release it."

"No. We can't let them release it."

"Cairo wants a headline, Marcus. They need a win."

"I get it, but not today. Not until we know who they are and what they're training for."

One by one, the rest of the team—Donny Callaghan, Geoff Stone, and Noah Daniels—filed into his office. As they did, Marcus skimmed the cables.

"The Egyptian thing, you got that from Langley? They're being cooperative."

"Not exactly."

"DIA?"

"No."

"Then where?" Marcus asked, reaching for the remotes on his desk and turning on the eight flat-panel TV monitors mounted on the far wall, all tuned to various cable and satellite news channels, even as he continued to read.

"Actually," Jenny said after a pause, "Pete got it for us."

Marcus looked at her, confused, and even more so when the man himself poked his head through the door. "Pete, what are you doing here?" he asked.

"I came to help an old friend," Pete said as he entered the cramped office. "Just to be clear, I'm still leaving on June 12. But I've got a month, and I figured, why not?"

"Then welcome aboard. Now, where'd you get this Sinai stuff?"

"A Mossad source tipped me off. But I confirmed it with a guy at the Egyptian embassy. He promised more as soon as he gets it."

"What do you make of it?"

"I don't know—it's too soon."

"Okay, stay on it. What else have we got? Noah, you're up first—go."

Noah Daniels was the team's tech guru. Marcus had met him in Jerusalem when they were safeguarding the first Israeli-Saudi-American peace summit that led to this treaty, and he'd been impressed. Only thirty-five, Daniels had joined the CIA when he was twenty-three after having graduated from high school at the tender age of sixteen, earning his bachelor's from MIT and both a master's degree and a PhD from Stanford. He still looked like he could be in high school, but his skills at setting up, hacking, or crashing any computer or phone system were undeniable.

"All our desktops are now up and running, and we've finally got encrypted email capability and secure phone lines," Daniels reported. "Our TVs are all operational, too, obviously, and I've set up our own dedicated satellite dishes on the roof. As of 4 a.m., we now have encrypted access to the mainframes at DIA, DSS, DHS, and Liberty Crossing. And Dell assures me we'll be patched into Langley's mainframe by COB."

"We'll see—but good job—stay on it."

"Will do."

"Agent Callaghan, tell me you have good news."

"Some," the former commander of SEAL Team Six replied. Callaghan explained that he'd spent yesterday afternoon discreetly meeting with various special forces commanders at the Pentagon who might have files on Kairos cells and operatives. "Now that we've got secure email, I'll let them know they can start flowing intel to us."

"And when we're ready to deploy?" Marcus asked. "Are we going to have access to choppers, weapons, ammo, comms gear, the works?"

"That's going to take more time."

"How much more?"

"I don't know yet. There's been no public announcement about our unit, so nobody knows we exist. And those who do, don't understand why we're not operating out of Langley or JSOC or CENTCOM."

"Call in every chit you've got, Donny," Marcus insisted. "When we get a hot lead—which may come quick—we need to be able to strike hard and fast."

Callaghan assured him he was on it, and Marcus had no doubt. Born and raised in south Boston, the son of a three-star Army general, Donny Callaghan was now thirty-six and a legend in the SEAL community. One of the best snipers in any branch of the U.S. military, he was even better known for his leadership and tactical brilliance on the battlefield. He was fluent in Russian and learning Arabic at night. He was also a hulk of a man—six foot three, 220 pounds of muscle, with closely cropped hair and a bushy beard that were both naturally red but that he'd dyed black to operate more effectively in the Middle East. Divorced young, he now had two small children from a second marriage to a Navy nurse, though this one wasn't going much better than the first.

"What about you, Agent Stone? Tell me something I don't know."

"I spent the afternoon at DSS," Stone began. "To be honest, their files on Kairos are pretty thin. But I did pick up one interesting nugget."

"What's that?"

"A couple of my guys on Secretary Whitney's detail are worried about the timing of this strike in Libya with the upcoming papal visit. Four cities. Four stadiums. Massive crowds, upwards of seventy-five thousand to a hundred thousand each. The secretary plans on attending all of them with His Holiness, and they're worried each Mass could become a target. With your permission, I think I should spend next week with them thinking through how to harden those sites."

Marcus shook his head. "Negative. DSS and Secret Service have the lead on all that. They're on defense. We're on offense, and we need to stay laser-focused on our mission. Find out everything we can about the Troika and whoever is left of Kairos. Give the president actionable intelligence on where they are. And be ready to go deep into enemy territory to take them out or at least to assist any SEAL team or Delta guys who are ordered to do so. That's it. Period. We don't have the time or the manpower to do anything else."

THE STATE DEPARTMENT

The side door to Meg Whitney's private dining room abruptly opened.

An aide stepped in, whispered in the secretary's ear, and then stepped back. Whitney immediately got up, apologized to her guest—the French foreign minister—and headed straight for her office. A moment later, her chief of staff burst in from the other side of the room, grabbed the remote off her desk, and turned up the volume on the main TV monitor.

"This is CNN breaking news. Now live from Washington, here's Carolyn Tam."

"The U.S. bombing of a facility near the Libyan city of Ghat on Saturday night now appears to have been a deadly and disastrous mistake," the Emmy Award–winning anchor began. "Rather than serving as the headquarters of the terrorist organization known as Kairos, the compound was actually a school for severely handicapped children."

Whitney gasped as the image cut from the cable network's D.C. studios to grainy, handheld video of mangled wheelchairs amid still burning and smoking rubble.

"CNN has obtained exclusive video taken by a Libyan doctor who lives in Ghat," Tam continued. "It contains images not suitable for children, and we urge extreme caution."

As the undersecretary of state and the chief of the Near East bureau now entered the room, Whitney found herself staring at the charred bodies of children and teachers, blackened and soot-covered stuffed animals, along with piles of burned, twisted, and mangled medical equipment.

Her eyes filled with tears. "Tell me this isn't happening."

"We've got to make a statement," her chief of staff said. "We have to get out in front of this and fast."

Whitney nodded but could not take her eyes off the screen. "Get me the president."

THE WEST WING

The national security advisor's private line lit up.

Maggie Allen, his executive assistant, picked up immediately. "Mr. McDermott's office. May I help you?"

"Maggie, it's Marcus. I need to talk to him immediately."

"Sorry, sir, but he just stepped into a lunch with—"

"Pull him out," Marcus ordered.

"I really can't do that, Agent Ryker; he's—"

"Maggie, you're not listening—pull him out now."

CIA HEADQUARTERS

Stephens was on a secure call with the Taiwanese chief of intelligence.

Dell burst into his office without knocking and broke the news. Just as she'd suspected, Stephens went ballistic, unleashing a torrent of profanity and ordering her to have his motorcade and protective detail ready to go in five minutes.

"Text me updates every ten minutes and pull together the senior team," he said as he grabbed his suit coat and headed to his private elevator. "I'm going to the White House."

★

THE U.S. CAPITOL

Robert Dayton had just cast his vote on the Senate floor when his phone rang.

"Make it quick, Annie, I'm already late for a luncheon with the majority leader."

"You're going to be later," she told him. "Head to the Cloakroom."

"Why?"

"CNN is reporting we bombed a school in Libya for severely disabled children, not the Kairos headquarters."

"That's impossible."

"They have video from inside the decimated compound, sir—the images are as macabre as anything I can remember. Burned body parts. Toys. Bunk beds. The remains of a playground—swings, slides—it's horrifying."

"How in the world did a CNN crew get there?" Dayton asked, racing off the Senate floor to find a television. "Isn't the sandstorm still going?"

"Yes, sir," Annie confirmed. "But it's footage taken by a local Libyan doctor. In fact, they just ran an interview with him, sobbing, enraged, trying to describe the scene, the stench. He's saying at least forty-two children are dead, along with at least a dozen teachers, possibly more."

Dayton entered the Cloakroom to find a half-dozen other Democratic senators watching the grisly images.

"I have to make a statement," he told her. "I'm heading to the press gallery."

"Senator, please don't—not yet. Let me gather more facts and—"

But Dayton hung up his mobile phone and entered the hallway. A gaggle of reporters, cameramen, and producers shouted questions at him. No other senators were in sight. He was the first.

"Senator Dayton, how do you respond to this breaking news out of Libya?" an MSNBC correspondent demanded as her network carried the moment live.

"Like all Americans, I'm sickened by the images we're seeing out of Libya and by the tragic loss of life," Dayton replied.

"Do you blame the administration?" a reporter for the *New York Times* shouted.

"Clearly, this is one of the worst intelligence failures in U.S. history since 9/11."

"But do you blame President Clarke personally?"

"Who else?" Dayton asked. "This is a diplomatic disaster for this administration, and I'm demanding immediate hearings into what the president knew, when he knew it, and how he could possibly have ordered the bombing of a special-needs school."

"Would you support the appointment of an independent counsel to investigate how this 'intelligence failure,' as you called it, happened?" a CNN reporter asked.

"I hope it doesn't come to that."

"But if the administration stonewalls?"

Dayton knew he could brush off the question as a hypothetical. He also knew he'd be scorched by his constituents back in Iowa if he didn't answer candidly. So he did.

"If President Clarke is stupid enough to stonewall a congressional investigation into how he bombed a school full of teachers and children, then an independent counsel will be the least of his worries. He'll be looking at a stampede toward impeachment."

Tarabulus
(Tripoli)
Tripolitania
Ghadames
Suknah
Maradah
Zellah
LIBIYA
(LIBYA)
Sebkha
Zighan
Serir Kalansho
El Juf
Ghat

PART TWO

28

BANDAR ABBAS, IRAN

Mahmoud Entezam's plane landed on a military airstrip at 7:44 p.m.

From there the commander of the Iranian Revolutionary Guard Corps was driven in a convoy of three armed SUVs from the airport through the port city of some half-million residents to Iran's main naval base, located on the eastern shore of the Strait of Hormuz. Just before 8:30 p.m., he entered the home of the base commandant and found Abu Nakba sitting in an overstuffed armchair, watching coverage of the fallout from the bombing in Libya on CNN.

"Ah, General, what a joy to see you," the old man said, rising to his feet with the help of his cane.

"Your Holiness, what a relief to see you, as well," Entezam replied, embracing the Kairos leader and giving the man the requisite kisses before they both took their seats and Entezam asked that they be brought some tea. "I trust your journey was pleasant."

"It has been some time since I have been out on the water, and it was a bit choppier than I would have liked, but otherwise, yes, it was most pleasant indeed."

"Thank you for accepting my invitation," the IRGC chief said. "You will be safe here and well looked after until your departure."

"I have no doubt."

"When did you arrive?"

"Just a short while ago, maybe twenty minutes before you."

"You must be tired. Would you like to rest and speak later?"

"How can I rest when the plan is just starting to come together? Let us speak now. Events are unfolding rapidly. We must make preparations."

"Very well," Entezam said, nodding to his bodyguards to exit the room.

When they were alone, the IRGC chief leaned forward. "Have you seen the latest out of Italy?" he asked.

"That the pope may consider canceling his trip to the Great Satan?" the Libyan said. "Yes. We must pray to Allah that he holds firm."

General Entezam nodded. "If his trip does continue, I have some good news. The specific cities on the pope's schedule have not yet been reported, but my men have obtained a working draft."

"How?"

"One of the benefits of having our operatives working in Iranian embassies in various parts of the world."

"Indeed."

"Let me walk you through what we know so far."

"Very well."

"The pontiff will land in Washington on Tuesday, June 2. He will be transported from Joint Base Andrews—a military airfield—to Blair House, directly across the street from the White House. We expect security to be airtight and see no opportunity to get near him at that juncture."

Abu Nakba nodded.

Entezam continued. "The pope has been invited to have lunch at the White House that day with the president and First Lady. That night, he will deliver an address to a joint session of Congress."

"At what time?" Abu Nakba asked.

"Nine Eastern."

"And you are convinced we cannot get him there either?"

"Impossible."

The old man shook his head. "A pity. That would be the ideal scenario."

"The perimeter will be hardened, and you simply won't have the manpower or firepower to break through."

"But every member of the House and Senate, plus the president and vice president, all in one place . . . ," the old man said, if only to himself.

Entezam waited a moment, then tried to redirect his guest's focus. "In my view, the following days provide our best opportunities," Entezam explained. "On Wednesday, June 3, the pope will fly to Miami, where he will hold evening Mass for an estimated sixty thousand people. He will stay in Miami overnight, then fly on Thursday, June 4, to Houston, where he will hold an evening Mass for seventy thousand. He and his entourage will stay overnight in Texas and then fly on Friday, June 5, to New York City to hold evening Mass at Yankee Stadium for an estimated eighty thousand people."

At this, Entezam opened his leather satchel and pulled out a map of the United States. He unfolded it and set it on the coffee table before them, pointing to each of the cities he had mentioned thus far.

"The final stop will come on Saturday, June 6," he continued. "That morning, the pope will fly from New York to Chicago, where we understand he will arrive at Soldier Field near midday. This will be the grand finale of the tour. They are expecting upwards of one hundred thousand people to attend—seventy thousand inside the stadium and another thirty thousand watching on large screens they will be setting up in the surrounding parking lots. The entire event will be broadcast live around the world."

Abu Nakba smiled. "That's promising."

"Promising, perhaps, but also problematic," the IRGC commander said.

"Why?"

"With the eyes of the world watching, security will be formidable. I believe Houston and Miami offer the greatest opportunities for maximum impact. These are two American cities that have never been hit by foreign terrorism. They will certainly have good security, but nothing like Washington, New York, and Chicago. They are in two of America's most populous states—Texas and Florida. My recommendation is that you send teams to both cities, analyze them for yourselves, and then pick the one you feel gives you the greatest opportunity to eliminate the most infidels."

"And you're committed to providing all the financing and logistical support we will need, which will be considerable?" the old man asked.

Now it was Entezam who smiled. "Take out Marcus Ryker, and I'll be happy to write you a check for $10 million."

Abu Nakba sat back and did not speak for a moment. Finally he said, "Ten million is not enough. Double that, and Ryker is as good as dead."

29

THE WHITE HOUSE

Flanked by his security detail, the CIA director stormed into the West Wing.

McDermott met him and ushered him into the Oval Office.

"What the hell is going on, Richard?" Clarke raged, on his feet and pacing as he watched the video now being replayed over and over on every American cable network with split-screen coverage of the U.N. secretary-general calling for an emergency session of the Security Council. *"This is a disaster. I want answers and I want them now."*

"Mr. President, this is all Ryker's doing," Stephens replied. "He's out of his depth. He pushed this thing too far, too fast, based on circumstantial evidence, and now you're about to reap the whirlwind."

McDermott saw Clarke wincing in pain and rubbing his temples. The president clearly had no interest in Stephens's *I-told-you-sos*. Yet the CIA director kept pushing hard for Ryker to be fired.

"Don't waste my time talking about ancient history," Clarke exploded. *"I want to know what we're going to do about it."*

"There's nothing you can do going forward, Mr. President," Stephens shot back. "Not unless you show the country and the world that you're as outraged as they are and willing to take decisive steps to make sure this will never happen again."

"I'm not ready to fire Ryker."

"You have no choice."

"After all he's done for this country, you want me to just sack him?"

"Mr. President, the ranking member of the Senate Intelligence Committee just went on national television and used the word *impeachment*. And I guarantee you he's only the first. You need to cut Ryker loose before he takes you down with him."

"There has to be another way."

"There isn't, sir."

"You're making him a scapegoat."

"No, sir—a scapegoat is an innocent party that gets sacrificed. Ryker is not innocent. Look, I know you like him. I know he saved your life with that Jerusalem peace summit debacle. But you've got to let him go and fast."

"It's not right," Clarke shot back, rubbing his chest and loosening his tie.

"Mr. President, Marcus Ryker is a drowning man. You can't save him. But you can save yourself, and for the good of the country you have to."

"What's that supposed to mean?"

"The country can't afford another presidential impeachment, and you know it. It'll be a bloodbath. And all the gains we've made against the Iranians, the Russians, and the North Koreans—it'll all be for naught. Our enemies will smell blood in the water, and who's going to stop them? If you go down, the Democrats are going to take the House and Senate in the midterms. They're going to take the White House after that. And then what? What happens to your legacy? What happens to the country?"

McDermott watched the two erupt in a full-blown shouting match. Worried others outside—especially the press—would be able to hear them, he tried several times to intervene and calm things down. None of it worked. The two were angrier than McDermott had ever seen them.

Suddenly the president collapsed, his head dropping to the *Resolute* desk.

McDermott rushed to his side. So did Stephens. Clarke was breathing shallowly, mumbling, still trying to speak, though his eyes were glassy and dilated.

McDermott reached for a button under the president's desk as Stephens shouted, *"Help—someone help. The president is down."*

30

OMNI SHOREHAM HOTEL, WASHINGTON, D.C.

The audience erupted in applause.

All 2,500 guests attending the annual conference of the National Federation of Independent Business were suddenly on their feet and giving the vice president a thunderous standing ovation.

"Thank you," the VP concluded. "Thank you so much. God bless each one of you. And God bless America."

The moment he stopped speaking, Stevie Wonder's 1970 hit "Signed, Sealed, Delivered" filled the ballroom. Basking in the rare glow of the spotlight, grateful to be back after so many months of recuperation and rehab after triple bypass surgery, Carlos Hernandez stepped back from the podium but did not immediately leave the stage. He waved to the tumultuous crowd to whom he had just laid out the administration's new tax reform plan, nodding to various friends and allies he spotted. Then Hernandez suddenly went off script. Rather than head back to the greenroom as planned, he jumped offstage—swept up in the emotion of the moment—and moved toward the metal barricades, shaking hands with those in the first and second rows and letting people take selfies while his Secret Service detail rushed to his side.

As a beaming Hernandez enthusiastically worked the proverbial rope line, an aide came up behind him and tried to whisper in his ear. It was impossible for the VP to hear over the music and the cheering, yet the twenty-eight-year-old aide hesitated to speak any louder on the off chance someone might overhear her.

Charlie Mitchell, the thirty-eight-year-old head of the detail, had no such hesitation. *"Mr. Vice President, we need to go—now,"* he ordered, physically pulling Hernandez away from the barricades and toward the back of the stage while the rest of the detail hardened up around him.

Soon the VP was being rushed through the kitchen, down a series of hallways, and into the armor-plated limousine known as the Beast. The moment the doors were closed, the nine-vehicle motorcade roared away from the hotel, led by an enhanced escort of D.C. Metro Police motorcycles and squad cars, lights flashing and sirens blaring.

"Havana is secure—I repeat, Havana is secure—we are inbound for Cloverleaf," the agent radioed over his wrist-mounted microphone, using the Secret Service code words for the VP and his residence. "ETA, three minutes."

Taking a left on Calvert Street, they soon took a right on Cleveland Avenue and accelerated.

"What in the world is going on, Charlie?"

"It's POTUS, sir."

"What about him?"

"He just collapsed in the Oval."

With traffic blocked off in all directions, the motorcade swerved onto Garfield, then onto Thirty-Fourth Street, blowing through red lights and whizzing past stunned onlookers. A moment later, they roared over Massachusetts Avenue and through the main gates of the U.S. Naval Observatory. Screeching to a halt in front of the residence, the detail rushed the VP inside as dozens of heavily armed members of the counterassault team took up positions around the VP's home, raised the security barriers at the main gate, and refused entrance to all visitors, even those with preapproved meetings.

Inside, Hernandez was taken to a secure conference room in the basement, where his two top aides were waiting, the looks on their faces saying it all.

"Tell me he's okay," the VP demanded.

Neither man could.

Marcus sat in his office watching the implosion of the Clarke presidency.

He told himself he should be working the phones, hunting down the rest of the Kairos network, but he couldn't do it. The images out of Libya were sickening, and now every other network was running with the story, not just CNN.

There was a knock at the door.

Jenny, clearly shaken, entered, and she had more bad news.

"Stephens is in the Oval."

"That was fast."

Jenny closed the door behind her and lowered her voice. "How did we get this wrong?" she asked, her eyes red and moist.

"I have no idea," he conceded, shaking his head.

He handed her a sheet of paper fresh out of the printer, still warm.

"What's this?" she asked.

"I wanted you to be the first to know," he told her. "I'm resigning."

Jenny read the letter, which Marcus had already signed. "Then I will, too."

"No, you need to stay. You need to run this office and see this thing through."

"I'm just as culpable as you are."

"Jenny, you're a rock star at Langley," he replied. "The president and VP like you. They trust you. More importantly, Stephens doesn't hate you. He wants my scalp, not yours. And Dell recruited you into the Agency. She'll have your back."

Jenny turned and looked up at the monitors. She was a strong woman, but it was clear that she was traumatized by the images of the small, burnt hands and severed, charred legs of one child after another, and the knowledge that she had played a critical role in convincing the president to order the strike.

Suddenly she began to hyperventilate. Marcus got up, came around his desk, and put his hand on her shoulder and urged her to sit down. Instead, she put her arms around him. They stood there for at least a minute, holding each other.

Until Pete knocked twice and popped his head in the door.

"Oh, uh, sorry, I . . ."

Jenny released Marcus, wiped her eyes, and headed back to her cubicle.

"It's Annie," Pete said as Jenny brushed by him. "She's on line two."

Marcus exhaled, then closed the door to his office after Pete had also left.

"Hey, you okay?" Annie asked when Marcus picked up.

"Honestly? No."

"Marcus, I'm so sorry."

"Yeah, well . . ."

"About Libya, of course, but also about my boss. I'm guessing you saw that."

"Hard to miss."

"I pleaded with him not to be first."

"Guess it's true what they say, right? There's nothing more dangerous than standing between a United States senator and a TV camera."

"It's despicable. I can't believe he did that."

"Did he say anything that wasn't true?"

"I don't care," Annie snapped. "It was wrong."

"It's okay," he assured her.

"No, Marcus, it's not."

"He didn't actually mention me."

"Not by name, but he knows full well that calling for an investigation is going to lead directly to you. And now . . ."

"What?"

"No, no, never mind."

"What is it, Annie? I'd rather hear it from you than someone else."

"You're sure?"

"Of course."

"Dayton just sent out a 'Dear Colleague' letter. He didn't discuss it with me. Didn't even give me a heads-up."

"What does it say?"

"It's signed by the entire Democratic caucus—forty-nine senators—calling for immediate hearings, beginning Monday."

Marcus said nothing.

"I just can't believe he would do this, Marcus," Annie said, her voice tense with anger. "After all you've done for him. After all *I've* done for him. Why would he take the lead on this?"

"You know exactly why, Annie. He's politically exposed. He hired me before his trip to Russia, or his PAC did. I'm dating you. He and Esther sat with us at the peace signing. The whole world saw us."

"And now you're radioactive."

"Exactly, and he's trying to create as much distance between us as he can, as fast as he can. He's saving his hide, Annie. That's how the game is played. No wonder you want out."

"Let's meet," she said. "Have you had lunch?"

"Maybe you should keep your distance too."

"Absolutely not. You made a mistake. But I'm not going to condemn you for it. And the more I think about it, the more furious I am that Robert moved so fast to throw you to the wolves. If I hadn't already resigned, I'd do it right now."

"Thanks," Marcus said. "Look, there's something I need to tell you."

"What?" she asked.

But just then his intercom buzzed.

"Just a sec, Annie," he said, putting her on hold and hitting his intercom button. "What is it, Pete?"

"It's McDermott."

"Let me guess—the president wants to see me."

"He didn't say that—not exactly."

"What did he say?"

"Drop everything and get over there now."

"Okay, I'm on my way."

"I'll go with you," Pete offered.

But Marcus wouldn't hear of it. "No, Pete—I'm toast, which means you're the new head of this unit, at least for the next month. It's gonna be up to you to find those Kairos bastards. Take them down. And keep a close eye on Jenny. I'm worried about her."

Then he took a deep breath, tried to steady himself, and took Annie off hold.

"I'm sorry but I can't talk right now. I've got to go."

"What now?"

"I've been summoned to the West Wing."

"That doesn't sound good."

"No, but it doesn't matter. That's what I wanted to tell you. I'm going to resign."

“What do you mean?” Annie asked, stunned.

“I mean quit. Leave. Step down. *Adios, muchachos.*”

“No, Marcus, you can’t do that.”

“Why not? You’re the one who wanted me to move on.”

“Move on, sure. But not fall on your sword. Look—if Clarke is going to fire you, fine, let him. But if you resign, you’re admitting this is your fault, not his.”

“It *is* my fault, Annie. I *am* radioactive. I need to protect him from the fallout.”

“No, you don’t, and it’s not your fault,” Annie shot back. “Look, I pored over all the same intelligence that you did. I read the full transcript of that NSC meeting. And it’s crystal clear that you brought the president and his team the best information you could.”

“But I was wrong.”

“You didn’t give the order to strike.”

“I may as well have.”

“But you didn’t—and there’s a difference.”

“You’re splitting hairs, Annie.”

"I absolutely am not. You told the NSC what you knew. You gave them the facts as best as you were able to determine them."

"And people died. Women, children . . ."

"Yes. And I know you feel sick about that. But that's not the point."

"On what planet is the death of innocent civilians not the point?"

"Marcus, the Central Intelligence Agency does *not* make policy. You do not make policy. The CIA does *not* recommend a course of action. The most the CIA can do is provide the president information, context, analysis, as best it can. It doesn't make decisions. That's black-letter law. If you withheld information from the president, then you should resign. If you lied to the president, then you should resign. If you willfully misled the president of the United States, then you should resign. But did you?"

After a long pause, Marcus said, "No."

"Agent Ryker, did you make the decision to bomb that compound?"

"I told them that—"

"Did. You. Make. The. Decision. To. Strike?"

Marcus now saw what Annie was doing. She was previewing the Senate intelligence hearing for which he would soon receive a subpoena. And despite the urgent summons to the Oval Office, he went along.

"No, Senator, I did not," he replied.

"Who did?" Annie pressed.

"The president."

"Did he have a full discussion of the facts first?"

"Yes."

"Did anyone object?"

"Yes."

"Who?"

"CIA director Richard Stephens."

"How would you characterize the nature of his objections?"

"They were vehement."

"Why?"

"Director Stephens said the information I was presenting was circumstantial and inconclusive."

"Did he ask the president to take more time, to gather more evidence?"

"Yes."

"Did Director Stephens warn the president of past examples of an American president making fast decisions with incomplete information that proved later to be a mistake and had deadly consequences?"

"He did."

"Did the president take a vote of the National Security Council prior to making his decision as the duly authorized commander in chief?"

"Yes."

"And what was the conclusion of that vote?

"The NSC voted unanimously to recommend that the president order a strike."

"No one voted against such a strike?"

"No."

"Not even Director Stephens?"

"As director of the CIA, Mr. Stephens was not legally permitted to vote to make such a recommendation."

"But there was no question that he was telling the president and the rest of the NSC that the available evidence was not sufficient to warrant a strike?"

"Essentially."

"One more question, Agent Ryker. Does Director Stephens outrank you within the Central Intelligence Agency, and thus does his input to the president of the United States carry more weight than an officer in the clandestine service?"

"Of course."

"Thank you, Agent Ryker," Annie concluded. "The witness is excused."

There was another long silence.

"A congressional investigation isn't going to bury you, Marcus," Annie added. "It's going to vindicate you. I'm not saying it's going to absolve you of the guilt and pain you feel. I'm just saying don't take the easy way out. Don't let the president or anyone else make this your fault. Not after all the sacrifices you've made to protect this country and its leaders. Twenty years from now, you need to be able to lay your head on the pillow at night and know that you did your best to 'support and defend the Constitution of the United States against all enemies, foreign and domestic,' that you bore 'true faith and allegiance to the same,' that you took that 'obligation freely, without any mental reservation or purpose of evasion,' and that you strove to 'well and faithfully discharge the duties of the office,' so help you God."

ISTANBUL, TURKEY

Zaid Farooq paid his driver in cash.

Exiting the taxi with just his carry-on bag, the thirty-nine-year-old Algerian native entered Sabiha Gökçen International Airport, Istanbul's second largest, and headed for the Air France counter. The lines were long. The air-conditioning was not working. Farooq felt trickles of sweat streaking down his back. But he was determined to remain calm.

Pairs of policemen seemed to be everywhere. Every several minutes, a member of the canine unit walked by with a German shepherd sniffing for drugs and weapons. Out of the corner of his eye, Farooq spotted a team of soldiers, each holding submachine guns, watching passengers warily. All the while, CCTV cameras scanned for trouble, no doubt running facial recognition software to identify wanted criminals and terrorists.

The last thing Farooq wanted to do was draw attention to himself. So he had chosen to wear a stylish pin-striped Western business suit, not his usual *galabia*, the traditional loose-fitting, long shirt he had grown up with and in which he felt most comfortable. He forced himself not to keep checking his watch or repeatedly mop his brow. To stay occupied and focused, he fished a set of earbuds out of his briefcase, connected them to his phone, and began listening to an audio recording of the Qur'an, hoping the words of the Prophet would give him the patience he needed.

During the cab ride to the airport, the Kairos intelligence chief had told himself there was no reason for worry. He did not have a criminal record. Nor, until now, had he ever directly participated in any of the group's operations, even those he had helped plan. He was not a known quantity. He was not on the Interpol watch list. So far as he knew, he was not even on the radar of the Turks, the Americans, the Israelis, or any other intelligence agency. This was precisely what made him invaluable in the eyes of his colleagues—most notably, Badr Hassan al-Ruzami—and why Ruzami had chosen him for this most important of all Kairos missions.

Finally reaching the counter, Farooq presented his real passport, real driver's license, and a credit card bearing his real name.

"Now is not the time to risk using false papers," Ruzami had insisted back in Yemen. "That will come. For now, you need to get into position and make all the critical preparations, minimizing any chance of detection or disruption along the way."

It was, to be sure, an enormous risk. But it was not one he had made on his own. From the earliest days of Kairos, Abu Nakba had entrusted the design and execution of nearly all operations to Ruzami. And if Father had trusted him, Farooq reasoned, so should he.

"*Bonjour*, Msr. Farooq," said the young woman behind the counter, a brunette with large brown eyes and a pleasant manner, speaking with a distinct Parisian accent. "May I have your passport and final destination?"

"*Oui, c'est ici*," he replied, sliding over his Algerian passport. "Mexico City, *s'il vous plaît*."

The woman smiled. "Business or pleasure?" she asked, typing his name into the computer.

Farooq was startled. Though he had traveled countless miles around the globe, he had never been asked that by anyone other than a security official.

"Uh, well, does it . . . ? I mean, does it matter?" he stammered.

"Oh no, of course not—forgive me—I was just making conversation," the woman said, blushing at the realization she had caused him any measure of discomfort.

The young woman was scrutinizing his passport and then typing something into her terminal. To his right, he noticed a pair of police officers watching him. More beads of sweat were forming on his forehead and neck. Finally she returned his passport and handed over his boarding passes and wished him a pleasant voyage.

Nodding his thanks, he headed for the security line. The first ticket was for an Air France flight that would take him from Istanbul to Paris. After a long layover, he would then board a second flight nonstop to Mexico City, landing at 4:55 p.m. the following day. To maintain his cover as a successful Moroccan businessman, he would travel first-class on a Boeing 777 wide-body jet. That, too, had been Ruzami's idea. Having never flown first-class before, Farooq had not argued.

ADEN, YEMEN

Once again, the warehouse erupted in laughter.

Tanya Brighton was laughing so hard she was practically snorting. So was Hannah Weiss. Even the guys were laughing, though they were supposed to be working. Then again, these dozen young men from a potpourri of Asian, African, and Latin American countries seemed to laugh at just about anything Mia Minetti said, even if English was not their first language.

Of the three American girls who had come to Yemen to volunteer for the year, Mia was the prettiest and most outgoing. The nineteen-year-old had long jet-black hair, dark-brown eyes, and lovely olive skin. Not a day went by when Mia didn't keep them all spellbound or cracking up with stories and jokes.

Then Hannah spoke up. "*Hardy har har*, Mia, but I can do you one better."

"In your dreams, Weiss," Mia teased to the cheers of the guys now gathering around the table.

"Oh, really, Minetti?" Hannah mused. "Care to make it interesting?"

"Absolutely," Mia said. "Name your terms, girl."

"Now, now, ladies, this isn't Vegas," said Tanya, the elder of the team at the ripe old age of twenty-seven. "You know the rules."

"Fine, fine, no money," Hannah said. "Let's play for dishes."

"Dishes?"

"That's right. If my joke is better than yours this time, then you're doing the dishes every night for a week. If not, then it's my dishpan hands, not yours."

"You're going down, Weiss," Mia laughed. "But fine, you're on."

The warehouse echoed with the *ooh*s and *aah*s of the sweat-drenched young men enjoying a welcome respite from their backbreaking work amid the hundred-degree temperature and brutal humidity. Tanya smiled as she pulled out a handkerchief from the pocket of her overalls and wiped her brow.

Hannah, who would turn twenty-three in a week, was an attractive brunette from East Texas. She was certainly a firecracker, smart as a whip and hilarious to boot. Tanya had been impressed with Hannah the moment she had arrived in Aden almost a year earlier, and even more so when she learned that Hannah had graduated summa cum laude from Liberty University and was going to begin medical school at Harvard in the fall. But first, she'd told her parents, she wanted to take a gap year and care for the poorest of the poor in war-torn Yemen. In less than a month, she'd be returning to Texas, and Tanya was going to miss her sass and can-do spirit.

"All right, Weiss, put up or shut up," Minetti said.

Standing, the Texan turned away from Mia and looked in the eyes of each member of her international jury.

"Okay, boys, now listen up," she began as she cleared her throat and the room settled down. "A German, an Italian, a Frenchman, and an American all walk into a bar, you see? And they all get talkin' about whose language is better. And of course, the American says, 'Come on, let's be real, English is the most beautiful language in the world. I mean, just take a word like *butterfly*. It's a beautiful word for a beautiful creature. *Butterfly*. Am I right?'

"But the Frenchman takes offense." Now Hannah shifted into her best Inspector Clouseau accent. "'What are you talking about, you fools!' he says. 'French is the loveliest language on planet earth. *Butterfly?* What kind of word is that? Nonsense. We say *papillon*. *Papillon*. Is there a more beautiful word than *papillon*?'"

Out of the corner of her eye, Tanya saw Mia smirk. But she also noticed how quiet the guys had become and how quickly Hannah had captured their full attention.

"Up to this point, the Italian has been quiet, but now he is becoming upset," Hannah said, then shifted into her best Italian accent. "'*Butterfly? Papillion?* You're both touched in the head. No, no, Italian is not just the most beautiful language; it is a work of art. For example, we say, *la farfalla*. Come, say it with me, *la farfalla*. So beautiful—*la farfalla*,' he says, touching his fingers to his mouth and tossing that kiss into the air as if he has just finished a most delicious meal and costly bottle of wine."

Hannah now raised her own finger as if to say, *Wait.*

"But the German is getting more and more angry by the minute," she said. "'*Vat are you talking about?*' he says. '*Haff you all gone mad?*' The German's face is red. His forehead is covered with perspiration. A vein in his neck is bulging. '*Butterfly? Papillon? Farfalla?*' he asks in disgust. '*And vat is wrong vit Schmetterling?*'"

Once again, the warehouse erupted in laughter. Even Mia was laughing. Until everyone heard the screeching of tires out front.

Two dust-drenched SUVs slammed to a halt.

Nasir Bhati stepped out of the lead vehicle, surrounded by four men in black hoods carrying Kalashnikovs. Both engines were still running as six more hooded men jumped out of the second vehicle and Bhati stormed through the front doors of the humanitarian relief center and into the reception area.

The first person he saw was a young woman behind the front desk.

"What are you—?"

Bhati raised his pistol and shot her in the forehead. Two male volunteers—a Spaniard and a South Korean, Bhati thought—suddenly rushed to the reception area from the warehouse. Bhati and his colleagues immediately opened fire on them, felling the men instantly.

Panic erupted throughout the building. Bhati could hear people screaming, scrambling for the exits, not knowing they were all covered. He heard squealing tires as a third SUV skidded to a stop beside the loading dock out back. Then he heard gunshots from outside—Yaqoub al-Hamzi and the three jihadists with him had just taken care of whoever was trying to escape in that direction.

Bhati strode farther into the warehouse and came upon two Filipino men taking cover behind a pallet of rice. Pointing his pistol at them, he ordered them to come out and show their faces. Trembling, they complied. Bhati then grabbed one and shoved the gun against the young man's temple.

"Where are they?" he shouted in English, though his Pakistani accent was thick.

"Who?" the man replied, as all color drained from his face.

"The Americans—where are they?"

When the man hesitated, Bhati pulled the trigger. The explosion thundered through the warehouse. Blood and bone and brain matter sprayed all over the other Filipino volunteer, whose entire body quaked with fear.

"Where are they?" Bhati shouted. *"The Americans. Tell me now."*

The man did not answer. He seemed to be mumbling to himself. Perhaps he was praying. Bhati heard the name of Jesus at least twice. He had no intention of hearing it a third time. So he pulled the trigger, killing the man instantly.

Throughout the building, Bhati's men were shooting everyone they found. They still had not located the Americans. Bhati reloaded his sidearm and headed for the restrooms. Rushing into the women's room, he found all the stall doors shut. He kicked each in, one by one, but they were all empty. Wheeling around, he brushed past al-Hamzi, who had come up behind him, and stormed into the men's room. But this, too, was empty.

Bhati cursed in his native Urdu, then heard one of his men shouting that they had found them. He headed that way immediately. The three Americans were hiding in a large pantry in the kitchen, located just off the east side of the warehouse. The women were sitting on the floor, huddled together, tears streaming down their faces.

"Get them in the truck," he ordered al-Hamzi as more gunfire echoed through the warehouse.

35

THE WEST WING

McDermott's assistant met Marcus in the basement of the EEOB.

She did not take him to McDermott's office. Instead, she led him through a tunnel few staffers knew about into the basement of the White House, telling him that she was under strict orders from her boss to keep him away from the prying eyes of the press corps. When they arrived at the presidential movie theater, she asked Marcus to step inside and wait.

Ten minutes later, McDermott arrived, stern-faced and impatient. "Take a seat," he said.

"We're not going to the Oval?" Marcus asked.

"No."

"Bill, come on, if the president is going to fire me, he should do it to my face. Haven't I earned at least—?"

McDermott cut him off. "Marcus, listen to me."

"No. I have the right to—"

"Marcus, sit down and—"

"I'm not going to sit down and take a lecture. If the president has something to say—"

"Shut up, Marcus—for once in your life would you just shut your mouth and listen to me?"

Marcus felt adrenaline surging into his system. He resented everything about McDermott's body language and tone and the feeling that he was suddenly back in the corps as a lowly recruit. But for the moment he would listen to what the man had to say.

"Twenty minutes ago, the president collapsed in the Oval."

Marcus could barely believe it, but it was obvious that McDermott wasn't kidding.

"He was having a screaming match with Stephens and then . . ."

"What?"

"He just keeled over."

"Why? What happened?

"We have no idea. And nobody knows what I just told you. Just Stephens, me, the president's detail, the chief of staff, his medical team, and now you."

"The press doesn't know?"

"Absolutely not."

"How could they miss him being whisked off to Walter Reed in an ambulance?"

"Because he wasn't whisked off."

"Why not?"

"The detail took him to the Residence."

"Why?"

"Because he ordered them to."

"He's still conscious?"

"He was at the time. I don't know about now. The president's physician is working on him as we speak. Specialists are on their way from Walter Reed."

"Where's the VP?"

"Stop."

"Why? What did—?"

"*Just stop*—you're acting like you're on his detail, Marcus. But you're not in the Secret Service anymore, and I'm not looking for advice. I summoned you because the president has suspended you without pay, effectively immediately."

"Suspended me?"

"Pending an investigation into your conduct and how badly you botched the intelligence and put this administration into the toilet."

McDermott handed Marcus an envelope. Marcus opened it and read the two-sentence letter, printed on White House stationery and signed by the chief of staff.

"Didn't Stephens tell the president to fire me?" Marcus asked.

"Of course."

"Which is why he rushed to the White House the moment he heard the news?"

"That surprises you?" McDermott asked.

"Hardly—but why isn't the president canning me? Why only a suspension?"

"Don't kid yourself, Marcus. I have no doubt the president is going to pull the trigger on you when the time is right. First he'll let Congress have its little investigation. Then he'll give them a scalp or two, including yours, but at a moment of his choosing, no one else's."

"That wasn't good enough for Stephens?" Marcus asked.

"Apparently not."

"And Stephens went ballistic?"

"That's about the order of things."

"Did you defend me?" Marcus asked, already knowing the answer.

"It wasn't my fight."

"Bill, I've known you for almost half my life."

"And you've resented me for most of it."

"That's not true."

"Of course it is, but that's immaterial," McDermott replied, his manner as cold as it was clinical. "How exactly was I supposed to defend you, Marcus? What exactly is the case you'd want me to make? This isn't about friendship. It's not about loyalty. It's about competence or the lack thereof. This thing is on you—all of it—and the best thing to do right now would be to submit your resignation and spare the president and this country a political witch trial it cannot afford."

"So just to make sure I'm hearing you correctly, Bill, the president of the United States made the decision to order the bombing, not me—since I work for an agency that is only allowed by law to collect and analyze intelligence, not make policy or take direct action—yet you want me to fall on my sword for the whole thing? And now the president has collapsed from some unknown ailment. But rather than be transparent with the world, you guys are keeping it a secret, lying to the press, lying to Congress, and lying to the entire country about his health. And you're telling me to '*do the best thing*'?"

"Get off your high horse. It wasn't my call to keep this secret. That's way above my pay grade. But that's not the point."

"What is?"

"The point is the president is under a tremendous amount of stress—and frankly you put him there. I'm not going to stand here and argue with you about it. You know what you told the president and the rest of the NSC. You know he made the decision based on your advice. And you know innocent civilians are dead because of it. So you're suspended. Soon you'll be fired. Right now, I need your White House hard pass, your CIA credentials, your DSS badge, and your gun. Next, you need to clean out your desk. Then you'll be escorted off the premises."

"You've got to be kidding me."

"Don't make this harder than it already is, Marcus."

Marcus stood toe to toe with McDermott, disgusted that after all they'd been through together, the man hadn't lifted a finger to defend him. Yet Marcus had no recourse. There was nothing he could do but comply. A shouting match wasn't going to get him anything except, perhaps, a night in jail. Marcus could see a uniformed Secret Service officer standing outside in the hallway. So he forced himself to keep his mouth shut and handed over everything to McDermott, even his Sig Sauer.

Then his phone rang. As he pulled it out of his pocket, they both looked down at the caller ID. It was Pete Hwang.

"You should take it," McDermott said.

Marcus wasn't going to, but McDermott insisted.

"He knows you're with me. He wouldn't be calling if it wasn't urgent."

Marcus held his tongue and hit Answer. "What?" he said, curt and defensive.

"Are you in the Oval?"

"No."

"Are you with the president?"

"No—Pete, this isn't the time."

"Are you still with Bill?"

"Yeah, but—"

"You both need to hear this."

"What?"

"Put me on speaker," Pete insisted.

Against his better judgment, Marcus did. "All right, go, but make it fast."

"There's been a terrorist attack in Yemen," Pete explained.

"What was the target?" Marcus asked.

"A Christian relief organization in Aden."

"When?" McDermott asked.

"It just happened."

"Casualties?"

"Five dead, maybe more—but it gets worse."

"How?"

"Three American aid workers—all women—have been taken hostage."

"Kairos?" Marcus asked.

"It's not confirmed, but it's got all the earmarks of them, yes," Pete replied.

"Well, isn't that lovely," McDermott sneered. "The one-two punch. First Kairos leaks their macabre video to CNN and humiliates POTUS in front of the entire world. Then they grab three American women to bury him alive. Congratulations, Marcus, the blowback for your Libya fiasco is well underway."

CIA HEADQUARTERS, LANGLEY, VIRGINIA

Martha Dell was in her office, working the phones.

She had just finished a secure conference call with the Agency's station chief in Sana'a, dispatching a CIA team to Aden to gather as much intel as possible. She'd spoken briefly with her counterparts in Riyadh and Abu Dhabi and asked them to vacuum up whatever they could on the attack in Aden and feed her anything and everything they found as fast as possible. But now her assistant had stepped in and turned up the sound on one of TV screens.

An MSNBC correspondent in Rome was reporting that Pope Pius XIII had just issued a statement asking Catholics around the world to pray for all the volunteers who had been attacked and for the speedy return of the three American aid workers to their families. The correspondent then explained that the Vatican was not commenting on a report in an Italian newspaper that the pope had decided to cancel his upcoming trip to the States, though he added that one cardinal who spoke to NBC News on the condition of anonymity said, "It is probably not appropriate to make the trip in light of all that has happened, but no formal decision has yet been made."

With that, another phone rang. Dell answered it. Stephens was back in the building and on his way up to the seventh floor. Dell muted her TV and headed into the director's adjacent office.

"Please tell me the news on POTUS hasn't leaked," Stephens said the moment he arrived.

"Not yet," Dell replied.

"You're sure?" he pressed as he removed his suit jacket and draped it around the back of his chair.

"We're monitoring everything."

"Who's *we*?"

"Three of my top aides—that's it."

"I don't want anyone else in this building to know—not until we know exactly what's happening with him and figure out how to proceed."

"Agreed."

"Because it's . . ."

Stephens suddenly slumped down in his chair and closed his eyes.

"What do you need, Richard? Seriously, let me help."

"Just give me five minutes to myself, Martha. I need to catch my breath."

"Of course—but before I go . . ."

"What?"

"What happened with Ryker?"

"Nothing."

"What does that mean?"

"I demanded the president fire him on the spot. The president said no, he'd suspend him but nothing more, not until a full investigation can be conducted. We got into a knock-down, drag-out shouting match . . ."

"In the Oval Office?"

"I'm afraid so."

"And?"

"And that's when the president lost consciousness."

Dell was speechless.

With his head still down and his eyes still shut, he asked her again to give him a few minutes and to have the staff direct all his calls to her for the time being. She agreed and returned to her office.

The moment the door was closed, Stephens opened his eyes again and turned on all of his TV monitors, keeping them muted with captions visible so he could read everything that was being reported. All the U.S. and European networks were still wall-to-wall with the kidnappings in Yemen and the ongoing coverage of the video footage from Ghat and the firestorm on Capitol Hill over it. Fortunately, he saw nothing about the president's health. But at the moment, Clarke was not his primary concern. Pulling out his mobile phone, he dialed an unlisted number. It rang four times; then a woman answered.

"Carolyn Tam."

"Carolyn, it's me."

"Whoa—didn't expect to hear from you today of all days."

"Got a minute?"

"I'm on a commercial break."

"I know. I'm watching."

"Sure, go ahead. Are we on or off the record?"

"When have I ever spoken to you on the record?"

"There's a first time for everything."

"Not today. Same rules as always."

"Fine. Talk fast. I've got a minute-forty-three left."

"I've got something for you, so long as you swear that you'll never reveal that I'm your source, not to your editors, not to your staff, not to your mother, not to God when you reach the pearly gates."

"Sounds juicy."

"Believe me, it is."

"Fine, you have my word. What is it?"

"Audio of the NSC at Camp David last Saturday."

"That's classified."

"Which is why you didn't get it from me."

"Then I'm guessing you weren't the one pushing the president to order the strike, even though everyone in town believes it was you."

"You'll hear exactly who pushed the strike and who pushed back."

"That's a big risk."

"And under any other circumstances, I'd never give it to you. But it's yours if you want it."

"Yes, of course, I'll take it."

"One more condition."

"Name it."

"You break this story today."

"That's crazy. You know I'm going to need several days to digest it, to do it justice. I can't just—"

"No—it runs today, preferably in prime time, or I move on to someone else."

"Why so fast?"

"Carolyn, do you want another Emmy or not?"

"Fine," she said. "How do we do this?"

"I'm sending it now through an anonymous, untraceable email account. It's a big file. It's going to take a few minutes."

"I'm on it," she assured him.

"You do this right, and believe me, I'll open the vault for you."

Seething, Marcus returned to the EEOB and gathered the team in his office.

"The president has suspended me," he said as he stepped behind his desk, bent down to pick up a box of copier paper, and dumped its contents.

"*Suspended?*" Pete asked. "You weren't *fired*?"

"Don't worry, he's going to fire me all right—but not until he gets maximum political credit for doing so," Marcus explained as he began to fill the box with books, papers, and other personal effects. "For now, I'm being 'suspended pending a complete investigation of Agent Ryker's alleged role in this tragic error,' but we know how this town works. They want me to resign to spare the White House from having to lower the guillotine. I said no. But whatever—I'm gone."

"Effective when?" Geoff Stone asked.

"Immediately," Marcus said, tossing the suspension letter onto his desk for them all to read.

"How immediately?" Jenny asked.

"Did you see the two uniformed officers I arrived with?" Marcus replied. "*Immediately.*"

The team began firing questions at him, but Marcus had neither the time nor the interest. Holding up his hands, he quieted them down.

"Look, Pete's in charge now—that's it," Marcus said. "Jenny, as my last official act, I'm appointing you Pete's deputy and heir apparent. Come Monday, you'll have a dozen analysts and admin staff to help you guys. So, Noah, make sure everything's ready for them to plug in and get to work. In the meantime, don't worry about me. Worry about those girls in Yemen. And show these idiots in the West Wing what you're made of. Outhustle everyone else in the intel community. Get these girls back home to their families. Then hunt down whoever's left in Kairos and blow them away."

"We're on it," Pete said. "In fact, Jenny just wrote a fast brief on who these women are. No one else has done it yet—not State or CIA."

"Good—send it now," Marcus replied.

"Don't you want to read it first?" Jenny asked.

"Wish I could, but I'm afraid my time here has come to an ignominious end."

Marcus gave each member of his team a quick hug, then followed the officers to the Northwest Gate and exited the White House grounds. Walking past the Blair House to the corner to catch a cab, he pulled out his phone and called Annie. "Hey."

"What happened?"

"I'm done. I'm out. Suspended," he said, briefly explaining what had happened though careful not to mention the president's condition.

Just like his team, she started firing one question after another at him, but he stopped her and said he couldn't discuss any of it on an open line. "Where are you right now?" he asked.

"Home."

"Home? What home?"

"My home. Where else?"

"You're not in the office?"

"I couldn't stay."

"Why not?"

"Honestly, I can't bear to see Dayton's face right now. Not after what he's just done. I'd totally lose it on him. So I took a personal day and came home."

"Can you meet me?"

"Absolutely. Where?"

"Walter Reed. I need to check in on Kailea. Then I'm leaving town."

Twenty minutes later, Marcus spotted Annie coming through the hospital's main entrance. He went straight to her, put his arms around her, and held her tightly.

"You okay?" she asked.

"I don't even know how to answer the question," he confessed.

Taking her by the hand, he found the elevators, and they headed up to the private room of his partner, DSS agent Kailea Curtis. They found her asleep—under heavy sedation. She was hooked up to an IV, a heart sensor, and various other devices and monitors. An oxygen mask covered her nose and mouth. As roughed up as Marcus knew he looked from their terrible ordeal in Lebanon, Kailea was worse. Though the swelling had gone down a bit since Marcus had first been to visit her on Sunday night, Kailea's face was badly distorted, and the bruising around her eyes and neck had grown. Her broken nose had a bandage visible around the edges of the oxygen mask. Her hands were almost completely covered with bandages as well.

They sat there for a while, not saying anything, just watching over her and each saying a silent prayer for her. When a nurse came in to give Kailea a shot, Marcus recognized her as the same woman who had been on duty Sunday night when he'd come to visit. "Good to see you, Betty," he whispered.

"And you, Agent Ryker," she whispered back.

"How's she doing?" Marcus asked.

"Whoever did this nearly killed her," the nurse replied. "But your partner is a fighter. Tough as nails. And I'd say she's nearly out of danger."

"Will she make a full recovery?"

"Let's hope so, though I'm not sure we can go that far at this point. But it's not what you can see that's the problem."

"What do you mean?" Marcus asked.

"Her face will heal—her nose and so forth. That's all superficial. There'll be scarring, but nothing a good cosmetic surgeon can't fix. The problem is that several of her internal organs were severely damaged. We almost had to remove her spleen, but the doctors held off on that. They want to give it more time."

"How much more?"

"Hard to say—it could be months until we know for sure and before she can go back home."

"And then?"

"She's got a long, hard road of recovery ahead of her."

THE NAVAL OBSERVATORY

The secure videoconference was now live.

Vice President Hernandez greeted Defense Secretary Cal Foster at the Pentagon, Secretary of State Meg Whitney at Foggy Bottom, CIA director Richard Stephens at Langley, and National Security Advisor Bill McDermott in the White House Situation Room. They were still waiting for the attorney general to come on the line, but with the clock ticking, the VP decided to start anyway.

After a quick prayer for the president, Hernandez asked Stephens to explain exactly what had happened in the Oval Office. Then he turned to McDermott for the latest developments at the White House.

"The Residence has been converted into an intensive care unit," McDermott began. "Dr. Jerome Lenkowski, head of Walter Reed, is on-site with his best people. They're bringing more diagnostic equipment—a CT scan machine and so forth—as we speak. It's being brought in through tunnels from Treasury to keep things quiet."

"And the president?" Hernandez asked. "How's he doing?"

"For the moment, he is under sedation and unconscious. Lenkowski says it's going to take some time to fully assess his condition," McDermott replied.

"But he's hopeful?" the VP pressed.

"I think we all need to be hopeful," McDermott said. "Given the president's family history, I suspect this is just a TIA. But we'll know more in a few hours."

"TIA?"

"Transient ischemic attack. Causes symptoms like a stroke but not as serious and usually only temporary."

The VP then turned to Foster, who assured the group that the military was detecting no changes in force status in Russia, China, North Korea, or Iran.

Whitney reported that nearly every country in the U.N. General Assembly had just voted minutes earlier to condemn the American strike in Libya. Only eight countries—Israel, Egypt, Jordan, the UAE, Bahrain, Sudan, Morocco, and Saudi Arabia—had voted against the resolution. Great Britain had abstained, as had South Korea.

Stephens said the massive sandstorm over North Africa was finally showing signs of abating. McDermott asked when it would be safe for U.S. special forces to get to the compound ncar Ghat to see the damage for themselves. Foster said it would still be twenty-four hours or so.

"Cal, we need to get our own people in there," Hernandez insisted.

"I understand, sir, but I don't want to lose a SEAL team and a couple of choppers over this. We need to take our time and do it right."

"I don't want more casualties either, but this isn't making any sense. If CNN can get a man in there, why can't we?"

"The CNN doctor was a local."

"Don't we have any local assets?"

"Frankly, no."

"What about the Brits, Richard?" Hernandez asked, turning to Stephens. "They've got a pretty robust intel operation in Libya, don't they?"

"Mostly near Tripoli, not out in the desert."

"Can't they send in a recon team and at least give us an initial read?"

"It's not going to pacify the jackals on the Hill," Stephens insisted.

"I wouldn't expect it to," Hernandez replied. "I just want the facts."

39

The vice president turned back to McDermott.

"Bill, brief us on the situation in Yemen."

McDermott began by showing a series of still photos of the crime scene—both the warehouse and the connected offices—taken by the local police in Aden. Next, he showed gruesome CCTV footage of the attack from inside the warehouse and front offices. Finally he displayed images of the three Americans who had been seized and gave a little background on each, using the briefing materials Jenny Morris had prepared.

The first image was of an attractive brunette. "Hannah Weiss," McDermott said. "Premed student from East Texas. Graduated summa cum laude last year from Liberty University, heading to Harvard Medical School next year, but wanted a gap year doing missionary work and chose Yemen. Wanted to make a difference, serve the poor and needy someplace where no one else wanted to go. She's been in country for more than ten months and was on track to return home to Tyler on the first of June."

Another photo appeared on the screen.

"Mia Minetti. Nineteen years old. Born and raised in Montgomery, Alabama. Planning to attend the University of Alabama in the fall to study psychology and intercultural relations. She's the oldest of seven children—five brothers and two sisters, ranging in age from nineteen down to the youngest at two and a half. Father, Bob, is a junior high PE teacher and football coach. Mom, Tracey, used to be a math teacher. Now homeschools Mia's siblings."

The woman in the last photo was older than the other two.

"Tanya Brighton," McDermott reported. "She's the overall team leader. Born and raised in Biloxi, Mississippi, but her family moved to Shreveport, Louisiana, when she was ten. Star varsity soccer player in high school, then played for Baylor on a full scholarship. Graduated with a degree in international relations and a minor in Arabic. She was hired right out of college by an NGO affiliated with the Southern Baptist Convention—the same group that sent all three women to Yemen. She's been in Aden for nearly five years. Has an older brother, Timmy, with Down syndrome, and she writes him once a week. The worst part is she recently got engaged to another guy from the warehouse—Rodrigo, a young man from Barcelona. The wedding was set for August 15. Rodrigo was shot and killed in the attack."

"Has anyone claimed responsibility?" Whitney asked.

"No," McDermott said.

"Has NSA picked up any SIGINT, any clues at all as to where these women were taken?"

"I'm afraid not."

"What are your people saying, Richard?" the VP asked.

"The timing of the attack so soon after Libya suggests Kairos, but the location suggests the Houthis or possibly the IRGC," Stephens replied, referring to the Iranian Revolutionary Guard Corps. "My analysts are divided on where the girls might have been taken. One scenario is that they've already been spirited out of Yemen, most likely by boat, most likely to Africa. Another is that they've been secreted away to Iran, perhaps taken across the Gulf in small speedboats. The third scenario is that they're still in Yemen but have been moved far from Aden, perhaps to a terrorist training camp in the mountains. But no one believes they're still in Aden."

Suddenly a new image came flickering onto the secure videoconference call. All eyes now turned to Attorney General Catherine Blackburn, the sixty-four-year-old former Harvard law professor and former governor of South Carolina.

Blackburn apologized for being late.

Hernandez gave her an update on Clarke's condition, then asked for her counsel.

"First and foremost, you have got to go public," the AG began. "If this leaks, combined with the white-hot anger on Capitol Hill over the Libyan thing, the administration is going to be crucified."

"We can't go public without a game plan," Hernandez said. "The medical details, as painful as they are, are the easy part. But the press is going to demand to know who's running the country and whether Clarke is still the commander in chief. What am I supposed to tell them?"

"Sir, we all wish the president a full and speedy recovery," Blackburn replied. "Hopefully he's back on the job in a few days, even if not at full strength. Maybe that takes a couple days more. Maybe a couple weeks more. I don't know. I have no doubt Dr. Lenkowski will walk us through all that soon. The challenge we face is that the president is not simply operating at less than full capacity. At the moment, he's still unconscious. Under heavy medication. Possibly in need of some major medical procedures over the next twelve to twenty-four hours. All of which means he is not capable of executing the duties of the office."

At this, Secretary Foster spoke up. "For the moment, Vice President Hernandez is in charge, right? I mean, we're not in a military emergency. We're not at war. We're not dropping bombs on anyone. Otherwise, I'd be in charge in the president's absence, but since that's not precisely the case, the VP takes point, correct?"

"Well, that's where things get murky," Blackburn replied. "Typically, when a president is undergoing a medical procedure of some kind involving anesthesia, he writes a letter in compliance with section three of the Twenty-Fifth Amendment, temporarily relinquishing his authority. Can we put up section three on the screen?"

An aide put up a PowerPoint slide as Blackburn put on her reading glasses and walked them through the text.

> SECTION 3. Whenever the President transmits to the President pro tempore of the Senate and the Speaker of the House of Representatives his written declaration that he is unable to discharge the powers and duties of his office, and until he transmits to them a written declaration to the contrary, such powers and duties shall be discharged by the Vice President as Acting President.

"We've all seen this happen a handful of times over the years," Blackburn said, removing her glasses. "But that's not what we're dealing with here. This isn't a planned procedure. There is no letter. Which brings us to Section Four."

> SECTION 4. Whenever the Vice President and a majority of either the principal officers of the executive departments or of such other body as Congress may by law provide, transmit to the President pro tempore of the Senate and the Speaker of the House of Representatives their written declaration that the President is unable to discharge the powers and duties of his office, the Vice President shall immediately assume the powers and duties of the office as Acting President.

"Now, to be clear, this provision of the Twenty-Fifth Amendment has never been activated since it was first passed by Congress and ratified by the States on February 10, 1967," Blackburn explained. "But I cannot see another way. We have to activate Section Four immediately."

Foster spoke again. "I don't know, Catherine," the SecDef said. "To many at home and abroad, that's going to smack of a coup d'état. Okay, so the president is ill. He's out of commission for a few days. But he's going to bounce back, right? Until he does, the VP runs the show."

"I hear you, Cal, but following the Constitution, by definition, is not a coup. It's not improper. It's certainly not illegal. The Constitution prescribes the exact remedy for a situation like this. To be sure, Section Four is a temporary measure. Once the president regains his faculties, then he can submit a letter to Congress stating that he's well enough to perform his duties, and that's it. The VP would no longer be in charge."

Secretary Whitney was shaking her head. "I'm sorry, Catherine, but I have to agree with Cal on this," she explained. "There's got to be another way. We're already heading into uncharted waters here. We're already in an emergency fraught with global uncertainty. And frankly, you're talking about an unprecedented constitutional action that's going to severely rattle the nation, spook the markets, unnerve our allies, and potentially embolden our enemies."

Yet Blackburn was adamant. "Madame Secretary, there is no other way. This is what the Constitution requires. You've all sworn an oath to uphold the Constitution. You can explain it to the nation and to the world. But you cannot ignore it."

WINCHESTER, VIRGINIA

Marcus and Annie headed west.

They spent the afternoon driving around the Virginia countryside, then went for a long walk in Shenandoah National Park, talking about anything and everything other than work, their relationship, or the crisis back in D.C. Eventually they pulled into a diner on the outskirts of Winchester to get a bite to eat. When the waitress seated them and brought them menus, Annie asked her to turn up the volume on the TV mounted over the counter.

"This is CNN breaking news," the announcer said. "Now from Washington, here's Carolyn Tam."

"Good evening. With the White House engulfed in multiple crises that seem to worsen by the hour, CNN has learned the identity of the official allegedly responsible for the disastrous bombing of a facility in western Libya, a facility that turned out not to be the base camp of the Kairos terrorist group but a school for severely disabled and mentally challenged children."

An image of Marcus flashed on the screen, and Annie gasped.

"CNN has exclusively obtained the audio recording and the official, classified transcript of the national security briefing at Camp David last Saturday," Tam continued. "They reveal unmistakably that a CIA officer named Marcus Ryker told President Clarke that Kairos founder and spiritual leader Abu Nakba was in the Libyan compound and pushed hard for Clarke to order the attack."

Marcus couldn't believe what he was hearing.

"Multiple sources in the intelligence community and the Pentagon tell CNN that Ryker—a highly decorated Marine combat veteran and former Secret Service agent—currently serves as a special agent with the Diplomatic Security Service, a division of the State Department. But our sources say that this is merely a cover and that Ryker actually works for the Central Intelligence Agency."

As Tam played the first sound bite from the NSC briefing, Marcus found himself being stared at by a dozen or more people who looked at him, then back to the screen, then back at him.

> "I have no doubt Abu Nakba is in that compound, sir. You have the brief. It's all there. The evidence may be circumstantial, but it is overwhelming. And I would remind you all that the Agency never had photos or phone intercepts of Osama bin Laden in that compound in Abbottabad. But he was there. And your predecessors made the right call sending in U.S. forces to take him down."

Then came the second sound bite.

> "Mr. President, you know my family history, and you know my service record. I am well aware of the risks you would be putting our pilots in, sir, and I do not believe I'm asking you to act recklessly. I'm following the evidence. Not my whims. Not my passions. But carefully gathered evidence. Evidence that leads to that building in Libya."

After the sound bites, the image switched to a CNN correspondent doing a stand-up report outside of Marcus's apartment in southeast D.C.

"We need to go," Marcus whispered. "Give me the keys."

Annie slid her keys across the table. Then they stood up, walked out, got back into Annie's Fiat 500L, and peeled out of the gravel parking lot.

"That's not all you said," Annie remarked as they pulled onto 66 heading east, back to D.C. "You told them about the 'massive and sophisticated compound' built 'in the middle of nowhere.' You talked about 'cinder block walls twenty feet high,' and guard towers in all four corners of the compound, and a 'steel reinforced gate.' You told them the NSA had picked up the signal of Abu Nakba's own satellite phone in the compound."

Marcus, hitting the accelerator and zigzagging through traffic at upwards of seventy-five miles an hour, glanced over at Annie.

"How do you know all that?"

"I told you I read the transcript."

"Yeah, but you remember those specific pieces?"

"I reread it all this morning."

"Why?"

"I wanted to know if I would've drawn the same conclusion you did."

"And?"

"I think I would have."

They drove in silence for several minutes until Annie asked where they were going. Marcus said he was driving her home; then he'd go back to his place to pack; then he was heading straight to Reagan National to catch the next flight to Colorado.

"You can't, Marcus."

"Why not?"

"Because you've just been accused on national TV of being responsible for the deaths of all those women and children. By the time we get back to D.C., it won't just be CNN. There's going to be a dozen news crews in front of your apartment and probably mine. And your mom's house is going to be next."

Marcus knew she was right. But he had no plan B.

Annie did. "What you need to do is get as far from the Beltway as possible and stay off the grid until we can figure out a plan. I'm coming with you. And I have just the place."

"Where?"

"A beach house."

"No, Annie, if we do this, we need to *really* get lost for a few days. Where no one can find us. Not Stephens. Not McDermott. Not the press. Or your boss. And you just said yourself that if the media is staking out my place, they're going to stake out yours."

"You're thinking of my place in South Carolina, the one my parents left me. What I'm talking about is completely different."

"You have another place?"

"Yes."

"Where?"

"North Carolina—the Outer Banks."

"You have a beach house on the Outer Banks?" Marcus asked, incredulous.

"Corolla—actually, a little north of Corolla—but it's not exactly mine."

"Then whose?"

"My aunt and uncle's place. They usually rent it out for the summer."

"How far is it?"

"We can be there in five hours."

"Isn't someone renting it now?"

"The season doesn't open until Memorial Day. What do you say?"

Marcus needed to think about it, but he didn't have long. They were rapidly coming up on I-95 south. If they were going to the OBX, he had to decide fast.

"It doesn't seem a little weird to you that we're barely dating and now you want to shack up together?" he asked.

"Look, you'll have your bedroom, I'll have mine, and never the twain shall meet," she told him. "You got a problem with that, then book yourself a room at the Hilton. But you'd better pay cash or all your friends from Moscow to Pyongyang to Tehran and beyond are going to track down your credit card and pay you a visit."

"Fair enough, Miss Stewart." Marcus nodded, smiling—just a little—for the first time that day. "I'm in."

He asked Annie to dismantle their phones, taking out their SIM cards so no one could reach them or track them. If they were going off the grid, they had to do it right.

Minutes later, he exited on I-95, heading south.

42

THE PRESIDENTIAL PALACE, TEHRAN, IRAN

"Mr. President, General Entezam needs to speak with you immediately."

"Now?" Yadollah Afshar, president of the Islamic Republic, asked his chief of staff. "He's back from Bandar Abbas?"

"Yes, and what he has to say is urgent."

"Very well," Afshar said. "Send him in."

A moment later, the commander of the Iranian Revolutionary Guard Corps—wearing his olive-drab uniform—entered the palatial corner office. Seeing the sober expression on the man's face, President Afshar stood, fearing the worst.

"General Entezam, what is it?" Afshar said. "You look like you've seen a ghost."

"Something has happened in the United States."

"What?"

"CNN is reporting that the man responsible for advising President Clarke for the bombing in Libya is Marcus Ryker."

"Ryker?" Afshar asked. "The Secret Service agent?"

"Former, but yes."

"The one you believe foiled our purchase of warheads from Pyongyang."

"Exactly, and the one the Russians believe was complicit in the assassination of its leadership," Entezam explained. "CNN is saying that Ryker is an employee of the Central Intelligence Agency."

"As you have suspected all along."

"Yes."

"Is it confirmed?" the president asked. "As you know, I put little trust in the American media."

"It is, Your Excellency, and that's why I came to you immediately," the IRGC chief said. "I believe it is time to double the bounty on Ryker."

"Double?"

"Yes."

"$20 million?"

"Mr. President, you remember the Supreme Leader's last words to us, how he made us promise to build, buy, or steal a nuclear arsenal and to assassinate the American president and the criminal Zionist prime minister?" Entezam recalled.

"Of course."

"We gave him our word."

"And we will succeed."

"I believe we will," Entezam said. "But let us be candid. No one has set these missions back further in recent years than Agent Ryker. He must face justice for the crimes he has committed against us. But I maintain it is still too risky for us to do the deed ourselves. It would be better, especially now in our time of such transition and potential vulnerability, for others to do the job."

"And by this you mean Kairos."

"I do. Look, Mr. President, I have not told you everything I am planning with Abu Nakba's deputies because I want you to have plausible deniability when the firestorm comes. But it's not enough. We need Kairos to take out Ryker. And believe me, $20 million is a small price."

"Very well, General Entezam," Afshar said. "You have your twenty million. Make it count."

RICHMOND, VIRGINIA

Nearly two hours later, Marcus and Annie stopped at a fast-food drive-through.

After getting their meals, Marcus drove into Richmond and stopped in front of the bus terminal. "Wait here," he said, then dashed inside before Annie could reply.

Exiting through the back of the terminal, he crossed the street and entered a UPS Store, where there were several rows of metal lockers. Accessing one he'd rented several years earlier, and for which he made regular cash payments, he pulled out a dark-green duffel bag and left the store. He ducked around the corner before opening it and finding everything still in place—a Glock 9mm automatic pistol with plenty of ammunition, fake IDs, passports, credit cards, and several stacks of currency in U.S. and foreign denominations. What's more, there were several changes of clothes and shoes, a cheap burner phone, a top-of-the-line satellite phone, and a set of car keys. Zipping up the duffel, Marcus quickly returned to the car, popped the trunk, and stashed the bag.

"What's that?" Annie asked when he got back in the driver's seat.

"Insurance."

Peeling away from the bus terminal, he drove to a junkyard on the edge of town.

"What are we doing?" Annie asked as Marcus punched a code into a keypad and an electronic gate opened.

"Switching cars," he said.

"Why?"

"Going dark isn't enough. Anyone who really wants to find us will soon discover my car is parked near the White House. Then they're going to look for your car at the Hart building and at your town house and see it's missing. They'll run your license plate and cross-check it through every traffic camera in a hundred-mile radius of D.C. Believe me, it wouldn't take long to find us. And we've still got three hours to go."

Locating his pale-blue 1996 Chevy Impala, he pulled Annie's forest-green Fiat alongside it. They transferred everything they had into the Impala.

"Are you going to wipe down my Fiat inside and out, like in *The Bourne Identity*?" she asked, smiling.

"You think this is a joke?" he asked.

"No, but come on—you've got to admit this is kind of cool, if a little weird, right? I mean, shouldn't we, I don't know, remove my license plates?"

"We don't have the tools. Anyway, your Senate parking permits are seared onto your windshield, and we don't have the tools to scrape those off either," he told her. "Besides, there aren't any CCTV cameras on the premises. That's why I chose this spot several years ago. And even on the remote chance that someone hunting us finds your car, the chance of them figuring out what kind of vehicle we've transferred to or where we've gone is remote at best."

"All right, you're the spy," she teased. "I'll take your word for it."

They got back on the road and continued driving south. But there was another matter on Marcus's mind. "Look, Annie, there's something you need to know."

"Okay, shoot."

"I should have mentioned this earlier, but I was told not to."

"Whoa, that sounds a bit ominous. What is it?"

"The president might be in a coma."

Annie was floored.

"I don't know if it was a heart attack or a stroke or what, but apparently he collapsed in the Oval Office," Marcus told her.

"When?"

"Just before I met with McDermott."

"Why haven't I heard anything about it?"

"They want to keep it secret."

"Who?"

"I don't know. The top brass at the White House."

"Are they idiots?" she asked. "The country needs to know."

Annie flipped on the radio and found a news/talk station. The CNN exclusive on Marcus was the only thing being discussed. More audio clips from the NSC meeting had been released by the network and were being picked up by every other news outlet.

Within minutes, though, the news anchor reported that three ambulances had just arrived at the White House.

Fifteen minutes after that, she reported that the president was being rushed to Walter Reed medical center.

At 7:43 p.m., the White House press secretary refused to discuss the president's condition but announced that the VP was en route to the White House and would be holding a press conference at nine o'clock Eastern time.

Annie turned off the radio. The sun was going down. The two took some time to pray for the president, the VP, and the girls in Yemen. Then Annie started scanning the dial again for more details. Every news station was covering the story of the president's collapse. Even most music stations had broken away from their regular formats and were broadcasting live feeds from C-SPAN and other networks.

So far, there weren't many new facts. For the next thirty minutes they mostly heard rumors and speculation and spin. Annie was tempted to call Senator Dayton to learn more, but Marcus advised against it. There was nothing they could do to help, and more information wouldn't benefit them. They just needed to stay dark and lie low.

Reluctantly Annie agreed. She turned off the radio, and they talked instead about the women who'd been kidnapped in Yemen. They talked about McDermott's betrayal and Dayton's.

Soon they were driving through Norfolk, the stars visible in the dark sky.

Just before the top of the hour, Annie turned the radio back on and settled on a Fox News affiliate.

At precisely 9 p.m., she turned up the volume.

"This is a Fox News alert. Good evening from Washington, this is Stephanie Baker for Fox News Radio. We are standing by for a White House press conference, which we will carry live. In case you're just tuning in, President Andrew Clarke was rushed to Walter Reed National Military Medical Center in Bethesda, Maryland, earlier this evening, having suffered what aides are privately calling a mild stroke.

"Unconfirmed reports by anonymous sources are telling Fox News that they believe President Clarke has experienced what's known as a transient ischemic attack, or TIA. If that in fact proves to be the case, medical experts say the president could very well be showing strong signs of improvement in the next twenty-four to forty-eight hours. But at this hour, there is great concern and much uncertainty. Asian markets are already reflecting this. The Nikkei is down 9 percent within an hour of opening. The Hang Seng and the Shanghai Composite are projecting down 6 percent and 4 percent, respectively, ahead of opening. Meanwhile, the *Wall Street Journal* is reporting that the opening of the New York Stock Exchange and NASDAQ could be delayed tomorrow morning to give investors more time to process developments and to keep the U.S. markets from tanking.

"Extended members of the First Family have been seen arriving at Walter Reed hospital in the past two hours. At the same time, Fox News can report that all members of the cabinet are currently holding a videoconference, which began about an hour ago. And the Speaker of the House and Senate majority leader have called on the nation to pray for the president and have asked members of Congress not to return home to their districts for the weekend until more is known regarding the president's condition.

"As we wait for the press conference to commence, let's now bring in White House chief correspondent Amy Rutledge and Fox News Sunday anchor Jack Murphy. Jack, let's start with you."

"Thanks, Stephanie," Murphy began. "Well, Clarke is an unconventional president. And this has certainly been an unconventional presidency from day one. Always twists and turns. Never a dull moment. And this is a serious development, but let's remember, it's not the worst health challenge this president has faced. He's battled prostate cancer and come through it with flying colors.

"Stephanie, let's underscore the point you made earlier. This is likely what's known as a TIA—a mild stroke, not catastrophic—and will probably not have any lasting health repercussions for Clarke. Politically, however, this could not come at a worse moment. The Libyan bombing and kidnappings in Yemen are proving to be disasters for this administration. And now we have the leak of classified audio recordings of the president and the National Security Council being briefed by a CIA officer named Marcus Ryker."

Annie squeezed Marcus's hand as they approached the North Carolina state line and continued south.

"Devasting stuff," the news anchor said. "What's the reaction been on Capitol Hill?

"Shock. Anger. Mounting calls for an investigation. Calls for the appointment of an independent counsel. I'm even hearing talk of impeachment."

"Even though this CIA officer, Marcus Ryker, appears to be the one at fault, having misled the president?"

"I've spoken to at least a dozen Senate Democrats who say it doesn't matter. They say it was the president who ordered the bombing. It was the president who disregarded the warnings of his own CIA director. And the result, as we've all seen, was a school full of dead teachers and children. So while Ryker will certainly be subpoenaed and called to testify, these Senate Democrats are aiming higher. As one told me, 'A fish rots from the head.'"

"But, Jack, won't the president's stroke, or TIA or whatever, create some much-needed sympathy for him?" the anchor asked.

"For a while, sure," Murphy replied. "But as the president recovers, the push to drive him out of office will intensify, especially as we move closer to the midterms."

"Thanks, Jack. Now, as we continue waiting for the cabinet meeting to finish and the press conference to begin, let's turn to Amy Rutledge at the White House. Amy, talk to us about Carlos Hernandez as he steps into the spotlight this evening."

"Absolutely. Hernandez is the first Latino in history to serve as vice president of the United States. What's interesting is that Clarke kept him on the ticket when they ran for reelection despite a series of heart attacks that Hernandez has suffered since taking office. He even underwent triple bypass surgery. And the irony is not being lost on anyone here at the White House that it's the health of Clarke, not Hernandez, that the nation and world are now focused upon."

"Ironic indeed, Amy," Baker said. "Thanks so much. And thank you, Jack. I want you both to stay where you are. I'll be coming to both of you immediately following the VP's remarks. But now Vice President Carlos Hernandez is entering the East Room of the White House, sporting a dark-gray suit, white shirt, and red tie. The fifty-seven-year-old Cuban American—born and raised in Miami—suddenly finds himself in a position he could never have anticipated, holding his first prime-time press conference as he stands in for an ailing chief executive. It's worth noting that it's the seal of the VP—not the president—affixed to the podium tonight. And Hernandez is not alone. He is flanked by Dr. Jerome Lenkowski, the chief physician at Walter Reed, the rest of the president's medical team, and—for reasons I assume will become clear in a moment—he is joined by Attorney General Catherine Blackburn.

"And now, ladies and gentlemen, the vice president of the United States."

THE WHITE HOUSE, WASHINGTON, D.C.

"My fellow Americans, thank you for giving me your time tonight," Hernandez began.

"Thanks, as well, to every member of the White House press corps who has assembled on such short notice. I wish I had good news to report tonight, but I must be honest with you. President Clarke has not experienced a minor TIA as previously suspected. Rather, he has suffered a massive stroke. Within the last ninety minutes, he has also suffered a very serious heart attack. He is alive, but I'm afraid he is in a coma and on life support at this hour.

"I ask all Americans wherever you are to pray for a miracle. I am declaring tomorrow a National Day of Prayer. And I will begin the day by attending a bipartisan prayer service at the National Cathedral with congressional leadership. For now, let me be clear: the president needs a miracle. Less than an hour ago, the president's medical team—the best physicians in the world—informed the First Lady, the rest of the Clarke family, the full cabinet, and me that they do not believe the president will ever come out of this coma. Nor do they expect him to survive for more than a week, despite the fact that he is receiving the best medical care possible."

Hernandez paused a moment to let the information sink in.

"Now, I realize this comes as a shock to all of you," he continued. "It certainly does to me. Over the past several years, Andy Clarke has become one of my dearest friends and closest political allies. And it is inconceivable to me to think that our captain may not be able to continue steering the ship in the right direction for the remainder of our term.

"That said, we must deal with the world as it is, not as we wish it to be. For that reason, I have been advised by the attorney general that we must activate the Twenty-Fifth Amendment to the U.S. Constitution. There has not been a single time in our nation's history—not once since this amendment was ratified by the states on February 10, 1967—that the Twenty-Fifth Amendment has been activated under circumstances such as these. Faced with no alternative, however, we have decided to act.

"Just moments ago, and after lengthy deliberations, the full cabinet signed a letter that is being delivered to the congressional leadership as I speak. They have declared President Clarke temporarily incapacitated and have appointed me to serve as acting president. Again, I am praying for a miracle, and I ask you to pray as well. I have no intention of staying in this role for a minute longer than necessary. The instant our beloved leader Andrew Clarke comes out of this coma and feels ready to resume his duties, I will immediately relinquish my temporary authority. For now, I want to assure you that our nation is strong, our government is unified, and our determination to keep the peace is unwavering. To our friends around the world, I ask that you stand with us during this challenging season. To our enemies, I want to make this crystal clear: Do not test us. As the commander in chief of the world's only superpower, a man who spent more than thirty years wearing the uniform of this great country, I will not hesitate to use all the might at my disposal to protect the American people and our allies from all enemies, foreign and domestic, so help me God.

"And now I'll take your questions."

EN ROUTE TO COROLLA, NORTH CAROLINA

Marcus and Annie kept driving.

But they were riveted by the discussion.

The first five questions were about Clarke's condition. For these, Hernandez deferred to Dr. Lenkowski and his team.

The sixth question was about the timeline of events and why the White House had taken so long to send Clarke to Walter Reed and not informed the public earlier. Hernandez took full responsibility for not being more forthcoming and said it had been necessary to keep the situation quiet until they had more answers.

The seventh question was aimed at the wisdom of invoking the Twenty-Fifth Amendment when it had never been invoked in this way before. For this, Hernandez turned to the attorney general.

"Congress took up this whole question of the temporary relinquishment of power by the chief executive after the assassination of President Kennedy," Catherine Blackburn began. "They asked, 'What if JFK had not died immediately from his wounds but had lingered on indefinitely? Would LBJ have legally been the president of the United States, with all the necessary powers to lead and protect the country?' At the time, there was no clear-cut constitutional answer. Death provided clarity. But incapacity—temporary or permanent—created a legal gray area. Yet in the coldest years of the Cold War, not long after the Cuban Missile Crisis and during the escalations in the Vietnam War, Congress decided that such legal ambiguity was dangerous. So the people's representatives moved to clarify the situation."

Blackburn noted that the question was not theoretical. Earlier in the century an assassin's bullet had severely wounded President James Garfield but had not immediately killed him. Unlike Kennedy, Garfield had lingered for eighty days, enduring unsanitary—and painful—attempts to surgically remove the bullet.

She also recounted the case of President Woodrow Wilson. After a nationwide speaking tour by train, Wilson developed a high fever and severe headaches. Yet he had refused to stop working or even slow down. Wilson's wife, Edith, found him collapsed on the floor after an address in Colorado, his face twitching uncontrollably. White House aides kept the president's condition private and got him back to Washington. But in the wee hours of October 2, 1919, Wilson suffered a massive stroke that left him partially paralyzed and barely able to function.

"Incredibly, the White House hid these facts from the press for the next several months," Blackburn said. "The story did not emerge in the papers until the following February. During that time, the president's health continued to deteriorate, yet Wilson refused to resign, and his VP—Thomas Marshall—refused to assume his powers. Thus, the nation was in limbo for more than a year until Wilson completed his term and left office in March of 1921, and neither the vice president nor Congress nor the American people had any recourse."

Annie had heard enough and was about to turn the radio off, but before she could, Carolyn Tam of CNN asked Hernandez for his reaction to her report and the NSC audio recordings of the presentation made by CIA agent Marcus Ryker.

"Carolyn, as you can imagine, I've had my hands full with far more pressing matters, so I'm afraid I haven't seen your report."

"But you were at the NSC meeting," she countered.

"I was."

"So you heard Agent Ryker tell the president that Abu Nakba was in that compound, correct?"

"First of all, this was an unconscionable breach of U.S. national security," Hernandez said. "I believe in the freedom of the press, so I don't blame you and your colleagues for reporting it. But whoever gave you such classified material is guilty of very serious crimes, and I guarantee you this will not go unnoticed or unpunished."

"But about Agent Ryker specifically, sir . . . ?" Tam insisted.

"Carolyn, I'm not going to comment on the specifics," he replied. "All I can tell you at this point is that President Clarke's last action before he collapsed was to suspend Mr. Ryker from government service, without pay, pending a full investigation."

Marcus's grip on the wheel tightened. He'd just been thrown to the wolves by the acting president of the United States, with all of his many enemies watching in delight.

EISENHOWER EXECUTIVE OFFICE BUILDING, WASHINGTON, D.C.—15 MAY

Marcus had given them their marching orders.

Which was why Pete and the team were in the office so early. None of them had been home to shower or even change clothes. What little sleep they'd gotten was from catnaps on the floor. But they weren't working literally around the clock simply because their friend had asked them to. The lives of three Americans hung in the balance, and they were determined to find them and bring them home as quickly as possible.

Hour after hour, through pot after pot of coffee, they combed through mountains of NSA intercepts, DIA files, CIA and State Department cables, and classified data from foreign intelligence services all over the world. They made phone calls, followed up leads, and fished for any scrap of information that could prove useful. They had no illusions this was going to be easy. They were searching for the proverbial needle in the haystack and doing so while battling growing anger at Stephens and Hernandez and McDermott and Dayton and everyone who had hung Marcus out to dry. Worst of all, they were having no success.

Pete made his rounds through the office, checking on everyone, asking for updates, and trying to cheer them up. "Come on, guys, this is why we make the big bucks," he told them.

Pouring himself another mug of Jenny's wretched sludge—how she could be so proficient with a Russian sniper rifle and still unable to make a pot of coffee was beyond him—Pete went back to his office, the one that twenty-four hours earlier had been Marcus's. He sat down, rubbed his eyes, and tried to steel himself to plow through the latest stack of Kairos files from Langley that Noah had dumped on his desk.

At precisely noon Eastern time, however, a news bulletin on MSNBC caught his attention. Scrambling to find the remote buried beneath all the paper on his desk, Pete turned up the volume on that particular monitor and shouted for the others to come in immediately.

"This is an NBC News Special Report—and now from NBC News headquarters in New York, here's Jim Zweigle."

"Good afternoon—an extraordinary development out of the Middle East this hour as NBC News has just received a video from the Kairos organization, claiming responsibility for the kidnapping of three American aid workers in Yemen," Zweigle began. "But what makes the video particularly important is who makes the announcement. Let's run the video, and then we'll have full coverage and analysis from our team of NBC correspondents and intelligence analysts in Washington, London, and Jerusalem."

The footage that now aired was raw and unedited.

But the face in the center of the picture was unmistakable.

Abu Nakba, the octogenarian terror master, was sitting on the floor, cross-legged, in what appeared to be the prayer hall of a mosque. As in all the other photos and video footage Pete had seen of the world's number one most wanted man, the jihadist wore a white tunic, covered by a classic brown Libyan robe, and sandals on his brown and bony feet. His long, flowing hair was almost silver, as was his beard.

"In the name of Allah, the All-Merciful, the All-Compassionate," the old man began in classical Arabic as someone working for NBC provided simultaneous translation. "Praise be to the Lord of All Worlds, and peace be upon our Prophet, and upon the Promised One—Imam al-Mahdi—the Long-Awaited One, and peace be upon his infallible household, and upon his chosen companions, and upon all the prophets and messengers and martyrs who work tirelessly for the sake of building the glorious final Caliphate."

The camera slowly zoomed in on Abu Nakba's weathered face and tired pale-brown eyes covered by the smudged gold spectacles he wore as he read from several typewritten pages of a prepared text.

"I hold in my possession three American virgins," he said, suddenly shifting into British-accented English and setting aside the pages and looking directly into the camera. "Tanya Brighton is twenty-seven and a native of Biloxi, Mississippi. Hannah Weiss is twenty-two and a native of Tyler, Texas. The youngest, Mia Minetti of Montgomery, Alabama, is only nineteen years old. I can tell you that for the moment all three are alive—but what happens next is up to the American government."

The video image now switched to the three women—two brunettes and one blonde—bound and gagged. Their faces were swollen and severely bruised. Their clothing was covered with blood, presumably their own. They were chained to what looked like a flagpole in the center of a courtyard of some kind.

Then the video cut back to the Kairos founder and spiritual guide.

"This is what they look like after only a few hours in my custody," he declared. "If their parents, families, and friends ever want to see these girls alive—indeed, if the infidel government of the Great Satan ever want to see their citizens alive—then they will pay us $50 million for each of their virgins in the next forty-eight hours. One hundred fifty million total. Payment instructions are being transmitted to the State Department at this very moment. And the countdown starts now. Pay what I ask, and you can have these women returned to you alive. Fail to pay, and I will add three American heads to the collection on a shelf in my office."

The final image of the video cut to a shelf of bloody heads. One Korean. Two Filipinos. Two Ethiopians. And four Spaniards.

COROLLA, NORTH CAROLINA

"It was Stephens, wasn't it?" Annie suddenly asked. "He leaked it, right?"

Marcus was doing laps in the small pool behind the house. The noonday sun was bright and warm. The sky was an azure blue. White puffy clouds could be seen out over the Atlantic. But thunderheads were rolling in from the north.

"Or am I missing something?" she asked as he swam over to her.

"No, that's where I come out too," Marcus replied. "But for the first time in my life, I don't know what to do. I know you want me to retire and move on with my life. And believe me, that sounds more and more attractive with every passing hour. But I don't believe in surrendering in the middle of a firefight. That's not in my DNA. Yet I can't see a way to fight back without making the situation worse."

"You want to know what I think?" Annie asked, sitting down on the edge of the pool and dangling her feet in the water.

"You have a plan?"

"I do," she said. "You need to launch a surgical counterstrike."

"Meaning?"

"You helped the Raven escape from Russia with a treasure trove of Kremlin secrets, right?"

"Right."

"But you also helped the Raven assassinate the Russian president and FSB chief."

Marcus stared at her. "What happened in Russia is classified beyond top secret, Annie. Those files aren't in any database you're authorized to access. So how do you know—or think you know—anything about it?"

"Have you forgotten that when all this was happening, Nick Vinetti asked Senator Dayton and me to take your mom and sisters out for dinner? He asked us to tell them some cockamamie story about how you'd flown back to D.C. with us from Moscow but came down with some mysterious disease and had to be hospitalized at Walter Reed. Any of that ring a bell?"

"You didn't buy Vinetti's story."

"Of course not. You left with us out of Moscow. But you got off the senator's plane in Berlin. You didn't say why, but later I could only assume you snuck back into Russia somehow to link up with the Raven and make sure all of his secrets came out with him."

Marcus didn't confirm the story, but he didn't deny it either.

"I don't know exactly what happened between you and the Raven," Annie continued. "And honestly, I don't want to know. Not because I blame you or think you were wrong. To the contrary. Whatever you did or didn't do, somehow you and the Raven—whoever he or she is—stopped a Russian invasion of NATO that could have really gotten out of control. You deserve a medal, not this high-tech lynching."

"I'm afraid I don't follow where you're going with all this," Marcus said.

"Of course you do," she said. "You're just too much of a gentleman to pull the trigger."

"Meaning what?"

"Didn't Stephens blame you for those assassinations in Moscow?"

"For the sake of argument, hypothetically, let's say yes."

"Didn't he want to silence you?"

"Let's say he did."

"He certainly didn't want the president to pardon you, right?"

Marcus didn't answer, astonished by how much Annie knew of a story almost nobody in the U.S. government, or any government, knew.

"At one point, you called into Langley from wherever you were on the Karelian Isthmus in the middle of that snowstorm and spoke to Stephens, right?"

Marcus said nothing.

"That gave Stephens your precise location at that moment. And you obviously suspected Stephens might give that information to the Russians so they could take you and the Raven out with a couple of drones."

"Seriously, where did you get all this?" Marcus asked, incredulous.

"Just answer the question. Did you suspect that Stephens might sell you out to the Russians?"

"More than suspect," Marcus finally confided. "I was certain."

"And you were right," Annie said. "The director of the Central Intelligence Agency picked up a phone and spoke to the head of the Russian FSB. He told him he had you on the line. He gave him your precise coordinates. And he told him to, quote, 'make the problem go away.' Am I wrong?"

Someone had to have told her this information. But who? Jenny Morris? She'd been sitting in the car next to Marcus when he made the call to Stephens. But why would she have told Annie? Pete Hwang didn't know any of this. Geoff Stone didn't. Nor did Donny Callaghan or Noah Daniels. His family certainly didn't know. McDermott knew, but again, why would he tell Annie?

"No, you're not wrong," Marcus said quietly.

"Yes, someone told me," Annie replied, reading the look in his eyes.

"Who?"

"I can't tell you that. But even if I could, it doesn't matter. What matters is that Stephens tried to have you killed, right?"

"Yes."

"He tried to have an American citizen murdered, on foreign soil, with the FSB's active assistance, without presidential authorization. Am I right?"

"I'm afraid you are."

"Then that's what we hang Stephens with."

"I'd love nothing more, Annie, but we'd need more proof than your say-so and mine."

"And I have it," Annie said.

Marcus followed Annie back inside the beach house.

She suggested they change and meet on the main level in five minutes. Marcus wasn't sure he could wait until then. Still, he took a quick, hot shower, changed into Bermuda shorts and a fresh T-shirt, and headed upstairs.

Annie was already waiting for him. She had put on a sundress and pulled her wet hair into a ponytail and was sitting at the dining room table, her reading glasses on, booting up her laptop.

When he sat down beside her, Annie held up a thumb drive.

"What's that?" he asked.

Annie inserted the drive into her laptop. "There are six different audio recordings on here," she explained. "One is a call of Stephens talking to you in Russia. Three are calls of Stephens strategizing with McDermott. Then there are two separate calls between Stephens and Nikolay Kropatkin, head of the FSB. In addition, there are several emails between Stephens and McDermott, then with the NMCC at the Pentagon, and finally with Kropatkin, both before and after the drone strikes. Each is more damning than the last. Believe me, it would hold up in any criminal or civil court. And make no mistake, if the Democrats on the Hill ever got ahold of this stuff . . ."

She didn't finish her sentence. She didn't have to.

"Annie, I'm blown away."

"Don't be. I didn't do a thing to get it. Didn't know it existed until it was literally dropped in my lap. All I was asked to do was hold on to it for safekeeping and hope it would never need to see the light of day."

"Someone was taking a terrible risk giving it to you."

"Maybe they calculated there was a greater risk in keeping it to themselves."

"When did you get it?" he asked.

But Annie didn't want to go there. "That's not important. The point is I know the source. They're unimpeachable—and I'm using that word advisedly. The material is authentic. It's unedited. And it's devastating. I never imagined having to use it. But it's time."

"We can't."

"We have to. Look, you're never going back into government service. That much is clear. But Stephens cannot be allowed to break the law. If you don't stop him, who else will wind up in his crosshairs?"

"This is highly classified material. Releasing it to the media would be a felony. We'd be guilty of the same tactics Stephens is employing."

"That's why we're not going to release this to the media," she replied.

"The Hill?"

"No. I wouldn't trust anyone in Congress with it either. Not right now. Things are too hot up there."

"Then I don't understand," Marcus said. "If we don't leak it to the media or give it to the Senate Intelligence Committee, how do you propose we use it?"

"We give it to the president," she said. "Well, the acting president."

"Hernandez."

"Exactly."

"But it'll be intercepted," Marcus protested. "There are too many gatekeepers. He'll never see it."

"No," Annie said. "Hernandez has a private email account. A back channel. Only a handful of people know about it. Senator Dayton has occasionally had me send things to him this way. When we were in Moscow, for example. And later in Riyadh. It's secure, and it's private. Only he ever checks the account."

"So you're saying we send the files to him as a couple of whistleblowers?"

Annie shook her head. "Not we. I."

"No, Annie, this is my problem. Not yours."

"It can't come from you. It has to come from a third party. And a staffer for a Democratic senator is ideal."

"It's too risky."

"Why? I've already resigned. What's the worst that can happen?"

"Seriously?" Marcus asked. "You're really asking me what could go wrong if you go nuclear on the director of the CIA?"

"Giving this to the media is going nuclear," she told him, shaking her head again. "Giving this to the acting president of the United States so he can make his own determination of how, if at all, he wants to act on this information and whether he wants to take the risk of it being leaked—that, my friend, is a surgical strike."

Marcus chewed on that for a moment, then made a counterproposal. "How about this?" he said. "We set up a fake email account and send it to Hernandez anonymously. I don't want you to get hurt."

"I won't get hurt," she told him, "but even if I do, it's worth the risk."

"We don't really know Hernandez's character," Marcus insisted. "We don't know how he'll react to any of this. I want to believe the best about him. But it might not be the right moment to stick your neck out of the foxhole. Let's send it anonymously and see what happens."

"Fair enough," she said.

Three minutes later the file was sent.

THE NAVAL OBSERVATORY

Thus far, Hernandez had refused to work out of the Oval Office.

Secretary of State Meg Whitney could understand why. The country was still reeling from the news of Clarke's stroke and a vice president they barely knew suddenly in charge. The optics were all wrong. Until further notice, he would work out of the VP's residence, his ceremonial office in the EEOB, and his Senate office. Except for press conferences and cabinet meetings, he would minimize the time he spent in the West Wing.

On this warm, mid-May Friday, Hernandez had commenced a working lunch on the back porch of the residence. Joining him were Defense Secretary Foster, National Security Advisor McDermott, and Whitney. CIA director Stephens was running late. No sooner had they started on their salads than the news broke that the Kairos leader was alive and well and running the show.

The group watched Abu Nakba's video in horror.

They were already on the defensive. A snap poll published that morning on the front page of the *Washington Post* found that only 26 percent of the country trusted Hernandez to lead the country effectively, and nearly seven in ten—68 percent—said the vice president was "morally and legally complicit" with Clarke in the bombing of the Libyan school. Nearly the same number supported the immediate appointment of an independent counsel to get to the bottom of the rocket strike and to ensure "the White House does not engage in a cover-up."

The news of Abu Nakba's veritable resurrection—combined with his ransom demand for $150 million—threatened to sink the administration before it even got started.

There was no question the video was authentic, McDermott pointed out. It had not been filmed before the raid near Ghat. It couldn't have been. Yet there were no clues where the girls were being held, much less whether Abu Nakba was with them or at some other location. They all agreed Hernandez had to make a statement and do it quickly. But what should he say?

"I know you're not going like this, sir, but I think we have to seriously consider paying the ransom," McDermott said.

"Bill, are you crazy—*$150 million*?" Foster shot back. "That's opening the floodgates to Americans being taken hostage all over the world. Where will it end?"

"Cal is right," Whitney added. "But paying off terrorists isn't just bad policy; it's terrible politics. It's political suicide."

McDermott pushed back. "How do you think it's going to play politically if Abu Nakba decides to execute these women on live television and we weren't willing to lift a finger to set them free?"

Hernandez asked Foster if a military rescue might be possible if they could buy some time and identify where the women were being held. When McDermott said that was ridiculous in light of their track record thus far on intelligence and special operations, the discussion became heated.

Then an aide slipped Foster a note.

"The sandstorm has finally lifted, Mr. Vice Presi—er, well, Mr. Acting President," Foster began, not accustomed to using the clunky new constitutional formulation of Hernandez's title. "With your permission, sir, I'd like to send a SEAL team into Libya immediately to scour that site and do an after-action report."

"Can you do it discreetly, without any press knowing about it?"

"If we move fast, then I believe we can, sir."

"Then do it," Hernandez ordered. "And while you're at it, pre-position Delta and SEAL teams throughout the Middle East and North Africa. The second we get a lead on where these girls are, I want rescue options ready to go on a moment's notice."

"Yes, sir," Foster said, already speed-dialing the Pentagon.

Hernandez now turned to his secretary of state. "Meg, get on the phone to the parents of those three girls. Tell them what's happening. Then get them all on planes to Washington immediately. I want them in the Oval Office by dinnertime—all of them. You and I are going to hold their hands and let them know precisely what we're doing to bring their daughters home alive."

"Absolutely, sir," Whitney replied. "And what is that, exactly?"

But Hernandez didn't hear her. Whitney could see the rage building up in the acting president. Knowing his history of heart problems, she wondered whether anyone was thinking about the continuity of government. The country had no vice president, and the Speaker of the House was a radical leftist who would be a disaster in the Oval Office.

Whitney was about to ask Hernandez what more she could do to help him when he turned sharply to a Secret Service agent and shouted, *"Where is Stephens?"*

SOMEWHERE IN YEMEN

The radio call came from the sniper on the roof.

"Are we expecting company?"

The kid in charge of communications on the top floor of the main house relayed the question to Badr Hassan al-Ruzami, Kairos's chief of operations.

Ruzami looked up from the maps spread out before him. "Is it a Range Rover?"

A moment later, comms nodded.

"Forest green?" Ruzami asked.

"No, sir," comms said. "It's gray."

"Then yes," Ruzami said. "Let them through."

Ruzami jumped up, strapped on his holster and sidearm, dusted off his uniform, and headed downstairs to meet his guests. His bodyguards went with him, but with several teams deploying to Mexico and Canada, the house was a little quieter now.

The dust-drenched Range Rover pulled to a stop. Ruzami could tell there were three men inside, though with the windows so filthy and smudged, he could not see their faces. The driver remained where he was. The man in the front passenger seat got out, an AK-47 thrown over his shoulder, and opened the back door. Out stepped an old man with a cane, and Ruzami smiled broadly. "Father, how good to see you," he exclaimed, bowing slightly.

Abu Nakba spread out his arms. The two men embraced and kissed each other on both cheeks and then headed to the front door.

"Come in, out of the heat and the flies," Ruzami said. "Would you care for some tea?"

"I would," the old man said.

Soon the two men were alone on the top floor. The communications operator was gone. So were the bodyguards, now standing post at the bottom of the stairs. The teakettle whistled. Ruzami turned off the stove and prepared the Kairos leader a cup of mint tea, adding a spoonful of honey, just the way the old man liked it. Setting it before him, Ruzami retreated to the other end of the large wooden table, took his seat, and watched his leader close his weary eyes and take his first sip.

Ruzami had only known Abu Nakba for a few years. But the stories of his cunning and cruelty were legendary. The time he'd cut the tongue out of the mouth of an Egyptian businessman who had double-crossed him. The night he had cut off the arm of a woman who dared serve him tea with her left hand. The Israeli tank commander he had gutted in Gaza in front of his fellow tankers. To say nothing of the jihadists he had persuaded with the sheer force of his personality to become suicide bombers, including those who had agreed to have the bomb surgically implanted inside their own bodies to avoid detection.

In his mideighties now, the man had certainly lost some of the vim and vigor he'd possessed in his younger days. Yet mentally he remained as sharp as ever, and Ruzami had no doubt this latest series of operations would go down as his greatest.

"You were right, Father," Ruzami said, turning to business.

"About what?" the old man asked, his eyes still closed.

"About everything. I know you've been on the move. But have you seen any news?"

"Very little, my son."

"Then you should know—the Americans are rattled. First, they were crowing that they'd killed you, taken you out in a huge air strike. Then you completely turned the tables on them. No one's talking about the peace deal anymore. All of Washington is talking about scandal. The word *impeachment* is in the air—if Clarke even recovers from his stroke. And now the kidnapping. And the video. Hernandez must think you rose from the dead. It's been something to behold."

The old man shook his head. "Parlor tricks, Badr. Enough to buy us much-needed time but little more. The hard work remains ahead. What news from Mexico? Have your men arrived yet?"

"Most of them, yes," Ruzami said. "Farooq is expected to land later today still."

"And the weapons?"

"The purchase was completed. My men have taken possession of them. They will go into Texas when the first team leaves tomorrow."

"What about the team going in via Canada?"

"They are all entering the country separately—Ottawa, Montreal, Quebec, and Vancouver. They should converge in Winnipeg in forty-eight hours."

53

DEEP INSIDE LIBYA

Four Black Hawk helicopters flew low above the desert floor in the dead of night.

The pilots flew by instruments, without running lights. Only a sliver of moon could be seen in the clear, cloudless, starry skies.

They were not coming from the north. Not from the *Nimitz* or any of the U.S. aircraft carriers patrolling the Mediterranean. Nor were they coming from NATO bases in Italy or southern Europe. Instead, the choppers—and the SEAL commandos they were carrying—were coming in from the south, from a base in Niger, a country emerging as an increasingly important counterterrorism partner in sub-Saharan Africa. Most of the joint missions the U.S. ran from Niger were against Boko Haram and other radical Islamist terror groups operating in the region. None of the SEAL forces deployed there had ever before conducted missions in North Africa, but this had suddenly become the White House's highest priority.

As they approached the Libyan city of Ghat, two of the choppers broke formation, heading west and hugging the Algerian border. The other two remained on course and were soon circling the compound. Using thermal imaging, neither the pilots nor their gunners spotted any signs of life. So one by one the commandos began fast-roping down to the desert floor. Once the two lead choppers were emptied, they moved eastward toward the Algerian border and were replaced by the other two birds that soon reached the compound and deployed their troops.

The first group established a secure perimeter. The second group set up generators and flood lamps, then began videotaping the scene, sifting through the sand and rubble, gathering body parts, taking DNA samples, and searching for anything that could provide a clearer picture of what had happened there.

What they found left them all stunned.

MEXICO CITY

Zaid Farooq finally landed.

The plane's departure from Paris had been delayed an hour, and by the time the Boeing 777 had taxied and parked at the gate, it was nearly 6 p.m. in the Mexican capital.

Farooq and his fellow first-class passengers were the first people off the plane. As he had not checked any luggage, he texted his contact and headed straight for the curb. Soon he saw the blue Mercedes sedan approaching. The license plate matched the one he had been given, so when the car stopped, he leaned into the open window of the passenger door and spoke several lines in flawless Spanish. When the driver replied with the precise agreed-upon phrase, Farooq climbed in, and they were on their way.

The two men said nothing for about twenty minutes until they had cleared out of the capital and were speeding north along Highway 57D.

"How was your flight?" Tariq finally said in Arabic.

"I'm here, that's all I'll say, praise Allah."

"And you were so worried."

"And you fault me for this?" Farooq asked. "When was the last time you traveled on your real papers?"

Youssef chuckled. "I cannot even remember."

"So is everything in place?" Farooq asked.

"Nearly so. We have secured a large villa in the mountains, just north of the city. The men have all been arriving on schedule."

"And the weapons?"

"Arranged."

"For the price we asked?"

"Not quite, but close."

"Including the SA-7s?" Farooq asked, referring to the shoulder-mounted surface-to-air missiles that Abu Nakba had been so eager to acquire.

Youssef smiled. "Yes," he said. "Including the 7s."

THE WHITE HOUSE

It was just after nine o'clock on Friday evening when the parents arrived.

Each couple had been picked up at home by a team of FBI agents—the Brightons from Shreveport, Louisiana; the Minettis from Montgomery, Alabama; and the Weisses from Tyler, Texas—and flown across the country on government planes to Joint Base Andrews. There they had been met by more FBI agents and brought to the White House. It had not been possible to keep any of this from the press. After all, each family had become the focus of global attention. Their houses and entire neighborhoods had been veritable media camps, teeming with dozens of local, national, and international reporters—print, TV, radio, and digital alike—along with camera crews, producers, floodlights, and satellite trucks.

Meg Whitney met the couples in the Cabinet Room, where they had some light refreshments and spent some time making awkward small talk. The secretary of state had already spoken to each of the couples by phone several times throughout the day, even during the flights, doing her best to get to know them, to comfort them, and to explain why the acting president had asked them to come to Washington. She already knew their faces from the last nine hours of nonstop television coverage. Still, it was different to meet them in person and to see the grief and fear in their eyes.

At 9:23 p.m., a Secret Service agent signaled the secretary. She nodded, rose, and asked the group of six to follow her into the Oval Office.

The first person they met upon entering the hallowed chamber was Defense Secretary Foster. Next in line was General James Meyers, the chairman of the Joint Chiefs of Staff, wearing his Marine dress uniform. Then came National Security Advisor McDermott, CIA director Stephens, the White House chief of staff, and the press secretary. It was too many, really, Whitney thought. She had advocated for a much smaller group, but Hernandez wanted a show of force. He wanted these folks to know they were getting the full attention of the most senior members of the American government. Whitney wasn't sure that was the message being received.

They all shook hands and then Whitney asked the couples to sit on the couches in the center of the room, Larry and Laura Brighton along with Tom and Kathy Weiss on the far couch, Bob and Tracey Minetti on the nearer couch, together with Secretary Foster and Whitney herself. The others sat in antique wooden chairs set up beside the couches. After they had all been seated and served hot tea and coffee by a steward, they stood again when Hernandez entered from a side door. The acting president greeted each of the parents one by one and asked everyone to take a seat.

For the first time since assuming his new role, Whitney realized, Hernandez did not sit in the vice president's armchair, positioned to the right of the couches, in front of the fireplace, but in the president's chair next to that. He didn't seem comfortable, she noted to herself, but then none of them did. The tension in the room was palpable. No one wanted to be there. All of them feared this story did not have a happy ending.

Hernandez thanked them all for coming on such short notice. He apologized for assigning FBI agents to protect each of them, their homes, and their families. He understood the imposition the agents represented in their lives but said that under the circumstances—the hostage situation, ransom demand,

and now a full-blown media circus—he felt he owed that to them. The families expressed their gratitude and said they were not annoyed but hoped it would all be over soon.

"That's our hope as well," Hernandez said, nodding to the cabinet and staff members around the room. "I want you to know that we are doing everything we can both to locate your daughters and to get them back to you safely and quickly."

"And what is that exactly?" Larry Brighton asked, his voice thick with emotion.

Whitney noticed Laura Brighton move her hand to her husband's knee. It struck her not as an act of tenderness but a discreet signal that it might be best if he restrained himself and let the meeting play out. Larry stiffened at the gesture; restraint might not be his chosen course of action, Whitney thought.

"Mr. Brighton, I have directed all seventeen U.S. intelligence agencies to find your daughters and those who are holding them," Hernandez replied. "We are working with numerous foreign intelligence agencies as well, and I have ordered the Pentagon to deploy a dozen special forces units to the region, ready to respond the moment we determine where the girls are."

At this, Bob Minetti spoke up. "You're planning a rescue operation?"

"Absolutely," Hernandez responded.

"But there's only thirty-eight and a half hours before the deadline," Kathy Weiss said. "Is that enough time?"

"No, it's not," Larry Brighton said, leaning forward and moving his wife's hand off his knee. "And it's too dangerous. What about the ransom?"

"Exactly," Tom Weiss said. "The ransom is the only way to make sure my Hannah and the others come back safely."

"I hear you," Hernandez said. "I do. And I haven't ruled out paying the ransom. Believe me, we've been discussing it nonstop. But there are enormous risks in going down that route, as you can imagine. First, it could create an open season, making Americans all over the world vulnerable to other kidnappers who want to cash in."

"I don't care about that," Tracey Minetti said, her eyes filled with tears. "Our government has the money. These thugs have our daughters. And you're the only one who can make this deal. So make it, Mr. President, please. I don't know how I could survive losing a daughter. I don't know if any of us could."

"Which is why I am actively considering paying the ransom—we all are," Hernandez assured her, though Whitney knew that wasn't completely true. "But it's not just the risks to others. It's the risk to your girls."

"What do you mean?" Larry Brighton asked.

"Yeah, what's that supposed to mean?" Bob Minetti asked.

"Please understand—Abu Nakba is the most ruthless terrorist on the planet," Hernandez explained. "There is a real concern in this room, and among my other top advisors, that even if I pay the ransom, Abu Nakba won't honor the deal."

Tracey Minetti gasped, her hands shooting to her mouth.

Larry nearly came off the couch, his face beet red. "You think that bastard will kill my little girl even if you pay?"

Out of the corner of her eye, Whitney noticed two Secret Service agents move almost imperceptibly, one closer to Hernandez, the other closer to the Brightons.

"That's my fear, Larry," Hernandez conceded. "And that's why my people are tearing apart heaven and earth to find your girls in the next twenty-four hours and launch a lightning-fast raid employing the best and the brightest special operators this country has ever deployed."

MONTERREY, MEXICO—16 MAY

Zaid Farooq felt himself being shaken.

"Farooq, wake up—quickly."

He grunted something unintelligible, then glanced at his watch. "Leave me alone, Tariq. I still have an hour to sleep."

"Wake up. We're here."

Farooq was in a foul mood. And Tariq Youssef did not outrank him. They were both deputy commanders of Kairos. Still, Youssef was their chief of internal security. If he said it was important, it probably was.

Youssef got out of the car and began shouting, waking everyone in the villa. *"Come, everyone—come now—quickly."*

Farooq grabbed his backpack and headed past the kitchen, through the dining room, and into the living room, where Youssef had tuned the TV to the Al-Sawt satellite network out of Qatar. Soon everyone had gathered, staring at the large plasma screen in shock.

It was Father.

He was alive.

For nearly a half hour, the men sat mesmerized as the video of Abu Nakba was shown over and over again. They listened as various analysts in the Doha-based studios reveled in the Kairos leader's ability to continually defy the Americans' efforts to hunt him down and discussed whether the White House would give Kairos the $150 million the most wanted man in the world was demanding.

Abruptly Zaid Farooq shut off the television and stood before them. "The truth is, Father was never in danger," he explained. "Brother Tariq and I, and Brother Badr back in Yemen, have been working on this plan that we are about to unleash. We designed it to lull Washington into a false sense that they had decapitated our leadership. We wanted to see them boast to the world of their perceived success in taking out the head of Kairos and his inner circle, and boast they certainly did. Then we embarrassed the Americans and sowed the seeds of chaos and political civil war in their capital. Allah has granted us favor beyond what even I had imagined. I confess, I had many doubts. But the plan is working. And now the Americans are reeling, trying to decide whether to pay us $150 million—three times our entire budget of last year, I would note—or to take their chances that they will find those three American virgins in time. But believe me when I tell you that Father has many more tricks up his sleeve."

Farooq sat on a chair by the fireplace.

"Let me now apologize to you all for letting you think, even for a few days, that Father had been killed," he told the men. "I know that was unfair to you all. It was not Father's idea. It was mine. We needed absolute operational security. For the illusion to work as long as it did, we couldn't afford a single leak. Not that I don't trust you, but we're at war, men. We are engaged in a holy war against the vilest of enemies, and we cannot take chances. But now you know the truth. You know that we have much to rejoice in, even if we have much hard work ahead. Come, it is time to pray."

Sobered by the gravity of their mission, yet emboldened by their leader's cunning, the men laid out their mats and bowed toward Mecca.

Soon it was time to move.

Energized by their success thus far, Zaid Farooq crossed through the rental villa and headed out to the van. He climbed into the front passenger seat as Youssef slid behind the wheel. Glancing behind him, Farooq nodded to his five comrades sitting in the back with all their crates of weapons and ammunition and the missiles. He took a swig of black coffee from the mug waiting in the cup holder for him, then told Youssef he was ready.

The drive from the hills outside Monterrey to the border was about 220 kilometers and took two and a half hours. When they arrived at a sprawling cattle ranch not far from Hacienda San José de Miravalle, the sun was up, but the roads were still quiet. Several armed guards met them at the gate and radioed back to the office for clearance before letting them enter and directing them to a barn a kilometer up the road. There they were met by more heavily armed Mexicans who exchanged prearranged code words with Youssef and told him to park the van inside the barn.

Zaid Farooq was in no mood to chitchat. Nor were the men they had come to see. They exchanged no greetings. No names. No conversation of any kind. Instead, Youssef and Farooq presented the Mexicans with a steel box containing one million American dollars in unmarked twenty-dollar bills. The ringleader—a thirtysomething mafioso with slicked-back hair and wearing a thousand-dollar suit—checked the money while his men stood guard in the lingering stench of fresh manure, their fingers on the triggers of their American-made submachine guns.

Satisfied, the leader asked one question in English. "What's in the crates?" he inquired, pointing to the back of the open van.

"None of your business," Farooq replied in Spanish.

The man smiled for the first time, revealing three gold teeth. Then he erupted in laughter and slapped the Algerian on the back. "*Very good, compadre, very good!*" he bellowed, then checked his watch. "*Vámonos—ándale*—there is no time to spare."

He snapped his fingers, and one of his men rushed to his side. He whispered in the young man's ear, then motioned for several others to lift the steel box into the trunk of his Range Rover. A moment later, he and his men drove off. Farooq's men wasted no time unloading the crates. After they did, Tariq Youssef gave his fellow deputy commander a bear hug and a kiss on both cheeks.

"May Allah be with you, *habibi*," he said.

"And you, *habibi*," Farooq replied, flush with nervous energy and determined to get moving. "God willing, we shall welcome the rest of you soon."

With that, Youssef climbed into the van, backed it out of the barn, and headed back to the villa.

Farooq watched the trail of dust dissipate. Then he turned and motioned for his men to grab the crates and load them into the bed of a large cattle truck. When they were finished, they climbed in the truck and covered themselves with blankets and bales of hay. Farooq joined them, and soon their lone guide, a lanky young man who could not be older than his late teens, was driving them into Nuevo Laredo, the Mexican border town nestled along the Rio Grande River.

There were no cattle in the truck, but evidence of them was everywhere. The odor was overpowering, and several of the men vomited. The rising heat did not help matters. But when the truck finally came to a stop, the rear gate was opened, and Farooq and his men found themselves inside the loading dock of a slaughterhouse.

The driver motioned for the six Arabs to follow him into a massive walk-in refrigerator. They ducked between bloody sides of beef hanging from hooks to reach the back of the cooler and pushed away several large crates, revealing a hatch door. The boy unlocked the padlock with a key hanging around his neck, then opened the hatch and scurried down a long metal ladder. It took some time to lower the crates of weapons and missiles through the opening, but eventually they all made it into the dimly lit and brutally humid tunnel. The boy closed the hatch above him and silently motioned for them all to follow.

Farooq hunched down and began the journey, finding it surreal to think that after so many months of planning and preparations, he and his men and their precious cargo were finally on their way. If all went according to schedule, in a few hours—working their way through a tunnel not yet detected by the Americans, a tunnel that would take them underneath the Rio Grande—they would be in Laredo, Texas. They would, for the first time in any of their lives, finally be in the United States of America. The Great Satan. And closer than ever to delivering the lethal strike for which they had all been chosen.

58

THE OUTER BANKS

"Anything yet?" Marcus asked when Annie came out to the pool.

She shook her head. "Nothing."

Marcus had already run five miles. And lifted weights. And done more than forty laps. Anything to keep busy and burn off the adrenaline that kept pumping into his system. Yet none of it was working.

Swimming over to the ladder, he climbed out of the pool. Annie tossed him a fresh towel, and he simply threw it over his shoulder. It was hot and breezy, and he figured he would dry off quickly enough. "It's almost been twenty-four hours, and he hasn't even opened the email?" he asked.

"He's got an awful lot on his plate," Annie offered. "And who knows what else is breaking? We haven't been watching the news. We're not checking our phones. Maybe we should."

"It'd just depress us," Marcus said. "If he opens it, you'll know it. And if he responds, it will only be through that new email address."

"What do you want to do?" she asked.

"Open the aperture."

"Meaning what?"

"We need to send it others, to people more likely to open it, read it, listen to the audio clips, and talk to the president."

"That's risky."

"I'd say doing nothing is riskier."

"Maybe," Annie said. "Okay, then who?"

"The attorney general. Blackburn is a straight shooter, and she could actually prosecute Stephens."

"Can we trust her?"

"I don't know."

"Can you even contact her? Do you have a private email for her?"

"No, but I can get it."

"Okay, who else?"

"Foster—him I know and trust. Maybe we go to him first, before Blackburn. And yes, I've got a private email address for him."

"What about Whitney?"

"Maybe."

"You know her better than the AG, right?"

"True. I briefly served on her advance team."

"And saved her life in Jerusalem."

Marcus only shrugged.

"Okay, so Foster and Whitney," Annie said. "And maybe Blackburn."

"No, definitely Blackburn," Marcus said. "We don't have time to be selective."

"It's your call. Anyone else? McDermott?"

Marcus stopped pacing and turned back to Annie. "You have to be kidding. He hates me."

"He doesn't hate you, Marcus. He was doing his job."

"You're wrong. He's never trusted me. Not really. I don't know why. And regardless, he's too close to Stephens. He's on those recordings. Some of those emails are his."

"You don't think he really wanted the Russians to kill you."

"I don't know what to think. Reading and listening to those files yesterday brought back a lot of ugly memories. We don't have time to process them now, but we're sure not going to give McDermott a heads-up that he's implicated with Stephens in all this. And besides, he would know instantly it was from me."

"Fine, what about Jenny?" Annie asked.

Marcus thought about it for a moment, then decided against it. His gut told him no.

"One more," Annie said. "What about Dell? She's a pretty straight shooter, isn't she? I mean, you know her better than me, but—"

"No," Marcus said. "Way too close to Stephens."

"You're sure."

"Yeah."

"Then we have our list."

"We do," Marcus said. "Let's get it out there."

Five minutes later, all the emails were sent.

59

GREAT FALLS, VIRGINIA

Allison McDermott noticed two Chevy Suburbans pull up out front.

"Bill?" she called out.

Her husband didn't respond.

Walking quickly to his study, she found him asleep on the couch, classified papers strewn about him and Fox News playing on the TV. He had been at the White House and the Naval Observatory most of the night, then had to appear on the Saturday morning news shows to discuss the hostage crisis and the administration's response. He'd come home less than an hour ago to shower and change and told her he was heading straight back to the Situation Room.

Allison was surprised to see him asleep. The clock was running, and those girls' lives hung in the balance.

"Bill, hey, wake up, honey—are you expecting guests?"

McDermott suddenly sat up and rubbed his eyes. "No, why?"

"Because the doorbell is about to ring."

The doorbell rang.

McDermott gathered up his papers and put them in his briefcase. Then he slipped his shoes on and went to the door.

To his astonishment, Cal Foster and his security detail were standing on the front porch.

"Now what?" McDermott asked, his stomach tightening.

"Got a minute?"

"Of course, come in. You know Allie."

"Sure, hi, good to see you again, Mrs. McDermott," Foster replied, smiling but clearly pressed for time.

"And you, sir—welcome."

Foster asked if there was someplace where he and the national security advisor could speak in private.

"Let's go in my study," McDermott replied. "Honey, would you bring us something to drink?"

The two men settled in the study and closed the door as one bodyguard took up a position in the hallway and several others guarded the front, back, and side doors of the house.

"Tell me you found the girls," McDermott said.

"I wish, but no."

"Then what's going on, Cal? You've never dropped by my house, much less on a weekend."

"The SEAL team just landed at Andrews."

"From Libya."

"Right."

"Wow—that was fast."

"We've got a problem, Bill."

"Why? What?"

"No children. No teachers. No wheelchairs. No playground equipment."

"What are you talking about?"

"My guys found none of it—*nada*."

"I don't understand," McDermott said. "Someone scrubbed the site?"

"No. Nobody scrubbed the site. There was plenty of evidence there. The compound wasn't a school."

"Come again?"

"You heard me—it was never a school, Bill. We've been played."

"So what did the SEAL team find?"

"Dead terrorists. Weapons. Laptops. Satphones. The whole nine yards."

"You mean . . . ?"

Foster nodded. "Yeah. Ryker wasn't wrong."

McDermott sat back in his chair, trying to take that in.

"And SEAL is absolutely certain? There's no chance that—"

But Foster cut him off. "They brought back an hour's worth of video—I just watched it all. Plus hundreds of digital photos. Mangled, half-melted computers. Body parts from at least twenty different Kairos operatives. They brought everything they could load on the choppers. And they've all signed sworn affidavits—classified, of course—that the compound was, without question, a Kairos safe house. Whether it was the main HQ or not, that'll take time to figure out. We've got to get into those computers and crack those phones. Given the condition they're in, it's not going to be easy. But the site was most definitely not a school for special-needs children. And I swear to you, there's going to be hell to pay for those who said it was."

"Who else knows about this?"

"You and me. A few of my senior staff. And the maintenance crew and security team that operate Hangar Nine at Andrews."

"That's where everything is now?" McDermott asked.

"Yeah."

"Does Stephens know?"

"Are you kidding?"

"He's going to hear about it soon enough."

"Not from me," the SecDef insisted.

"None of your guys will leak this to the press?" McDermott asked.

"Not on your life."

"Why didn't you just call me?"

"I didn't want to take the risk that the NSA might intercept the call. This changes everything, and we need to manage it and release it in our way and on our terms."

"We need to take this straight to the president and let him make the call," McDermott said.

Just then there was a knock. The door opened and Allison brought in a tray of drinks along with some snacks.

"I'm so sorry, honey. We've got to go."

60

THE NAVAL OBSERVATORY

Twenty minutes later, they were sitting in the acting president's dining room.

Foster recounted for Hernandez what he had just told McDermott. Then he set up his laptop on the dining room table, played about fifteen minutes of video, and showed some digital photographs the SEAL team had taken.

"So the video leaked to CNN was fake," Hernandez said.

"Yes, sir," Foster confirmed.

"And the Libyan doctor?"

"Probably a Kairos operative."

"This was all a psyop?" Hernandez clarified. "A diversion?"

"And a good one, too, unfortunately," Foster said.

"We were set up," Hernandez said, standing now and pacing the room.

"Yes, sir."

"Abu Nakba knew we'd sweat his guy at Gitmo," Hernandez continued. "He expected him to talk—planned for it, in fact."

"That's the way I figure it, sir," Foster agreed. "My guess is he left his satellite phone in the compound—turned on and pinging—so we'd find it. But by that point he was long gone to another safe house, probably in Yemen. They must have had the video of the bombed-out school racked and ready to release, and the plan to attack the warehouse in Aden and grab the three American girls, well in advance."

Hernandez ran his hands through his hair, seemingly torn between rage and relief. "Tell me we at least got some of his top guys."

"Too soon to say, sir. The SEAL team brought back every intact body and every body part they could find. They're running the DNA as we speak. It might take a day or two until we know for sure who we've got, but I'll tell you the moment I know."

"No one can know we have this until the DNA results are in," Hernandez insisted. "We can't say anything publicly that isn't 100 percent truth. Fact-checked. Bulletproof."

"Yes, sir."

"Meanwhile, we've got to get into those phones and laptops and see if there's any salvageable intel on them," Hernandez continued. "But I hate to involve NSA, much less CIA. The more people who know about this, the faster it's going to leak. And I want to break this news myself. Understood?"

Foster and McDermott said they did.

"And Stephens can't know," Hernandez stressed. "Nor Dell. Not yet. Not until we have all our ducks in a row. But who do we use to get into those devices?"

McDermott spoke up. "Noah Daniels," he said.

Hernandez stopped pacing.

"Daniels?"

"He's one of the best tech guys Langley has."

"I know who he is, but doesn't he work for Ryker?"

"For a time, yes. Now he works for Hwang and Morris in the new—"

"No, no, I've got that, Bill," Hernandez interrupted. "I'm talking about the optics of having anyone connected to Ryker anywhere near this."

"I realize that, sir," McDermott acknowledged. "But the game has just changed. You have conclusive proof that Ryker was right and Stephens was wrong. So it's not like Ryker's team can be accused of cooking this thing up. But

I'm telling you no one is better qualified to get access to those hard drives and SIM cards, whatever their condition, than Daniels. His skills are second to none, and his reputation is unimpeachable."

Hernandez raised an eyebrow. "Not exactly the word I'd be using right now."

"Sorry, sir," McDermott said. "But—"

"Stop," the commander in chief said. "You've sold me, Bill. But don't call Daniels. Go find him in person and drive him out to Andrews yourself. Don't leave his side. Spend the night if you have to. Watch everything he does. And the moment you have anything, come straight back here. And don't tell anyone else what you're doing. Got it?"

"Yes, sir, but . . ."

"But what?"

"What about Ryker?"

"What about him?"

"Doesn't he deserve to know this, sir? That he's been vindicated?"

"And Jenny Morris, too," Foster added.

Hernandez nodded. "They do. So who tells them?"

McDermott looked at Foster. "You're a little too high-profile for that job."

"Probably right," the SecDef said. "But you're going to be at Andrews all night."

"What about Pete Hwang?" Hernandez asked.

"I thought you didn't want anyone else read in on this, sir," McDermott said.

"Don't tell him the specifics. Just tell Pete the acting president needs him to track down Ryker and get him to the Oval Office ASAP. Tell him it's a matter of the most urgent national security. Then get your tail over to Daniels's place, drive him to Andrews, and get cracking on those computers."

EISENHOWER EXECUTIVE OFFICE BUILDING

It didn't take McDermott long to find the team.

He knew they were hunkered down in the EEOB, working every possible lead to find the hostages. He also knew he wasn't exactly welcome in their suite of offices. But he didn't care. The clock was ticking, and he had his orders.

The conversation was brief. McDermott didn't exactly apologize, but there would be time for that later. Daniels immediately agreed to go to Andrews. Pete and Jenny immediately began working the phones, hunting down Marcus.

The rest of the team went back to searching for Brighton, Weiss, and Minetti.

COROLLA, NORTH CAROLINA

Marcus and Annie had made their play.

Now all they could do was wait.

To keep their minds off the multiple firestorms engulfing Washington, they'd thrown themselves into opening the beach house for the season. They'd given the place a thorough cleaning from top to bottom. They'd washed all the linens and towels, mowed the lawn, and weeded the flower beds out front and in the side yards. Marcus had even sanded down each of the decks and the front porch in order to restain them and spent several hours fixing the air-conditioning system that was on the fritz. It was exhausting yet satisfying work.

They wanted to keep a low profile, so they hadn't gone into town or out to dinner or even to the grocery store. Instead, they'd ordered groceries and other supplies to be delivered directly to the house, paying for them out of Marcus's fat stacks of cash. They cooked meals together, alternating between Annie's family recipes and Marcus's.

They'd been resolute in not watching TV or listening to the radio. With their phones still off and dismantled, they had no access to social media, and Annie had been careful not to use her computer to check her personal or work emails, even while setting up their anonymous account and monitoring it closely.

They knew none of the neighbors, and even if they had, there were precious few people around this time of year. The locals didn't live in the multimillion-dollar homes directly on the beach, and the summer surge had not begun. They had effectively cut themselves off from the world, and now that all their work was done for the day, they tried to relax.

To celebrate their accomplishments as the sun went down, Marcus made Annie a candlelight dinner. He grilled a couple of steaks, boiled two fresh Maine lobsters as well as several ears of sweet corn, made a big bowl of fruit salad, and dusted off a bottle of merlot he'd found on a rack in the basement.

They talked about baseball, especially the Nationals, and Marcus was blown away to learn that Annie was a season ticket holder, though she rarely had time to use them and usually gave the tickets to friends.

They talked about teachers they loved and hated growing up. About the kids they loved and hated growing up. About books and movies they loved and hated right up to the present.

After dinner, they dried and put away the last of the dishes, then stepped out onto the top deck and sat in matching Adirondack chairs. They gazed out over the Atlantic and a million stars spread across the darkening sky as the waves gently lapped upon the shore.

"Penny for your thoughts?" he said, seeing Annie lost in her head.

She smiled. "Is that all they're worth?"

"That's all I have on me right now."

"Yeah, right—I saw those wads of cash."

"All government money, I'm afraid. But seriously, you looked far away."

"Guess I was," Annie said.

"Washington?" he asked.

Annie shook her head. "Charleston," she said.

"Homesick?"

"A little."

"Do you wish we'd kept driving—gone there instead?"

"No, I love the Outer Banks. Actually, I forgot how much I love it. My aunt and uncle used to invite us every year, starting on Memorial Day weekend, and my parents would always take the whole week off and pull me out of school and we'd just come up here and play. Every day. All day. Swimming and making sandcastles and hunting for crabs at night and playing miniature golf and grilling out. No crowds, no traffic—it was like we had the whole island to ourselves. When I was really young, we'd come up for the entire month of June along with all my cousins and their families, and we'd play volleyball in the front yard and go on long bike rides up to the lighthouse and even farther to see the wild horses. Did you know there are wild horses that live on the beach north of here?"

"Sounds magical," Marcus said. "All of it."

"It was," she said. "And then it all vanished."

"Why?"

"I told you my parents died in a plane crash, right?" Annie asked.

Marcus nodded.

"I've hardly told anyone in D.C.," she said, staring out over the ocean. "My dad loved to fly. I can still remember the day he told my mom and me he'd bought this single-engine Piper Cub. It was a dream come true for him, and he went everywhere in it. But after Senator Dayton hired me, I sort of got pulled into the D.C. vortex, and that was the end of coming to the Outer Banks. When my parents died a couple of years after that, it was like all my childhood memories—the sweetest memories of my life—were just ripped away." She sighed. "Let's talk about something else. Tell me something about you."

"What would you like to know?"

"Anything."

A Coast Guard Seahawk helicopter came patrolling down the coastline. Marcus watched it closely as it flew north to south, just a hundred feet or so off the sand.

"It's kind of strange, isn't it?" he suddenly asked.

"What?"

"That both of our dads were pilots, that both of them died in plane crashes?"

Annie didn't respond.

"I mean, your dad flew as a hobby and mine as a career. And I know the circumstances were completely different, but . . ."

His voice trailed off as the roar of the chopper faded and they could once again hear waves below. He could feel Annie's eyes on him, but he kept staring out at the ocean.

Then she looped her arm through his and pulled him close. "It's hard to lose a dad at any age, but you were just a kid," she said.

Marcus nodded, afraid to speak lest his voice should crack.

"I was lucky," she said. "I got to have my dad until I was thirty."

"But you lost them both—I can't imagine not at least having my mom."

"Yeah, but you know, it was better that way."

"Better?" he asked, turning to her.

"Not for me—it was horrible. I don't think you ever get over something like that. With God's help, and your friends' help, you make your peace with it, or try to, and do your best to go on. What else can you do? But I mean for them, for Mom and Dad, I've always thought it was merciful that they went home to be with the Lord on the same day, at the same moment. They loved each other so much. I don't think my mom could have survived long without, you know, without my dad. If she couldn't be with her one true love, she wouldn't have wanted to go on another minute."

"How about a walk on the beach?" Marcus asked, needing a change.

"Love to," she said.

They stepped out onto a long wooden walkway leading to the dunes.

"North or south?" he asked as they kicked off their shoes and dug their feet in the now-cooling sand.

"You pick," Annie insisted.

"All right then—let's go north," Marcus concluded. "Maybe we'll find those wild horses."

Basking in the moonlight and determined to keep the world at bay, they talked about nothing and about everything. Annie asked him how he had developed such a love for Russian literature. Marcus asked her how she had developed such a love for English poetry. She asked him about his favorite places to snowboard in the Rockies. He asked her favorite places to water-ski in South Carolina. She asked him what kind of lunch box he had in elementary school (metal, from *The Empire Strikes Back*). He asked her what it was like to see scenes of *Forrest Gump* being filmed in Port Royal, the town where her parents had first met.

What kind of playlists did she have on her iPhone?

How many American states and foreign countries had he visited?

Their conversation never felt awkward, never forced, never hit a lull. They had known each other for nearly twenty years, and the occasional silence—be it to savor the natural beauty of the ocean and dunes or to ruminate on each other's stories or to sidestep the ubiquitous crabs—did not bother or threaten them. Somehow, over the past three days, they'd been transported far from their fears, and neither wanted this escape to end.

"Annie, can I ask you something personal?" Marcus asked as they continued to stroll, not another soul to be seen.

"Should I be worried?"

"No, no. Don't answer if you don't want, but well, I'm just curious."

"Ask away," she said, gently splashing the water with her feet. "I've lived in Washington long enough to say, '*No comment, next question.*'"

Marcus couldn't help but laugh.

"Fair enough. I guess I was just wondering how come you never got married. I mean, you're smart and you're beautiful, and I can't figure out how it is that I get to be here with you, enjoying every moment of your company, when you should've been taken off the market long ago. I know that's a terrible question, and I really shouldn't ask it, but I just can't get my head around how that's possible."

Annie winced. "You weren't kidding," she said. "That *was* personal."

"I'm sorry."

"It was going to come up at some point, but it's just, you know, a little tough to talk about."

"Then forget I asked," Marcus said. "You don't have to tell me—really. Not now. Not ever."

"Ever?"

"Not if you don't want to."

"Well, eventually I'd have to, right?" she said. "If there's any future for us, I'd need to come clean on all that, wouldn't I?"

"It's early yet," Marcus demurred.

"Is it?" she asked. "Didn't you tell me the other day that the only reason you'd ever date someone was to see if God meant for you to be married?"

Marcus nodded, a bit sheepishly.

"I was grateful for that," she said. "Don't get me wrong—I'm scared to be honest with you, Marcus, but I definitely want you to be honest with me."

"Why would you be scared?"

"It's not *you* that scares me."

"Then what?"

"It's *me* that scares me."

"I don't understand."

"I'm not used to being—you know—open, vulnerable, honest, with a guy, anyway. It's never gone well for me."

Marcus stayed quiet and they kept walking.

"You just said it's early yet in our relationship, but that's not really true, is it?" she asked. "We've known each other a long, long time. And we know a lot about each other, don't we?"

"We do," Marcus said.

"And I agree with you," Annie continued. "I don't want to goof around. I'm not interested in just casually seeing each other. Life's too short. But that means that either this is all going to fall apart quickly, or this thing could go from zero to sixty in 2.2 seconds."

"It could."

"I don't usually go off-grid with guys that I'm interested in. Or correspond with their mothers. Or invite them to spend a weekend at a beach house I haven't laid eyes on in a decade. That's not me. That's not how I roll. And with you, I'm in real danger here."

"Danger?"

"Yeah, in danger of getting hurt pretty badly if things don't work out," she confessed. "And don't get me wrong. I don't know any more than you do what God wants from us, if he wants us to be together. But . . ."

"But . . . ?"

"But it's nice to think about."

Marcus turned them around and they started walking back down the beach.

"I dated a lot of guys in high school," Annie began. "Football players. Soccer stars. Handsome. Popular. Nominally Christian. But they didn't take their faith seriously. Then again, neither did I. And I got burned. Over and over again. And it didn't get better in college—not my freshman year, anyway. But it was at AU that I finally started really growing in my faith, and as I did, I made a decision that I needed to stop dating for a while until I was ready for a serious relationship. By graduate school, I just had no interest in dating."

She paused for a bit, though they kept walking. Marcus sensed she was trying to decide what to tell him and what to leave out.

"After Senator Dayton hired me, I immersed myself in my job. There was so much to learn, and I finally started to come out of the darkness and feel like myself again. But that crash and all that happened in Afghanistan, that really threw me."

"How could it not?"

"I went into an emotional tailspin," Annie confessed. "I'm not ready to tell you all of it, not yet, but it was . . . dark. The senator kept me on the payroll, thank goodness, and that's when Esther and I really bonded. But I was a mess. Emotionally. Physically. Let's just leave it at that for now. And to be honest, between that and my parents' plane crash . . . it ate up a lot of years. So yeah, there were guys in my life—colleagues, friends—but nothing serious. For a long time, I didn't date at all. I was too busy and too much in pain."

"But then . . . ?"

"But eventually there was this guy. And he was sweet, you know? Kind. Funny. Smart. Really smart. Yale grad. Harvard law. Deputy director of the Senate Intel Committee. A few years older than me. Not pushy. Not showy. Just nice. And . . ."

"And you began hanging out."

"For a while, yeah, and then he asked me out. And so we started dating. And dating. And dating. And well, five years went by and we were still together."

"He never proposed?"

"That's what my friends kept saying. That's what Esther Dayton kept saying."

"But he never did?"

"No, no, he eventually, finally, inevitably, I guess, popped the question."

"And you said no?"

"Au contraire," she said wistfully.

"You said yes?" he asked, surprised.

"I did," Annie confirmed. "And we were engaged for a year, and then . . ."

"What?"

"He broke it off."

"Just like that?"

"Oh yeah, and quit his job and moved away—Seattle, I think, or Portland. I don't know. I never heard from him again. I was devastated. I thought things were finally coming together. I was actually starting to enjoy life again and trust people and laugh. And then, boom, it was all over. He cost me a lot of wasted years."

"I'm so sorry, Annie."

"Yeah, well, what are you going to do, right?"

Both were silent for a time, lost in their own thoughts, their own memories.

"So," Marcus said finally.

"So," Annie responded.

"You don't have this guy's current mailing address?"

"No."

"Email?"

"No."

"Phone number?"

"Marcus, seriously, I haven't seen or heard from him in years, and I don't want to ever be in touch with him again. Why do you think I'm not on Facebook or Instagram or any social media?"

"But I need to track him down."

"What? Why? No, that's crazy. Why would you want to track him down?"

"To thank him, obviously."

"*For what?* The guy's a grade A jerk."

"Maybe so, but he's the reason you're single and on this beach with me right now."

LAREDO, TEXAS

Zaid Farooq awoke an hour before sunset.

Slipping out of the bunk bed to which he had been assigned, he headed to the kitchen, turned on the stove, and filled a large pot of water for coffee. He called his men into the kitchen for a meal. As per Farooq's orders, they all remained silent as they ate, but there was a nervous energy in the air as they tidied up their temporary quarters, headed into the garage, loaded their crates into a white Chevy box truck, and climbed in themselves. All except Mansour bin Badr, whom Farooq told to join him up front.

Farooq pulled down and locked the truck's rear door, then climbed into the driver's side, hid his loaded pistol under the seat, and turned the key. Checking his mirrors, he programmed the portable GPS device mounted on the dashboard. Then he nodded to their young host, and the boy pushed a button on the wall. The garage door opened, and they rolled out into the toasty evening air.

The Algerian took Highway 59, heading northeast. Using the vehicle's cruise control feature and determined to do nothing to draw attention to themselves, he maintained the posted speed limit. Only when Laredo was fading away behind them did he finally relax and begin to speak.

"I am sorry about your mother, Mansour," he began. "She was a pious woman, and she raised three courageous warriors."

"Thank you, Brother Zaid," the young man replied.

"You must miss her very much."

"I do—we all do," Mansour said. His older brothers, Jibril and Ali, were staying behind to travel with the second group, led by Tariq Youssef. Mansour seemed obviously slighted at being left out.

"It must be very hard on your father to be alone."

"Perhaps, but he does not speak of it."

The moment was awkward, so Farooq said nothing, and they drove on in silence for a while.

Then Mansour said, "I never imagined I would ever leave Yemen," as he stared out at the cattle grazing and the oil derricks pumping for as far as the eye could see.

"Your father is very proud of you."

"My brothers, for sure."

"And you, as well."

Mansour shrugged. "Perhaps."

"What do you mean, *perhaps*?" Farooq asked, determined to shake the boy out of his melancholy. "Your father is a great warrior. And he is one of the wisest men I have ever known. He could have chosen any of his men for this mission. He could have sent your brothers and left you home. But he didn't, did he?"

Mansour said nothing, just continued gazing out the passenger window.

"Jibril is as brave a young jihadist as I have ever met, rivaling your father," Farooq continued. "And Ali is nearly as courageous. But you are smarter than them both, Mansour. Shrewder. More cunning. That is why I asked for you by name."

That surprised Mansour. He turned and faced Farooq. "You asked for me?"

"Of course."

"But why?"

"Was it not you who proposed kidnapping those three aid workers? Was it not you who planned the mission with such precision?"

"But *he* doesn't know that," Mansour shot back. "He thinks it was you."

"I am more than happy to tell him it was your idea, when the time is right."

"He never would have listened if you'd told him earlier."

"Which is why I never told him," Farooq said. "But you know the truth, and so do I. You have greatness within you, Mansour. That's why I want you at my side—especially on this mission. We are about to make history. We are about to be immortalized. For all eternity, every Muslim in the world will know your name."

THE WHITE HOUSE SITUATION ROOM—17 MAY

In fifteen minutes, the room would be filled with NSC principals.

But for the moment, at the unholy hour of three in the morning, the only people in the room were Bill McDermott, Martha Dell, and Peter Hwang.

"Please tell me you've found these girls," McDermott began, his tie loosened, his face unshaven, his eyes bloodshot.

"Bill, I'm sorry," Dell replied, looking just as disheveled. "We've talked to every intelligence agency. Pored over every cable, every satellite image, every intercept, every dispatch from the region. But there's simply no sign of them. Whatever trail there was has gone cold."

"I can't accept this," McDermott said, slamming his fist on the table. "We have to do better."

"Bill, look, we have to face facts," Pete said. "We're out of options and almost out of time. The best thing you can do now is advise the president to wire the money. Hopefully, Kairos will release the girls. In the meantime, we can follow the money and pray it leads us to them or at least to the Kairos high command."

"That's not your call, Pete," McDermott said. "And we still have nine hours before the deadline."

"Come on," Pete shot back. "Even if we find them, there's no time to mount a rescue operation, and you know it. I know Foster and Whitney are telling the president it's political suicide to pay off terrorists. But the truth is, it's political suicide not to. You guys in this White House may think you're in enough trouble with the American people right now. But that's nothing compared to the storm that's going to hit if you let those girls go to their deaths without having done everything you possibly could to save them. No one else is going to say this to the acting president, but it's the truth. It's your job to tell him. And time is running out."

McDermott shifted in his seat, then glanced up at the world clocks on the far wall. "What about the other thing we discussed?" he asked Pete.

"What other thing?" Dell asked.

"Nothing," McDermott said. "It's a private matter."

"I'm working on it," Pete replied.

COROLLA, NORTH CAROLINA

Annie woke up to pounding on her bedroom door.

Rolling over, she saw the alarm clock read only 6:14 a.m.

"What is it?" she asked, fumbling for her glasses. "What's the matter?"

"We need to go," Marcus said through the door. "Don't worry about packing. We don't have time for that. Just put on—"

Annie opened the door, wearing her pajamas, her hair a tangled mess. She was stunned to find Marcus showered, shaved, and wearing a freshly pressed suit and tie. "What in the world is going on, Marcus?"

"I'll tell you on the way. Right now, I need you to take a superfast shower and put on the best thing you've got with you."

"I don't have anything with me, just what we bought on the way. And where'd you get the suit?"

"The duffel bag I grabbed in Richmond. Forget it. It doesn't matter. Just meet me in the car in ten minutes."

"Why?"

"Because we're wheels up in thirty."

"Where are we going?"

"The Oval Office."

Eight minutes later, Annie climbed into the passenger seat. Marcus handed her a travel mug of coffee and a toasted English muffin. Then he hit the accelerator. Ten minutes after that they were parking at the Pine Island Airport in Corolla, where Annie was stunned to see Jenny Morris waiting for them.

"What is she doing here?" Annie asked.

Marcus took a deep breath and signaled Jenny that they would be there in a moment. Jenny pointed to her watch, then backed off and went into the tiny airport, used exclusively for private aviation.

"I couldn't sleep, so I went for a run," Marcus began. "When I stopped for a bottle of water at the gas station—you know, the one on the corner—the front page of the *USA Today* stopped me cold. Abu Nakba is alive."

"What?"

"He released a video on Friday saying that Kairos has the three kidnapped aid workers. He's demanding the White House pay him $150 million by noon today or he's going to kill them all. I used a pay phone to check my voice mail. As you might imagine, it's full. And not just from my mom but from Pete and Jenny desperately trying to track us down. Apparently Hernandez is summoning me to the Oval Office."

"To arrest you?"

"They don't know. All Hernandez said was that it's a 'matter of urgent national security.'"

"And you believe him?"

"Honestly, I don't know what to believe. But when I got back to the house, I booted up your computer, created a new Gmail account, and sent Pete an encrypted email saying I'd gotten his nineteen messages but wasn't anywhere near Washington. He wrote back immediately, asking where I was and could he send a plane to get me. I asked why. He said it's a madhouse up there. He doesn't have the full picture. But yes, he thinks I should come immediately and hear Hernandez out. What's more, he said if they were going to arrest anyone, Jenny would already be in custody."

"So you told him yes."

"I did—but I also insisted that you had to come with me."

"And then you told him where my family's beach house is."

"No," Marcus assured her. "I said you and I had gone south for a few days, but it wouldn't be hard to head north again. He asked where the nearest private airport was. I told him we could definitely be in Corolla in two hours. He said fine, he'd make all the arrangements, and Jenny would meet us."

Annie shook her head. "Never a dull moment with you, Ryker. Not even one."

WASHINGTON NATIONAL AIRPORT

The unmarked government Learjet was wheels down at 7:52 a.m.

Three black armored Chevy Suburbans were waiting for them on the tarmac.

"Why all the firepower?" Annie asked as they deplaned and saw federal agents take up positions around them and the jet.

"I have no idea," Jenny said over the roar of the engines.

The three were patted down for weapons or explosives by several of the agents, even though they had gone through security back in Corolla. The lead agent then asked the three to get into the middle SUV. The rest of the agents piled into the first and third vehicles, and they were off.

On the drive into the city, none of them spoke, cognizant that anything they said could later be used against them. Even on the plane, they had not spoken much. Rather, using an iPad Jenny had brought with her, they wrote messages to each other, then erased them immediately. Jenny conceded that she, too, was in the dark over why they were being summoned. In light of Abu Nakba's apparent resurrection, the imminent danger to the three aid workers, and the stampede on the Hill for congressional investigations and even the appointment of an independent counsel, they all braced for impact.

At 8:16 a.m., the motorcade pulled onto the grounds of the Treasury Department. Once again, they were taken through metal detectors and their personal items scanned through an X-ray machine while a bomb-sniffing dog did its own due diligence. Jenny's iPad was taken from her, as were their mobile phones and satellite phones. They were then given visitor badges and taken through the tunnel from Treasury into the basement of the East Wing.

At precisely 8:30 a.m., they were ushered into the Oval Office, where they were greeted by the acting president. Hernandez remained seated behind the *Resolute* desk. He did not smile nor offer to shake their hands. He asked them to take a seat on the far couch. Sitting across from them were McDermott and Martha Dell, an empty space between them. Sitting in the armchairs usually reserved for the president and vice president were Secretary Whitney and Attorney General Blackburn. Sitting in antique chairs against the far wall were the White House counsel and chief of staff. To Marcus's surprise, and no doubt Annie's, Senator Dayton was also in the room.

Several minutes later, CIA director Stephens arrived. Marcus noticed that he didn't apologize but silently took his seat next to Dr. Dell.

"Okay, we're all here," Hernandez said. "First, let me say that we have only three and a half hours before the deadline is up. Given that Langley has been completely unable to locate the women, I see little choice but to transfer the money. Already, the insurance company working with the missionary organization that the women were sent by are prepared to send $30 million. I have authorized them to wire the funds to Kairos at ten o'clock. I've asked the treasury secretary to be prepared to wire the additional $120 million at eleven o'clock to make sure there is enough time for Kairos to receive the funds and factor in enough time for any complications or delays."

"Excuse me, sir, may I?" Stephens suddenly asked.

"This isn't a discussion, Richard," Hernandez said. "I've noted your disapproval, but I've already made my decision."

"No, it's not that, sir," Stephens replied. "What I want to know is why Marcus Ryker is in the White House at all, much less sitting in an NSC principals meeting in the Oval Office."

Marcus stiffened but held his tongue.

"First of all, this is not a principals meeting," Hernandez explained. "Second, I asked Agent Ryker to join us, along with Agent Morris and Miss Stewart. And third, since you're so eager, let's get right to the heart of the matter."

"Sir, with all respect, it is completely inappropriate to have Ryker on White House grounds after you suspended him, pending a full investigation. I for one—"

But Hernandez cut him off. "Shut up, Richard."

"I beg your pardon?"

"You can beg all you'd like but the decision has been made," Hernandez shot back, leaning forward in his chair, his arms on the desk.

Marcus had no idea what was going on here, but the tension in the room was palpable. Stephens's face reddened, and he was about to come off the couch. But Hernandez preempted him.

"Richard, I want your letter of resignation, effective immediately."

"My *what*?"

"You heard me. In fact, I've taken the liberty of drafting a one-sentence letter. I want you to sign it while I watch."

At this, the White House counsel stepped over to the *Resolute* desk, picked up a sheet of CIA letterhead stationery, and handed it to Stephens.

"What exactly is going on here?"

"Resign, Richard, right now, or I will have no choice but to fire you for cause," Hernandez said.

"Fire me? On what grounds?"

"The attempted assassination of two American citizens."

All color drained from Stephens's face. He turned to Marcus, then to Jenny, then back to Hernandez and the bulky reel-to-reel tape deck Marcus now noticed sitting on the desk.

"Shall I play for you the most damning phone calls between you and the FSB, or should we save that for the grand jury?" the acting president asked, his voice remarkably calm and even, given the circumstances.

Marcus felt Annie stir beside him and knew exactly what she was thinking. The emails had not only been received, they'd been read and were now being acted upon.

Stephens sat silently for a long moment, then pulled a Montblanc pen from his breast pocket, signed the letter, stood up, and stormed out of the Oval Office.

Hernandez turned to the head of his detail and ordered him to have Stephens escorted from the building, his security clearances revoked, and his access to Langley and all other U.S. government offices barred.

Then he turned to Dell. "Martha, you're the new acting director of Central Intelligence. Will you accept?"

Dell was in shock. "Unless you want me to resign, as well, sir. You deserve your people running the show, especially now."

"I appreciate that, but I think we both know why I trust your judgment," Hernandez replied. "I wouldn't ask you to serve otherwise."

Dell nodded her gratitude. "Then I accept, Mr. President."

At that moment, Marcus finally realized who had entrusted those files to Annie.

Hernandez turned to the secretary of state.

"Meg, I'd like to appoint you to serve as my acting vice president. Would you do me, and the nation, the honor and accept?"

It was clear by the stunned expression on her face that this was the first Whitney was hearing of Hernandez's plan.

"We may have a bruising confirmation battle ahead of us," Hernandez added. "But I'm willing if you are."

"I'd be honored, Mr. President. Thank you. Thank you so much."

"Good, so that's taken care of," Hernandez said, turning to Senator Dayton. "Robert, I need a secretary of state. Someone with world-class experience. Unquestioned integrity. Independent judgment. And a bipartisan spirit. If I appoint you, would you accept?"

Now it was Dayton's turn to be blindsided. "You're sure?" he asked.

"Absolutely," Hernandez said.

"After what I've been saying publicly for the past few days?"

"Because of what you've been saying for the past few days."

"I don't understand."

"Bill, do you want to tell him or should I?" Hernandez asked McDermott.

"It's your show, sir," McDermott replied.

"Very well," Hernandez said. "The SEAL team is back from Libya. The compound we bombed was indeed the Kairos headquarters, not a school for disabled children. In a moment, we'll head down to the Situation Room, and I'll show you the videos the SEALs took, the photos, video interviews with SEAL team members on the ground, all of it. We were played, Robert. Abu Nakba wasn't there, but his phone was. The SEALs recovered it. It's burned pretty good, but we have it, and we've got an expert unlocking it right now. We also have a treasure trove of burnt and damaged laptops and other electronics. From what I've seen already, the data we'll pull off those devices in the next forty-eight to seventy-two hours should be astounding and, let's hope, actionable."

"I—well, I don't know what to say, Mr. President," Dayton stammered.

"Say yes, Robert. I need you at my side, and so does the country."

Marcus exhaled and instinctively took both Annie's and Jenny's hands and squeezed them. Glancing at Annie, he could see the relief in her eyes. When he looked at Jenny, he could not see her eyes at all. Her head was down, and she was trembling ever so slightly. He let go of both women's hands. It was the Oval Office, after all. But he nudged Jenny and whispered, *"We're good."*

She nodded but couldn't speak. Not yet.

"Very well, Mr. President," Dayton finally said. "Assuming everything you say checks out, I would be honored to serve as your secretary of state."

"Excellent," Hernandez said. "I very much look forward to that announcement and confirmation process. I suspect it may be the fastest in Senate history."

"Let's hope so, sir."

Hernandez got up, came around the desk, pulled up a chair, and turned his attention to Marcus and Jenny.

"You two were right," he said. "We may not have gotten Abu Nakba, but you were right. I'm sorry I doubted. I'm sorry we all did."

"Thank you, sir," Marcus replied.

"Yes, sir, thank you," Jenny said.

"The investigation into your conduct is no longer pending," Hernandez said to Marcus. "It's over. I'm fully reinstating your security clearance and pay. What's more, I'm promoting you to director of Near East operations at Langley. Agent Morris, I'd like you to serve as deputy. I want you to bring your full team back to Langley and serve under Dr. Dell here, but with direct access to me at any hour of the day or night. We're going to get these aid workers back safe and sound. But then I want you to unleash everything you have into hunting down Abu Nakba and his entire network and raining the full fury of the American government down on their heads. You'll have an unlimited black budget. Anything you need. But before you accept, I do have to tell you something you're not going to want to hear."

Marcus once again braced for impact.

"We've picked up signals intelligence that the Iranians have doubled the bounty on your head. They're offering $20 million to anyone who kills or captures you. And we believe Kairos has already signaled back to Tehran that they want that contract. There's all the reason in the world for you to want to walk away from this life, and I would respect that. You've given everything you have to serve your country and paid a very high price in the process. If you turn down my offer, I will understand. And I will sign an executive order authorizing a protective detail for you and your family for the rest of your lives. But my preference, frankly, is that you accept this promotion and take the fight to Kairos yourself. You know as well as anyone in this room that the best defense is a good offense."

Marcus nodded and was about to speak when Hernandez added something else.

"One more thing. Miss Stewart, I'd like you to take Dr. Dell's job as deputy director of the CIA for intelligence. I know you want to leave Washington. I know you've submitted your letter of resignation to Senator Dayton. But we need you. I need you. The country needs you—for a little bit longer."

The room was silent.

Marcus could barely process all that was happening.

"I know these are big decisions," Hernandez said. "But we don't have much time. If you need to think it over, talk it over, pray about it, do so. But do it quickly. Personally, I can't think of three people more qualified for these jobs. So I leave it to you."

Hernandez leaned back in his chair and was about to stand when Jenny spoke up. "I don't need twenty-four hours, sir," she said. "I'm grateful for your confidence and your apology, and I accept your offer."

"Very well, Agent Morris. I'm honored to have you on the team."

"As am I," Dell said.

"Good for you, Jenny," Marcus said. "You're going to be amazing. But I'm going to need more time, Mr. President. I understand the pressure you're under, but I've got a lot to think through, and I've only just started my recovery after Beirut."

Hernandez nodded and was about to speak, but Annie spoke first.

"Actually, Mr. President, we don't need more time," she said. "Marcus and I would be honored to accept."

Marcus turned to Annie in shock. "What are you saying?"

"I'm saying you were born for this job, for this moment, and maybe I was too. I'm not so sure about that part, but—"

"Annie, don't do this for me. I heard everything you were saying and—"

"I'm not doing this for you," she told him. "I'm doing this with you. You're right. Abu Nakba is a monster. They all are. Now let's get him and bring him and Kairos to justice before they rob, kill, and destroy everything we hold dear."

Marcus felt his heart racing. He kept his eyes on Annie, unsure what to say. Finally he turned back to the new commander in chief. "Okay, sir. We're in."

Tarabulus
(Tripoli)
Tripolitania
Ghadames
Suknah
Maradah
Zellah
Libyan
LIBIYA
(LIBYA)
Sebkha
Zighan
Serir Kalansho
El Juf
Ghat

PART THREE

WINNIPEG, CANADA

Everyone was now present and accounted for.

They'd entered the country over the past week via Ottawa, Montreal, Quebec, and Vancouver, without so much as a raised eyebrow from Canadian authorities. They'd found the vehicles pre-positioned for them and picked up the weapons and ammunition waiting for them in various storage facilities across the country. For Nasir Bhati, commander of the cell, their success thus far was a welcome sign of Allah's favor, but he knew far more success was needed to accomplish their mission, and time wasn't on their side.

Gathering the team in a rented basement flat, Bhati served his men a classic Pakistani stew dish flavored with a spicy yogurt his mother had taught him to prepare. Only after breakfast, as the men sipped their tea, did he pull out the maps.

"Brothers, the first team departs within the hour," he began. "The second leaves at ten. The last leaves at noon. The drive ahead of us is long, nearly 1,700 kilometers. Factoring in breaks to refuel or relieve yourselves, it should take about seventeen hours."

"Where are we going, sir?" one of his men asked.

"Grand Rapids."

"Where is that?"

"Michigan."

"Why are we going to Michigan?"

"You'll find out when we get there," Bhati said, continuing to compartmentalize all critical mission planning. "We'll be driving in teams of two. Ibrahim, you'll come with me. Daoud, you're with Syed. Aziz, you'll go with Abdullah."

The men nodded, pleased with their assignments.

"Study your maps carefully—and go over your cover stories until you know them by heart," he continued, handing out thick manila envelopes. "Here are your passports, driver's licenses, credit cards—all Canadian, all clean. But I guarantee you'll be questioned at the border, so be ready. And stay calm. The Americans aren't only listening to your answers. They're watching your eyes. Studying your body language. So no mistakes."

GEORGETOWN MEMORIAL PARKWAY

The press conference began at 11 a.m.

Marcus and Annie didn't stay to watch. There was far too much to do, and they couldn't afford to be seen by reporters. Instead, they listened on a local news radio station while they raced back to CIA headquarters.

"Let me begin by saying I've already authorized $30 million to be transferred as a down payment, a signal of goodwill that we want all three Americans returned safely and immediately," Hernandez began from behind the presidential podium in the East Room. "Furthermore, I've directed the secretary of the treasury to release the rest of the funds within the hour.

"Yes, there was a good deal of debate within my inner circle as to whether the U.S. should negotiate with terrorists," Hernandez continued. "I've long agreed with the position of my predecessors not to do so. But I've also looked into the eyes of the parents of these three dear women—Tanya Brighton, Hannah Weiss, and Mia Minetti—and promised them I would do everything in my power to get their daughters home safely. And I want the American people and the world to know that I am a man of my word."

Reporters started shouting questions, but Hernandez was not finished.

"To Abu Nakba, let me say this: I expect you to keep your word and immediately release these innocent American citizens, free from further harm. Too much blood has been spilled in our fight against one another. Let this serve as the beginning of a truce between us."

Marcus had serious reservations about the policy Hernandez was pursuing. He understood the politically fragile position Hernandez found himself in in the first fateful days of his accidental presidency, though he feared paying the ransom could lead to a risk of additional attacks against Americans everywhere. But Hernandez had made his decision. The Agency's role now wasn't to question it but support it.

Rather than take questions, Hernandez now made more headlines. Big headlines. He announced that he was nominating Margaret Whitney as his vice president and Robert Dayton as his new secretary of state. He also announced the resignation of Richard Stephens and proudly named Martha Dell as his choice for the new director of the Central Intelligence Agency. Any one of these would have been front-page news on a normal day, but today was far from normal.

Senator Dayton's explanation of his decision to join the Republican administration despite his untarnished record as a loyal member of the Democratic Party—combined with his startling revelation that the compound in Libya had, in fact, been the Kairos headquarters and not a school—was a significant moment in helping Hernandez establish some desperately needed legitimacy for his new administration. Both Marcus and Annie also found Dayton's description of Hernandez as a faithful husband, loving father, patriotic military commander, and loyal friend quite moving. They knew the senator's words would not calm all partisan passions in D.C., much less the country, but they believed they could very well begin to turn the tide in the new president's favor.

Even more moving was the profound gratitude Martha Dell expressed to Hernandez for appointing her as the first African American ever to serve as the director of the CIA. Dell recalled the bitter racism she'd experienced growing up in Atlanta and the degradations her single mother had been subjected to as a child in Mobile, Alabama, in the 1950s. She also shared about her grandparents, who'd been sharecroppers in Alabama, and her great-great-grandparents on both sides of her family who'd been slaves.

"No one can ever tell me this country is perfect," Dell told the reporters. "But nor can anyone tell me this country isn't changing, isn't improving, isn't trying to make things right. We have a long way to go and much to do to truly establish liberty and justice for all. But America is moving in the right direction, and today is further proof."

"Not a bad way to hit reset," Annie said as they pulled through the front gates of CIA headquarters.

"Not bad at all," Marcus agreed.

SOMEWHERE IN YEMEN

Abu Nakba watched the press conference with great interest.

His men cheered when the American president announced he was transferring the funds. They cheered again when Ruzami confirmed that the entire sum of $150 million was now in their accounts and ready to be withdrawn.

"It's time," the Kairos founder said.

Badr Hassan al-Ruzami nodded and ordered that the women be brought to the courtyard as he and a bodyguard helped the old man down the stairs.

When they arrived, Abu Nakba saw the three Americans for the first time. They weren't simply bound and gagged and dripping with perspiration in the sweltering Yemeni heat. They were bloodied, bruised, and trembling. The old man felt no pity for them. They were Americans and Christians and therefore infidels of the most heinous kind.

They were also the best fundraising tools he'd ever seen.

For the Libyan, this operation had never been about money, though that was a serendipity. It was about humiliating the American people and their leaders in

Washington. It was too bad Andrew Clarke was out of the picture. Abu Nakba had designed this mission with Clarke in mind. But Hernandez, the Cuban, would suffice. By transferring the funds, Hernandez had already demonstrated how weak he really was, no matter his accomplishments in the Navy. Who knew what other compromises he could now be compelled to make?

The cameras were in place.

Wearing a traditional white robe, brown vest, turquoise horn-handled knife, and black- and white-checkered turban that covered his face, revealing only his eyes, Ruzami said nothing as he leered at the women. It was a pity they had to be eliminated, he thought to himself as he took the last drag on his cigarette. He'd given his men permission to beat the virgins but not to defile them. Now he wished he'd defiled them himself. The blonde, anyway. He didn't recall her name. Nor did he care. But there was something about her figure that at once inflamed and revolted him.

Since his three wives had been killed in a Saudi air strike six months earlier, he had not been with a woman. It was time. He was barely fifty. Still young. Still virile.

No, he suddenly remonstrated himself. Such were the lies of the devil. How cruel Satan was. And how crafty. He could turn himself into shapes so pleasing, so alluring as to be almost irresistible.

Such was the trap of fleshly temptation, Ruzami scolded himself. But this was no time to be distracted. They were at war, and he had a strict timetable to follow.

Drawing a .45-caliber pistol from his belt, he strode toward his prey. They were weeping now, but he refused to look at their faces. Rather, he walked behind them and thrust the barrel in the back of the head of the first girl. Ordering all three cameramen to begin rolling, he shouted praise to Allah and pulled the trigger. The girl's body slumped into the dirt.

He moved to the next girl. She was sobbing, begging for her life. He again raised his pistol but this time shouted, *"Death to Israel! Death to America!"* Then he fired a second time.

The third girl, the blonde, fainted. This would not do. She had to be awake.

Viewers had to see the fear in her eyes. How else were the American people going to be shaken, shown there was no place they could hide, no amount of money that could ever protect them? They were criminals, all of them, destined for the fires of hell, and the sooner the better.

One of Ruzami's men—his face also covered—rushed over with a bucket of ice-cold water. The shock brought the stricken girl back to consciousness. Though gagged, it was obvious that she, too, was pleading for her life, and he let her continue for several moments. It was good television. The panic in her eyes. The tears streaming down her face. Her friends' blood and brain matter all over her.

Ruzami raised his pistol and pressed it into the back of her skull. But just then a thought came to him. Abu Nakba had never specified the precise manner in which the girls were to be executed. Grabbing this one by her filthy blonde ponytail, Ruzami dragged her kicking and screaming across the courtyard until he reached the metal flagpole at its center. There, he called for a rope. Someone rushed one to him. Together they tied the girl's chest, waist, and legs to the pole.

As they did, Ruzami shouted something to yet another man, who quickly grabbed a beat-up wicker chair off the back porch and brought it over to them, tilting it against the pole. Then he gathered up all manner of sticks, garbage, plus the bodies of the other two girls, positioning them at the base of the pole.

At Ruzami's direction, someone went into the garage and brought back a can of petrol. Ruzami poured the contents all over the whimpering aid worker, over the chair and the bodies and the garbage and the kindling. Then he looked directly into the camera, which was still running. This time, he did not shout. Rather, he walked straight up to the lens and said in heavily accented English, *"We are coming for you—all of you—every enemy of Allah shall burn. You have been warned."*

Then he turned, walked back to the flagpole, stared one more time into that beautiful face—now pale as a ghost—and tossed his cigarette onto the bodies of her colleagues. As the flames began to spread and lick at her feet, Ruzami pulled the dagger from its sheath.

"Goodbye," he whispered, cutting away the scarf that had been gagging her.

Walking to the porch, Ruzami took his place beside Abu Nakba.

One of the cameramen circled around the flagpole to capture Abu Nakba's reaction and prove that he was really there. The old man watched in delight as the flames quickly engulfed the girl. Then he looked up into the heavens, closed his eyes, and smiled as he drank in her cries of terror and pain, knowing they would be heard in the citadels of earthly power all over the globe and particularly in the White House itself.

LANGLEY, VIRGINIA

At precisely 3 p.m. Eastern, the video was released on the Al-Sawt network.

Simultaneously, it was uploaded to YouTube.

None of the senior staff gathered in the new director's seventh-floor corner office was surprised that Abu Nakba had taken the money and not released the women. This was exactly what Dell, Marcus, and Annie had told Hernandez was likely to happen. Still, the sheer horror of seeing Hannah Weiss and Mia Minetti being shot to death so coldly was more revolting than anything they'd personally witnessed in wartime, much less in a time of peace.

Marcus's jaw clenched as he focused on the figure that he suspected was Badr Hassan al-Ruzami, though his face was covered. He tried to dissociate from the cruelty itself. He searched for any clue that might give them a location and thus a target. But there was nothing.

His blood boiled as he watched Tanya Brighton tied to the flagpole, doused with gasoline, and set ablaze. He had seen terrible things in his life and in this job. But nothing had prepared him to look upon men smiling while they engaged in acts of such wickedness. Every instinct in his body wanted to look away, as Annie now did. Or leave the room, as two other staffers did. Yet Marcus forced himself to watch. It was his duty, he told himself, especially as Ruzami said, *"We are coming for you—all of you—every enemy of Allah shall burn. You have been warned."*

When he saw the man draw his dagger, however, and cut away the rag and pull it out of her mouth, toss it into the fire, and walk out of the picture, he knew what was coming, and this was more than he could bear. He did turn away as the flames engulfed Tanya, but it hardly shielded him. The screams that followed were unlike anything Marcus had ever heard before, unlike any sound he'd thought a human capable of making.

Dell suddenly shot out of her chair and into her private restroom and vomited.

None of this barbarism was new.

All of it, Marcus knew, had its roots in the ISIS playbook, *The Management of Savagery*, written by an obscure jihadi strategist from Egypt by the name of Abu Bakr Naji. The book was gruesome enough. But Marcus now recalled an analysis of the book by two professors working in the Department of War Studies at King's College in London. He pulled out his phone, looked up the text, and read:

> Jihadism counterposes a belief in life with a cult of death. This is not a reversion to medieval cruelty. It has modern origins. Fascism, as Umberto Eco observed, possesses a taste for political necrophilia: elevating slaughter and martyrdom to theater, symbolism, and modus operandi. The Islamist version is similarly obsessed. . . . Adoring and serving death provides the movement with its fundamental rationale. . . .
>
> In essence this fetishizing of death defines itself against secular, Western, Enlightenment assertions of life.

"Whatever truce the president imagined, it's over," Marcus said, breaking the silence and putting away his phone. "We're at war, and it's time we got back on offense."

"Amen," Dell said as Annie and several others reentered the room, all color drained from their faces.

"I need one thing," Marcus said.

"Name it," Dell said.

"I can't go into battle without knowing my family is safe," he replied. "I'd like to bring my mom, my two sisters, and their families to Washington and house them on a military base here in the city, preferably Bolling."

Joint Base Anacostia-Bolling—previously known for decades as Bolling Air Force Base, but forever pronounced "bowling"—served as the headquarters of the Defense Intelligence Agency as well as the base for Marine One and the fleet of other helicopters used by the president, the VP, and senior government officials. Bolling was a highly secure facility set on 905 acres, located just across the Potomac River in southeast D.C.

"Will they come?" Dell asked.

"They will now," Marcus replied.

"Then do it," Dell said. "Come to think of it, I want you and the rest of the team there too. And you, Annie. I'll relocate there as well for the time being. We've got to get on a war footing. There's no way we can stay in our private homes with this kind of threat out there, though I suspect we'll all actually be spending most nights here for the foreseeable future."

Everyone agreed, and Dell told Marcus to make arrangements for his mom and sisters to come right away.

Then she turned to Annie. "Call Pete and tell him to bring the team back here immediately. In the meantime, take over my old office next door. There's already a foldaway cot in there. But I'll get fresh linens sent up right away. Let me show you around."

"Thanks," Annie said as she followed Martha into the deputy director's office.

Marcus headed down the hall to set up shop in the suite of five offices, a dozen cubicles, a conference room, a SCIF—secure compartment information facility—and a kitchen for his team's own private use.

Once Marcus and Annie were taken care of, Dell returned to her office and worked the phones, stepping up satellite coverage of Yemen and checking with the head of the NSA to see if the ransom money had been moved out of the bank in Zurich where Treasury had wired it. Not yet, she was told, but they were monitoring it closely.

Next she participated in a secure videoconference with NSC principals. Hernandez explained that he'd just called the families to express his condolences and vow to bring down Kairos once and for all. He said he planned to address the nation that evening and call for another National Day of Prayer for the following day. He would set the example, he said, by attending Mass first thing in the morning.

Dell was ashamed that she didn't have any new leads to give the president, any hope to provide for her colleagues. She was struck, however, by the reports Whitney, Foster, and McDermott shared of the wave of phone calls, emails, and cables coming in from members of Congress on both sides of the aisle, from allies, and even from some unaligned nations. And they were offering more than sympathy. Outraged, they were offering any assistance they could to end the Kairos reign of terror.

Something profound was underway. The geopolitical ground was shifting beneath their feet. The question was, how could she marshal it and use it to America's advantage?

MONUMENT, COLORADO

Marjorie Ryker was pulling into her driveway when her cell phone buzzed.

Assuming it was one of her daughters, each of whom checked in on her once a day, she put the car in park and fumbled through her purse for the phone. "Can I call you back, honey?" she said. "I just need to get these groceries inside."

"Marj, it's me."

Marjorie recognized the lovely Southern drawl instantly. She'd known Maya and Carter Emerson ever since Marcus and Elena had moved to Washington and begun attending Lincoln Park Baptist Church, where Carter had been senior pastor. They'd been through dark times together. The Emersons had taken Marcus and Elena through more than a year of counseling when their marriage was on the rocks. Carter had preached the eulogy at the memorial service for Elena and Lars. Marjorie had attended the service for Carter after his murder by Kairos terrorists. Over the years, Marjorie and Maya had grown close. They called each other often to swap stories, share Scriptures, and pray together. Over the last several weeks when Marcus had been taken hostage in Lebanon, they'd called several times a day. Still, Marjorie was surprised to hear from her old friend so soon after they'd been together at the White House.

"Maya, what a pleasant surprise. I thought you were Marta or Nicole."

"Have you talked to Marcus?" Maya said with no pleasantries.

"Not today. Why?"

"You haven't seen the news?"

"No, I've been doing errands this afternoon."

"But you're home now?"

"Yes, I just pulled in. What is it, Maya? What's wrong?"

"Go inside, turn on the TV, and then call Marcus and—"

Suddenly they were disconnected, but Marjorie didn't take the time to call Maya back. Nor did she grab her groceries. Instead, she raced into the house and flipped on the TV. Sickened by the ghastly video, she turned off the TV just as quickly and called Marcus's mobile number. As usual, she got voice mail. She left him a message, then got down on her knees and began to pray for him, for the families of those women, and for the country.

Her phone rang again. Opening her eyes, she noticed her caller ID said, "UNKNOWN NUMBER." Her first instinct was to let it go to voice mail, but something prompted her to take the call.

"Mom, it's me."

"Marcus? I just tried to call you."

"Sorry, my cell phone doesn't work here at Langley."

"Langley? I thought you were fired."

"I was, but I've been exonerated and reinstated," Marcus replied. "It's a long story. I'll tell you later. Are you okay? Are you safe?"

"Yes, yes, I just walked in the door. Maya called and told me to turn on the TV."

"So you've seen what's happening?"

"It's so horrible, Marcus. I'm physically ill."

"So am I, Mom. That's why I need you to listen."

"Okay. What is it?"

"I need you to get in your car and leave immediately."

"Why? Where?"

"Head directly to the airport, but to the private aviation terminal."

"What's going on, Marcus?"

"A credible threat has been made to my life," he told her. "I can't tell you the details now. But given what's happened to those three women, I'm worried the people who are after me could come for you, too. I'm going to call Marta and Nicole as well. You all need to come right away."

He explained that FBI agents would escort them to D.C., that housing was being arranged for them in secure facilities, and that technically he would be staying there too, as would Annie, though they were likely to be at Langley most nights.

"It's really that serious?"

"It is, Mom—now head to the airport. Don't pack. Don't bring anything. Get on the plane and I'll see you soon."

HANGAR NUMBER NINE, JOINT BASE ANDREWS

Noah Daniels had no idea how many cups of coffee he'd downed.

Operating on barely four hours of sleep, he poured himself another—black, no sugar—took several sips, then went back to work. Gone were the jet planes and helicopters normally housed in this mammoth facility. Instead, strewn across the concrete floor was every burnt, charred, gnarled, and twisted fragment the SEAL team had brought back from Libya.

Strewn was not, perhaps, the right word. The items were all organized in square grids, marked by duct tape on the floor, according to where they had been found in the ruins of the compound near Ghat.

The pace, though excruciatingly slow, was finally picking up now that he was no longer alone. At Dell's direction, Noah had a hand-selected team. Some were specialists from the CIA's Directorate of Science and Technology. Others were members of the FBI's Evidence Response Team Unit. All of them were Noah's friends, and having just seen the Kairos video, they all understood the stakes.

Walking over to grid 24, Noah donned a fresh pair of latex gloves, knelt, pulled a pair of tweezers from his pocket, and began to pick through the wreckage. The first item was the remains of a wristwatch. Half the leather strap was missing. The other half was burnt to a crisp. What was left of the metal buckle was partially melted. The plastic case over the dial was cracked and splattered with dried blood. But to Noah's astonishment, it was still ticking. Noah checked his own watch, calculated for the difference in time zones from Maryland to Libya, and realized this thing was keeping perfect time.

He found the mangled remains of a Kalashnikov, dusted it off with a makeup brush, and identified a serial number. Snatching his phone, he took a snapshot and texted it to a colleague back at Langley, along with the grid number, requesting it be run through the Agency's database to find out where it had been made, where it had been sold, and to whom. He had little expectation that the search would reveal anything important. But every lead had to be followed, however seemingly insignificant.

To Noah's shock, Marcus Ryker entered the hangar just before 11 p.m.

"Whoa, hey, what are you doing here, boss?" Noah said, standing upright. "I thought . . ."

"No one told you?" Marcus asked.

"Told me what?"

"That I've been totally cleared."

"Seriously? That's great."

"Did you know that Stephens resigned or that Dell is the new director? Or that Annie is the new deputy director?"

"What? No. Why? How?" Noah stammered.

Marcus lowered his voice and briefly explained.

"Wow, well, welcome back," Noah said with a weary smile.

"It's good to be back," Marcus replied. "How's all this going?"

"Honestly? Slow and frustrating. Is that why you came all the way out here, just to check up on me?" Noah, fatigued as he felt, was touched.

"Well, no," Marcus conceded. "My mom, my sisters, their husbands, and all their kids are about to land in a few minutes."

"Here?"

"Yeah, we're putting them at Bolling for safekeeping. Actually, we're all moving there. You, too, when you're done here."

"Sounds good," Noah said.

"I hear you found Abu Nakba's satphone."

"We did, and I'm glad because like everything else you see around here, it certainly vindicates you. That said, it hasn't provided much else, I'm afraid."

"You couldn't pull anything useful off it?"

"Sadly, no—but don't worry. We remain on the hunt."

"I know. And I'm grateful, buddy."

Noah nodded, then turned and went back to work.

Marcus headed to the flight line.

Twenty minutes later, a Gulfstream V landed and taxied to a nearby hangar.

Marcus met his family on the tarmac. He was about to apologize to them for turning their lives upside down. But the looks in their eyes told him it wasn't necessary. They had seen the video, or clips of it anyway—the adults, at least—and it was clear they understood what Marcus was demanding was for their own good. They didn't say as much, but the intensity with which they all hugged him told him everything he needed to know.

MONTERREY, MEXICO

Tariq Youssef grabbed the phone off the nightstand beside him.

Rolling out of bed, he stepped out onto the veranda and took the call.

"*Aló, José?*" came the voice at the other end.

"*Sí, señor?*" Youssef replied.

"*Todo bien.*"

"*Todo bien?*"

"*Sí.*"

And with that, the line went dead.

Youssef stared out over the lush green mountains and forest spread out before him in every direction thinking it was too bad to have to leave this place so soon. Still, he breathed a sigh of relief. Zaid Farooq and his cell had made it to Miami.

Now it was his turn.

He roused his men and made sure they all had something to eat and plenty of water. Then he insisted they wipe the villa down one more time to leave no trace of their ever having been there. When they were finished, he fired up the truck and they were off.

When they reached the ranch not far from Hacienda San José de Miravalle, Youssef was furious to learn that the cattle truck they would be traveling in would be full. He told the young driver this was unacceptable. His colleagues had not had to endure such unpleasantries on the previous trip, and for him and his men to do so would be an insult.

The boy had no answer. He had his orders. There was nothing he could do. He suggested Youssef call his boss and have it out with him, then offered to let Youssef make the call in the office in the main ranch house rather than in the barn for privacy.

Youssef accepted the offer, called his contact, and argued heatedly that he was paying a fortune for this run, twice the normal rate. He and his men should not have to lie in a bed of manure, in the back of a truck packed with cattle, that stank to high heaven. But the more he yelled and cursed over the phone, the less headway he was making. The contact already had his money. The night was already wasting away. The tunnel was getting more humid by the hour. Plus, there were other paying clients who wanted to move their people and cargo through the tunnel, as well. It was now or never, he was told, and then the contact hung up on him.

Youssef was livid but he was also a realist. There was nothing more to be done. He stepped outside the ranch office, rejoined his men in the barn, told them it was time to go and that no grumbling would be permitted. Dutifully, the six of them loaded their crates and themselves on the floor of the last several stalls. The driver covered them with blankets and bales of hay, then filled the rest of the stalls with a head of cattle each. A moment later, Youssef heard the truck's engine roar to life, and they were moving. It was all he could do to suppress his gag reflex. But in the darkness, under the cover of the scratchy wool blankets, he put in his earbuds, found a playlist of classical Arabic music on his phone, and cranked up the volume.

He had already come to terms with the likelihood that he would be martyred in this operation, that he would not see his daughters get married, never hold his grandchildren. It was a steep price, but it was one he had decided he was willing to pay. Becoming a *shahid* while waging jihad against the infidels was the only way to guarantee eternal life for himself and his family. He would shed his own blood so that his wives and daughters would never have to fear burning in the fires of hell. And he would still see his children and grandchildren, of course. They would spend eternity together in paradise. What greater gift, what richer inheritance, could a father bequeath to those he loved the most?

77

THE VATICAN—18 MAY

"Get me the president," Pope Pius XIII said as he watched the Mass on TV.

Commander Gianetti was surprised. "Which one?" the security chief asked.

"Hernandez, of course."

"But why, Your Holiness?"

"He's a Roman Catholic. He's calling his nation to prayer. And I must stand with him in this terrible hour."

"You mean at the White House—a meeting, a photo op—and then right back here to the Vatican," Gianetti said, more a suggestion than a question.

"No, I want to go ahead with the tour."

"Your Holiness, with respect, that is not wise."

"We walk by faith, Commander, not by sight. At least I do. Your eyes I want open and vigilant, at every moment, especially while mine are closed in prayer."

Gianetti continued to protest, but his warnings fell on deaf ears.

Ten minutes later, he reluctantly told the old man to pick up the phone.

"Hello? Is someone there?" the pope asked.

"Your Holiness?" came a woman's voice on the other end of the line.

"Yes, it is I."

"What an honor. Please hold for the president."

A moment later, Hernandez came on the line. "Your Holiness, thank you so much for the call."

"I was just watching you on television. You are handling the crisis well."

"Thank you, but which one?" Hernandez demurred.

"All of them, my son. I was touched that you began this day by attending Mass. You are setting a good example."

"I hope so, but honestly, it was more to fortify my soul than for any kind of example."

"You are walking through the valley of the shadow of evil, Mr. President. But you shall fear no evil."

"You are kind to call with so much else on your plate."

"This is more than a condolence call, though I plan to call each of the families, if you will permit me."

"I think they would appreciate the gesture. My staff will get you their numbers."

"I also want to come to the States next month, to see you, to pray with you, to congratulate you, to thank you for all that you and your predecessor have done for the cause of peace. And I want to lead Mass in all four cities, as planned."

Hernandez was silent for a moment, as if taken aback. "It would be a personal honor for the First Lady and me to host you, but I must caution you that now may not be the best time. The security environment going forward may not be conducive to such a high-profile visit."

"I am not afraid, Mr. President. The Good Shepherd goes before me. He sets a table in the presence of my enemies."

"That's exactly what I'm afraid of, Your Holiness," Hernandez quipped, but the pope did not laugh, so Hernandez changed his tone. "You're really serious? You want to come here, with all that is taking place, despite the advice I am certain you are receiving from your security staff and the rest of your inner circle?"

"What was it that John A. Shedd once remarked? '*A ship in harbor is safe, but that is not what ships are built for.*'"

"True," Hernandez said. "But wasn't he a Presbyterian?"

Now the pontiff did chuckle. "No one's perfect," he said.

CIA HEADQUARTERS

Martha Dell had worked through the night.

She had finished calling all the spy chiefs in the Middle East. Now she was working her way through the NATO allies.

One by one, she assured them that Carlos Hernandez was firmly in control of the U.S. government. She also made it clear that the Libyan compound had, in fact, been the Kairos HQ, answered any questions they had, and informed them that Marcus had been vindicated, exonerated, and promoted.

This cleared the way for Marcus to begin working the phones himself. What's more, his team had arrived, and Marcus welcomed them in his new conference room.

"Guys, I want to thank each of you for believing in me—and Jenny—when almost everyone else cut us loose," he began. "I can't tell you how much that has meant to me. To both of us. And I know how defeated and exhausted you feel right now, because I'm feeling the same way. It seems like no matter how hard we work, Abu Nakba is always three steps ahead of us. We weren't wrong about the Libyan compound. But nor did we get him. We didn't bomb a special-needs school. But we were condemned for doing so. We haven't lied to the nation or the world about how dangerous Kairos is. We haven't exaggerated the threat. But we've been treated like pariahs. And I know how much it saps your strength and makes it seem like what we're doing doesn't matter and isn't appreciated. But that kind of thinking is not only wrong, it's poison. Don't go there. Stay focused."

Marcus paused for a moment and scanned the room. He could see his message hitting home, even in the younger support staff who were new to his unit and only knew him by reputation, for good or ill.

"I'm sickened that we couldn't find and weren't able to rescue these girls in time," he continued. "And candidly I'm sickened by how the previous director ran this organization. But he's gone. It's a new day. I have the utmost admiration for Dr. Dell and the highest confidence that things are going to be different on her watch. She's cut from a very different bolt of cloth, and I know she's going to impress you, as she has me. What's more, I think you're going to come to love our new deputy director, Annie Stewart, as much as I do."

There was a slight murmur in the room.

"Okay, maybe not as much as me, but that's a different story," he said with a smile, lightening the mood slightly. "Listen, she's a consummate professional. Worked on Senator Dayton's staff for the past fifteen years. Worked on the Senate Intel Committee for more than a decade. She's played an indispensable role in numerous operations that I've been involved with in recent years. So I'm asking you to give her and Dr. Dell everything you've got. Understood?"

Everyone did.

"Good. Now, one more thing," Marcus added, turning to Jenny. "I want to say a very special thank-you to my friend and colleague Agent Morris. We have quite a history together. We don't always see eye to eye. And I appreciate that about her. I also appreciate her professionalism. I trust her judgment. And I'm deeply grateful for her loyalty. No one on this team has impressed me more, and there's no one I'd rather have as my deputy to hunt down Abu Nakba and the Troika than her. Except, of course, Pete, who is abandoning us in our darkest hour. But again, that's probably a different speech for a different time."

A ripple of laughter moved through the room as Pete shook his head in mock surrender but for whatever reason chose not to shoot back. Marcus assigned Jenny the large office directly next to his. He assigned the other three smaller offices to Geoff Stone, Donny Callaghan, and Noah Daniels, though for the moment Noah was still at Andrews and wasn't expected back anytime soon. Since Pete was only with them for a few more weeks, Marcus asked him to work out of one of the cubicles with the rest of the support staff, whom he now met and greeted for the first time.

There wasn't much more to say. They all knew what they had to do, and Marcus urged them to settle in and get back at it. They had terrorists to track and target, and the clock was ticking.

"Do you have a minute?" Pete asked when the meeting was adjourned.

"Of course," Marcus said, heading to his office. "But you know I'm just kidding you. Mostly."

"Yeah, but that's what I want to talk to you about," Pete said as he followed Marcus into the spacious corner office and closed the door behind them.

"What's up?"

"That video," Pete replied. "I've never . . ."

Pete couldn't finish his sentence. He suddenly became more emotional than Marcus ever remembered.

"Look," Pete said finally, gathering himself. "Would you be open to me staying on, you know, at least until we've got Abu Nakba's head on a platter?"

"Seriously?"

"Seriously," Pete assured him. "I'd never be able to live with myself if I walked away now."

"And you're not just saying this because I assigned you a cubicle?" Marcus said with a slight smile.

"Maybe a little."

"Welcome back," Marcus said, giving his old friend a bear hug.

"It's good to be back."

"Take the office I just gave Noah. I'll sort him out later."

"Sounds good."

Just then there was a knock on the door. It was Geoff Stone.

"You guys should see this," he said when Pete opened the door.

They stepped back into the conference room, where everyone was watching a breaking news bulletin from the BBC. The Vatican had just confirmed that the papal visit to the United States was still on.

Marcus tensed. He said nothing to the others but caught Jenny's eye and knew she felt the same way.

The timing could not be worse. This was an invitation to disaster.

HANGAR NUMBER NINE, JOINT BASE ANDREWS—19 MAY

Noah opened his eyes and stared up at the cavernous ceiling.

He was lying on a cot, stripped down to his boxer shorts and covered with sweat. The air-conditioning unit had apparently blown a fuse, and the temperature inside the hangar had spiked during the day. Having no idea what time it was, but no longer able to sleep in this makeshift blast furnace, Noah forced himself to his feet, pulled on his jeans and T-shirt, then went back to the men's room to brush his teeth and plunge his head into a sink full of cold water. He toweled off, went to the kitchen, made himself another cup of coffee, snagged the last piece of stale coffee cake left in a box on the counter, and headed back out to the floor and powered up the portable lights positioned at grid 34.

No one else was awake. He had the whole place to himself. He shrugged, donned a fresh pair of latex gloves, squatted down, and got back to work. Eyeing a new pile of garbage—most of it wholly unuseful and thus arguably not worthy of having been transported halfway around the world—Noah pulled out a walkie-talkie. It was covered in soot but in decent shape overall.

He examined it, even pulled it apart, but found nothing of value. So he set it aside and kept hunting.

At first, the remains of a DVD player struck him as promising. But upon closer examination, he realized that it had been so melted by the missile-induced fires that even if there had been a DVD inside the device, and even if he could pry it out, it would be entirely unviewable. On he went, poring over a twisted pair of glasses, a scorched ammunition belt, and the remains of several wallets so badly burnt that none of the IDs, bills, or credit cards inside were legible.

Two hours later, soaked with sweat, Noah found a large, burnt steel box. He brushed off the soot and ash and used a bolt cutter to snap off the padlock. Inside, he found stacks of cash in four currencies—Iranian rials, Russian rubles, Turkish lira, and piles of euros, but curiously no U.S. cash of any denomination. As Noah methodically counted all of it, the overnight shift arrived. One of the FBI's supervisory agents came over and helped him finish counting the money and put the currencies in separate evidence bags, marking and photographing everything and handing it all off to the appropriate team members. All told, the funds added up to more than a quarter of a million dollars. What did not make sense—not to Noah or the FBI agent, at least—was why Kairos had so much cash on hand and why more than two-thirds of it was in Russian, Iranian, and Turkish currencies.

Mopping his brow, ready for a break—and more importantly, a shower—Noah spotted under another pile of debris what looked like the remains of a computer. He pulled it out and found it was, in fact, a laptop. The problem was it was half-melted and, thus, fused shut. Rifling through a box of tools, he found a screwdriver and began trying to force the laptop open like an oyster. After repeated failed attempts, he gave up and walked it over to a metal cutting saw stationed on a large worktable not far from the kitchen. He donned protective eyewear and thick work gloves, then proceeded to slice into the laptop until he could pry what was once its cover from the motherboard.

On the left side was what remained of the cooling fan. Toward the front he found the optical drive connector and two speakers. Off to the right he was able to identify the power jack. And then Noah smiled, for there it was, the pearl for which he had been diving—the RAM memory cards.

Newly inspired, he forgot all about the shower.

SOMEWHERE IN YEMEN—20 MAY

Abu Nakba woke before dawn.

Dressing himself in his usual robe, he took his cane and hobbled down the stairways of the house he had been given for the duration of his stay. His knees ached. So did his back. And he was winded by the time he reached the living room. Nevertheless, he opened the front door and made his way—slowly and with a great deal of discomfort—to the small mosque across the street. As he did, the muezzin began the call to prayer.

The founder and spiritual father of Kairos entered the simple stone structure, performed his ablutions, then removed his sandals, padded his way into the sanctuary, and bowed his face toward Mecca in prayer. When he was finished, he reversed the process and eventually got himself back to the house. He made himself a small pot of tea and sat down at the kitchen table before putting on his reading glasses. Opening his laptop, he entered various passwords, clearing several levels of security, until he found the latest batch of encrypted messages from operatives around the world. Ignoring most for now, he zeroed in on the two most important to him.

The first was from Tariq Youssef.

The Kairos security chief's scouting report was lengthy—nearly nineteen pages, including photos and maps. Abu Nakba read every word on every page. He watched every video and scoured every map. He could not help but smile, however faintly, with a sense of pride at his man's thoroughness and attention to detail, yet what interested him most was the simple conclusion.

NRG Stadium in Houston is an attractive target.

It can hold up to 72,220 people. Local media anticipate a full crowd.

The stadium has a retractable roof, though it is rarely open and will likely be closed due to the forecast heat during the pope's visit.

My team and I have no doubt our rockets will easily penetrate the translucent fabric roof.

Further, we believe the stadium's unique design will amplify the shock waves of our explosives and trap most of the gas and radiation of our weapons, killing or at least maiming every single person inside.

Downsides include the fact that there are not any high-rise buildings near the stadium. This means we would not have the ability to shoot from a high angle down at the stadium's roof. There is the risk, therefore, that we could misjudge some of our fire, sending our rockets over the stadium and into the surrounding parking lots rather than into the heart of the facility.

However, George Bush Intercontinental Airport is only twenty-two miles north of the stadium.

Since President Hernandez will not be attending, it is unlikely that antiaircraft missiles will be positioned around the stadium during the event.

It is likely, however, that a number of police helicopters will be patrolling the airspace near the facility, and a UH-60 Black Hawk helicopter and H125 A-Star helicopter from U.S. Customs and Border Protection will be on hand as well. Whether they will be armed with live rockets or missiles is unknown at this point.

Nevertheless, we conclude that should you authorize the airborne option, we can still secure a jet and fly it into the stadium. This would likely give us the highest chance of maximizing the death of the pope and most, if not all, of those attending the Mass.

There was something very attractive about the idea of launching a series of major attacks in the heart of one of America's "red states," the Libyan mused. Was it not Republican presidents who had initiated the most wars and "counterterrorism operations" in the Muslim world? Afghanistan. Iraq. And his home countries of Libya and Palestine. To name just a few. And had it not been a Republican—Andrew Clarke—who had thwarted Tehran's operation to acquire nuclear warheads from the North Koreans? Had it not been Clarke and his operatives who had killed his plot to blow up the so-called "peace summit" in Jerusalem? And interfered with his plans in Lebanon?

Allah had already punished Clarke through his massive and almost certainly lethal stroke, and for this he was to be praised. But was there not so much more to avenge?

Intrigued and heartened by the prospects in Houston, Abu Nakba turned to the report from Zaid Farooq.

Might the Miami option offer more?

Once again, Abu Nakba devoured every word.

Watched every video. Scoured every map and photo. He found himself impressed by the report's length, breadth, and depth.

Sipping his tea, he focused on the report's conclusion.

> Miami's Hard Rock Stadium is a good target, though not ideal.
>
> Of the various sites we are assessing, it is the smallest. Originally, it was built to hold up to 75,000 people. Over the years, it has been modified a number of times. Local media reports indicate that with the staging being planned, event capacity will be only 64,000.
>
> On the positive side, the stadium is an iconic American landmark. It is the home of the NFL franchise known as the Miami Dolphins. It has hosted six Super Bowls (football), two World Series (baseball), and numerous other major sporting events.
>
> Also on the positive side: the roof is open, and our rockets would have nothing to penetrate.

> However, there are four spires on the roof, one in each corner. If we do not fire accurately, some of our rockets could hit one or more of the spires, potentially knocking them off course and reducing or eliminating their lethal impact.
>
> It should be noted that there are no skyscrapers or high-rise apartments or office buildings anywhere near the stadium. While my men have a great deal of experience with these kinds of rockets, you should be aware that they would not be able to shoot down into the stadium. While I assess the risk as minimal, it is possible the team could overshoot the stadium with some of the rockets, reducing the death toll inside an already-smaller facility with fewer attendees than other cities.
>
> Regarding the airborne option, the stadium is only eleven miles from Miami International Airport.
>
> Thus far, there have been no reports of plans to shut down the airspace over the event, particularly since President Hernandez and the First Lady are not expected to attend.
>
> We do not believe that antiaircraft missiles will be set up to protect the stadium, though we expect federal, state, and local law enforcement helicopters to be in the air well before and during the event. Whether any of them would be armed with munitions capable of taking down the Dassault Falcon 900LX that the IRGC has acquired for us is not known, but we deem this unlikely.

Abu Nakba took another sip of tea as he watched drone footage and other video Farooq and his team had taken of the stadium and its surroundings. He still believed that outside of attacks on the White House and the Capitol Building—far and away his preferred targets—Yankee Stadium was the best available option. New York City was the media capital of America and arguably the world. Al Qaeda had taken out the Twin Towers because they lay at the center of America's most populated, wealthy, and wicked city, the American Babylon, the beating heart of the Great Satan. Should not Kairos strike there, too?

Not according to General Entezam.

The IRGC commander was adamant that security in the so-called "Big Apple"—however rotten to its core—would be so tight that the first team would never be able to get the first shot off. Moreover, Abu Nakba had to admit that there simply was no airborne option in and around the New York–New Jersey region. Because of the annual opening of the U.N. General Assembly each September, among other events, federal, state, and local authorities had too many years of experience protecting high-level dignitaries in and around Manhattan. Keeping the pope safe would not be difficult for the New York authorities.

The old man finished his tea. He was certainly captivated by both reports. On balance, he found himself leaning somewhat toward Miami. But what about Chicago? They still had some time. There was still a window—however brief—to send some of his men to the Windy City, and he wondered if he should take the risk to see if the winds there might actually be blowing in Kairos's favor.

LANGLEY, VIRGINIA

Marcus woke up in a sleeping bag on the floor of his office.

He glanced at his watch and saw it was 5 a.m. He'd only gotten three hours of shut-eye, and that was all he was going to get. But there was no point in complaining. Everyone else on his team was keeping the same hours. So were Dell and Annie, though they had foldaway cots in their offices, a luxury the rest of them didn't have.

He closed the blinds in his office and changed, grateful to Pete for having sent some guys over to his apartment to grab a bunch of clothes and some toiletries. Stepping out to the men's room, he washed up and brushed his teeth but didn't shave. He welcomed any growth that could cover up what Kairos had done to his face in Lebanon.

When he reached the kitchen, planning to make a pot of coffee, industrial strength, he found Jenny had beaten him to it.

"Bless you," he said as she handed him a mug.

"Have you checked your messages yet?" she asked.

"No, why?"

"Noah called you about twenty minutes ago. When he didn't get you, he called me. He's on his way."

"What's he got?"

"He didn't want to say on an open line."

By 5:30 a.m., the senior staff gathered in the conference room. The support staff wouldn't be in for another hour.

Noah looked terrible. His shirt was wrinkled and stained. He hadn't had a haircut in weeks. The dark circles under his eyes worried Marcus most. Nevertheless, Noah was in high spirits.

"We have a lead," he began, almost breathless. "Five, actually."

Powering up the audio-visual system, Noah patched in his Agency laptop and uploaded a file. An instant later, images of digital memos in Arabic flashed on the plasma screens.

"I found a computer belonging to Zaid Farooq in the mountains of garbage that the SEALs brought back from Libya," Noah explained.

"The Kairos intelligence chief?" Jenny asked. "Part of the Troika?"

"That's the one," Noah confirmed. "Whether he was killed in the strike remains to be seen. But regardless, this computer was badly damaged. Partially melted, even. Still, I was able to pull some fragments of files and even some emails. The most recent stuff I could find dates back almost six months, so this was probably not Farooq's current computer. In fact, it's an older model from Dell that—"

"TMI, Noah," Marcus said.

"Right, sorry. Anyway, so this document, the one here on the screen, describes five Kairos training bases spread out across Yemen."

New images flashed on the screen.

"These emails describe significant activity at three of the camps, including upcoming travel plans by Badr Hassan al-Ruzami."

"When were they sent?" Marcus asked.

"Some last July. Others in August. Another in October."

"So the camps could all be abandoned by now," Callaghan said.

"Or this could just be more of the Libyan's diversions," Pete said, "breadcrumbs they hope we'll find to lead us on not one wild-goose chase but five."

Marcus ignored the cynics. "Jenny, get Prince Abdullah on the line at Saudi GID. Let's see what they know about these locations. Pete, talk to NSA, and, Geoff, talk to DIA. Let's pull together any satellite imaging the U.S. government has on this. And, Donny, wake up your buddies at the Pentagon. I want drones up over each of these sites by noon."

Everyone sprang into action.

Then Marcus said to Noah, "Walk with me."

He led the younger man to the kitchen and poured him a fresh CIA mug of coffee. "Good work."

"Thanks."

"Now go take a nap on the floor in my office. I've got a new sleeping bag in there and a great down pillow."

"I can't. I need to get back to Andrews. There's more out there. I can feel it."

"No, you need to sleep. That's not a request. It's an order. When you wake up, we'll get you a good hot meal and then you can go back. Got it?"

"Yes, sir," Noah said, visibly grateful despite his protests.

When Noah had turned off the lights in Marcus's office, Marcus went back into the conference room. Jenny already had Prince Abdullah on the line.

"So glad to hear you've been cleared, *habibi*," the prince began, addressing Marcus, "and you, too, *habibti*," he added for Jenny. "You Americans have a crazy system of government. I don't know how you get anything useful done over there. You really would do well to ditch democracy and establish a kingdom."

"Been there, done that," Marcus replied. "Didn't work so well for us. But listen, Jenny and I might have something, and we need your help."

At 7 a.m., Martha Dell met with her senior managers in her office.

Marcus nodded to Annie as they took their seats, each a bit unsure how to interact now that they were working together. Worse, Annie outranked Marcus, a point that she had not yet ribbed him about, but he had no doubt she would soon.

Dell apologized that their meeting would have to be brief. She was supposed to deliver the PDB—*The President's Daily Brief*, a summary of the most pertinent overnight intelligence—to Hernandez and Whitney at nine. "Agent Ryker, you have news?"

Marcus nodded and walked them through what he'd learned from Noah and what he'd requested of the Pentagon, the other U.S. intelligence agencies, and the Saudis. Everyone agreed it was promising, but Annie went further.

"You and your team should be on a plane, not here," she said, the urgency in her voice surprising to everyone, Marcus included.

"To Yemen?" Marcus asked.

"No, to Riyadh," Annie said.

"Why? We don't know anything yet—nothing solid," he protested.

"But in six or eight hours you will," she pushed back. "Why wait? Get in the air. Martha and I can light a fire under everyone here. By the time you get to Saudi Arabia, you may have an actionable lead. And isn't time of the essence? Don't we all fear that if the White House had ordered the strike in Libya earlier, we might have gotten Abu Nakba?"

Marcus considered that for a moment, then turned to Dell. "The woman has a point," he said.

"She does," Dell agreed. "How fast can you guys deploy?"

"As soon as we're done here," Marcus said.

"Then go now," Dell ordered. "Gather your team and head straight to Andrews. I'll have vehicles waiting downstairs in fifteen minutes and a G5 warming up on the tarmac with all the equipment you'll need."

"You sure?" Marcus said, as much to Annie as to Dell.

Both women nodded and wished him well, as did the rest of the senior staff.

"Can I borrow her for just a moment?" Marcus asked Dell, glancing at Annie.

Dell nodded. "Make it quick. I'll call Jenny and get the team moving."

Marcus thanked her, then took Annie into the hallway and pulled her into the director's conference room and shut the door behind him. "You know how crazy this is?" he asked, taking her hands, standing so close to her he could feel her warm breath on his neck. "Not very many days ago, you were on your way out the door and wanted me to go too. Now you're the deputy director of the freaking CIA and dispatching me to Saudi Arabia and almost certainly to Yemen."

"I know," she said. "But what choice do we have? You know Kairos isn't going to stop at those three girls. We can't ever let that happen again."

"I love you, Annie Stewart," Marcus suddenly blurted out, as surprised at himself as she was, judging by the look in her beautiful green eyes.

"You do?"

"Yes."

"Well, I love you, Marcus Ryker. So don't get yourself killed out there, or I'll never forgive you."

"Annie?"

"Yes."

"Would it be okay if I kissed you right now?"

"It's about time you asked."

But just then Jenny burst into the room. "The plane is ready," she told him. "We need to go now."

JEDDAH, SAUDI ARABIA—21 MAY

The G5 touched down at King Abdulaziz International Airport at 4:19 a.m.

Once they had taxied into an unmarked hangar and the doors were shut, Marcus and his team emerged from the plane and were greeted by officials from the GID. Then they were hustled into two armor-plated black Mercedes SUVs and whisked across the airfield to a squat, nondescript office building not far from the maintenance hangars. In short order, they were led inside the air-conditioned facility to a windowless but beautifully appointed dining room, where they were greeted by Prince Abdullah bin Rashid, the chief of the kingdom's General Intelligence Directorate.

"Welcome, *habibi,* it is an honor to see you again," the prince said to Marcus, embracing him and giving him a kiss on both cheeks. "Welcome to all of you. Please, sit down."

The table was set for a meal with a crisp white linen tablecloth, fine china, and golden goblets. At each seat was a nameplate. Stewards in white gloves led the team members to their assigned places. The prince sat at the head of the table with Marcus immediately to his right, Jenny to Marcus's right. They were all served hot mint tea, followed by a small cup of Arabic coffee. Then the stewards stepped out of the room, and the prince spoke again.

"His Majesty the king and His Royal Highness the crown prince both wanted me to express to you their personal greetings, as well as their condolences," he began. "We are still reeling from the news of President Clarke's sudden affliction. The crown prince has taken it especially hard, having just been with the president at the White House, where he seemed so vigorous and full of joy and on top of the world."

"It has been a shock to us all," Marcus agreed. "Please thank His Majesty and His Royal Highness for their kindness and concern."

The spy chief then added the royal family's condolences, and his own, for the deaths of the three American women in Yemen. It had been a week of whiplashing emotions, he noted. Marcus and his team agreed.

At this, the doors to the intimate dining room reopened, and platters of eggs and pastries and bowls of yogurt and hummus and olives and much more were brought in and served. Marcus knew how things were done in the kingdom. Relationships came first and were fostered over meals, not intelligence briefings. The specifics would come, but they would not be front-loaded. Still, Marcus couldn't bear the thought of feasting when they should be hunting their prey.

"Your Highness, we're all grateful for your hospitality," he began. "But at the risk of offending you, we need to know everything you've learned since we were in the air."

"Anxious to get moving, are you?" the prince said.

"We are."

"Very well. Since you and I spoke last week, our intelligence teams have been tracking Kairos's possible allies. On Thursday, General Entezam of the IRGC flew from Tehran to Bandar Abbas, stayed for two or three hours, and then flew immediately back to Tehran. The next day we began hearing chatter that the price on your head had doubled."

"So it's possible Entezam met with Abu Nakba in Bandar Abbas," Marcus said.

The prince hesitated. "We have no hard evidence, but I think it's very possible. Unfortunately we also believe Nakba is no longer in Iran."

"Where do you think he went?" Marcus asked.

"It's likely he made his way into Yemen, to oversee the executions of the American women personally. So it is very good that you are here now. I suspect you know that I spoke several times to Director Dell while you were en route?"

"Yes."

"And that she told us it's going to take longer than she'd expected to retask one of your spy satellites to photograph the five camps that Agent Daniels has identified? And that she did not have any drones nearby that could provide coverage of those camps? And that she asked me to provide the drones until she could move more assets into the region?"

"Yes," Marcus said. "She called us about an hour ago. What she didn't say was whether you'd learned anything yet."

"As a matter of fact, we have," the prince said. "We've ruled out three of the camps. No one is there. They look like they may have been abandoned several months ago. Of the other two, both have activity, but only one has a courtyard and a flagpole."

"Seriously?" Marcus asked, his pulse quickening.

"The reason we never noticed it before is that the camp is in a very rugged section of mountains in northeastern Yemen. Not a place we've ever seen Houthi activity, much less Kairos. If it wasn't for Agent Daniels, I don't know if we would have ever noticed it."

"Do you have live images coming from your drone now?" Jenny asked.

"Sadly, no. The drone had been operating over Aden. We redirected it the moment Dr. Dell called me. But it was running low on fuel, so we had to bring it back. It should be here in about ten minutes. Then we'll top off her tanks and send her back out."

"How quickly can you get us there, Your Highness?" Marcus asked.

"You can leave right after breakfast," the prince replied. "I will order my team to make preparations and you can be on a helicopter to the southern seaport Jazan as soon as you are finished eating."

THE RED SEA

By noon, the team was finally steaming southward.

Marcus stood on deck, close to the bow, taking in the scene as a slight breeze blew from the east. Jenny, Pete, Geoff, Noah, and Donny Callaghan were down below, cleaning their weapons and triple-checking their gear. Two teams of Delta operators and a fleet of Black Hawk helicopters were on standby—one team in Riyadh, the other in Jeddah—ready to assist. Marcus felt they had a better chance of succeeding if they went in as a small, discreet ground team rather than roaring in by air with a huge show of force. It was a risky decision, but everyone agreed, including Donny Callaghan, the former SEAL Team Six commander.

Marcus watched as they slipped along the coastline of Eritrea on their starboard side, with Yemen on their port side. With the prince's help, they were traveling aboard an Iranian-flagged oil tanker. It was not, of course, owned or operated by Iran at all. Rather, it was a Saudi intelligence vessel, but it did give them a cover story for what they were about to do next.

Around 5 p.m., Marcus went up to the bridge and conferred with the captain. He confirmed they were right on schedule. Coming up on their left was Kamaran Island, Yemen's largest but sparsely populated island with barely two thousand residents.

"It's time," said the captain, a GID veteran.

Marcus thanked the man, returned to his team, and gave the signal. They lowered speedboats disguised as fishing vessels into the water. Then they loaded the boats with wooden crates of communications gear, RPGs, AK-47s, ammunition, and other light arms—all bearing Iranian markings in Farsi—then boarded the boats themselves. Last aboard were two young Saudi intelligence officers who would accompany them to shore before driving the boats back to the tanker.

Firing up the engines, they sped quickly around the stern of the tanker, heading for the leeward side of the island toward Al-Salif.

Located on the peninsula behind Kamaran, Al-Salif was a coastal fishing village in the northwest section of Yemen. There were fewer than seven thousand residents living there, and as they zipped through the choppy seas, salt water spraying in his face, Marcus prayed that his team would be able to avoid too many questions from any officials they came across.

As they rounded the tip of Kamaran, they could see Al-Salif's small port. They had discussed landing a bit northward, farther up the peninsula, where it was more sparsely populated. In the end, however, they had opted against it, believing their chances of coming across someone with a vehicle they could steal or commandeer, certainly of the kind and specs they needed, were better at the port.

The prince had insisted that they play the part of Iranian arms smugglers. Arrive in the port late in the day. Unannounced. Show the harbormaster false papers. Pay a small fee. And a large bribe. Break into a nearby garage or warehouse. Steal a vehicle or two. Hope that their generous supply of Iranian dinars was enough to get them out of Al-Salif and past the several Houthi checkpoints they would encounter as they headed inland. And pray they did not get caught. Such tradecraft had worked for decades. Marcus hoped it would serve them well now.

No matter how good Jenny's Arabic, Farsi, and Russian were, the prince warned them it was not going to be enough. He had assets inside the country who could assist them, people who could help them talk their way through checkpoints and run point on buying fuel, food, water, and whatever other supplies were needed. The problem was that the assets he trusted most were nowhere near Al-Salif just now. On such short notice, he'd had to turn to two other men who were younger and less experienced. But they would have to do.

Callaghan had recommended waiting until the veteran assets were in place. But Marcus had overruled him. Yes, there were serious risks of getting stopped and caught anywhere along the route. But there was a greater risk, he'd argued, that the targets they had identified would not be there if they waited. The prince agreed.

Docking was no problem. Nor was greasing the palms of the old man who stumbled out of the harbormaster's office to welcome them, an AK-47 dangling from his bony shoulders. The man was barely coherent, though Marcus was not certain if this was from fatigue or if the man was simply spaced-out from chewing *qat*, the Yemenite drug of choice. Either way, he posed little threat. He pocketed his payment, wandered back toward his office, and disappeared.

Marcus scanned the port in all directions and saw only a handful of people who appeared to be wrapping up a long day on the docks. No one seemed to be watching his team. Moving quickly, the team heaved the crates of weapons onshore, then signaled the two Saudis to hightail it back to the tanker. Marcus spotted a warehouse about a hundred meters from the docks and went over with Geoff to investigate. The warehouse's bay doors were padlocked, but Geoff pulled out a bolt cutter from his backpack while Marcus protected his flank.

Inside it was pitch-black. Marcus pulled out a flashlight and entered first, gun up and ready to fire. No guards were on duty, so he came back and helped Pete, Geoff, and Callaghan carry in the crates. Noah closed the door behind him and stood guard, while Jenny and Marcus proceeded to search the facility.

They found tire marks and oil stains on the floors. Vehicles were typically housed here. But there were none there now. Breaking into the office, they found hooks on the wall where keys usually hung, yet nothing was dangling from them this evening. Jenny went through the desk and the file cabinets, looking for anything useful. She found nothing and reported that to the group.

"All right, look, we're going to need to move deeper into town," Marcus said. "I say we ditch the crates. We can hide them behind some of those pallets over there. We'll move faster without them. Once we find some vehicles, we can come back."

A man stepped from the shadows. "Welcome to Yemen, Mr. Ryker."

AL-SALIF, YEMEN

Marcus whipped around, as did the others, their AK-47s at the ready.

"Don't shoot," said the man standing in the doorway, speaking English with a thick Arab accent.

"Who are you?" Jenny demanded in Arabic.

"Colonel Abdul-Malik al-Hakim, at your service," the man, who appeared to be roughly Marcus's age, replied in English. "I work for Prince Abdullah. He asked me to meet you here and make sure you had everything you needed."

Marcus was suspicious, having been told to expect a younger man. He asked a challenge phrase to see if the man was legit. When the man gave the right response, Marcus asked a second challenge question. Once again, the man nailed it. Marcus ordered Geoff to get the man's credentials. With every gun pointed at the colonel, Geoff retrieved his papers and tossed them to Jenny. She read them carefully, then nodded, returned the papers, and backed away.

"Is this really your man, Your Highness?" Marcus said into his whisper microphone, knowing that the prince was watching everything they did and said through the tiny camera mounted over his right ear. "Otherwise, it's not going to go well for this guy."

Marcus heard a hiss of static. They all did. Then the prince confirmed that this was, in fact, his man and to please not pump him full of lead. At this, Marcus lowered his weapon. Slowly, cautiously, everyone else did too.

"So you're not here to kill us?" Marcus asked.

"By no means," the colonel said, then asked permission to send a text to his men, not far away, with the vehicles. Moments later, two jeeps pulled up, mounted with .50-caliber machine guns.

"We have Houthi uniforms for you," the colonel explained. "You'll dress like us, then take the two jeeps. I'll drive in the lead vehicle with you. Two men in the back. The rest of your team will follow in the second jeep. Good?"

"Yes," Marcus said, finally beginning to breathe.

"Then let's pick up the pace. The sun will be going down soon."

Colonel Malik dismissed the two young drivers, and they ran off. Marcus and the others changed quickly. Then the colonel climbed behind the wheel of the lead jeep. Marcus rode shotgun. Jenny sat in the back, dressed as a man, ready to jump on the fifty if need be. Noah sat beside her, trying to get their comms connected to Langley. Behind them, Geoff drove. Pete served as his wingman. Callaghan had the back to himself, also ready to unleash the .50-caliber machine gun on any threat that presented itself.

They headed down the peninsula and soon reached a military checkpoint at the intersection of the coastal road and Highway 2. As the colonel slowed to a stop, he told the Americans to have their papers ready.

"What papers?" Marcus asked. "We came posing as gunrunners from Tehran, not Houthi rebels."

"Never mind," the Saudi said. "Too late."

It didn't matter. Of the five rebels manning the checkpoint, all but one were too occupied eating dinner to pay attention to the approaching vehicles. The fifth man waved the first jeep forward, took one glance at Abdul-Malik in his Houthi uniform, and waved him on. Marcus worried that Geoff's jeep would be stopped, but he too was waved past the checkpoint without issue. Both vehicles turned left and headed north through Al Hudaydah Governate, the Houthi stronghold hugging the Red Sea.

"Forgive me," Marcus said. "But you don't look Saudi."

"Forgive me," the colonel responded. "But you don't look Persian."

"Touché," Marcus said with a smile, enjoying the salt air and grateful for the slightly cooler evening temperature.

"I'm a Saudi citizen today, but my family is all originally from here," the colonel said.

"Al-Salif?" Jenny asked.

"No, the capital—Sana'a," he replied. "My grandfather was recruited by Saudi intelligence during the wars in the 1960s. He quickly became a very valuable asset for Riyadh, and they offered to move him and his entire clan to the kingdom. But my grandfather did not want to leave. He told the Saudis he was helping them to save his country, not trying to leave it himself, and we have remained here ever since. My father was recruited, as well. My brothers wanted no part of it. They headed to Dubai and Manama and got into business. But I was fascinated by my grandfather's tales of spy craft. So what can I say? It has not been boring."

"I was expecting someone half your age," Marcus said as they approached the town of Az Zaydiyah and turned onto Highway 45, heading northeast.

"His Highness the prince thought I wasn't going to be able to get here in time. But I was closer to the port than he realized."

"Glad to have you with us."

"It is my honor, Agent Ryker. I have heard of you. Many stories."

"Not all bad, I hope."

"To the contrary, no one has put Abu Nakba on the run like this before. You are doing God's work, my friend."

"Then why do I also feel like the Libyan is on offense and I'm constantly on defense?"

The colonel laughed. "How do you think the old man became your country's most wanted man? He's a crafty one. Now we must beat him at his own game."

There were few vehicles on the roads in these late hours of the day, and they made good time. The goal was to pass through the Hajjah Governate but to skirt the Saada Governate. That, the colonel explained, was the home base of the Houthis, overcrowded and thus far too risky, even now. At the village of Jahniyah, they took a right onto Highway 2311, heading southeast. After about an hour, they crossed into the Amran Governate and pulled into a gas station and 24-7 convenience store near the junction.

"Wait here," Colonel Malik said, shutting down the engine.

He began filling up the jeep with gas and waved Geoff up to the adjacent fuel tank to top the other jeep off as well. Then he headed inside and out of view. Marcus gripped his AK-47 and scanned the faces of the truckers gassing up their big rigs. As he did, he noticed that Callaghan was now standing, his hands on the fifty, just in case. Marcus motioned for Jenny to do the same.

"Hey, we're finally online," Noah whispered a minute later.

Grateful to be reconnected with the ops center, Marcus whispered back that Noah should give their eyes in the sky an update on what was happening and why and where they were now.

"Already done, boss," Noah replied, just as the colonel returned with an armful of bottled water and freshly baked pita, right out of the oven.

Two hours later, they had reached their objective: Wadi Amlah.

Just south of Kitaf, a small city of about forty-three thousand, the long-parched riverbed had been a favored route for smugglers and bandits of many kinds for centuries. The two jeeps entered through a narrow canyon at the wadi's western end, then traveled over hardscrabble and often-bumpy terrain for about four kilometers before coming up on a small stone mosque tucked into the side of a mountain. To Marcus, it looked like it had been abandoned for years, but the colonel said it was still very much the center of religious life for the families who dwelt in the caves and outcroppings of this region.

"The sun will be up very soon," he noted as they eased past the structure. "The call to prayer will follow. Keep your eyes sharp and your weapons at the ready."

Seeing no movement anywhere around them, they proceeded eastward, then did a U-turn and pointed both vehicles in the other direction. The colonel shut down the engine and said they would have to proceed on foot to maintain the element of surprise.

They did a comms check, with each other and with Langley. All good, they attached suppressors onto their weapons and loaded up on ammo while Marcus reviewed the plan they had sketched out on the oil tanker. Then, just as the sun was peeking up over the ridge, everyone headed out to take their assigned positions.

WADI AMLAH, YEMEN—22 MAY

They no longer had the cover of darkness.

But the plan was built around the premise that no one at the camp was anticipating an American raid at dawn. Or at all.

Jenny, Geoff, and Callaghan headed up a mountain range to the right. Colonel Malik—carrying a light machine gun with a sniper rifle and tripod slung over his back—led Marcus to the left, down a narrow ravine, with Pete and Noah following. About two hundred yards in, they began climbing a steep path to a craggy mountain ridge that ran along the southern side of the wadi.

Roughly halfway to the top, they came to a fork. The colonel motioned for Pete and Noah to take the left path while he took Marcus to the right. The sun was now fully up and blazing hot. By the time they reached another fork, twenty more minutes had elapsed, and Marcus's shirt was soaked through. This time, they took the path on the left and soon they were sneaking up to an outcropping that gave them a commanding view of the facility the Saudis believed belonged to Kairos.

Marcus pulled a pair of binoculars from his backpack and surveyed the compound. It was comprised of three buildings. The main house was a simple two-level structure built out of cinder blocks with a satellite dish mounted on the roof, positioned between rusted strands of rebar sticking out of the concrete, evidence that someone had once hoped to build a third level. He could see two guards standing watch, stationed on the back porch, one at each corner.

To the left of the house and running perpendicular to it was a long, squat, single-story rectangular building. It was also built of cinder blocks but had no rebar on its roof. Marcus assumed it contained offices or was a bunkhouse of sorts, but he saw no movement inside. The final building was a weathered wooden structure that appeared to be a barn or garage. In the center of the dirt courtyard created by the three buildings was a single metal flagpole. There was no flag flying. But at the pole's base was a pile of soot and ashes, clearly the remains of a bonfire.

Just then, the colonel tapped him and pointed to the near side of the barn. There were three shallow graves, both apparently recently dug. Even in the heat of the early morning, Marcus felt his blood run cold. The Saudis were right. This was it. Marcus was certain.

For the first time since they had split up, Marcus adjusted his headset and spoke over the whisper microphone. Once he had established that everyone was in place, he reminded them that they were here to gather intelligence, not exact revenge. They would take out the guards and kill anyone who presented an immediate threat, but they needed hostages, people they could interrogate. Still, he admitted to himself that it was going to take all the discipline he could muster not to kill everyone inside.

"Hold tight, and wait for my command," Marcus radioed the team. "I'm moving into position."

"Copy that," came the response from Callaghan. "On my way as well."

As the colonel set up his tripod and sniper rifle, Marcus took a swig of water, then retraced his steps down the path until he once again reached the fork. This time he took the other path. This one was steeper and narrower, but in time it led him down to the floor of the wadi. From here, he was just a stone's throw from the back side of the wooden barn. Hugging the mountain and crouching in the shadows, Marcus double-checked his Kalashnikov. Then he radioed the team to make sure neither of the guards on the porch of the main house was looking in his direction.

When he received the all clear, Marcus sprinted across the wadi, reached the barn, and pressed himself against the back wall. Sixty seconds later, Callaghan radioed that he was inbound and not to shoot. Once he, too, got the green light, he came sprinting in from the north side.

"We're going in," Marcus whispered to the team. "Cover us."

Callaghan slowly pulled the back door open and took a quick peek inside. Shaking his head, he confirmed what the drone coverage had revealed—there was no one there. Marcus nodded and headed in first, weapon up and sweeping to the left, just in case. Callaghan was right behind him, sweeping his Kalashnikov to the right. Inside they found the chassis of a rusted Toyota 4x4 with no tires, mounted on cinder blocks. Car and truck parts were everywhere. They did not find any members of Kairos.

Approaching the smudged windows near the front of the barn, Marcus peered into the courtyard while Callaghan watched their six. Marcus could see the two guards on the porch, roughly fifty yards away. They were young, wiry men, probably in their mid- to late twenties, with full beards and thick mustaches. Both were wearing filthy T-shirts, tan camouflage pants, and combat boots, but no balaclavas or kaffiyehs.

A door opened, and another man—an older one—stepped out onto the porch and handed both men steaming mugs of coffee or tea.

This was it, Marcus thought. It was now or never.

He radioed to Jenny and learned there were two more guards posted at the front of the building. She had one in her sights. Pete confirmed that he had the other. Marcus checked in with Geoff, who confirmed that he had the guard on the right side of the porch in the courtyard in his sights. The colonel confirmed he had the other.

"Noah, you good?" Marcus asked.

When Noah said he was, Marcus gave the order.

The suppressors did their work.

Marcus heard none of the shots. He did, however, see the heads of both men in his field of vision snap back in a puff of pink mist. When both men dropped to the ground, Marcus ordered Noah to fire as well. These shots he heard, along with the shattering of glass, and soon he could see thick clouds of tear gas pouring out of the house in every direction.

Donning their gas masks, Marcus and Callaghan threw open the front doors of the barn and sprinted across the courtyard. As they did, the sound of automatic weapons fire erupted from their right. Now the colonel—the only member of the team with eyes on the windows of the long rectangular building—opened fire. It was instantly clear from the sound that the Saudi had shifted from the suppressed sniper rifle to the light machine gun. Abdul-Malik was strafing every window of the office with everything he had and buying them badly needed time.

Callaghan reached the porch first. Marcus was steps behind, winded, nowhere near recovered from his ordeal in Lebanon. Whoever had been shooting at them had stopped, at least for the moment. So both men proceeded with the plan. Pulling grenades from their backpacks, they each pulled their pin, lobbed the grenades through the filthy windows next to them, then flattened themselves on the porch and covered their heads.

The explosions were deafening. Glass and chunks of concrete flew everywhere. A moment later, Marcus and Callaghan rinsed and repeated. Tossing two more grenades into the house, they again hit the deck and two more explosions ripped through the structure.

Callaghan jumped to his feet and kicked in what was left of the back door. Marcus was right behind him. They found themselves in a kitchen. Water from a shattered sink pipe was spraying all over the room. Through the tear gas, the smoke of the explosions, and the collateral dust, Marcus could see what looked like two mangled bodies. Moving deeper into the house, he saw Callaghan disappear into what appeared to be a dining area. Marcus turned around and watched their six. Then he heard combat boots rushing down the stairs behind them.

Pivoting, he unleashed a burst into the chest of the first man to hit the landing, killing him instantly. The man went sprawling. The second man, right behind and coughing up a storm, lost his footing and tripped over the first. Callaghan pounced on him immediately, smashing the back of his head with the butt of his rifle, knocking him out cold, and kicking the man's weapon out of reach. Callaghan moved quickly to cover the jihadist's mouth with a gag and fastened plastic flex-cuffs around his hands and feet.

Marcus kept his weapon aimed up the stairs. The air was already clearing somewhat on the second floor, and he could hear sounds up there. Slowly, carefully, Marcus crept up the steps, weapon at the ready, waiting for someone to come around the corner. No one did. When he reached the top, Marcus took a quick peek down the hallway to the right. As he did, someone unleashed a hail of gunfire.

Pulling back, Marcus weighed his options. They had one prisoner now. But they needed more. Saudi intelligence said anyone on the second floor would be a high-value target, as the men on the ground floor were mostly there to guard the senior Kairos commanders. Still, it was going to be almost impossible to reach the second floor and whatever computers, phones, and other treasures were up there if the stairwell was being guarded. Marcus radioed to his team, explaining where he was and asking if any of them could see through the windows and had a shot. None of them did. Callaghan radioed to him to use another grenade. Time was running out. Someone in this canyon was hearing all this gunfire, which meant reinforcements were on the way.

Marcus pulled a flash bomb from his backpack. Just before he pulled the pin, he ordered Noah to fire another tear-gas canister through the windows in the southeast corner of the building. When Noah did, Marcus raced back up the stairs, leaned into the hallway—now filled with clouds of gas—and rolled the device down the hall. Once again, an explosion rocked the house. But rather than kill everyone on the second floor, the device emitted an intense energy flash, disorienting everyone in its range.

Marcus immediately pivoted back into the hallway and unleashed a full burst of automatic weapons fire. Then he ejected the empty mag, popped in another, and charged forward. Callaghan charged up the stairs right behind him. What they found was a bloodbath. But as the gas and smoke and dust began to dissipate again, they also realized they had hit the jackpot.

They found him slumped against a wall in the far corner of a back room.

The man was hiding behind a large wooden desk. His left leg was badly wounded, and he was bleeding out. Writhing in pain, he was feverishly trying to wrap a black- and white-checkered kaffiyeh around his left leg as a tourniquet. He was surrounded by shattered glass, chunks of drywall, overturned chairs, and bullet casings everywhere. On a wooden table in the center of the room, covered in dust, were a half-dozen open laptops, multiple satellite phones, pistols, and ashtrays filled with cigarette butts. On one wall was a reinforced metal shelf upon which sat four television monitors, screens cracked and black, none working anymore.

Callaghan trained his AK-47 at the man's chest. Marcus slung his own Kalashnikov over his back and drew his Glock 9mm. Approaching the jihadist warily, Marcus kicked away the Colt .45 by the man's left hand and studied him closely. The face was bearded but no longer shrouded by the kaffiyeh. The man's hair was jet-black, with a few flecks of gray around the temples. It was uncut and matted with sweat. Marcus pegged him in his late forties or early fifties, a hard man who had lived a hard life.

It was the man's eyes, however, dark and cold, filled with an unnerving mixture of pain and hatred, that gave him away. Marcus would know those eyes anywhere. The clothing helped too. The man was wearing a traditional white robe, now covered in blood, and a brown vest. A thick leather belt circled his waist. Tucked into the belt was a sheath that held a large, curved dagger with a turquoise horn handle.

There was no question now. This was him. This was the man who had spoken into the camera, the one who had shot the two aid workers in the back of the head, the one who had set the blonde woman on fire and laughed as she burned to death.

But where was Abu Nakba?

Saying nothing, Marcus snapped a photo of the man's face with his satphone, uploaded it to Langley, and waited. The facial recognition software did its magic, and a moment later, Marcus and the rest of the team heard the voice of Dr. Martha Dell in their earpieces.

"*Mabruk, habibi,*" she said. "You just bagged Badr Hassan al-Ruzami."

"Roger that," Marcus replied, returning the phone to the clip on his belt.

Ruzami just sat there bleeding, his eyes darting back and forth from Marcus to Callaghan, clearly wondering who was going to speak first and what was going to happen next.

Marcus was wondering that too. He knew this man needed medical attention. He just wasn't certain he wanted to give it to him quite yet.

Stepping away from Ruzami, Marcus stood up from the crouch he'd been in and walked over to the blown-out windows overlooking the courtyard and the flagpole.

"Wait here," he said to Callaghan, "and put two bullets through his eyes if he gives you any trouble."

"Will do, boss."

Then Marcus went back downstairs where he could be out of earshot of their prize prisoner, the leader of the Troika. He ordered Geoff to help him drag the bodies of three dead jihadists over to the flagpole. He also ordered Noah and Jenny to come to the house quickly and bag up all the loot. Pete and the colonel he told to remain on overwatch. Company was coming. They did not have much time. But he had a feeling this just might work.

When everything was set, Marcus went back upstairs, crossed the room, and stood over his prey.

"Commander Ruzami, you are now a prisoner of the United States government," he began.

The man's eyes flashed with surprise.

"That's right," Marcus said. "I know who you are. And I know what you've done. So here's how this is going to work."

Without warning, Marcus smashed his boot down on Ruzami's injured leg. The man shrieked in pain even louder than before and tried to push Marcus away. But Marcus shoved his automatic pistol into the man's forehead, driving his head back hard against the concrete wall.

"You're going to tell me what I want to know, and you're going to do it right now," Marcus said. "Where's the man you call Abu Nakba?"

Gritting his teeth, Ruzami tried to speak but could not. Marcus noticed Callaghan raise his eyebrows and took the hint. He eased his boot off the wound ever so slightly, providing a small measure of relief.

"It's too late," Ruzami spat in guttural but understandable English. *"You cannot stop what Father has set into motion."*

"And what is that?" Marcus demanded.

Ruzami didn't answer.

"Where is Abu Nakba right now, right this minute?" Marcus demanded.

"Arrogance," Ruzami shouted. *"You will pay for your arrogance—all of you. I told you. You cannot stop this. We are coming for you. Infidels. Enemies of Allah. You shall burn. All of you. And soon. Very, very soon."*

Marcus smashed his Glock across Ruzami's face, creating a gash above the man's right eye. Blood poured from his forehead, nose, and mouth. Yet the man's eyes grew more defiant.

Just then Jenny and Noah entered the room. Marcus paid no attention to them other than to order them to do their work fast. Then he drove his boot into Ruzami's stomach and forced him to double over. Holstering his pistol, Marcus put a pair of plastic cuffs on the jihadist's wrists and removed the man's dagger from its sheath, stuck it into his own belt, and dragged Ruzami upright. Then he drew the Glock again and shoved it into the man's right kneecap.

"Listen to me very carefully," Marcus told Ruzami. "I'm going to count to three, and you're either going to tell me what Abu Nakba is planning and where he is, or you are going to experience more pain than you ever thought possible."

Ruzami said nothing.

"Right now," Marcus said again. *"Do you hear me? Here we go."*

The voice of the colonel suddenly crackled over the radio. He reported that a fleet of Range Rovers was racing down the wadi from the northwest, at least a dozen of them, filled with fighters and kicking up a cloud of dust.

"How far?" Jenny asked when Marcus didn't answer.

"A kilometer," the Saudi said. "Maybe two but no more. We need to move."

Marcus ignored them all. *"One,"* he shouted in the man's face.

Ruzami refused to speak.

"Two."

The man was struggling to get free.

"Three."

Marcus waited a beat, but Ruzami said nothing. Instead, he looked up and spat in Marcus's face.

Marcus pulled the trigger, and the gun went off. The explosion echoed through the canyon, as did the screams.

90

Again, the colonel came over the radio.

He insisted they had to leave the compound now or die. The convoy of jihadists was almost at the base of the mountain. But Marcus did not reply.

Ruzami's blood was spraying everywhere. But Marcus was not done. He grabbed the man by the hair and dragged him over to the window.

"Talk," Marcus demanded. *"Tell me what I want to know."*

"No," the man shouted back as he gasped for air. *"Never. NEVER!"*

"Talk or your sons will die. All three of them."

For a split second, this seemed to stop Ruzami in his tracks.

"That's right," Marcus screamed. *"We have them—all of them. Jibril. Ali. And Mansour. And if you don't talk, they all die. Right now."*

"You're lying," Ruzami cried.

"We're going to kill them unless you tell me where Abu Nakba is and what he's planning."

"You're lying. You're lying. My sons are—"

Again the colonel came over the radio. The convoy was almost there. They had to move. But no sooner had he said the words than an explosion shook the entire house. Then a second. A third. And a fourth.

Everyone but Ruzami turned and looked out the windows. They were expecting to see the barn and the offices obliterated by Houthi mortars or artillery shells. But before anyone could speak, the voice of Martha Dell came back over the radio. It was not the Houthis doing the shooting. Two of the CIA's Predator drones had just arrived on scene and fired their Hellfire missiles, taking out the convoy of approaching jihadists. And the strikes had been precise, she reported. All the vehicles had been destroyed and there were no survivors.

"Now finish this," Dell ordered Marcus, knowing exactly what he was up to.

So Marcus turned back to Ruzami. He could see the man was beginning to crack. He glanced back and found Callaghan helping Noah finish bagging up the computers and phones. He told them both to take everything downstairs. He could take it from there. When he heard them descending the stairs, Marcus again stomped on Ruzami's leg. The man cried out and gasped for air.

"Listen to me carefully," he said, speaking softly now. He pressed his pistol against the man's temple. "This is it. Your last chance. I'm going to count to three one more time. And you're going to talk, or your sons are going to die."

"No—you can't," the man screamed.

"One."

"Not my sons."

"Two."

"Have mercy—please."

"Three."

The man was howling in pain. Tears streamed down his face. He was shaking his head and trying to curl up into a fetal position. But Marcus refused to let him. He looked out the window and nodded to Geoff Stone. Then he grabbed Ruzami's hair, yanked him up, and forced him to look out the window.

Chained to the flagpole were the three bodies that he and Geoff had just dragged there. Surrounding them were scraps of furniture Geoff had brought out of the house. He had doused all of them in gasoline and now lit a cigarette, took a drag, and tossed it onto the kindling. The whole thing burst into flames.

For several seconds, Ruzami stared in disbelief. But then the commander began laughing through his pain.

"Liar," he screamed. *"You're a filthy liar. Those aren't my sons. My sons are twelve thousand kilometers away. Ready to execute the plan. And there is nothing—nothing—you can do to stop them."*

Suddenly, in a burst of rage-filled adrenaline, Ruzami drove his handcuffed fists into Marcus's groin. The force and the wrenching pain instantly dropped Marcus to his knees. His gun dropped from his hands and went skittering across the floor. Blindsided, Marcus tried to stand but could not get up. Dropping to his side, he tried to speak but could not get out the words. The wind had been knocked out of him. He was struggling to breathe. Struggling to think clearly. But in a blur of color and movement, Marcus now saw the man's hands move toward the dagger tucked into Marcus's belt. He saw Ruzami raise the dagger and saw, too, the vengeance in his eyes.

Marcus instinctively raised his hands to block the coming strike. Yet in that instant, he knew he had neither the strength nor the breath to stop what was coming. For a split second, he had foolishly—stupidly—let down his guard. Why had he imagined even for a mere moment that he could force a man such as this to talk, much less trick him into doing so? And now this madman was going to take his life.

Just then, however, gunshots exploded behind him.

Marcus saw Ruzami's head and chest explode. The force of the bullets drove the man backward. The dagger fell from his hands. His eyes rolled up in his head, and he slumped to the floor.

As startled as he was relieved, Marcus just stared at Ruzami for what seemed like an eternity. Finally he turned his head, expecting to see smoke curling out of Callaghan's Kalashnikov. But it was Jenny holding the smoking weapon.

"Come on," she said, grabbing Marcus's arm and pulling him to his feet. "We need to go."

No one spoke on the way back.

They were too exhausted and still unsure if they had come away with any actionable intelligence. They had, however, taken out a member of the Troika. And everyone agreed that even if Jenny hadn't shot Ruzami dead, a man like that was never going to talk. If there was anything of value in that compound, it was in the computers and phones they'd grabbed, not the one prisoner they'd taken alive. He was just a bodyguard. A small fish. The big fish had, once again, slipped their grasp.

The colonel drove the lead jeep. Marcus sat beside him, cleaning his weapons. Noah was in the back, uploading the contents of one laptop after another to the Global Ops Center. Jenny was back there too, sending updates to Dell and Annie at Langley via a series of encrypted text messages.

Geoff drove the second jeep. Pete sat beside him. Callaghan rode in the backseat, weapon at the ready, keeping a close eye on their prisoner, bound, gagged, drugged, and lying on the floor, covered in blankets.

Marcus popped a new magazine into his Kalashnikov. It wasn't ideal to be driving across Yemen in the bright light of day. Yes, the two Predators were still watching over them. But neither had more missiles. If they got in trouble, they were on their own.

Moreover, it was approaching noon. The sun was at its peak. They had no AC, and the air was a blast furnace. Marcus could barely breathe. He and his team were drenched with sweat. The bottles of water they had bought were so hot now they were undrinkable. And it would be hours, he knew, before they were back in Jeddah, and nightfall by the time they were in the air, headed for home.

THE WHITE HOUSE, WASHINGTON, D.C.

Dell rose as the president entered the Situation Room.

Hernandez greeted her, as did Bill McDermott, who entered right behind him.

"Please, Martha, take a seat," Hernandez said, taking his own at the head of the conference table. "How did it go?"

"Depends how you look at it, Mr. President," she replied, donning a pair of reading glasses and reviewing her notes. "They killed nine tangos, including one of the deputy commanders of Kairos."

"Which one?"

"Badr Hassan al-Ruzami."

"The chief of operations?"

"Yes, sir."

"That's fantastic," Hernandez said.

"I would have preferred him alive."

"Ruzami? Come on, Martha. You know he'd never talk. Marcus and his team just saved the American taxpayers a boatload of money and no small amount of grief."

"Hope you're right, sir."

"Did they get any prisoners?"

"One."

"Is he talking?"

"Not yet."

"Are they bringing him home?"

"I told Marcus to leave him with the Saudis," Dell said. "We think he was a bodyguard for Ruzami, not anyone senior. But if there is anyone who can get the guy to talk, it's the Saudis."

"Any loot?" McDermott asked.

"Lots of it, actually," Dell replied.

"And?"

"Too early to say. The team uploaded everything in the computer hard drives and satphones to us. I've got a task force poring over it all now. Everything is encrypted. It's going to take some time for us to get in and see what we have."

"But you're confident you can do it?"

Martha hedged. "Fifty-fifty."

It was not the answer the president wanted to hear.

JEDDAH, SAUDI ARABIA—23 MAY

For the first time, Marcus began to fear that he'd met his match.

Abu Nakba wasn't the leader of a country. He wasn't a president, prime minister, king, or crown prince. The man was a street thug. A common criminal. A cold-blooded murderer. And yet a tactical wizard, Marcus thought. Always two steps ahead of him, if not more. And innocent people were dying because Marcus couldn't outsmart this guy.

Marcus pulled out his satphone and dialed Annie's mobile phone but got no answer. He tried her home number, then her office line, to no avail. Finally he left her a brief message, telling her they were all safe and heading back, having exhausted Noah's leads in the region.

He saw Jenny crossing the tarmac to the Gulfstream and caught up with her. "Hey, I just wanted to say thank you for everything you did back there."

"Don't mention it."

"Seems like you're always getting me out of a scrape." He smiled.

She smiled back. "Seems like you're always getting me into one."

Jenny turned and boarded the plane. Marcus was about to do the same when he heard a familiar voice. Wheeling around, he found Prince Abdullah, dressed in his traditional robes, striding across the tarmac.

"Agent Ryker, the crown prince asked me to thank you."

"For what? I'm not sure we accomplished anything."

"You took down Ruzami. That is enough for now."

"I hope you're right."

"His Royal Highness invites you to come back when this is all over to visit him."

"I'd be honored," Marcus said. "In the meantime, don't kill my prisoner."

"Never," the prince laughed. "But I will definitely make him sing."

"How's the king?" Marcus asked.

The smile faded from his friend's face. "Not well, I'm afraid. Say a prayer for him."

"I will."

"Goodbye, *habibi*," the prince said, giving Marcus a bear hug and a kiss on both cheeks. "And Godspeed."

The pilots dimmed the cabin lights as they cleared Saudi airspace, heading west. Soon they had reached their cruising altitude of thirty-two thousand feet and were flying over Cairo. When the lights of the Egyptian capital disappeared behind them, Marcus stared into the black void, punctuated only by the small flashing red light at the end of the left wing.

Feeling miserable, Marcus decided to make a checklist of all that had gone right with the mission. It might not be much, but he needed to see it written down. In a small leather-bound journal that he'd brought with him from the States, Marcus made his list.

I didn't die.
I didn't get arrested.
None of my colleagues died or were captured.
None of my team was injured.
We captured a prisoner—he could end up knowing something useful.
Nine terrorists met their Maker.
Badr Hassan al-Ruzami was one of them—his reign of terror is over for good.
We even hauled in a few oysters—maybe Noah can find a pearl of great price.

Suddenly they hit a patch of severe turbulence. The Gulfstream began to shudder and pitch. The cabin lights flickered. It was over quickly, and when it was, Marcus tucked his journal away in his backpack and headed to the galley. There was no way he was going to be able to sleep no matter how exhausted he was. The only thing he wanted to do now was review everything they had seen and heard and try to redeem this trip. There had to be something they were missing, some clue to Abu Nakba's whereabouts or plans they had stumbled upon, however small, however seemingly insignificant. There had to be. Or the entire exercise could prove to have been an enormous waste of time and money.

He grabbed a cold bottle of water from the refrigerator and returned to his seat. Taking a swig, he closed his eyes again and mentally walked back through the compound in the wadi. The Saudi intel had been accurate. There had been a Kairos cell on-site. With a high-value target. Badr Hassan al-Ruzami was a big fish. One of three deputy commanders of the group. And arguably the most important.

Marcus knew he was going to catch hell back in Washington for not bringing him in alive. But only a fool could believe this guy was really going to talk. Hopefully the man's phones and computers would.

Marcus didn't regret Ruzami's death, but he had no doubt Ruzami had known all. He'd known everything Abu Nakba was planning and the details of the plan. Abu Nakba was the group's CIO, the chief inspiration officer. But for all the hype, he was not a world-class strategist. Nor a brilliant tactician. That was Ruzami's forte. That was why Abu Nakba had recruited him in the first place.

Yemen was too small a stage for Ruzami to play on. The man longed to be a global player, and in the sick and perverted world of international terror, he deserved to be. He was that good. Up there with al Qaeda's KSM—Khalid Sheikh Mohammed—and the Islamic State's Abu Bakr al-Baghdadi. Maybe better. And Ruzami knew it. He had already pulled off some of the deadliest and most spectacular attacks in recent memory and done so in some of the biggest and most secure cities in the world. Washington—twice. London. The Israeli-Lebanese border. Beirut. Aden. And if that had not been enough, he had nearly pulled off the mother of all terror attacks in Jerusalem, coming this close to blowing up the president of the United States, the prime minister of Israel, and the king of Saudi Arabia, and doing so amid a Middle East peace summit that was being broadcast live around the globe.

Having been thwarted at the last possible moment, what would Ruzami want next? Revenge, of course. But not so much against Israel. The Jewish state was just the Little Satan in Ruzami's eschatological worldview. The United States was the big prize. America was the Great Satan. Yet shooting up a church in the American capital or murdering three Christian aid workers was small potatoes for such a man. The chief of operations for Kairos had to be planning something far bigger. Was that not what he had told them in the video released to Al-Sawt and on YouTube?

"We are coming for you—all of you—every enemy of Allah shall burn," Ruzami had shouted. *"You have been warned."*

That, of course, was standard operating procedure. It was what all terrorists said. Yet in Ruzami's final moments, with Marcus's gun to his head, knowing he was certainly going to die—or at least spend the rest of his life in solitary confinement—he had said essentially the same thing. Marcus pressed his eyes shut tighter and rubbed his temples, trying to bring back the exact words.

There was something about being prideful. Paying for their pride as Americans. Paying their due, or . . . no, Marcus recalled.

Arrogance.

That was the word Ruzami had used.

"Arrogance! You will pay for your arrogance—all of you. I told you. You cannot stop this. We are coming for you. Infidels. Enemies of Allah. You shall burn. All of you. And soon. Very, very soon."

It could all be rhetoric, of course.

Boilerplate.

A "Terrorist TED Talk."

Yet the more Marcus played the words over again in his head and recalled the tone and visualized the body language, the more convinced he was that this was not an idle threat. The man was not pontificating. He was boasting. He had a plan. It was already in motion. The target was unquestionably the United States. And the plan was going to be executed soon.

The question was: *Where?*

Marcus had no memory of falling asleep.

But now he heard someone walking past him and it woke him up. Checking his watch, he discovered hours had passed. He unbuckled his seat belt, got up, and found Callaghan pouring himself a cup of coffee in the galley.

"Want one?" the former SEAL asked.

"Sure," Marcus said. "Thanks."

"In your shoes, I would have done the exact same thing," Callaghan said out of the blue, then paused a moment and corrected himself. "Well, I would have set Ruzami on fire, filmed it, and posted the video on YouTube. He was never going to talk. It would have been a waste to let him leave that house alive. But hey, that's just me."

Callaghan finished his coffee and returned to his seat. Marcus returned to his. Every muscle in his body ached. Yet he could not stop replaying the conversation with Ruzami in his head. And as he did, something bothered him. If there really was going to be a major operation inside the United States, why was Kairos's chief of operations in Yemen? And where were his sons? Why were they not all together inside the States, preparing to execute whatever plan he had concocted?

Then again, how would Badr Hassan al-Ruzami enter the U.S.? He was the second most wanted man in the world. He couldn't just fly into an American airport. Even in a disguise, even with forged papers, he had to know that the CBP—Customs and Border Protection—would nail him right away. That explained why the father was not in the U.S., Marcus concluded. But the sons were a different story. The CIA knew there were three of them. Jibril was the oldest at twenty-seven. Ali, the middle boy, had just turned twenty-five. The baby of the trio was Mansour, only twenty-one. But that was about all the Agency had on them. No pictures past or current. No fingerprints. No DNA samples. Barely even a file on them. They only knew this much because Al-Sawt had done a full profile on Ruzami once the CIA identified him as Abu Nakba's second-in-command. It had been a big story in the region.

Come to think of it, Marcus realized, that profile had been produced by none other than Hamdi Yaşar. Now it made more sense how Yaşar could have had such unusual access to one of the world's most notorious criminals. Marcus briefly mulled the prospect of going back to Gitmo to interrogate Yaşar again, this time about Ruzami's family, but concluded the man was never going to talk, and Marcus didn't have time to waste.

It was then that Marcus remembered something else Ruzami had said. His bluff to convince the Kairos operative into thinking that the U.S. had captured his sons had been unsuccessful. But for a moment there, it was clear Ruzami thought Marcus might just be telling the truth. It was only when Marcus had forced the man to look out the window at the three bodies chained to the flagpole and set ablaze that Ruzami had realized his sons were not in American custody.

"Liar," the man had screamed. *"You're a filthy liar—my sons are twelve thousand kilometers away. Ready to execute the plan. And there is nothing—nothing—you can do to stop them."*

In the heat of the moment, Marcus had incorrectly assumed Ruzami's sons would have been at their father's side, somewhere in the compound. If so, it would have made sense for his team to have captured them alive and tied them to the flagpole. But rather than just being relieved at calling Marcus's bluff and knowing his sons were fine, Ruzami had given away an important detail. His sons were not with him. They were already in the United States or on their way.

Marcus pulled out his phone and connected to the G5's Wi-Fi. Choosing the Yemeni capital of Sana'a as his reference point, he did a Google search of the distance to New York City. It turned out to be 11,105 kilometers. He did the same with Washington, D.C. That turned out to be 11,430 kilometers. Neither were precise, but they were close, and there was no reason to think Ruzami was trying to be technically accurate. Tokyo was 9,501 kilometers from Sana'a. Seoul was only 8,343 kilometers away.

No, the U.S. was the target. That much was certain. Ruzami had not lied in his final moment. He had been proud of what his sons were doing, and with his last words he had chosen to boast of it. New York and Washington made sense as targets. These had been Khalid Sheikh Mohammed's strike points. Why not Badr Hassan al-Ruzami's?

Someone's satphone rang. It was not his. Scanning the cabin, he saw Noah rouse.

"Hello?" he heard him say. "Say again? You sure? Okay, I'll let him know."

Noah rose from his seat and came to the back of the plane. "That was the watch officer at Fort Meade."

Marcus was all ears. "Tell me they broke into Ruzami's gear."

"No, that's going to take a couple of days."

"Then what?"

"They've actually just broken into one of the damaged satphones the SEAL guys recovered from the compound near Ghat."

"And?"

"That particular phone was used only six times and only to call one number."

"Abu Nakba?"

"No."

"One of Ruzami's sons?"

"No—listen to me, Marcus," Noah replied in exasperation.

"Fine but spit it out, man," Marcus pressed.

"NSA says it's a private number belonging to a wealthy Mexican businessman. He owns a huge mining and agriculture conglomerate, though DEA has long suspected he also makes and launders money from drug running and human trafficking. They have never been able to build a solid case against him. And the guy is completely wired into the Mexican government. Donates massive amounts to the current president and top senators, no doubt to buy protection. But it doesn't make much sense. What would Kairos need from a Mexican mining magnate?"

Marcus knew immediately. "They need a tunnel into Texas."

Heading to the front of the plane, Marcus ordered the pilots to refile their flight plan. They were no longer going to Washington.

Tarabulus
(Tripoli)
Tripolitania
Ghadames
Suknah
Zellah
Libyan
LIBIYA
(LIBYA)
Sebkha
Zighan
Serir Kalansho
El Juf
Ghat

PART FOUR

GRAND RAPIDS, MICHIGAN

Nasir Bhati awoke before dawn.

He washed and said his morning prayers.

Then he made himself a cup of instant coffee and stepped out onto the balcony of the Holiday Inn Express & Suites. Located some thirteen miles southeast of the city—on Highway 37, near the corner of Patterson Avenue—it was ideally situated, giving him and his men a clear view of Gerald R. Ford International Airport, both the passenger terminal and its two concourses and the two parallel runways, running east to west.

Michigan had the second highest Arab population of any American state, with nearly four hundred thousand residents born in Arab countries or born to Arab American immigrants. Another seventy-five thousand Muslims from India and Pakistan lived in the state. And though most lived in or near Detroit, and along the border with Indiana, several thousand Muslims from Asia and the Arab world lived in the Grand Rapids area.

This, Bhati knew, was why Abu Nakba and Badr Hassan al-Ruzami had chosen the city in the first place. He was under strict orders not to make contact with any local residents. Ruzami had said some might be friendly to their cause, but too many were loyal Americans. But at least Bhati and his men did not look out of place. Nor were they likely to raise suspicion staying for the week, so long as they paid their bills, obeyed the local laws, and kept their heads down. Better yet, Bhati thought as he sipped the piping hot brew, the city had halal restaurants and markets. Not every town in America did.

Ruzami had been adamant. Neither Bhati nor his men were to use binoculars or take photographs of the airport, as this would draw suspicion if noticed. Still, from this vantage point, Bhati had identified nine different airlines that flew to and from the airport, as well as several cargo services. DHL's main facility, located a stone's throw from the airport grounds, drew his particular attention.

Just then, there was a knock at his door. Bhati found it was Ibrahim.

"It's shaping up to be a lovely week," the young jihadist said, handing over a copy of the local paper and a box of pastries. "Warm and sunny with daily highs around seventy. Perfect weather for flying."

"And perfect for sending a package," Bhati replied with a slight grin. "Come, Ibrahim. Let's pay a visit to DHL."

MONTERREY, MEXICO

The G5 landed just before noon.

The Gulfstream taxied to a private hangar, where Marcus and his team—with the exception of Noah Daniels—disembarked. Marcus needed Noah to get back to Washington immediately with the computers and phones they had grabbed and to crack them open with the help of his colleagues at Langley and Fort Meade. The rest of them were greeted by a security detail and Miguel Navarro, the thirty-seven-year-old CIA chief of station. Climbing into a caravan of three bulletproof SUVs, they were whisked off the airport grounds to a safe house about thirty minutes north of the airport.

On the drive, Marcus made two calls. The first was to Annie to let her know they'd arrived safely. She was glad to hear from him and said she was doing well but things were moving fast. She was en route to the Pentagon at that moment and couldn't talk, but she promised to call back later.

The next call was to his mom. She had no idea he'd been to Yemen, nor that he was currently in Mexico. Nor was Marcus going to tell her. She knew he was working for the CIA. Then again, the entire world now knew that. She also knew he was intensely busy, under tremendous pressure, and that enemies of the United States were gunning for him. She did not know the specifics, and Marcus was careful not to discuss his work with her. She certainly didn't have the security clearances for him to talk shop with her. More important, he didn't want her to worry more than she already did. So he kept things light. Asked if she and his sisters were settling into life at Bolling. She assured him that they were, though the kids missed their friends and schools, and his sisters were not exactly big fans of being forced to homeschool them, especially so late in the school year. Marcus said he sympathized, but he reiterated that it was important they be kept safe.

Jenny, meanwhile, was chatting with Navarro. Though she, too, had been a station chief—the Agency's youngest, based in Moscow—the two operatives had never crossed paths. After saying goodbye to his mom, Marcus listened in on their conversation. He heard Navarro say that he had been born in Houston of Mexican immigrants and was fluent in Spanish and Portuguese. After graduating from West Point, he had served as the commander of an Army Ranger unit in Operation Enduring Freedom in Afghanistan, and later in Operation Iraqi Freedom, operating mostly in Fallujah. After being wounded by an IED, he had recovered for several months at Walter Reed before he was recruited by Martha Dell to join the CIA. Navarro explained that he had been sent on missions into Venezuela and Colombia before being assigned to the U.S. Embassy in Brazil as a State Department political officer, then to the American embassy in Nicaragua, and was eventually promoted to lead the CIA's work in Mexico.

Finally they pulled onto a placid, tree-lined street. Several blocks in, they passed through a set of steel gates and into the driveway of a walled compound. On the outside, it looked like any large hacienda that might be owned by a wealthy Mexican CEO. Inside, however, they were led down to the basement, where they found a sprawling underground operations center humming with staff not only from Langley but from the FBI, Drug Enforcement Administration, Customs and Border Protection, and the Pentagon.

Marcus declined the tour Navarro offered, explaining they were already dangerously behind. Kairos operatives could very well be inside the American homeland at this very moment, yet they had no idea where or what they were planning. Navarro took them down a hallway, punched in a passcode, submitted to a retinal scan, and opened a vault-like door. He had everyone take a seat around a small conference table. On the walls were large TV monitors, and laptops linked to the Agency's mainframe were positioned at each spot around the table. Once they were all served fresh coffee, the station chief picked up a phone and dialed Langley. Moments later, a live video feed from the office of acting Director Martha Dell flickered on the screens around them.

Marcus braced himself for a dressing-down for not bringing Ruzami in alive. But that was not the case.

"Agent Ryker, I want to congratulate you and your team on a job very well done in Yemen," Dell began. "The president will address the nation tonight and announce—well, let me just read an excerpt from the prepared text."

They watched as she sifted through several papers on her desk.

"Here it is," Dell continued. "'I am pleased to announce tonight that U.S. forces have successfully hunted down and taken out Abu Nakba's chief of operations in Yemen. They have also captured or killed all the members of a major Kairos terrorist cell in Yemen that was plotting attacks against the United States and our allies around the globe.' The president won't mention the Agency's involvement in any of this. But I met with him this morning, and he asked me to convey his gratitude for everything you did in Yemen."

Marcus tensed and was about to say something, but Dell wasn't finished.

"I received a call from Jeddah this morning, from your friend Prince Abdullah," she added. "Apparently, the one guy you didn't kill in Yemen was not just a bodyguard. The Saudis have been working him over pretty good. His nom de guerre is Abu Jihad. His real name is Ismail al-Houthi."

Dell explained that he was the eldest son of the founder of *Ansar Allah*, the formal name of the Houthi rebels, which translated to "Supporters of God."

"He's thirty-two years old, born and raised in Aden, and trained by his father in the art of tribal warfare," Dell continued. "Went on to train his six younger brothers but was severely wounded by a Saudi air strike about eighteen months ago. Nearly died. Lost a kidney. Apparently, at the Houthis' HQ, he was constantly at his father's side and constantly pushing his father to transform the Houthis into a global terrorist organization focused on killing Christians and Jews and establishing a global Caliphate, not simply taking over Yemen. When his father repeatedly refused, Ismail defected to Kairos and became an aide to Abu Nakba. The Saudis say they have no doubt this guy is going to spill his guts soon, and when he does, you and your team will be among the first to know."

The unexpected information came as significant encouragement to a group that badly needed some good news.

But Dell had more.

A new image flashed on the plasma screens.

It was the photo of a suave if balding Latino man in his midfifties, trim and impeccably dressed in a finely tailored suit.

"As you can imagine, the president is eager to see what's on the hard drives and satellite phones you guys recovered, as are we all," Dell noted. "In the meantime, we've learned a great deal about the Mexican businessman whose phone number Noah found on that burned satphone from Libya."

She now addressed the photo on the screen.

"This is Joaquín María del Castillo. He owns one of the largest and most profitable companies in Mexico—Castillo Holdings International—headquartered in a twelve-story building in the capital. But our friend Joaquín spends most of his time at his villa just outside of Monterrey. We have a drone watching the villa right now." She turned to an aide and asked, "Can we bring up the live video feed?"

Now Marcus trained his attention on a black-and-white image of a sprawling home built into the side of a mountain, surrounded by a lush and dense forest.

Dell pointed out the two armor-plated Range Rovers parked in the driveway and two more in the open garage, the armed sentries guarding the front, back, and side doors, the guard booth at the front gate at the base of the mountain, and the CCTV cameras monitoring all movement around the villa. Then she showed the team thermal images displaying the heat signatures of a group of people in a room on the back side, or northwest corner, of the hacienda.

"We know Castillo is there," Dell said. "We don't have a visual on him, but for the last several hours, we have been monitoring all phone calls in and out of the house. Castillo has made or received six calls so far, and we have positively ID'd his voice. Moreover, we know he is presently holding court in that back room with five associates, though we have not been able to ascertain whether these are bodyguards or business colleagues. We are assuming the latter because all of them are sitting, while three men outside the door to his office are standing. Those are the bodyguards, we believe."

"How many total guards are in the house and on the grounds?" Marcus asked.

"Twenty," Dell replied.

Jenny shot Marcus a look of concern, as did Geoff and Callaghan.

"And you're certain this Castillo guy has been in direct contact with Abu Nakba?" Marcus asked.

"Certain? No," Dell conceded. "And in contact with Abu Nakba directly? I can't say based on what we have so far. But Castillo—or someone using his personal satphone—has definitely been placing and receiving regular calls with people who were working at the Ghat compound while Abu Nakba was there. The first call was placed from Castillo's phone on February 9. The calls picked up in frequency in late April. The last call from Libya to Castillo was placed on Friday, May 8."

"The day before President Clarke ordered the air strike," Jenny said.

"That's right," Dell confirmed. "Which is why Castillo has suddenly become a person of interest to this Agency."

"Right," Marcus said, "but there's no way he was talking directly with Abu Nakba. Or at least, the satphone Noah found could not have been Abu Nakba's only phone, or even his main one. Otherwise, the SEALs would never have found it at the Libyan compound. Abu Nakba would have taken it with him.

And we now know he and his closest advisors had bugged out by then, probably to Yemen."

"Or to Mexico," Geoff said.

"You think Abu Nakba came here?" Jenny asked her colleague.

"What if he did?" Geoff asked. "And what if he is now inside the U.S. with the rest of his men?"

"No, that doesn't make sense," Callaghan protested. "The man is in his eighties. I can't see Abu Nakba climbing through a tunnel into the U.S. to run some operation in person, no matter how big it is."

"Then where is he?" Marcus asked.

Dell chimed back in.

"There's only one person who can tell us why he placed and received so many calls from Abu Nakba or his closest associates, and that's Joaquín María del Castillo," she said. "That's why you guys need to go see him and find out what exactly he knows."

"*See him?*" Geoff asked. "With all due respect, Madame Director, what makes you think he'll accept a house call from us?"

"Don't worry about that," Marcus interjected. "I've got an idea."

"I'm sure you do, Ryker," Dell said. "But let me be crystal clear on this point. This man is a prominent foreign national. He's personal friends with the president of Mexico and most of the congress. He's also personal friends with the owners of all the major media outlets in the country. I trust you've heard the phrase 'Don't pick a fight with someone who buys ink by the barrel'? It applies. Rough this guy up, and he will unleash a media firestorm against the U.S., against the president, and against the Agency, none of which we can afford. Look, I have every confidence that we can help the FBI build an airtight legal case against him and have grounds to arrest him. But that will take weeks—time that we simply do not have. So I need you guys to be on your best behavior. Ryker, I'm specifically talking to you. Don't get me wrong. You need to be persuasive. Very persuasive. But you cannot physically harm this man. And you certainly cannot harm, much less kill, any of his people. Is that understood?"

"It is," Marcus said.

Everyone else nodded, though Marcus knew they were all looking at him. He did not want the reputation of using heavy-handed tactics, nor of using more force than appropriate to get people to talk. But how much force was too much against terrorists plotting to kill innocent American citizens? There was a line one should not cross. Of this Marcus was certain. The laws of the United States constrained him. So did the Geneva Convention. So did the Scriptures. But where exactly was the line?

"What if Castillo provides us intelligence that leads us back into the U.S.?" Marcus asked.

"That's exactly what I'm hoping he gives you," Dell replied. "The man runs a mining company. We've suspected for some time that he's been digging tunnels from Mexico into the U.S., but we haven't been able to prove it."

"And you're hoping we can?"

"Of course."

"Then what are our rules of engagement if we find ourselves in a tunnel or back on American soil?" Marcus pressed.

It was an important question. Legally, the CIA was not supposed to operate inside the United States.

"Let's blow up that bridge if we get to it," Dell replied.

"I'm sorry, ma'am, but I can't do that," Marcus insisted. "My team and I need to know what you will and will not allow. Otherwise, I don't see how we can proceed."

"I'll check with the lawyers and get back to you, Ryker," Dell finally said.

This, however, was only one of Marcus's concerns. "Fair enough," he began, trying to choose his words carefully. "But I'm wondering if we could double back to the first point you raised at the start of our call."

"The president's address?"

"Yes, ma'am."

"What about it?

"With respect, Madame Director, I would caution against any public announcement that we have taken down Badr Hassan al-Ruzami."

"Why's that?" Dell asked.

"Don't get me wrong, ma'am. I realize that the president wants and needs—and deserves—a big win, especially in his first days of taking office. Nevertheless, right now, so far as we know, Abu Nakba and the rest of the Kairos network have no idea Ruzami is dead. The other two deputy commanders don't know. And maybe more importantly, none of Ruzami's sons know. The longer we keep that a secret, the better."

Dell was visibly surprised, possibly even offended. "Jenny, how do you see it?" she asked.

"If Marcus hadn't said it, I would have, ma'am," Jenny replied. "We've just caught several important breaks here. Abu Jihad. Castillo. Now is not the time to tip our hand."

Dell was quiet for a moment. Finally she said she would take the team's advice to the president immediately. "But he may have already requested airtime from the networks," she warned. "If so, then the genie is out of the bottle."

Marcus glanced at the clocks on the wall above the main screen displaying Dell's image. If the speech was happening, it would take place at 9 p.m. Eastern. It was presently 1:36 p.m. in Monterrey—the Central time zone—so that was 2:36 p.m. back in Washington. It was almost impossible for Marcus to imagine that the White House press secretary had not already requested time from the major broadcast networks for a prime-time presidential address only six and a half hours from then. He suggested they sign off and get moving. Dell agreed.

Once the screens had gone dark, Miguel Navarro turned to Marcus. "So, Agent Ryker, you said you had an idea?"

"I do," Marcus said.

Explaining that he was borrowing from an old CIA playbook, he described exactly what he had in mind. The station chief, a shrewd and experienced Agency hand, was more than ready to oblige.

Within the hour, Navarro's team had procured a van and a number of uniforms from the local power company. These in hand, the team executed a cyberattack on the power grid in Castillo's neighborhood and in several neighboring *municipios*, or municipalities. Simultaneously, the team hacked into the local phone company and automatically routed all calls coming into the power company to the local CIA offices. A junior officer played the role of switchboard operator. She was soon taking hundreds of angry calls and routing them all back to the actual power company. All but one.

When the irate manager of the Castillo residence called, she explained that the outage was an area-wide problem. However, because Mr. Castillo was such a valued customer, she would dispatch a team immediately to hook up a temporary generator and make sure he was the first to get his service restored.

Suited up in the appropriated coveralls, Marcus and his team raced to the hacienda while Dell monitored the entire operation in the ops center at Langley from the drone several miles above them.

When they reached the front gate, Navarro explained in flawless colloquial Spanish that they were expected. The guards, each bearing a sidearm, and one holding a submachine gun, asked to look in the back of the van. There, they found Marcus and the others putting on their tool belts. Another guard used a mirror attached to a long pole to make sure there were no explosives under the chassis. Yet another walked a bomb-sniffing dog around the perimeter of the van Soon, they were given the all clear signal. The wrought iron gates opened, the steel barriers lowered, and they drove up the half-mile-long driveway.

Several more armed guards met them at the front door along with a short, wiry man who said he was the house manager. The man's manner was irritated and brusque, and Marcus took him to be the one who had placed the call to the power company to begin with. Navarro did all the talking. Marcus and his colleagues simply carried boxes of equipment, including a portable generator, inside the vestibule and kept their eyes down. They were shown to the basement, where all the fuse boxes and electrical connections were located. Using flashlights and headlamps, they followed the manager down the steps. Geoff was in the rear and closed the basement door behind them.

When they reached the bottom of the stairs, Pete jabbed the manager in the back of the neck with a hypodermic needle, injecting him with a narcotic that knocked him out cold. Helping him to the floor, Pete checked his vital signs and gave everyone a thumbs-up. The man was alive and would not reawaken for several hours. Just in case, Callaghan put the man in handcuffs, gagged him, and chained him to the water heater.

This accomplished, Marcus opened his toolbox, emptied most of the contents onto the floor, then pulled out a Taser and a Glock pistol to which he attached a silencer. The others followed suit. Then they hooked up the generator and connected it to the house's circuit breakers. The entire process took less than three minutes. But they waited close to twenty before turning on the generator. All the lights in the basement flickered back to life. This, they hoped, would give everyone upstairs a sense of relief. The lights were back on. The air conditioner roared back to life. The TVs and computers were working again. It was time to move.

Hiding their weapons in the pockets of their coveralls, they reloaded their toolboxes and headed upstairs, though Marcus asked Pete to stay behind to monitor the manager's vital signs and to serve as a backup in case the plan began to fall apart. When they reentered the vestibule, Miguel Navarro asked the guards where the main power lines entered the hacienda from the street. He also asked if he could speak to the owner of the house, saying that there were some complications that he very much needed to be aware of. When one of the guards asked where the manager was, Navarro explained that he was monitoring one of their colleagues who was still trying to fix one of several problems downstairs.

Shrugging his shoulders, the guard directed a younger man to take Geoff and Callaghan outside. He then guided Navarro, Marcus, and Jenny through the beautifully appointed living and dining rooms to Castillo's home office. Three armed guards stood outside the door but stepped aside as the supervisor knocked and heard Castillo's permission to enter.

When the door opened, Marcus saw Castillo sitting behind a large oak desk, hunched over his laptop. He pulled his Taser from his pocket and fired fifty thousand volts into one of the guards, felling him instantly. Jenny and Navarro did the same with the two others, and as they did, Marcus disabled the supervisor and rushed into the room.

99

"Hands," Navarro shouted in Spanish as he and Marcus aimed at the man's head.

The blood drained from Castillo's face as he raised his hands over his head.

Navarro ordered the man to step out from behind the desk and lie on the floor, facedown, spread eagle. The man complied immediately. Jenny used flex-cuffs to secure Castillo's hands behind his back. Then she put a black canvas bag over his head and pressed the barrel of an empty Glock against his neck.

"Money?" Castillo asked. "Is that what you want? Because I can—"

"Silencio," Marcus snapped.

Castillo instantly shut up.

Marcus motioned to Jenny, who hurried off to find where the CCTV recordings were kept and to gather all the tapes for the last six months. When she had left the room, Marcus knelt and pressed his Glock into the back of Castillo's skull. Then, telling Navarro exactly what he wanted him to ask Castillo, he listened carefully as the station chief repeated his questions in Spanish and translated the answers into English.

"We want you to get us across the border," Marcus began.

At first, the man said nothing.

Marcus shifted his pistol several inches away from the man's right ear and fired into the floor. The silencer prevented anyone else in the house from hearing the shot. But Castillo instantly got the picture as Marcus returned the heated barrel to the back of the man's head.

"Yes, yes, of course," Castillo replied.

"How many crossing points do you have?"

"Just one."

"Where?"

"Laredo. We have a tunnel."

"Under the river?"

"Yes."

The man was talking freely now. Then again, Marcus realized, this was not a trained and hardened jihadist. Castillo might be a mafia boss of sorts, but he was not a terrorist. He was driven by greed, not radical, violent fanaticism. He wanted to live, not die. He was convinced that Marcus and his men would kill him if they needed to. And not being a Muslim, the Mexican had no illusions of going to paradise to spend eternity in the arms of seventy virgins.

"From where?"

"I own a meatpacking plant in Nuevo Laredo. The entrance to the tunnel is there."

"Inside the plant?"

"Yes."

"How long has that tunnel been operational?"

"Six months. Maybe seven."

"How much does it cost?"

"To cross through the tunnel?"

"Yes."

"It is free, *señor*—for you and all your people, it would be free."

"For others."

"It depends."

"On what?"

"How much I think I can get."

"Meaning what?"

"This is not for migrant workers, *señor*. This is for . . ."

"For what?"

"People who have the means."

"Drug runners?" Marcus asked.

Castillo was silent.

"Human traffickers?"

Again, Castillo said nothing.

"Terrorists?"

"Please, *señor*—I'm just a—"

"Arabs," Marcus snapped.

"What about them?"

"When did they come?"

Castillo said nothing.

Marcus pressed the gun harder against the man's skull.

"A few days ago."

"When exactly?"

"I . . ."

"When did they come?"

"Last Saturday."

"The sixteenth."

"Yes, yes."

"How many were there?"

"Two groups."

"How many in each group?"

"Six."

"So twelve men total?"

"Yes."

"Who were they?"

"We never ask that question."

"I bet—how much did they pay?"

"A lot."

"How much?"

"A million dollars."

Marcus was stunned.

"A million for the two groups?"

"No, *señor*—a million each."

"What did they have with them?"

"They were carrying boxes."

"Describe them."

"They were long—cases, really, not boxes."

"Of what?"

"I did not ask."

"Why not?

"They were dangerous men, *señor*. They would have killed me had I started asking too many questions."

That clinched it. Marcus had no doubt these had been Abu Nakba's men. No one else would have paid so much, nor been able to put the fear of God into a man as wealthy and powerful as Joaquín María del Castillo.

There was a knock at the door. Navarro continued to guard Castillo as Marcus took up a position to the right side of the door, weapon at the ready. Marcus asked who it was in passable Russian. Jenny gave a false name, but there was no question it was her voice. Marcus asked a challenge phrase, just to be sure she was not being held at gunpoint. When she responded properly, Marcus cautiously opened the door to find that the coast was clear. Pete was standing at Jenny's side.

Jenny whispered that she had been in touch with Geoff and Callaghan. All the guards had been neutralized. She had shut down the CCTV system. She had confiscated all the tapes. They were good to go.

Marcus and Navarro hoisted Castillo to his feet, then rushed to the garage and loaded him into the back center seat of an armored Range Rover. Jenny and Pete sat on either side of Castillo. Geoff Stone and Donny Callaghan climbed into a second Range Rover while Miguel Navarro returned to the van they had arrived in. Radioing ahead to the guardhouse at the end of the driveway to lower the steel barricades and open the gates, Navarro drove the van out first, telling the guards that their boss was apparently leaving momentarily as well. Moments later, Marcus drove off the compound's grounds at high speed.

About a mile from the meatpacking plant, Marcus found the van pulled over to the side of the road. Slowing to a stop, Marcus got out and met Navarro, who emerged from the driver's seat.

"Did you talk to Dell?" Marcus asked.

"She was on a call with the Israelis," Navarro replied. "But I briefed the shift leader at the ops center on what we've learned and where we're headed."

"And they'll make sure forces are pre-positioned to back us up on the other side?"

"Absolutely," Navarro said. "And I have more good news."

"What's that?" Marcus asked.

"The president just named your old Secret Service friend, Carl Roseboro, the new head of DSS, and Roseboro is sending one of his SWAT teams to Laredo. In fact, they're setting up a joint task force with FBI, DEA, and CBP."

"That's great news," Marcus said. "And the rules of engagement?"

"Nothing yet," Navarro said. "The Agency's chief counsel is reviewing the matter, but no word so far."

"They know we're very likely going to encounter resistance down there, right?" Marcus said. "I mean, this is the Mexican mafia we're talking about here, and this tunnel is making a fortune for them. They're not going to just turn it over to us without a fight."

"I made the risks very clear," Navarro insisted.

"Okay, good. We need to move."

Marcus climbed into the front passenger seat of the Range Roger while Navarro got behind the wheel. Weapons drawn but out of sight, they followed Castillo's instructions on how to radio ahead to the guards at the plant and get them to open the front gate and let them through. It was a risk. Castillo could betray them. But Marcus could think of no other way, and they were under strict orders not to go in guns blazing.

As they approached, they could see the barriers had been lowered.

They blew past the guardhouse too quickly for the men to see anyone through the tinted windows. When they reached the main facility, the barn doors were open, and they entered without a problem.

Pete and Jenny guarded Castillo while Marcus and the rest of the team spread out to search the facility and the nearby offices, tasing every armed guard they came across. Within minutes, they found where the plant's CCTV footage was stored. With no time to search through the files, they ripped out the hard drives, stashed them in a backpack, and gave them to Navarro. They also found a cache of automatic weapons and boxes of ammo and helped themselves.

Returning to the vehicles, they dragged Castillo at gunpoint into the refrigeration unit and demanded he show them the entrance to the tunnel. When he did, Marcus nodded to Pete, who drew another hypodermic needle and jabbed it into Castillo's neck. With the bag once more over his head, the man went limp, and they lowered him to the floor. The Justice Department could sort out later whether the U.S. government was going to charge and arrest the man and his many associates. Marcus certainly hoped they would. But for now, Castillo was deadweight. They did not have the luxury of taking him with them, so they left him behind.

Marcus thanked Navarro for all his help. He directed Jenny to hand over to the station chief her backpack full of CCTV footage from the hacienda. Navarro, in turn, promised to have his team erase all the footage of their raid and forward to Langley whatever images they might find of Abu Nakba's forces. Then he returned to the Range Rover and sped off into the afternoon sun.

Marcus led his team into the tunnel, an M4 in his hand and his Glock on his belt. The temperature was ghastly hot—at least a hundred degrees, he figured—and the humidity made it feel worse. Why Castillo, with all his millions, had not set up an air-conditioning system, or at least a proper ventilation system, was beyond him. Then again, Marcus figured, once Castillo had his money, he probably could not care less what the conditions were in his tunnel. He had no doubt spent a small fortune to build the tunnel under the Rio Grande in the first place—and do it without attracting the notice of either the American or Mexican governments. Any further improvements or creature comforts simply were not in the budget.

One thing Castillo had spent money on was lighting. There were electrical wires running along the left wall that powered hanging lamps every five yards or so.

What struck Marcus most was how deep they descended. About two hundred yards in, they reached a ten-by-ten-foot hole, a shaft that went straight down. A steel ladder had been drilled into one side of the bedrock, yet even shining a flashlight into the hole, Marcus could not see the bottom. Throwing his M4 over his shoulder, he headed down the ladder first. Jenny was next, followed by Pete and Geoff. Donny Callaghan brought up the rear, staying on special alert lest Castillo or any of his men wake up in time to send forces after them.

At the bottom of the shaft, the tunnel leveled out and headed north, under the river. It was much cooler at this depth. They stopped a moment, caught their breath, and consumed the bottled water and PowerBars that Miguel Navarro had given them for their journey. Then Marcus picked up his weapon and led the way forward. They were not moving quickly. Callaghan had cautioned them that the tunnel could be booby-trapped. There could also be armed men coming in the opposite direction.

After an hour, they reached the end of the tunnel without finding either. They had come to another shaft, another ladder bolted into the bedrock, and a long climb upward.

But to where?

101

They changed order before climbing up the shaft.

Marcus was still in the lead, but Callaghan now followed directly behind him. Then came Geoff, and then Jenny, while Pete brought up the rear. They kept their flashlights off and maintained complete silence on the climb, taking care not to let their weapons clang against the ladder or the rock.

At the top of the shaft, Marcus cautiously poked his head up. Seeing no one in the tunnel ahead, he scrambled off the ladder, raised his M4 to provide cover, and whispered for Callaghan to do the same. When they were all in this significantly wider tunnel, they took a moment to again catch their breath and replenish their fluids. After several minutes, Marcus motioned for Callaghan to move to his side since this section was broad enough to proceed two abreast.

Marcus was surprised by how long this stretch was. Rather than just a few hundred yards, he estimated they had walked nearly a mile before reaching an opening back up to civilization. The heat and humidity were also once again in force. They were continually wiping sweat from their brows and hands. They had no resin, nothing to prevent their weapons from slipping, and they had no idea where they were or what they were about to encounter.

More problematic was that they had been incommunicado with Langley for well over an hour. There was no Wi-Fi in the tunnels. No cell phone coverage. Nor could they use satellite phones. Marcus took some degree of comfort in the fact that Dell and her team at the ops center knew that they would be emerging somewhere in the Texas border city of Laredo. While the CIA itself was not permitted legally to operate in the U.S., Navarro had informed him that U.S. Customs and Border Protection had put two helicopters in the air, along with three drones, and were closely monitoring activity on and near the Rio Grande. An FBI hostage rescue team had been deployed in the city and was driving around Laredo in three unmarked box trucks, waiting for a location and instructions. A DSS special weapons and tactics team had also been deployed from Dallas and should now be on-site, along with DEA units. All of them should be able to respond to a distress call within minutes.

The bigger problem was that Marcus still had not received clear rules of engagement from Dell or the Agency's chief counsel. While he was relieved that they had not run into trouble down in the tunnel, with no way to hear from Langley before they potentially encountered hostile forces guarding the tunnel's other end, Marcus had to make the call on his own. During one of their water breaks, he informed his colleagues that for legal purposes they had all just officially resigned from the Agency. He told Pete that he should now consider himself a sanctioned DSS officer. So would he. Geoff was DSS anyway. As for Jenny and Callaghan, Marcus took a moment to deputize them into the DSS, even having them raise their right hands and take the DSS oath. He had no idea if any of this would hold up in a court of law. But they all agreed that if they were fired upon on American soil, they were not going to use Tasers. They were going to shoot to kill.

Convinced he had done all he could, Marcus took one more swig of water and steeled himself for the mission ahead. He could not help but think about the last tunnel he'd been in. Just weeks earlier, he had been dragged unconscious through a previously unknown Hezbollah tunnel from Israeli territory deep into Lebanon, far behind enemy lines, into the single most terrifying experience of his life. His escape had been nothing less than the grace of God. He could try to pass it off as the result of good training and cool nerves, but he knew better. It had not, apparently, been his time to die. God had more plans for him on this side of eternity.

Did those plans include Annie? he wondered. The very thought of Annie both inspired and haunted him. Yes, she was praying for him. That much he knew, and for this he was grateful beyond words. But how could she ever forgive him if he did not make it out of this thing alive? Hadn't she suffered enough pain and loss and loneliness in this life? Didn't she deserve a fresh start, danger-free, up in those glorious Rocky Mountains he so loved?

Suddenly he felt a jab in the ribs. It was Callaghan. This was no time for daydreaming or second-guesses. It was time to move.

Wiping his forehead one more time, Marcus said a silent prayer. Then he slung his M4 over his back, drew his silenced Glock, and reached up to open the hatch. Doing so made more noise than he'd intended, but there was nothing he could do about it now. Rather than throwing it open, however, he raised it just slightly.

As he did, he saw movement. A bearded man in his twenties whipped around, brandishing an AR-15. Marcus did not hesitate. He fired two shots to the man's head and one to his chest. The shots made little noise. The man crashing to the floor certainly did.

Marcus saw no one else—yet.

But he was certain reinforcements would be coming quickly. Marcus now threw the hatch wide and climbed through the opening, finding himself in a bunkroom of sorts. No sooner was he on his feet than another armed man came around the corner and through the door. Marcus double-tapped him as well.

Moving quickly to the doorway, Marcus made sure both men were dead, then reloaded while Callaghan came up behind him. Together, they pivoted into the hallway, Marcus facing east, Callaghan facing west. Marcus found no one ahead of him but heard his colleague fire twice, also from a silenced pistol.

When the rest of the team were through the hatch and ready to move, they spread out in two directions. Marcus took Jenny. Callaghan took Geoff. Pete again hung back to provide backup to either team, or medical assistance if, God forbid, it was needed. Now back at ground level, their comms were working again. Pete was in charge of calling the Global Ops Center and providing Dell with a situation report and their precise coordinates. He was told one of the FBI's tactical teams was less than five minutes away, which he immediately radioed to the others.

Callaghan soon radioed back that he and Geoff had cleared a series of additional bunkrooms but found no one else there. They were now retracing their steps and would link up with the others momentarily.

Marcus and Jenny, however, were radio silent. As they came around the corner, up a flight of stairs, and through a closed wooden door, they found themselves entering a kitchen that was connected to a spacious if sparse dining facility where a half-dozen armed men were eating and drinking. It was clear that the men had not heard anything that had happened on the floor below them. The stunned looks on their faces told Marcus all he needed to know. But as they moved for their weapons, Marcus switched from the Glock to the M4. He fired two bursts to the left as Jenny followed suit, firing two bursts to the right. Each felled a man, but only wounding, not killing, either. Both Marcus and Jenny got off another burst each but had to back through the door and down the stairs as the return fire now came hot and heavy.

The door was being shredded to pieces. Splinters flew everywhere. Marcus and Jenny continued backward into the hallway. They were met by Callaghan and Geoff. Marcus motioned for each to step into a different bedroom and wait. It was the right move and just in time. They heard a grenade clattering down the stairs, followed by an explosion that knocked them all to the floor. Blinded by smoke and dust and covered in bits of concrete and drywall, Marcus knew he had to stay quiet and get back on his feet. But he started coughing violently and could not stop.

Just then, he heard boots rushing down the stairs. An instant later, he heard automatic gunfire in the hallway. But this was an AK-47, not an M4. Then he heard another grenade rattling down the hallway. Grabbing Jenny, he threw her into a side room and pushed her to the ground, covering her with his own body. This second explosion rattled the building and brought more smoke and dust surging into the bunkroom where Marcus lay, his back in severe pain, covered in rubble, ears ringing, and struggling to get back up.

Rolling off Jenny, he could see wires dangling from the ceiling, sparking wildly. Water from a burst pipe was spraying everywhere. A silhouette suddenly appeared in what was left of the doorway. Was it one of his or one of theirs? Marcus saw a weapon coming up. It was aiming at Jenny. Marcus grabbed his pistol and fired six shots. The figure collapsed to the floor.

He felt around in the dark for his own M4, and when he found it, he pulled it close to his chest, then scrambled to his feet and holstered his Glock again. Then he reached down and grabbed Jenny's hand and pulled her up. He motioned for her to follow him. They were going hunting again.

The firefight in the hallway was brutal. But by the time the FBI arrived, it was over. Marcus and his team were all standing. Filthy. Exhausted. But alive and largely uninjured.

There was just one problem.

Two, actually.

All of the men they'd just encountered were Mexican drug runners, not Kairos operatives. They were on the payroll of Joaquín María del Castillo, not Abu Nakba.

And all of them were dead.

Marcus had no witnesses. There were no CCTV cameras on the premises. No files. No computers. Nothing to tell them where the Kairos operatives had gone or what they had in their possession.

JOINT BASE ANACOSTIA-BOLLING

Marjorie Ryker was cleaning up after dinner when her cell phone rang.

Drying her hands, she put on her glasses and checked the caller ID. When she saw the call was coming from Louisa Garcia, she answered it immediately.

"I had to call, Marj," Mrs. Garcia said. "Javier and I have been seeing so much about Marcus in the news, and we can't imagine all you've been going through. It's so terrible what they've been saying about him."

"It has been pretty rough, but don't believe everything you hear."

"No, no, of course not. And obviously Marcus has been exonerated and all. But still, the media is atrocious. I've rarely seen Javier so mad. He keeps throwing things at the television. As though that'll fix anything. So how are you holding up? I heard you'd left town for a bit?"

Marjorie tensed a bit at this. Marcus had told her not to tell anyone why she was living in Washington for a while. But she wasn't used to concealing the truth from friends, especially old friends like the Garcias, especially since she was so grateful for the reconciliation slowly unfolding between them. So she ignored the question and turned the conversation to how the Garcia girls were doing.

About ten minutes into the conversation, Mrs. Garcia caught her completely off guard.

"Javier's law firm got him tickets to the papal Mass two weeks from now in Chicago as a birthday present since he's the oldest partner on the payroll. And they're great seats. The firm represents United Airlines, so the seats are in the United skybox. It'll be air-conditioned, and we'll have an amazing view. The girls have a birthday sleepover party that weekend they don't want to miss. So we have two extra tickets. I know you're not Catholic. But Javier and I thought you still might find it interesting, and we'd love for you to come as our guest. You could bring a friend. Maybe Maya Emerson. We'd even like to cover your flights and hotel. We could make a long weekend of it. What do you say?"

"Oh, Louisa, I don't know what to say. That's too much. Too kind. I couldn't possibly say yes."

"No, no, you must. We loved having you over for dinner and catching up after far too long. This is going to be a once-in-a-lifetime event. And it would really be our honor to have you come."

"Really? You're serious."

"Absolutely. Please. We insist. Unless, of course, you have something else going on."

"Not at all. Just babysitting the grands. But as much as I love that, I could always use a little weekend away, right?"

Mrs. Garcia laughed. So did Marjorie.

"Well, I'm touched. Please tell Javier I accept. Thank you."

"That's wonderful, Marj. He'll be thrilled, as am I. Would you like to bring someone—Maya or someone else?"

"Yes, I think Maya would love to come. I can call her right now."

"Perfect. Let me know, and then I'll book your flights. Javier and I will be arriving on Thursday. We thought it would be fun to, you know, explore Chicago a bit before the big day. We've already booked a suite at the Four Seasons, and we've held an adjoining room, just in case, since rooms are going very fast in Chicago."

"I bet they are. I saw on the news they're expecting one hundred thousand people or more."

"It's going to be quite something."

"Well, thanks again for inviting me."

The moment they hung up, Marjorie called Maya, who was as stunned and delighted as Marjorie. And Maya was no Catholic either. She was true-blue Southern Baptist. Her husband had even been a Baptist pastor. But the truth was their theological differences with the pope didn't even occur to them. Both women saw the invitation as an answer to many years of prayer for healing between the Ryker and Garcia families, and they were grateful not only to be able to accept but to be able to go together.

By the time Marjorie put her head on the pillow that night, read the Scriptures, prayed, and turned out the lights, all the details were set. The trip was booked. She was going to Chicago.

104

THE WHITE HOUSE—24 MAY

Martha Dell and Annie Stewart cleared security just before 7 a.m.

At their side was Marcus Ryker, fresh off a red-eye from Texas.

They entered the Oval Office and were greeted by the president, McDermott, and Carl Roseboro, the new head of DSS.

Ryker and Roseboro went way back. Now fifty-three, Roseboro was Marcus's senior by more than a decade. The new DSS chief had not cut his teeth in the Diplomatic Security Service. Rather, Roseboro, like Marcus, had spent his entire post-military career in the Secret Service. He began as a special agent, first busting counterfeiters and later serving on the elite Presidential Protective Detail at the White House. When Marcus first met him, he was heading up the Service's intelligence division before being promoted to the agency's deputy director. Roseboro was a twenty-seven-year veteran of the Service, and Marcus considered him the quintessential federal agent. Crazy off-the-charts smart. Fearless. Counterintuitive. And a consummate professional. Now he was the head of DSS—the first African American ever to serve in the post—and Marcus could not have been more pleased.

"Welcome back, Agent Ryker," Hernandez said, coming around the *Resolute* desk to shake Marcus's hand. "Great work out there. You've been busy."

"Thank you, Mr. President," Marcus replied. "And thank you, especially, for not going public yet with Ruzami. I think that was wise."

"That was a close one, Ryker. We were fifteen minutes away from contacting the networks. Even still, I'm concerned the story will leak. But tell me what happened in Mexico."

"I will, sir, but first, Carl, congrats." Marcus shook Roseboro's hand.

"You look like crap, Ryker," the DSS director quipped, punching Marcus in the shoulder. "And weren't you fired?"

"Ouch," Marcus said.

"Too soon?"

"A little."

"Well, good to see you too, my friend."

Once everyone was seated, Marcus turned back to the president. "Sir, the CCTV footage from Castillo's office and meatpacking plant are clear," he began. "We know for certain that two teams of Kairos operatives—a total of twelve jihadists—have entered the United States."

"Have we established their identities?" Hernandez asked.

"Some of them, yes," Marcus replied. "Using facial recognition software—and with the help of Saudi, Emirati, and Israeli intelligence—we've ID'd two of the men so far. One is Tariq Youssef, a member of the Troika and the organization's chief of security."

"That's a big fish."

"Very big, sir, but so is the other man we've ID'd—Zaid Farooq. He's the third member of the Troika, and Abu Nakba's chief of intelligence. Now, our best guess is that three of the young men with them are the Ruzami boys—Jibril, Ali, and Mansour—but we have not been able to confirm this yet as we don't have any photos of them on file. Would you turn to pages four and five in the PDB?"

Hernandez opened his copy of *The President's Daily Brief* and found screen captures from the various CCTV cameras of all twelve Kairos terrorists. Then Marcus directed him to the next page, which contained images of both cells transporting large, rectangular boxes into the tunnel.

"What's in those?" Hernandez asked.

"That's what worries us, Mr. President," Marcus replied. "We don't know yet."

Now Annie spoke up. "Sir, the CIA and FBI found traces of radioactivity in the Castillo home, the meatpacking plant, throughout the tunnel, and in the safe house in Laredo."

"Meaning what?"

"Neither the bureau nor the NEST guys they brought in last night from DOE think the traces are strong enough to suggest full-blown warheads," Annie replied, referring to the Department of Energy's Nuclear Emergency Support Team.

"But?"

"They're still conducting tests," Annie continued. "But their preliminary assessment suggests some form of dirty bomb."

Hernandez turned to Dell. "Capable of what?"

"We should know more by the end of the day, Mr. President," Dell replied. "But a dirty bomb could spread radioactive material that is highly toxic to humans. Built right and with the right kind of fuel, each device could cause mass death and injury. But they would also create mass panic and economic devastation in whatever city in which they were deployed."

The room was silent for several moments.

Then Roseboro spoke up. "When did they arrive in the country?" he asked.

"The sixteenth," Marcus replied.

"So Kairos has had an eight-day head start on us?"

"I'm afraid so."

"Any leads on where these two teams went?" the new DSS director asked.

Annie took that one. "No, sir—the FBI is canvassing every car rental facility in and around Laredo, every new and used car dealer, every taxi and Uber driver, but nothing's turned up yet."

"If you were them, what would you be doing with that time?" Roseboro asked Marcus.

"I'd be buying burner phones," Marcus replied. "Weapons. Ammo. Bomb-making supplies. More vehicles. Renting safe houses. From what they paid Castillo, we know money is no object. And from what they did to the three aid workers in Yemen, we know they are planning a true bloodbath."

"Where? When?" Roseboro pressed. "I mean, in his video, Abu Nakba said they were going to strike soon. So did Ruzami. Do you think they're planning to strike this weekend? Memorial Day would make sense for an attack."

"It's possible," Marcus agreed. "It's also possible they need more time to prepare for whatever they're planning."

"They could be going for another significant date, like the Fourth of July," Annie suggested.

"Or the arrival of the pope," Roseboro said. "Right now, that worries me most."

"Let's talk more about that," the president said. "Where does the pope go first?"

McDermott took that one.

"He lands at Andrews on June 2 at noon and takes a motorcade into the city."

"He's staying at Blair House?" Marcus asked, referring to the presidential guesthouse across the street from the White House.

"Yes," McDermott confirmed.

"What then?"

"His Holiness is scheduled to have lunch here at the White House with the president and First Lady, followed by a press conference in the Rose Garden," McDermott said. "That night he will address a Joint Session of Congress. The following day, Wednesday the third, he flies to Miami to hold an evening Mass. He and his entourage will stay there overnight. On the fourth, he flies to Houston, where he will hold another evening Mass, then stay at the governor's mansion in Austin. On Friday, he flies to New York City to hold a Mass at Yankee Stadium."

"Where's he staying?" Marcus asked.

"The Waldorf," McDermott said. "Then on Saturday the sixth, the pope will end his tour by flying to Chicago. That will be the grand finale, an afternoon Mass at Soldier Field."

"How many people?" Marcus asked.

"We're expecting a hundred thousand—the most of any site," Roseboro said.

"I didn't realize Soldier Field was that big."

"It's not," Roseboro replied. "They'll be set up for seventy thousand inside the stadium, including seats on the field. The stage will be small, and the Eucharist will be served at people's seats. No one will be coming forward, like in the other cities. They will also be setting up jumbotrons and thirty thousand chairs in the parking lots all around the stadium."

"Will they be served Communion as well?" Marcus asked.

"Yes."

"But if they're using the parking lots for overflow seating, where will people park?"

"All parking will be at sites far from the stadium," Roseboro said. "The only access will be via public buses that will shuttle people to and from the designated lots."

"That will also keep all the streets around the stadium closed to private traffic so they're clear for the Secret Service," Dell added.

"You mean DSS, for the pope?" Marcus asked.

"No," the president said. "For me."

Marcus was surprised. "You, sir?"

"That's right—the First Lady and I will be heading out to Chicago to be part of it all," Hernandez confirmed. "His Holiness is going to serve us the Eucharist. It should be quite something."

"I should say so," Marcus said, the look on his face giving him away.

"You don't approve?" the president asked.

"Of you and your wife taking Communion? Of course I do. Of the pope coming here based on what we now know, absolutely not."

"You think Kairos is going to target the pope?"

"Why not?"

"Why go through all the trouble of coming here? Why not hit Rome? Why not the Vatican?"

"Because hitting him here—and you, as well—gives them a double whammy,"

Marcus replied. "A devastating attack against the Great Satan *and* against the head of the Roman Catholic church. And come to think of it, it's during the week of the anniversary of the Six-Day War. That makes it a triple crown."

"Why is the anniversary significant?" Hernandez asked.

"June 5 to the tenth, 1967," Marcus recalled. "The Israelis defeated five Arab armies, tripled their land, seized control of the West Bank—what they would call Judea and Samaria—and reunified Jerusalem. Remember whom we're dealing with here, Mr. President. Kairos was founded by a man who calls himself Abu Nakba, meaning 'Father of the Disaster.' We think of him and refer to him as 'the Libyan' because his father was Libyan and because his base camp was in Libya. But don't forget his mother was Palestinian. Born and raised in Gaza. Abu Nakba identifies as a Palestinian. And while we may not have thought of the upcoming anniversary of the Six-Day War while planning for the pope's visit, I can assure you that Abu Nakba is thinking about it night and day."

The room was silent for a moment. Then Hernandez turned to Dell. "What do you think?"

"It's certainly plausible, Mr. President, though we haven't seen any reporting on specific threats to the pope. NSA isn't picking up any chatter pointing in that direction. My analysts haven't ruled out the possibility, but they haven't considered it likely."

At this, Annie spoke up. "True, but in the last twenty-four hours, I've been doing some research on this, Mr. President. The fact is, there hasn't been a serious plot to assassinate a pope since 1995. That's when the Filipino government unearthed a plot by radical Islamists to attack Pope John Paul II in Manila. Before that, you'd have to go back to 1981, when the Soviets tried to take out the same pope using a Turkish gunman who shot him four times at point-blank range in St. Peter's Square. That said, in both cases extreme Muslims were involved in the planning and operations against the pontiff. I think we need to look more closely at this."

Dell disagreed.

"Mr. President, those plots are ancient history. Most of my analysts—Annie and Marcus apparently excepted—believe it's far more likely that Abu Nakba wants to blow up a major American landmark or set off a dirty bomb in a major city, killing many but terrifying even more. We'd rank Washington at the top of the target list with Manhattan second."

Marcus couldn't accept this. "Mr. President, please, at the minimum you need to speak to His Holiness again, let him know the gravity of the situation, and let him make his own decision."

Hernandez looked to Dell. "That's probably right, sir," she replied. "But it might be better for me to brief the Vatican security chief first before you make that call."

"Fine, but do it fast," the president said.

Marcus, Dell, and Annie rode back to Langley together.

Jenny was waiting for them outside Dell's office when they arrived. "Prince Abdullah just called from Riyadh," she said. "It seems that our prisoner Abu Jihad has begun to sing."

They gathered in Dell's office and shut the door.

"Anything useful?" Dell asked.

"Interesting but not actionable—not yet," Jenny replied. "He says Abu Nakba was in that compound near Ghat for years and confirmed that it was his headquarters. However, once the old man heard that Hamdi Yaşar had been captured, he fled to Iran within days."

"To Bandar Abbas?" Marcus asked.

Jenny nodded. "That's what the Saudis think. When Abu Nakba left Iran, he spent several days at the Ruzami compound in Yemen. He left only about twenty-four hours before we arrived, and that's where the trail goes cold again."

"Is it possible he went back to Iran?" Annie asked.

"Let's task a satellite to scour every inch of that naval base," Dell said. "If Abu Nakba is still there, we'll know soon enough."

"That's all well and good," Marcus said, "but it doesn't put us any closer to figuring out where these Kairos cells are, or where they are going to strike, or when."

Six hours later, however, there was a new development. This time the entire team met with Dell and Annie in the director's conference room, and the guest of honor was Noah Daniels.

"We've cracked the *Dead Sea Scrolls*, and they're finally revealing their secrets."

"The *Dead Sea Scrolls*?" Dell asked.

"That's what I've nicknamed all the stuff brought back from Libya, together with what we brought back from Yemen," Noah explained.

He directed everyone's attention to the plasma screens. Photos of various microchips, SIM cards, and other scraps of digital data flashed on the various screens, but on the center monitor, a video began to play. It was a message from Abu Nakba. He was speaking in Arabic, but Noah's team had translated it and added English subtitles.

"We are coming for you—all of you—every enemy of Allah shall burn," the old man began. "We will destroy your idols. We will elevate the crescent and break your crosses. Listen, O infidels. Hear me, O pagans. Allah has prepared the earth for the bloodiest battle before the hour of our redemption. Make no mistake: the purposes of Allah shall come to pass. He will see his slaves sweat in spilling their blood as they wage jihad and prepare for the Coming One. He will also see the blood of his enemies flowing like rivers upon the earth because they have rejected the Holy Qur'an. Because they have rejected his last and final Prophet, peace be upon him. The time has come. The prophecies are coming to pass. The end of days is upon us. The beloved forerunner to the Mahdi—Jesus, son of Mary, peace be upon him—is coming at any moment. He will bring justice to the earth. He will smite all liars and murderers and fornicators and all the enemies of Islam. He will debunk once and for all the cruel and deceptive myth that he was once hanged on a cross and crucified. He will curse the deluded and the blasphemers who claim that he and Allah are one, who make claims of his resurrection and divinity. He will expose such diabolical lies with a sword and fire. Behold, when Jesus returns to earth in the final days of human civilization, he will adhere to the Law of Muhammad, peace be upon him. He will proclaim and advance the Law of Muhammad, peace be upon him. He will wage jihad for the cause of Allah. And until that day—that glorious day—Allah commands his servants to begin spilling the blood of the Christians and their leaders. Make no mistake, O pagans, we are coming for Rome. We are coming, and we cannot be stopped."

When the video ended, Noah turned back to the group.

"We recovered this video from one of the charred laptops in Libya. We know from the time stamp embedded in the video that it was recorded on May 8. Therefore, we now know that Abu Nakba was in that compound near Ghat until at least then and shot the video there. What's interesting is that NSA also just found a copy of this video on one of the laptops we brought back from Yemen. It was sent by an encrypted email on the eighth to a Yahoo account used by Ruzami."

"That's pretty chilling stuff," Dell said.

"I'll say," Annie noted. "But isn't it odd that Kairos never released it?"

Marcus agreed.

"What do you make of it, Noah?" Dell asked.

"My best guess is that Abu Nakba recorded it to release to the media—almost certainly through Al-Sawt in Doha—but only after he and Ruzami had confirmation that their cells had successfully entered the United States. But then came the bombing of the compound in Libya. And our raid in Yemen. And killing Ruzami. And us grabbing Ruzami's laptop. Everything has happened so fast. It's very possible that no one else in Kairos has this—or even knows it exists."

"Maybe yes, maybe no," Marcus replied. "At the very least, it adds a great deal of weight to the notion that the Kairos cells are in the States to target the pope."

"You may be right," Dell said. "But then again, Abu Nakba says he and his men are coming to Rome to 'break your crosses.' So it's possible the Kairos cells have other targets in mind here in the U.S. and that Abu Nakba has planned a separate operation to hit the pope when he returns home to the Vatican."

As everyone considered that possibility, Dell turned to Annie, who had taken the remote from Noah and was replaying the video on mute. "Deputy Director Stewart, what are you thinking?"

Annie hit Pause and turned to Dell.

"What strikes me is that Abu Nakba does not actually say that he and his men are coming *to* Rome—he says they are coming *for* Rome," Annie noted. "That is, they are coming against Roman Catholicism, which is effectively his way of saying he is coming to destroy Christendom. I mean, look at the language he's using. He's making a direct attack on the essential theology of Christianity—the historicity of the cross, the crucifixion, the resurrection, the divinity of Christ."

Further, Annie pointed out, the Kairos leader was claiming Jesus would return to earth as a jihadist for Islam and as a forerunner of the Mahdi. "So I don't get the impression this is about an attack on the physical city of Rome. He's essentially making a declaration of war on Christianity itself. And that has to make the opportunity to assassinate the pope—and do so on the soil of the 'Great Satan'—irresistible to Abu Nakba and his disciples."

The room was quiet.

"What about you, Ryker?" Dell finally asked.

Marcus remained quiet for a long moment, still processing the video and everything his colleagues had just said.

"Well, ma'am, as I told the president, I strongly believe we should postpone the pope's visit. Clearly, there's a circumstantial case that Kairos is gunning for the pope. It's no 'slam dunk,' to cite a previous CIA director. After all, the fact that the Kairos cells entered the U.S. even when there was doubt over whether the pope was coming suggests Abu Nakba has multiple targets in mind. I absolutely agree with Annie that Abu Nakba would love to deal a death blow to the pope, one that will be felt by all Americans but especially by a billion Catholics around the globe. But he clearly knows how heavily protected the pope will be. So why take the risk? Why not hit a series of softer targets, sites not guarded at all?"

"Like what?" Dell asked.

"Let's not forget the attack that Abu Nakba ordered in the Lincoln Park Baptist Church a year and a half ago," Marcus said. "An unprotected sanctuary. Hundreds of worshipers. And look how many they killed. Look how many they wounded. And but for the grace of God, it could have been much worse. But look at the headlines that generated—not just here but around the world. That church shooting really rattled people. Christians, observant Jews attending synagogues, even devout Muslims attending mosques. Every person of faith in the country suddenly felt vulnerable."

"So what are you saying?" Dell pressed. "Is Kairos going to target the pope or not?"

"I think we have to consider multiple scenarios," Marcus replied. "If it were me, would I wait to attack four heavily defended stadiums? No. Why not hit a dozen churches and synagogues in each those four cities—plus Washington—this Sunday, the day before the pope even lands on American soil? What would happen then? The pope would almost certainly cancel his trip. The stadium Masses would be canceled. And nobody would want to go to church or synagogue for months to come. Think about it. During the pandemic, many state governments forced houses of worship to shut their doors for public health reasons. In this scenario, all houses of worship would likely close themselves. And even if they remained open, who would go?"

Again the room fell silent. No one wanted to contemplate such a ghastly scenario, yet they all knew it was plausible.

"That's what I would do," Marcus said. "But I'm not Abu Nakba. He isn't looking for the easy way out. He's old. He's frail. He's on the run. And he wants to pull off something bigger than 9/11, more spectacular than what Osama bin Laden pulled off. That's why I lean toward thinking that Annie's right. He wants to assassinate the pope, but he certainly has backup plans if that proves impossible."

"What would you recommend?" Dell asked.

"Pull the plug on the trip entirely."

"But if it goes forward?"

"It shouldn't."

"But if it does, Ryker, what then?"

"We'd need to go public."

Dell blinked. "You just told the president to stay quiet."

"Look, if the pope understands the threat against him and still decides to come, and the president still wants him to come, then that's above my pay grade. But then the public needs to know what we know. The FBI director—or the president—should hold a press conference. Give the public the facts. Go ahead and reveal that we've taken out Ruzami. Take that win. But also release the photos of the twelve Kairos operatives we know are in the country. Raise the national threat level. Put up an 800 number for people to call in leads. And ask every mayor and governor to assign local police and state troopers to protect all houses of worship this weekend. Deploy the National Guard. Then flood these four specific cities with federal agents in a massive manhunt until we roll up these cells and the threat can be neutralized."

"That's a pretty big risk," Dell said. "It could very well create a national panic."

"And it's going to overwhelm the system with people calling in false leads and wild rumors," Callaghan added.

"Marcus is right," Jenny suddenly said. "We need to go public. It's honest, and it could save countless lives, including the pope's."

Annie was nodding vigorously. "I agree. After all, imagine what happens if we *don't* inform the country."

"Unforgivable," Marcus said.

"Pardon?" Dell asked.

Marcus was not sure if she really had not heard him or simply had not liked what he had said. Either way, Marcus did not hesitate to repeat himself. "It would be unforgivable, ma'am."

THE WHITE HOUSE, WASHINGTON, D.C.

It was almost nine o'clock in the evening before the president could meet.

Marcus was growing frustrated. Precious hours were going by. Time they could not afford. Only when he and Dell cleared through security and entered the West Wing did they learn what was holding things up.

The president and First Lady had been meeting for the last several hours with the families of the three aid workers who had been murdered in Yemen. This was not a photo op. The names of the families were not on the president's public schedule, and they hadn't been recorded on the official White House visitor log. The meeting was not held in the Oval Office or the Roosevelt Room but upstairs in the Residence, and the families had been secreted into the White House through the underground tunnel running from the Treasury Department so they would not be seen, much less mobbed by the press corps. The visit was only supposed to last an hour, Bill McDermott whispered as he led Dell and Marcus into the Situation Room, but it had gone much longer than expected, turning into dinner and lasting well into the evening.

Marcus's frustration now turned away from Hernandez and onto himself. He was grateful the president had given so much time to the families and had done so off-the-record. He only wished he could have been there himself to look each mother, father, sibling, and grandparent in the eye and apologize that he hadn't rescued these women or stopped them from being seized in the first place.

Entering the Situation Room, Marcus took a seat in one of the chairs against the wall that were reserved for staff, right behind McDermott and Dell, who were at the table. The entire NSC was there, including Carl Roseboro. The vice president's chair remained empty as Whitney's appointment had not yet been taken up by Congress.

At 9:13 p.m., the president finally entered the room. "Please take your seats," Hernandez said as he took his. "Martha, where are we?"

Dell showed the Abu Nakba video and updated the group on the intelligence Marcus and his team had gathered thus far. Then she described her call with Alphonso Gianetti. The Vatican security chief was aghast and said he would strongly recommend that the Holy Father postpone the trip. But she added that an hour later, Gianetti had called back to say that the pope was determined to come anyway. "Now is not the time to surrender to madmen," he'd said.

It was a good line, Marcus thought, but a bad move.

To his surprise, however, she did not request that the president go public with what they knew. Why not? Wasn't that why they were here?

Hernandez went around the room, asking each principal for an update on what they were doing to prepare for the pope's arrival.

His frustration mounting by the minute, Marcus could not keep his silence any longer. "Excuse me, Mr. President, may I speak?" he said when it appeared Hernandez was wrapping up the meeting.

All eyes shifted to him. It was a breach of protocol. This was a principals meeting. Staff were not supposed to speak unless called upon. But Marcus had no time for such formalities. Too much was on the line.

"Agent Ryker," Hernandez said, looking tired and now a bit peeved. "Were your contributions not covered by acting Director Dell?"

"Not entirely, sir, no."

"Very well—proceed, but make it quick."

"Yes, Mr. President," Marcus replied, making his case as concisely as he possibly could.

Hernandez leaned back in his chair.

"As you know, Agent Ryker, I appreciate all you have done and all that you are doing for the country. And I could not be more pleased with your contributions, especially today. That said, I suggest you stick to counterterrorism, not public relations. Going public right now is only going to trigger a national panic, and that's the last thing we need."

"With respect, Mr. President, I'm not talking about public relations," Marcus countered, leaning forward in his chair. "This *is* counterterrorism, sir."

The room was still.

"Look, sir, we have the most serious threat in a generation on our hands. The lives of tens of thousands of Americans lie in the balance. If Kairos succeeds in what we think they're planning, we could see a death toll twenty or thirty times greater than 9/11. Possibly more. We don't know precisely where these Kairos teams are, and we're running out of time. We need to deputize the American people and ask them to help us. And we need to do it now."

"Absolutely not," the president replied. "I have every confidence in you and your team and the thousands of law enforcement professionals assigned to this visit to make sure it goes off smoothly and without a hitch. What's more, I believe the *Dead Sea Scrolls*—as Agent Daniels has so memorably dubbed the intel cache—will reveal more critical secrets. I have no doubt that we are going to find and stop these cells and safeguard the lives of the American people. But the last thing I'm going to do is create mass panic, shut down social and economic activity in five major American cities, and trigger a crash on Wall Street, all the while providing a win for Kairos whether they hit us or not."

MIAMI, FLORIDA—25 MAY

Zaid Farooq stepped onto the balcony to enjoy his Turkish coffee and the view.

He was surprised that he had not heard from Ruzami in several days, but he was grateful for the arrangements the Kairos operations chief had made. The accommodations were ideal.

The Oak Grove apartment complex was located directly across the Snake Creek Canal and less than a mile from Hard Rock Stadium, with an unobstructed view. Long known as Joe Robbie Stadium, it was the home of the Miami Dolphins football team and site of numerous Super Bowls and other major sporting events and high-profile concerts since it opened its doors in 1987.

From the tenth floor of the adjoining apartment suites, Farooq and his colleagues had been able to study all the security preparations being made at the stadium in minute detail, day and night, in good weather and in the brutal thunderstorm that had just swept through. The Patriot missile battery, for example, was almost directly in front of them, and they had taken careful note of how many men operated the system and exactly when their shifts changed.

They also now knew where all the sharpshooters were going to be positioned and could see the makeshift hospital as it was being erected.

Pretending to read that morning's edition of the *Miami Herald*, Farooq was in fact focused rather intently on an exercise underway at that hour by first responders training for some sort of crisis—perhaps the very sort of crisis he and his men were planning to inflict. Sitting beside him was his young aide-de-camp, Mansour bin Badr, hunched over his laptop and scouring news reports and social media for any scrap of information on the logistics for the upcoming Mass.

"Brother Zaid, a new message has just arrived for you," Mansour whispered, suddenly looking up.

"From your father?" Farooq asked, not taking his eyes off the exercise.

"No, from Tariq."

"Everything all right?"

"Hard to say," the young man said. "You'd better read it yourself. There seems to have been a change in plans."

DSS HEADQUARTERS, ARLINGTON, VIRGINIA

"Agent Ryker, the director will see you now."

Marcus nodded his thanks to the man's executive assistant and glanced at his watch. It was precisely 10 a.m. Marcus had come alone, urging Jenny to crack the whip back at Langley and keep their team focused on hunting the Kairos cells.

Carl Roseboro greeted him with a bear hug. "Didn't think this would be a good idea last night in the Sit Room," he said with a laugh.

"No, probably not," Marcus agreed. "Especially after I crashed and burned."

"It wasn't a pretty sight," the director said as he motioned for Marcus to take a seat near the plate-glass windows overlooking the Potomac River and the Lincoln Memorial and Washington Monument on the other side.

"The president is making a serious mistake."

"I agree," Roseboro said. "But it's his call, not mine, and certainly not yours."

"Doesn't he realize this story is going to leak?"

"It better not come from you."

"It's not me or my team he needs to worry about. Four governors have now been read in on the intel. Four big-city mayors. Police chiefs. The circle of people who know what's happening is expanding rapidly."

"You don't need to like it, Ryker. You just need to accept it and do your job."

Marcus didn't like it, but he let it go for now and focused on the mission at hand.

For the next several hours, Roseboro took Marcus through the precise itinerary Pope Pius and the cardinals and Vatican staff traveling in his entourage would be taking. He showed him photos and bios on everyone in the delegation. He walked him through the results of all the background checks they had already done on each and intelligence they had from the Vatican's own security service.

Then Roseboro reviewed the accommodations for the accredited members of the American and international press corps who would be covering the pope's visit. He explained the steps the DSS and Secret Service were taking to prevent weapons from being smuggled into the stadiums. He described the new magnetometers, X-ray machines, and other technologies that were being deployed at each location to detect body-cavity bombs like the one that had been so deadly at 10 Downing Street eighteen months earlier, as well as the one that had nearly taken out the U.S. president, Israeli prime minister, and Saudi king.

Marcus's phone buzzed. Glancing at it, he saw it was his mother. He declined the call. He would have to get back to her later. There was too much that the director had not covered, and Marcus had questions.

111

"Cell phones," Marcus said.

"What about them?" Roseboro asked.

"Shouldn't you turn off the towers anywhere near the stadiums during each Mass? You know—no calls, no Wi-Fi, no way for anyone inside or out of the stadiums to communicate with each other, much less activate a device? Remember what happened in Jerusalem."

"You're right," the director said, jotting something down on a notepad. "We'll have all security services operating on encrypted radios and satphones. And everyone will be told ahead of time that phones and other electronic devices—aside from digital cameras—won't be allowed in."

"Good," Marcus said. "Now what are you doing to prevent airborne attacks?"

"Foster is lending us Patriot antiaircraft batteries, one for each stadium."

"Only one?"

"It's all the Pentagon has stateside. All the others are deployed overseas."

Marcus wasn't satisfied, but there wasn't time to bring additional Patriots back home. Instead he asked about medical facilities, how they were being staffed, and what type of backup plans were in place if the primary medical teams on-site were killed, injured, or otherwise incapacitated in an attack.

Roseboro explained that they were setting up multiple mobile field hospitals in tents, paired with fleets of ambulances, on the outer edges of the parking lots. These would be located well away from the stadiums themselves but still much closer than local hospitals, as he feared the prospect of ambulances having to thread their way through mass-panic traffic jams. Roseboro also explained that helicopter landing pads were being established next to the field hospitals in case patients with severe injuries needed to be transported to local hospitals. Plus, he was putting fleets of National Guard and Coast Guard choppers on standby to assist in any rescue efforts.

Marcus turned to the radiation that had been detected in the tunnel under the Rio Grande. What was being done to prevent the detonation of a dirty bomb in or near the sites?

Roseboro told him that the Department of Energy's NEST unit was deploying rapid-response teams to New York, Houston, Miami, and Chicago, as well as beefing up their activity in and around Washington, D.C. By the following morning, NEST would be conducting 24-7 patrols of the grounds of each stadium and surrounding neighborhoods with state-of-the-art sensors capable of "sniffing" radioactivity that could suggest the presence of nuclear weapons.

What's more, Roseboro explained, they were also working with Homeland Security's Domestic Nuclear Detection Office and the Pentagon's Defense Threat Reduction Agency to install special weapons-detection sensors throughout the stadiums, throughout all parking facilities, and on all bridges, train tracks, and intersections within a five-mile radius of the stadiums. The sensors were capable of detecting not just nuclear devices but chemical and biological weapons as well.

The new director then had a question for Marcus. "I'm heading to Miami tomorrow to review the site and plug any holes. Why don't you and your team come with me and give me your take?"

"We can't tomorrow. We've got conference calls all day starting with Saudi intelligence, then the Emiratis, the Bahrainis, and the Jordanians. It's nonstop. What about later this week? Where will you be?"

"Chicago Friday and Saturday," Roseboro said. "Houston on Sunday. Then straight back here to prepare for the pope's arrival on Tuesday."

"All right," Marcus said. "Let me talk to my guys and get back to you."

112

CHICAGO, ILLINOIS—30 MAY

United flight 1800 landed at O'Hare at 8:05 a.m. local time.

As the Boeing 737-700 taxied to the gate, Marcus forced himself awake and texted Annie to let her know he and the team had landed safely. Thirty minutes later, they had retrieved their luggage and equipment at baggage claim and were met by a young DSS advance man driving a large white rental van. By 10 a.m., they had checked into the Hilton Garden Inn on East Cermak Street, just a mile from Soldier Field.

Once that was done, the advance man gave them keys to two Jeep Wranglers that had been rented for them and were parked in the hotel's underground garage. Marcus took the keys to the gray one, leaving the red one for Geoff. Then the advance man gave them his mobile number, excused himself, and explained that he needed to head back to the airport to pick up another DSS team that was landing at noon.

They were to meet Roseboro at the stadium, so they dropped off their luggage and met in the parking garage. Marcus took Jenny with him. Geoff took

Pete and Donny Callaghan. It was a short drive but complicated. Though it was a full week before the Mass, roadblocks were already up, sealing off the perimeter five blocks from the stadium. That would soon be extended out to ten blocks, but even now, no nonessential traffic was being permitted in this part of the city, angering every Chicagoland resident who had a daily commute into downtown.

Even on a Saturday, traffic was still a nightmare. The first checkpoint was guarded by a dozen reservists in full battle gear and an armored personnel carrier from the Illinois National Guard, topped by a .50-caliber machine gun. Marcus slowed to a stop. They showed their DSS badges and photo IDs and were eventually cleared, but they had to repeat the process at three more heavily defended checkpoints before finally parking in front of the stadium.

Roseboro and his detail met them in the lot.

Marcus shook his friend's hand and introduced his team, then asked, "How's it looking?"

"Aside from the fact that we have two terrorist cells on the loose and no idea where they are?" Roseboro said, pretty much setting the tone for the morning.

For the next hour, the director gave them the grand tour. They began inside, examining the stage where the president and pope would be speaking and the multiple routes Roseboro and the Secret Service had planned in case the principals needed to be evacuated. From there, they went up on the roof to see where all the sharpshooters and spotters would be positioned. It was a gorgeous, sunny morning with barely a cloud in the deep-blue sky. The view of Lake Michigan and the Chicago skyline—notably the Willis Tower, formerly called the Sears Tower, once the tallest building in the world—was spectacular.

"Any thoughts on bringing in Coast Guard cutters to keep an eye on the shoreline?" Jenny asked.

"Absolutely," Roseboro said. "Three of them arrive tomorrow."

"Director, I'd love to see the field hospitals you told Marcus about," Pete said.

"Absolutely, Dr. Hwang. Let's do that now. Then I'll take you to the command center and introduce you all to the watch commanders."

No sooner had they headed downstairs and gone back out into the parking lot, however, than a Black Hawk helicopter with National Guard markings came roaring into view. It set down on an empty section of pavement about fifty yards from where they were standing, and the side door slid open. To their astonishment, Bill McDermott was sitting in the back and waving them over.

"Get in," he shouted over the roar of the rotors.

"Bill, what are you doing here?" Marcus shouted back. *"What's going on?"*

"Get in—now—I'll explain on the way."

Marcus's phone rang as they all piled inside the chopper. It was his mother. Marcus silenced the call. He felt guilty, but it couldn't be helped. When the side door was closed and locked, McDermott gave the pilots a thumbs-up. The Black Hawk lifted off the ground about fifteen feet, rotated 180 degrees, then rapidly gained altitude, heading north by northwest. As the Chicago skyline blurred past, Marcus realized they were heading back to the airport.

"What's going on?" Marcus shouted again.

"A NEST team just picked up two radioactive signatures in Houston," McDermott shouted back. *"One was at an apartment complex about five miles from NRG Stadium. The other was at a parking garage three miles from the stadium. The FBI has cordoned off both areas. HPD is in the process of evacuating everyone. And DOE is deploying more NEST teams to Houston as we speak. We need to get you there right away."*

Soon they were landing at the Signature Flight Support center at O'Hare and boarding a government G5. As they taxied toward the runway, Roseboro and McDermott were speaking urgently into their phones. Marcus was hunched over his phone, scanning social media. The news had not yet broken in either the local or national media. Marcus knew the FBI and other agencies would do everything possible to keep the story contained, but part of him wanted the media to blow the story wide-open. He certainly understood the president's desire not to create a national panic that foreign terrorists were on American soil and had in their possession nuclear weapons, or at least radioactive material. But the American people had a right to know. And Marcus still thought Washington needed to mobilize the public to find these Kairos cells before it was too late.

Then, just as they were about to take off, Marcus's phone rang again. Hoping it was Annie, but assuming it was his mother, he checked the caller ID. To his surprise the call was coming from Aspen, Colorado. That could only be one person: Oleg Kraskin, aka the Raven, and given all that was happening, it could not be good news.

HOUSTON, TEXAS—2 JUNE

Three days later, Marcus and his team were still in Houston.

They had been working eighteen- to twenty-hour days, yet neither they nor the five hundred other federal agents spread out across the city had discovered, much less captured, any Kairos operatives.

That said, there was no question the NEST teams had found convincing evidence of radiological devices in both an apartment building and its parking garage. What was particularly odd, and deeply troubling, was an analysis by the top nuclear scientists at both the Defense Department and the Department of Energy verifying that the particular uranium signature detected was from material originally produced in Russia.

That finding, highly classified and known only to nineteen people in the entire federal government, had been a thunderclap. However, on a secure videoconference of the National Security Council, Defense Secretary Cal Foster cautioned that this apparently damning evidence did not necessarily mean the Russians had given uranium to Kairos. Foster noted that the traces could very well have come from uranium that Moscow had once provided to Iran for their civilian nuclear reactor at Bushehr. The IRGC, in turn, might have provided it to Abu Nakba. At this point there was no way to be certain.

It was then that Marcus felt compelled to share the new information that he had learned from Oleg Kraskin and had been trying to confirm for the past several days. By hacking into the Kremlin's computer system, the Raven had uncovered evidence that the FSB had bankrolled Kairos in its early years with a series of complicated wire transfers through various shell corporations in the Caribbean. The transfers totaled more than 100 million rubles. While that was the equivalent of only about one million U.S. dollars, it was still a bombshell to the National Security Council given all the Americans Kairos had already murdered and Kairos's attempt on President Clarke's life in Jerusalem.

"I thought Kairos was being bankrolled by the Iranians," Hernandez said over the secure conference line.

"They are, sir," Marcus confirmed, "but what the Raven has uncovered indicates Abu Nakba has been soliciting funds from multiple sources. I've suspected this for years, but this is the first hard confirmation we've ever found."

Martha Dell and Annie Stewart verified that the Raven's evidence was airtight and had been cross-checked by the Agency's top Russia analysts.

The revelation sparked an intense debate over what this meant and how to handle it. Foster, the SecDef, argued this was an act of war. Whitney agreed but laid the blame at the feet of former Russian dictator Luganov, not Russia's current president, Mikhail Petrovsky. Annie suggested that Hernandez send Whitney to Moscow immediately to confront Petrovsky both with the evidence of his predecessor's support for Kairos and the evidence of Russian uranium being used by Kairos to build one or more dirty bombs.

"The last thing I want to do is start a war," Hernandez said.

"Exactly, sir," Annie replied. "The secretary can make it clear that you want a fresh start with Moscow. But to do so, you need Petrovsky to help us identify and stop these terrorists—immediately. And she should also make it clear that if a nuclear device made with Russian uranium is detonated on American soil, you will consider this an attack by the Russian Federation on the United States of America."

Marcus concurred but suggested a slight alternative. "Mr. President, I'd recommend that Director Dell fly to Moscow instead. A visit by Secretary Whitney would attract too much attention. But Dell can go quietly and serve as a back channel. No press. No leaks. Just lay out the facts, as Annie suggested, and present a crystal clear ultimatum. If Petrovsky is serious about peace, he can help us stop these terrorists immediately without the public knowing. If he refuses, Mr. President, then we'll all know what we're up against."

This, too, sparked a heated debate. Telling the Russians what the U.S. now knew about the imminent Kairos threat posed a serious risk. What if the Kremlin was, in fact, using Kairos to retaliate against the U.S. for alleged U.S. complicity in the assassinations of former President Luganov, former FSB chief Dmitri Nimkov, and former Prime Minister Maxim Grigarin? If so, they might verbally agree to help the Americans thwart any coming attack yet not actually provide any useful information. Worse, they could tip off Abu Nakba to accelerate his attack.

But they were fast running out of time, and both Marcus and Annie argued that Petrovsky, while no friend of the U.S., was not as evil as Luganov. He certainly didn't want to spark a nuclear war and could very well have intel about Kairos that might prove critical.

In the end, Hernandez was persuaded and ordered Dell to fly to Moscow immediately. Then he apologized for having to end the NSC call. The pontiff's plane had just landed on American soil and he would be arriving at the White House within the hour.

"Agent Ryker, you have a call from Agent Daniels."

Marcus and his team were in the DSS command center in Houston eating Chinese takeout and watching the pope's address to Congress, but he immediately muted the TV, took the call, and put Noah on speakerphone.

Noah reported that he had just broken into a file on Ruzami's hard drive. It contained detailed blueprints for each of the stadiums in all four cities where the pope would be speaking. These were not commercial blueprints, Noah said. They could only have come from the architectural firms that had designed the stadiums in the first place.

What's more, Noah and his colleagues at NSA had also just decrypted files containing JPEGs of Google maps and satellite imagery of Miami, Houston, New York, and Chicago. Alone, these were not proof that the pope was, in fact, Kairos's target. Nor did they provide hard evidence of which city was being targeted—unless they all were. Still, the material at least indicated that the four cities were the focus of Abu Nakba's planning.

"Good work, young man," Marcus said.

"Thank you, sir."

"Get this to Dell and Annie and to Roseboro at DSS."

"Yes, sir."

No sooner had Marcus hung up than Roseboro called on another line. "Ryker, get yourself to Miami now," he ordered.

"Why? What's going on?"

"A NEST team has just found a new hot spot."

"Where?"

"Barely a mile from the stadium," Roseboro said. "And the pope flies to Miami in less than twelve hours."

MIAMI, FLORIDA—3 JUNE

Marcus and his team landed in Miami in a private jet just before 3 a.m.

A DSS advance agent met them at the Signature Flight Support center and drove them to the Oak Grove apartments, though it was a nightmare to get to the actual evidence scene. The entire area was blocked for a half mile in every direction, and residents were still being evacuated.

Even when they cleared through the checkpoints, they found the streets near the building clogged with emergency vehicles. Specialists in hazmat suits were everywhere. Police and FBI choppers buzzed overhead, though there were no TV news helicopters; the governor, in coordination with DSS and the Secret Service, had just declared a no-fly zone over the stadium.

Marcus eventually found the special agent in charge and received a full briefing. No other hot spots had been found in the city, though NEST teams were going neighborhood by neighborhood in search of more. A massive manhunt was underway but so far had turned up no one associated with Kairos. The only sliver of good news was that the city was not panicking, since most of its residents were sound asleep. The deadline for the morning edition of the *Miami Herald* had already passed, and so people would not be waking up to headlines screaming anything like "Feds Hunt for Nuclear Terrorists ahead of Papal Visit." For now, officials were telling the media there had been fears of a gas leak in an apartment and that out of an abundance of caution, residents were being evacuated until the situation could be resolved.

That story worked for a while, but by sunrise, TV and radio news broadcasts were leading with unsourced rumors that federal authorities were searching for a "foreign terrorist cell" allegedly operating in the Miami area.

At 9 a.m., the governor and mayor held a joint news conference to say simply that there had been a bomb threat at the apartment complex—not a gas leak—but that the situation was under control. Asked by reporters if rumors of terrorists coming to Miami were true, the governor adroitly deflected the issue by saying, "As with any major event in our city, we are dealing with many rumors and allegations." He added that he and the mayor had great confidence in the work law enforcement was doing, that the city was not in danger, and that the people of Miami remained "very proud to welcome His Holiness" to their city.

Shortly before 10 a.m., Marcus arrived at the DSS command post, located on the top floor of a high-rise hotel not far from the stadium. He placed a call to Dell to basically report that they hadn't found anything Kairos related yet.

"I think you need to get on a plane to New York next, then," Dell said, speaking from a SCIF in the American embassy in Moscow. "If there's nothing more you can do in Miami, and Houston is already on high alert, we need boots on the ground near Yankee Stadium."

Marcus couldn't think of a reason to disagree. The pope was on his way to Miami even now. NEST and the other agencies had things under control, as much as he could predict.

At 10 a.m., Marcus joined a secure videoconference with the president and the NSC.

Defense Secretary Foster opened the briefing by telling the group that the Pentagon and DOE were able to confirm overnight that the unique radioactive signatures found at the Miami apartment complex could, in fact, be traced back to Russian uranium. However, the evidence was conclusive that this was a different batch of Russian uranium from the traces found in Houston. That was significant, he said, because it meant the Miami hot spot had not been created from the same set of bombs as the Houston one. That, in turn, meant these bombs were being transported by a different Kairos cell.

Hernandez called on Dell, who was participating in the call from the SCIF. "What time are you meeting with Petrovsky?" he asked.

"In about ninety minutes."

"Add this to your brief, Martha."

"I will, Mr. President."

Hernandez ordered the SecDef to take U.S. nuclear and conventional forces to DEFCON 2. Then he turned back to Dell. "I don't want to give the Russians any room to misunderstand the gravity or the urgency of the situation, Martha. And I want you to use the language Annie suggested yesterday. Make it clear that if any nuclear device containing uranium mined, processed, or enriched in Russia is detonated on American soil, the U.S. government will consider this an act of war by the Russian Federation. Understood?"

"Yes, sir," Dell said. "But what if Petrovsky argues the material was given to the Iranians or stolen or was out of the Kremlin's control for some other reason?"

"Tell him I don't care, and neither will the American people. If nuclear weapons with Russian fingerprints kill American citizens, we are going to war."

Every muscle in Marcus's body tensed. The situation was deteriorating rapidly. A Kairos attack inside the American homeland would be bad enough. But this thing could get far worse. Aleksandr Luganov—Petrovsky's predecessor—was dead, but the evil that Luganov had set into motion was taking the great powers to the brink of global thermonuclear war. And unlike the Cuban Missile Crisis, the only parallel he could think of, no one outside this call had any idea of the danger.

CHICAGO, ILLINOIS—4 JUNE

United flight 743 from Reagan National landed at O'Hare at 9:55 a.m.

Marjorie Ryker and Maya Emerson gathered their suitcases from baggage claim, then took the private car service that the Garcias had arranged. By noon they had checked into their suites on the top floor of the Four Seasons Hotel. Both Marjorie and Maya had repeatedly protested the extravagance, but the Garcias were insistent. They wanted this to be a weekend to remember and said their guests should stop worrying about the cost and just enjoy themselves.

The ladies finally gave in and accepted the lavish generosity, with one exception. Rather than eating something fancy at the hotel, Maya wondered if they could simply get some famous Chicago-style deep-dish pizza for lunch. The Garcias laughed and accepted her conditions.

In a cab on the way to the original Pizzeria Uno, Marjorie tried to reach Marcus again. She had been trying to reach him for days, but he never answered his phone. She did not want to leave a voice message or send a text. She wanted to tell him personally, to surprise him, and encourage him that such a sweet and unexpected reconciliation between her and the Garcias was really in motion. But yet again, Marcus did not pick up.

She was not particularly worried about her son. And she was grateful no one back at Bolling had stopped her from traveling on her own. The chief of security on the base had told her that neither the Iranians nor Kairos had any idea where she was now and couldn't possibly track her personally. It was staying in Colorado in houses that could be easily identified that presented the main threat to the family.

That said, Marjorie had to admit she was growing irritated. The boy was busy. This much she understood. But too busy to return his mother's calls?

THE BRONX

As they feared, the day had been a complete waste.

"This thing is airtight," Callaghan said of the security in and around Yankee Stadium. "The NEST teams haven't turned up anything here. If these guys are going to strike, it's going to be in Chicago."

Jenny agreed. "It's almost midnight," she told Marcus. "We're wasting time. We should be in Illinois."

Geoff concurred. Pete, however, made the case to stay in New York until the Mass on Friday night was over. He had family in the area, and he wanted to do everything in his power to protect the lives of his kids.

Marcus was conflicted. He and the team were bone-tired. They had spent another fruitless day hunting ghosts. Now they were back at some lousy Best Western eating cold pizza and accomplishing nothing. There had been no attacks in Washington. Nor in Miami. Nor in Houston. So far, the papal visit was going smoothly, safely, and on time. But they were hardly in the clear. The event at Yankee Stadium was set to begin in eighteen hours. And then there was Soldier Field.

To their bewilderment, the imminent threat of attack by two and possibly more Kairos cells had still not made the news, aside from a plethora of rumors and heightened threat alerts that kept people buzzing on social media. Miraculously, the presence of two sets of nuclear devices on American soil had also not made the news.

With nerves strained, the discussion over whether to stay in the Bronx or head immediately to Chicago was becoming heated. Then Marcus's secure satellite phone rang. It was Annie.

"Martha just landed at Andrews," she said without small talk.

"And?"

"Her talks with Petrovsky were about as tense as they get, but in the end, they may have worked. The second she stepped off the plane, she got a call from Nikolay Kropatkin," she explained, referring to the Russian spy chief. "For starters, he confirmed that until recently, Abu Nakba was in Iran, but he departed for the Hindu Kush region of Afghanistan two days ago."

The team was arguing so loudly now about whether to stay in the Bronx or leave for Chicago that Marcus could barely hear Annie. Stepping out onto the balcony, he asked her if the Russians were tracking the Kairos leader.

"Kropatkin says no. What's more, he insists that the IRGC doesn't know where he is or how to contact him. The old man contacts them when he wants to communicate; otherwise it's radio silence."

"Liars."

"My thoughts exactly," Annie said. "But Kropatkin gave Martha a half-dozen satellite phone accounts that they know for a fact are used by Kairos operatives."

"How do they know?"

"Because apparently Luganov ordered the FSB to provide Russian-built satphones to Kairos for the exclusive use of Kairos's top command. Kropatkin claims that this all happened under his predecessor, Dmitri Nimkov, without his knowledge. But regardless, Noah just cross-checked the serial numbers of the phones. He says one of the phones was used by Abu Nakba himself in Libya. He also says the SEALs pulled the remains of a second Russian satphone out of the Ghat compound, but it was too damaged to get any data off it."

"What about the other four?" Marcus pressed.

"I just spoke with NSA," Annie replied. "They say three of the phones have not been used in weeks, but they'll start monitoring them and checking past usage."

"And the fourth?"

"That's why I'm calling," Annie said. "The account is active. The phone was used yesterday, and it's in Chicago."

117

CHICAGO—5 JUNE

They landed in the Windy City just after 9:30 a.m.

No one was there to greet them. Everyone was too busy making final preparations for the arrival of Air Force One the following day.

By the time they had retrieved their luggage and gear, caught some cabs, and made it downtown through the snarl of traffic, it was nearly noon. Their cabdrivers were not permitted to pass through the checkpoint at the outer edge of the security perimeter around the stadium. So the team had to wait for three Chicago PD patrol cars to drive them to their destination, the Hilton Garden Inn on East Cermak Street. The whole process was an enormous waste of time, pushing the team's already-frayed nerves to the limit.

Once checked into the hotel, they were able to retrieve the two Jeep Wranglers that the DSS advance man had returned for them from the stadium parking lot to the hotel parking garage. Their first stop was the Joint Security Task Force command post, being run out of the basement of a museum located a block north of the stadium. By the time Marcus arrived, the daily NSC videoconference was already in progress. Dell had just briefed the president on what she'd learned from the Russians. Now Roseboro was briefing him on the early morning raid DSS and FBI agents had conducted at the JW Marriott in the heart of Chicago's financial district. The presidential suite on the hotel's twelfth floor was the last location of the Kairos satphone. Unfortunately, no one had been in the suite at the time of the raid, but its last guests had left behind several clues.

While the NEST team on-site found no traces of radioactive materials, Roseboro explained, CCTV footage from the lobby revealed that the man who had checked in was none other than Tariq Youssef. Other CCTV footage of the twelfth floor showed six men entering and exiting the presidential suite at various hours of the past two days and nights. They also found multiple sets of fingerprints in the room, belonging to Youssef as well as two others, possibly two of Badr Hassan al-Ruzami's sons.

It was a significant breakthrough. For the first time, they had confirmation that at least one of the terror cells was in the city. But the knowledge only increased Marcus's anxiety. Why was there no evidence of nuclear devices in the hotel or in the garage? Why was the satellite phone now no longer functioning? When had the men checked out? Where were they now? And where was the other Kairos cell?

Marjorie, Maya, and the Garcias had a lovely breakfast at the Four Seasons.

They spent the morning touring the National Museum of Mexican Art. After a light lunch in the food court of the Sears Tower—Marjorie knew it was no longer called that, but to her it would always be the Sears Tower—they bought tickets to the Skydeck and took the elevator to the 103rd floor, their ears popping on the way up. When they got there, Louisa was terrified. So was Maya. But Marjorie loved it. Heights had never bothered her. "I married a fighter pilot, and I live in the Rocky Mountains," she said.

Getting change for a ten-dollar bill, Marjorie paid for them all to look through the big viewfinders positioned on all four sides of the building. With the weather so beautiful and the skies so clear, she was tickled by the concept of being able to see a good forty or fifty miles in every direction, and into three neighboring states. She also found it fascinating to watch all the security preparations being made at Soldier Field, which she could see clearly through the viewfinder. It made her wonder if Marcus was down there or back in Washington. Either way, she was relieved at how safely and smoothly the pope's visit to the States was going. Wherever Marcus was, she was sure he was playing a critical role.

While Louisa and Maya perused the gift shop in the center of the open and spacious floor plan, determined to stay away from the massive plate-glass windows, Marjorie and Javier got in line behind a group of squealing teenage girls and stepped into "the Ledge," one of several large glass boxes that jutted out from the side of the tower. That might have been a bit too much. Even Marjorie was scared to look straight down—1,353 feet—to the streets and tiny people below.

She stayed in the box for less than a minute before asking Javier to help her step out. But she was proud of herself for having done it. She had read that several years earlier the glass bottom of the box had cracked. It had been repaired, of course, and there had probably never been any real danger. Nevertheless, Marjorie could not think of a more terrible way to die than plunging a quarter of a mile out of the sky only to—

She shuddered, not daring to finish the thought.

She and Javier soon joined the others in the gift shop. Marjorie bought some T-shirts and other knickknacks for her grandkids and a book about the building of the tower for herself. Finally she bought several postcards, including one for Marcus. If her son was too busy to answer her calls, perhaps he would at least read his mail and learn that his mother was living her life and not sitting around waiting for him to pick up the phone.

After the NSC call, Marcus and Roseboro walked back to the stadium.

"What are you thinking?" the director asked. "What am I missing?"

Scanning the horizon, Marcus noticed the line of commercial jetliners and private planes stretching out over Lake Michigan, on approach to land at O'Hare.

"Why hasn't the president declared a no-fly zone over the city?"

"He says that would be an overreaction."

"The governor did it in Miami."

"That was just over the stadium itself. And that was Miami. This is Chicago."

"So?"

"So O'Hare is the one of the busiest airports in the world—900,000 flights a year, an average of 2,500 flights a day, one takeoff or landing every thirty to forty seconds. And then there's Midway."

"And?"

"And the president doesn't want to shut them down."

"Then that's the biggest risk I see right now."

"We don't have any threat reporting of an airborne attack," Roseboro said. "Besides, there's the Patriot battery right over there. That should suffice."

"Carl, come on. Let's say the worst happens, and there's another 9/11 scenario," Marcus pressed. "Are you really going to order a missile attack on an unarmed jumbo jet on live global television?"

Roseboro was quiet.

"No, you're not," Marcus said. "And even if you did, you'd only authorize the launch at the last possible moment, when you were absolutely certain the plane was heading for the stadium, and then it would be too late. That's too big a gamble. You have to tell the president to shut down all air travel in and out of Chicago tomorrow, except of course for Air Force One and the pope's plane. Personally, I'd shut it down today as well."

"It's not going to happen."

"Then put up a CAP," Marcus insisted, speaking of a combat air patrol of armed fighter jets over the city.

"That's out of the question."

"You're not even going to request it?"

"I did request it," Roseboro said. "The president said no, the Patriot battery is enough."

"You asked me what you're missing. That's it, Carl. And if things go badly tomorrow, you'll never forgive yourself."

Annie called around dinnertime.

"Hey, I've been trying to reach you for hours," Marcus said. "Everything okay?"

"Of course. Didn't you get my message?" Annie asked.

"No, where'd you leave it?"

"I kept trying you on your Agency phone, but it was always busy. So I left a message on your personal phone."

"That explains it," Marcus said. "I left it in the hotel this morning."

"Then you don't know that I'm here," Annie said.

"Where?"

"In Chicago—I just landed."

"Seriously?"

"Martha sent me. With you guys out in the field, she wanted one of her own in the command post to keep tabs on everything for her and serve as a direct liaison to Roseboro and the others."

"That's great. But brace yourself."

"For what?"

"The mood around here is pretty grim."

"No breakthroughs since I've been in the air?"

"Hardly. We know one of the cells is here. We suspect both are. And there may be more. We know the attack is coming tomorrow, and we have absolutely no idea how to stop it."

Tariq Youssef's ears were popping all the way up.

When he reached the 89th floor of the Willis Tower, he checked his new Breitling watch. It was 4:47 p.m., nearly closing time. Adjusting his silk tie and sweeping away a piece of lint from his Brooks Brothers suit, he stepped off the elevator and took a right. At the end of the hall was the law firm of McClintock, Bannister & Locke.

"May I help you?" asked the attractive young redhead at the front desk.

"Yes, I have an appointment with Mr. McClintock."

"Are you Mr. Aden?"

"I am," Youssef said.

"And you're here to discuss the bankruptcy matter?"

"Yes."

"I'm so sorry, Mr. Aden, but Mr. McClintock was expecting you at three o'clock," the receptionist said. "When you didn't show, we called you and texted you several times."

"I'm so sorry. With all the security for the event tomorrow, it has been almost impossible to get here. I had to walk nine blocks, and my mobile phone hasn't worked since I entered the security perimeter."

"Oh yes, of course. Unfortunately, Mr. McClintock has just left for the day."

"But I've flown in from L.A. especially to meet him, and I fly back there tomorrow. Is there anyone else I could speak with?"

"At this hour? I'm afraid not, sir. Everyone has gone. It's just a paralegal and me now, and we're leaving soon too. May I reschedule something for next week?"

Just then the paralegal came down the hall, a brunette no older than thirty.

"May I help you?" she said.

"Apparently I've missed Mr. McClintock. But is there really no one here I could speak with?" Youssef asked.

"Sorry, there isn't. It really is just the two of us. But—"

The paralegal never finished the sentence. As she spoke, Youssef unbuttoned his suit coat, drew a silenced pistol, and double-tapped her to the head. Before she'd even hit the floor, he'd done the same to the stunned receptionist. Dragging their bodies to the ladies' room, he grabbed a stack of paper towels, returned to the lobby, and wiped up the blood. Then he picked up an office line and called a brand-new burner phone.

Ali bin Badr, sipping a latte at a Starbucks in the atrium, answered on the second ring.

"Come on up," Youssef said. "The meeting is on."

With his team on their way up, he now called down to the loading dock. "Hello? Yes, hi, this is Gary McClintock in 8109. A client tells me he sent several boxes to me by FedEx earlier in the week, but I never got the message."

"Yes, sir, Mr. McClintock," said the on-call manager. "We've got six boxes here. Fairly big, too. Would you like to have my guys bring them up?"

"Would you?" Youssef asked. "That would be great. But I'll be on a conference call and my staff has just left for the day. Would you mind having them left by the front desk?"

"No problem, sir. They'll be right up."

CHICAGO—6 JUNE

The alarm on his phone went off at 5 a.m.

Marcus hit Snooze, then thought better of it and forced himself out of bed, heading straight into a long, hot shower. There would be no time for a run this morning. He and Annie had had a quiet if brief dinner when she'd arrived at the hotel. Then he'd taken her to the command center and introduced her to the senior members of the joint command. That, however, had been the best of his night. It had gone downhill from there.

Closing his weary eyes and breathing in the steam, he replayed in his mind the last secure videoconference of the evening. Beginning at 9 p.m. Washington time and running almost two hours, it had been planned as a final briefing on what little new intelligence they had as well as a checklist of items that needed to be finalized before the president and Pope Pius XIII arrived at O'Hare. But the meeting had erupted into a fight over whether to impose a no-fly zone over Chicago.

To his credit, Roseboro had made a clear and convincing case that the biggest flaw in their otherwise-airtight security plan was keeping the airports open. The president had not been convinced. To the contrary, Hernandez had argued that with the exception of the one-hour window when Air Force One and the flight DSS had dubbed "Vatican One" touched down, closing the rest of Chicago's air operations would be a terrible mistake that would trigger panic rather than appear as prudent protection efforts.

Roseboro had pushed back hard. When his arguments did not seem to be working, Marcus had jumped into the fray as well. Hernandez got angry, but Marcus refused to be shut down.

"Mr. President, the other day you told me to stay out of PR and stick to counterterrorism," he'd said. "But I have to say now what I told you then. This isn't public relations. It's counterterrorism. Keeping the skies over the event at Soldier Field open is a serious mistake, and with all due respect, sir, I believe you know that. The only reason you have given us for saying no to our recommendation is due to PR concerns. But that is unacceptable, sir. I pray to God nothing goes wrong tomorrow. But if it does, the American people will not forgive or forget a commander in chief who does not do everything in his power to safeguard the country from a threat you still refuse to tell them even exists."

That had sucked all the air out of the room. McDermott had defended Hernandez and told Marcus he was out of line. Marcus shot back that the national security advisor was out of his mind to put the president of the United States and the head of the Roman Catholic Church and one hundred thousand innocent American citizens in harm's way. He came dangerously close to calling the decision a potentially impeachable offense but caught himself at the last moment.

In the end, the defense secretary weighed in that the presence of the Patriot battery would "probably be enough" to secure the event. Marcus tried to respond to that but found his microphone had been muted.

When the meeting ended, Marcus expected his phone to blow up with McDermott and other members of the NSC calling to ream him out. Instead, not a single person called. Except, of course, his mother, whose call he did not take.

Now spent and operating entirely on adrenaline, Marcus turned off the shower, toweled down, and decided to cut off his beard. As lousy as he felt overall, he wanted to be clean-shaven again. The bruising on his face and neck had mostly faded now. He still had scars, but they were fading too.

He opted against a business suit and instead threw on a pair of old blue jeans, a black T-shirt, and his shoulder holster and Sig Sauer. Over this he donned the well-worn leather jacket that Elena had given him on their last Christmas together. He texted his team to go casual as well. They would not be on any of the protective details. They were going hunting.

The team ate breakfast together in the lobby at six. Annie joined them. By seven, they were loading their weapons and gear into the backs of both Jeeps. Then they hit the road, dropping Annie off at the command center.

At Roseboro's insistence, the security perimeter had been extended even farther overnight. Now, only Chicago Transit Authority buses and law enforcement vehicles were permitted to operate between the stadium and the I-90 highway to the west, I-55 to the south, and the Merchandise Mart and the river to the north. Marcus asked Geoff Stone and Donny Callaghan to head to the city's south side, beyond Chinatown, to patrol the neighborhoods around the Illinois Institute of Technology. Meanwhile, he, Jenny, and Pete would patrol Lake Shore Drive.

The stretch of the iconic road that was inside the perimeter was off-limits to normal traffic. But Roseboro had not, in the end, received permission to clear all the pleasure crafts out of the nearby harbors. This had infuriated Marcus nearly as much as the president's refusal to order a no-fly zone. The good news was that the Coast Guard had positioned five well-armed cutters offshore, not just three. They also had divers triple-checking the hulls of every boat in the harbor, as well as helicopters keeping a close watch of the shoreline. Armored personnel carriers mounted with .50-caliber machine guns were positioned every two hundred yards along Lake Shore Drive, facing the water.

Marcus felt they were as prepared as they could be for an attack from the lake. He also felt certain that was not where the attack, if it came, would originate. They still were insufficiently prepared for an air assault.

Once again it was shaping up to be a gorgeous late spring day in Chicago.

Sunny. Blue skies. White puffy clouds. A light breeze coming off the water. Nearly unlimited visibility. And Marjorie Ryker could not have been happier. It had been far too long since she had done something spontaneous and crazy like this. Well, it was not exactly spontaneous. The Garcias had put a great deal of thought into making every detail special, and they were spending a fortune. But for Marjorie and Maya, it was the craziest thing they had done in years, and they were loving every minute.

Though they were not far from the stadium, they learned they couldn't take a cab to the big event. Rather, they had to take a series of special CTA buses. The concierge at the Four Seasons made all the arrangements to get them to the right place at the right time, which meant early. It was a good thing, too, because the buses were backed up for nearly a mile. None of them minded, however. All four of them found the process fascinating as they peered out the bus windows at the National Guard troops lining the streets.

When they finally pulled up to their designated checkpoint, every guest got off the bus and entered one of seven enormous white tents. There they were directed by U.S. Secret Service and DSS agents to show their tickets and a valid photo ID, pass through magnetometers, and put their belongings through X-ray machines and past K-9 units with explosive-sniffing dogs. Marjorie marveled at all the CCTV cameras, remembering what Marcus had taught her over the years about how these images were fed through state-of-the-art facial recognition software and run through a database of terror suspects jointly maintained by the Secret Service, DSS, FBI, Homeland Security, the CIA, and no doubt even more mysterious agencies too. Once they were cleared, they were each given a wristband indicating that they had been through the process. Then volunteers directed them back onto the buses to be taken right up to the front doors of the stadium.

It was exciting to be part of something so grand and historic, Marjorie thought, and while Maya and the Garcias were chatting about it all, she dashed off a text message to Annie, kicking herself for not having thought of doing so before.

Hi, Annie, she typed. **Guess where I am? Chicago! Going to see the pope with Maya Emerson and the Garcias. Crazy, right? I know. It's a long story. Will tell you and Marcus all about it when you guys have time. Give him my love. Have been trying to reach him all week. But I'm sure he's busy keeping us safe. Call when you can. Praying for you both!—M**

Only then did she remember she wasn't allowed to bring her phone into the stadium and the thought that security was going to confiscate it made her ill.

GRAND RAPIDS, MICHIGAN

Nasir Bhati parked his van in front of the DHL terminal.

He and Yaqoub al-Hamzi, both wearing new Zegna suits and carrying small crates, entered the lobby.

"Good morning, may I help you?" the clerk asked.

"Yes, we'd like to ship these to Seattle," Bhati said. "And my colleague could use a men's room."

"Of course. Down the hall and to the right."

The moment al-Hamzi disappeared around the corner, Bhati unbuttoned his jacket, drew a silenced pistol, and shot the clerk twice in the chest and once in the head. It was lunchtime, and most of the staff—four warehouse workers, a driver, and two pilots—were in the break room as they were every day at this time, eating pizzas and laughing about something. Bhati never caught the topic. Nor did it matter. By the time he reached the break room, al-Hamzi had already shot them all in the head and grabbed them both a slice.

Bhati tossed it aside. There was no way New York–style pizza was going to be his last meal. Al-Hamzi stripped one of the dead employees of his bright-yellow-and-red coveralls and his ID badge and put them on. Then he headed into the warehouse to finish off the remaining staff. Bhati, meanwhile, stripped the pilots of their uniforms, IDs, and wallets. Next he removed his expensive suit and put on one of the uniforms.

Once he was certain there were no other living souls on the premises, Bhati pulled out a new burner phone and called Zaid Farooq. "Your order is ready, sir."

"Good, I'll be right there."

A moment later, Farooq entered the DHL premises, locked the front door behind him, and hung the We'll Be Right Back sign in its place in the window. Then he strode through the front offices and found the break room, where Bhati was waiting for him with his uniform. It didn't fit exactly. But for their purposes, it would do.

"Vatican One" touched down at O'Hare International Airport precisely at noon.

Fifteen minutes later, Air Force One was wheels down as well.

Using high-powered binoculars from the position they'd taken near Navy Pier, Marcus, Jenny, and Pete watched both planes come in on approach. As each jet roared past, the three agents scanned the city's three most prominent office buildings, looking for anything out of the ordinary.

Marcus focused on Willis Tower. Completed in 1973 with 110 stories and standing a dizzying 1,450 feet tall, it was the tallest building in the state of Illinois and the second tallest in the United States. That made it both a potential target and a theoretical launching pad for terrorist attacks. Marcus, like many Americans, still thought of it as the Sears Tower. But the building was renamed in 2009, years after Sears—once the biggest retailer in the world with 350,000 employees—sold the building and its naming rights, eventually filing for bankruptcy.

Jenny, meanwhile, zoomed in on the Trump International Hotel & Tower. Completed in 2009 and named after its brash and colorful owner, the building was home to not only a luxury hotel but apartments, condos, and business offices. It stood 92 stories and a whopping 1,398 feet including its spire.

Pete monitored the St. Regis Chicago, which had broken ground in 2016 and was completed in 2020. It was now the third tallest building in the city, clocking in at 101 stories and an impressive 1,191 feet.

The other two buildings didn't have balconies. Nor did they have windows that could be opened. Neither Marcus nor his colleagues saw anything that concerned them, but that hardly settled Marcus's nerves.

Now that the president and the pope had landed safely, Pete suggested they find a position overlooking the Jane Byrne Interchange between I-90/I-94 and I-290 to monitor the incoming motorcade. Marcus agreed, and they decided to join a team of DSS agents positioned on the roof of the Student Recreation Facility on South Halsted Street, located on the edge of the campus of the University of Illinois Chicago. That was the tallest building close to the city's central freeway interchange and would provide them with the best vantage point.

With no traffic, the drive—even with several checkpoints—was quick, and they soon found themselves with their colleagues.

Marcus wished the principals were taking Marine One to Soldier Field. The presidential helicopter would certainly have been faster. Typically, it was also considered the safest means of transportation for the president and his guests. Marine One did not travel alone. Rather, it flew in a package of three choppers that constantly rotated in flight to confuse any would-be terrorists as to which aircraft the president was actually in. Roseboro, however, felt a motorcade would be safer, arguing that if the Kairos operatives possessed surface-to-air missiles and had located themselves outside the security perimeter to avoid detection, they might be able to fire simultaneously and repeatedly on all three helicopters, potentially exhausting the choppers' onboard anti-rocket defenses and scoring a direct hit.

Hernandez had been skeptical, and Roseboro had conceded that there were risks to keeping him and the pope on the ground as well. On balance, however, he was convinced it was the right thing to do. After all, the principals would be traveling separately in limousines dubbed "the Beast." Specifically designed for the Secret Service, the limos were essentially luxury battle tanks, impregnable and capable of surviving a direct hit even by an anti-tank missile.

Both I-90 and I-290 were empty. They had been closed to all civilian traffic at midnight and had been thoroughly checked for IEDs and other explosive devices. Soon Marcus saw the first detachment of police motorcycles roaring toward them from the west. The rest of the motorcade would not be far behind.

His stomach in knots, he called Annie. "Anything?" he pressed, his voice thick with tension.

"Nothing," she replied, her voice just as tense. "Stay sharp. I'll call you if something breaks. Dell is calling. I've got to go."

Chicago PD and Secret Service helicopters crisscrossed the skies overhead. So did a dozen surveillance drones. Marcus and his team used their binoculars to scan every building lining the highways, looking for snipers or anything out of the ordinary. The problem was that windows of almost every apartment building close to the president's main route were open. People were hanging banners out of them, welcoming the leaders to Chicago. Some were waving and cheering and leaning out their windows. Others were cursing and shouting protests. Clusters of people were massing on rooftops. Some sat in lawn chairs. Others stood at the edges of their buildings, eager to catch a glimpse of history in the making.

Now a formation of CPD squad cars came into view, trailed by six identical black limousines. These were followed by a fleet of black SUVs carrying members of the Secret Service counterassault team, electronic jamming equipment, and plainclothes agents. Next came a line of black sedans carrying White House staff. These, in turn, were followed by white vans ferrying the White House press corps, a line of ambulances, more police squad cars, and another formation of police motorcycles.

Moments after the motorcade passed his position, Marcus watched it reach the next exchange and exit onto I-55, known as the Stevenson Expressway. From there, it turned without incident onto South Lake Shore Drive and then onto the grounds of Soldier Field.

Now what? Marcus thought. Had all their efforts spooked the Kairos teams? Or were they waiting for a more opportune moment?

Tariq Youssef and his team had slept on the floor of the law firm's conference room.

They'd awoken early, bowed toward Mecca, and made their final preparations. Now dressed as a FedEx driver, Youssef and one of his men took several elevators to get down to the tower's basement level and found the building's command center. Holding a large package in his arms, Youssef knocked twice. When the door opened, he said he had a delivery for the head of security.

"Neil, package for you," the man shouted back toward his three colleagues manning a bank of video monitors.

Youssef dropped the package, raised his silenced pistol, and shot all four men before they had any idea what was happening. Then he ducked back into the hallway and told his colleague to take over the center, lock the door behind him, call the law firm, and tell the rest of the team to meet him on the 103rd floor.

That done, Youssef headed to the freight elevator just down the hall. Six minutes later, the door opened on the 103rd floor. Exiting the elevator, Youssef drew his pistol, but there was no need. His team had already murdered everyone on the Skydeck.

"Good work, boys," he said. "Now open the crates and I'll be right there."

Walking over to the enormous plate-glass windows on the east side of the building, Youssef powered up his satphone and dialed a number from memory. "We're in place, Father," he said in Arabic. "Do we have authorization to proceed?"

"You do, my son," said the familiar voice, crystal clear though he was on a mountain half a world away. "And may Allah welcome you into paradise as the most worthy of *shahids*."

Marcus's phone rang.

It was Annie.

"One of the NEST teams just picked up a radioactive trail at O'Hare," she said.

"Near Air Force One?"

"No, in the parking lot outside the Signature Flight Support terminal."

"How strong is the reading?"

"Not that strong, actually. And so far, they haven't found anything inside the Signature offices or hangar. But they're still looking."

Marcus relayed the news to his colleagues.

"We should go check it out," Pete said.

"Why?" Jenny asked. "We don't bring any expertise to the table, and if there is an attack, we'd be twenty to thirty minutes out of position."

"Then what do you suggest?" Pete sniped. "We can't just stay here."

"I don't know. I don't like this any better than you do," Jenny shot back, growing visibly more frustrated by the minute.

"Now that the principals are in place, let's get ourselves back across I-90, within striking distance of the stadium," Marcus told them. "If there is an attack, we're not going to do any good on this side of the highway."

Jenny and Pete agreed. They quickly moved to the stairwell, got back down to the ground floor, and jumped into the Wrangler. Marcus took the wheel while Jenny checked in with Stone and Callaghan.

By the time they finally cleared through all the checkpoints and were back on the stadium side of I-90, the Mass was underway. They listened to live coverage on WGN, Chicago's leading news/talk radio station, which reported that there were now 109,426 people in or around the stadium, the largest crowd in Soldier Field's recent history. Typically, when the Bears were playing, the stadium held no more than 62,000.

Heading east on Ida B. Wells Drive toward Lake Michigan, they were just about to cross the river when Marcus's phone rang. With Marcus driving, Jenny answered it on the first ring.

"Annie, it's Jenny. No, he's driving. . . . What? . . . Here? In Chicago? You're sure?"

"What's the matter?" Marcus asked.

Rather than explain, Jenny put Annie on speaker. "Tell him."

"Marcus, it's your mom."

"What about her?"

"She's there."

"Where?"

"In Chicago, at the stadium."

"What are you talking about?"

"She sent me a text message a few hours ago on my personal phone. I just noticed it now. She says she's there with the Garcias and Maya Emerson."

"That's impossible. She never goes anywhere."

"She says she's been trying to reach you, to tell you, for days."

Marcus suddenly felt sick. "Can you call her?"

"Sure," Annie said. "But say what?"

Marcus had no idea. When he glanced at Pete and Jenny, it was clear they didn't either. "Just tell her you spoke to me and that she and Maya and the Garcias should leave the stadium immediately. Don't tell her why. Just tell her time is of the essence. They should leave and walk to the center of the city immediately."

"Marcus, that's not possible," Pete said from the backseat.

"Just do it, Annie—quickly—please."

"Marcus, she can't," Pete protested.

"Why not?"

"Don't you remember? There's no cell phone service in the stadium. You told Roseboro to turn off the local towers and cut off all service during the Mass."

Now Jenny's phone rang.

It was Dell at Langley. "Where's Marcus?" she demanded. "I can't get through."

"He's right here," Jenny said. "We were on the phone with Annie."

"Put me on speaker," Dell ordered.

Jenny did.

"Marcus?"

"Yeah."

"NSA just got a hit on that Kairos satphone."

"Where?"

"It was active for less than a minute, then went dark again."

"Where, Martha?" Marcus pressed.

"We're triangulating it now. Somewhere near the corner of West Adams and South Franklin."

"That's three blocks from here," Pete said. "Take a right."

Marcus turned the wheel hard, sliced across two empty lanes, and took a loop that soon put them on South Wacker Drive. Meanwhile, Jenny speed-dialed the Chicago PD operations center and relayed their location and destination. The last thing they needed now was to be stopped by some overzealous and misinformed cop.

Hitting the accelerator, Marcus blew through a red light at the intersection with West Van Buren Street and then another one at the intersection with West Jackson Boulevard.

Half a block farther, however, he had to slam on the brakes to keep from running a roadblock guarded by two APCs and about two dozen troops from the Illinois National Guard. Looking up, they suddenly saw why. They were directly out front of the Willis Tower. Every soldier was now pointing an M16 at their heads and chests. They were ordered to get out of the vehicle slowly, with their hands raised. Marcus shouted back that they were DSS agents, but for the moment, no one believed them. Using a bullhorn, the commander of the Guard unit ordered them all to lie down in the middle of the street, facedown, arms out. There was nothing they could do but comply. To argue at this point was to risk some overanxious Guardsman opening fire.

They were handcuffed. Searched. Their weapons were taken from them. So were their DSS badges, wallets, and phones. All of these were set on the hood of a vehicle that appeared to belong to the on-scene commander. Taking his own sweet time, the commander called into the Joint Task Force operations center near the stadium, explaining the situation and relaying the names and badge numbers and other relevant details.

Marcus's phone began to ring again. He could see it shifting and vibrating on the hood of the vehicle. But the commander was not looking at it, much less answering it. A few moments later, Pete's phone rang. Fifteen seconds later, Jenny's phone began ringing, too. None of them were answered. They just kept ringing, and Marcus was livid.

Marcus began to silently count down from fifty.

He had to calm himself down or he was going to make the situation worse. Another minute passed. Then two. Then three, though it seemed like an eternity. Finally Marcus could hear just enough of the conversation to tell him that the commander was now on the line with Roseboro.

Even from several yards away, Marcus could hear the DSS director screaming bloody murder at the commander, who was of course just trying to do his job but had no idea how much damage he was doing. Soon Marcus heard the commander apologizing profusely. Then he hung up.

"*Uncuff them—now—move,*" the commander barked at his men, who tried to apologize to Marcus and the others as well.

Marcus had no time for that. The moment he, Jenny, and Pete had their weapons and other possessions back, they sprinted for the front doors of Willis Tower. As they ran, Marcus called Roseboro back.

"NSA has isolated the signal," Roseboro told him. "103rd floor—east side. It's the Skydeck."

Outside the main lobby, they once again had to show their badges and IDs to police officers and National Guard troops standing post out front of the massive skyscraper.

Pete unleashed a torrent of profanity at the officers, demanding they let him and his colleagues through. But they were not listening. They said they needed to check everything Pete was saying with their superiors. This only further set Pete off. Even when Marcus put the lead officer on the line with the head of DSS, it was not enough. The officer claimed he needed to hear from the watch officer at the Joint Task Force. Turning red, Pete screamed that the head of DSS was in charge of the JTF and—

Marcus grabbed Pete, pulled him aside, and told him to shut up. He was not helping.

Stunned, Pete stopped talking.

Marcus apologized to the officer and calmly explained that they were federal counterterrorism officers. They were responding to a credible threat, and the officer and his men needed to stand down immediately or all be arrested.

At this, the officer carefully studied each of their badges again.

Just then the watch officer at the JTF center called the officer on his mobile phone. Marcus could not hear what the man was being told. Nor did he need to. When the brief call was over, the officer apologized, handed Marcus his own personal M4 automatic rifle and belt filled with extra magazines. He took off his bulletproof vest, gave this to Marcus as well, and told his colleagues to do the same for Agents Morris and Hwang. Then the officer opened the doors into the Willis Tower and stepped out of the way.

"Have your team guard the lobby," Marcus told him. "No one but federal agents allowed in. Got it?"

"Yes, sir," the officer said.

"And call the building security command center," Marcus added as he strapped on the ammo belt and pulled the vest over his head. "Have them call every office from the 102nd floor down. Tell them to evacuate immediately, but don't tell them why. And tell them they must take the stairs and keep the elevators clear for first responders. Clear?"

"Clear, but what about the Skydeck and above?"

"Everyone on the Skydeck is dead or a hostage."

With that, Marcus bolted past the metal detectors, across the lobby, and up one of the escalators near a Starbucks. Donning their equipment, Pete and Jenny soon did the same and raced up behind him.

Jenny's phone rang.

"Roseboro says we've got a DSS tactical unit inbound, along with a Secret Service CAT unit and a NEST team," Jenny told them as they approached the bank of elevators. "But he says not to wait."

Marcus hardly needed to be told that. He entered the number sixty-seven into the digital touch pad that directed the elevator control system. When one of the doors opened, they all stepped inside and ordered every employee and visitor stepping off the elevator to evacuate the building immediately. On a typical weekday, upwards of twenty-five thousand people worked in the building or passed through to visit, shop, or dine. Marcus had no idea how many would be here on a Saturday when traffic was so restricted, but he asked Jenny to call Roseboro back and have him reinforce the order to clear all floors under the Skydeck and not allow anyone new inside the building.

Then they were on an express elevator, heading to the 67th floor at 1,600 feet per minute. Marcus's ears popped.

Though the NSA believed the call had come from the 103rd floor, Marcus told Jenny and Pete they were not going there directly. It was too risky. They could be shot the moment the door opened. Instead, once they got to the 67th floor, they should each take separate elevators. He directed Jenny to the 101st floor and Pete to the 104th. Marcus told them that he would go to the 102nd. Once they got off, they should pick a stairwell and converge on the 103rd floor from all three directions. They had no idea how many terrorists they would be up against, but they had to move fast.

The elevator bell rang. Marcus swung the M4 over his back and drew his Sig Sauer. They still had nearly fifty floors to go, but he did not want to frighten civilians working in the building more than necessary. As the doors opened, a crowd of startled employees and a couple of maintenance people greeted them. Marcus flashed his badge and ordered them to tell everyone on their floor to evacuate and get out of the building as quickly and as quietly as possible, using only the stairs. Jenny added that they should text anyone else they knew on floors under 102 to evacuate as well. They did not say why. They just spread out and moved to separate banks of elevators.

Just then, however, Marcus's phone rang again. It was Dell.

"We're too late," she said. "They just fired."

128

Keeping Dell on the line, Marcus turned and raced down the hall.

It took a moment to find a window looking eastward, but when he did, he saw the contrail of an SA-7 shoulder-mounted rocket streaking toward the stadium. It did not, however, go through the open roof and into the stands. Instead, it scored a direct hit on the sole Patriot missile battery. The size and force of the explosion was like nothing he had ever experienced outside of combat.

Marcus sprinted back to the elevators. Boarding the first one that came, he headed upward, praying for his mother, for Maya, for the Garcias, and for every other soul in that stadium.

Alone in the elevator, his ears popped again. He was once more moving at 1,600 feet per minute, but it wasn't nearly fast enough.

The explosion shook the stadium violently and knocked the president off his feet.

Secret Service agents instantly responded. Amid the deafening screams of one hundred thousand people, they raced to Hernandez's side, lifted him under his arms, and manhandled him off the stage, his feet barely touching the floor. Simultaneously, Commander Gianetti and a team of DSS agents grabbed the pope and raced him out a separate exit and down a separate tunnel.

Marcus could feel his rage building as he passed the 98th floor.

Then the 99th and the 100th.

Telling Dell that he needed both hands free, he asked her to patch in through the DSS comms network and hung up. Through his earpiece, he could hear DSS agents shouting updates from multiple vantage points. The president, First Lady, and the pope were now in the Beast, tearing out of the parking garage and racing back to O'Hare and Air Force One. Holstering his Sig Sauer, Marcus grabbed the M4 from his back as he reached the 102nd floor.

"Carl, can you hear me?"

But Annie spoke instead.

"He's busy, Marcus. What do you need?"

"A dedicated channel." There was no way he could focus with all that was unfolding on the ground below.

"Got it. Hold on."

By the time the elevator doors opened on the 102nd floor, Marcus and his team were all switched to a secure and solo frequency. Bracing himself against the left wall of the elevator, he took a quick peek to the right and saw no one there. Pulling back, he waited a beat, then crossed to the other side of the elevator and took another fast look to the left. It, too, was clear, so Marcus moved into the hallway, weapon up and sweeping side to side. Reaching the closest stairwell, he threw the door open. He saw no threats and bounded up the steps two at a time.

When he reached the Skydeck, he paused, caught his breath, and rechecked his weapon. Suddenly he felt the building swaying. Some movement was typical from the fifty- to sixty-mile-an-hour winds that typically buffeted a skyscraper of this height, but this was far from normal. Glancing through the small square window in the door, he saw no one. To the right was a large pillar. He opened the door slowly and sprinted to the pillar. Now he heard the screaming howl of wind surging through the building and knew instantly what was happening. The terrorists had blown out at least one of superthick windows when they'd fired the rockets. With the roaring winds, Marcus didn't need to worry about not having a silencer. But his aim would be severely affected.

Then again, so would theirs.

Looking around the right side of the pillar, he had a clear view down the north side of the observation hall. He could see Lake Michigan and the gift shop. He saw no terrorists. He did, however, see the lifeless bodies of at least one uniformed guard and six visitors, including two small children, lying on the floor, pools of crimson soaking into the gray carpeting around them.

About twenty yards ahead, he could also see six long, rectangular boxes. He'd seen these before on the CCTV videos in Monterrey and Laredo. They were the ones Kairos had smuggled into the U.S., and they were all open.

129

In any other situation, Marcus would have advanced with stealth.

He had no idea how many Kairos operatives he was confronting or what kind of firepower they had, aside from the SA-7s. But there was no time for stealth. The terrorists had already fired one rocket and taken out the stadium's only air defense network. The next rocket was going to kill a lot of people. So Marcus said a silent prayer and charged forward.

Staying low, he sprinted toward the open cases. When he reached them, he stopped and ducked behind a shelf of books and knickknacks in the gift shop. Five of the six cases were empty. Only two rockets remained in the sixth case.

Suddenly he found a target. Not twelve feet ahead and off to his right was one of the terrorists. Sure enough, he had just reloaded a rocket launcher and was now taking aim. The stadium was less than two miles away. And the SA-7 had a range of almost three miles. From this height and angle, the man had a direct shot into the seats on the facility's western and northern sides.

Marcus opened fire. His first burst went wide. But the second hit its mark.

The man's head exploded just as he pulled the launcher's trigger. The man's body began to collapse to the ground, but the rocket had already erupted from the launcher. Marcus raced to another pillar, one from which he could see the rocket's trajectory. He didn't need to follow the contrail. The explosion told the story. The makeshift hospital on the far side of the west parking lot had just been obliterated, along with all the medical staff inside it.

Marcus stood there for a moment, staring at the carnage—until multiple rounds started tearing up the pillar he was crouching behind. Ducking down farther, he switched the M4 to full automatic, pivoted it around the pillar, and sprayed everything he had down the hallway. The incoming fire stopped, but so did the M4.

Ejecting the empty magazine, Marcus popped in another. Then he swung around the edge of the pillar and fired another burst. But no one was standing. He saw two bodies down next to another rocket launcher.

The pause lasted only a moment. More Kairos operatives—each carrying handguns, not automatic rifles—began firing back. Marcus ducked right, taking cover behind another pillar. He scanned the hall behind him but saw no sign of Jenny or Pete. He had no idea how many terrorists were out there, but they all now knew where he was.

Switching back to semiautomatic, he swung around the right side of the pillar and fired a quick burst. Then he made a dash for the west side of the hall, working his way around the far side of the gift shop. Everywhere he looked, he saw more dead bodies. Visitors. Skydeck employees. Two security guards. And several maintenance people. It was a bloodbath. Marcus berated himself for not getting there faster.

Glancing behind to make sure he was in the clear, Marcus sprinted ahead. Two terrorists were coming around the corner. He opened fire and dropped them both, then fired another burst into their lifeless bodies, just to be certain. Kicking their pistols away from them, more out of habit than necessity, Marcus wheeled around again, hearing footsteps behind him. Sure enough, someone was racing through the gift shop and charging toward him, firing two pistols at once. Marcus instinctively dropped to his right knee and opened fire. The first volley went wild, but the second burst ripped the man to shreds. He collapsed to the floor. His pistols went flying. And then, despite the roar of the wind, Marcus heard a hail of gunfire coming from behind him. He dove to the floor, and the shots missed him but the window behind him was blown out.

Suddenly the sixty-mile-per-hour Chicago wind coming off Lake Michigan swirled through the Skydeck. The terrorist rushing toward Marcus was still firing, but before Marcus could fire back, he watched the man get swept off his feet and blown out through the window frame and down 103 stories.

Facedown on the carpet, Marcus pressed himself as flat as he could.

Yet he could feel the gale-force wind pushing him toward the gaping hole in the side of the building. His M4 was the first to go, getting blown out of his hands and into the atmosphere, and Marcus feared he was next.

Grasping desperately for anything solid, Marcus's left hand found one of the bookshelves. If it was freestanding, Marcus knew he was about to die. Instead, he found it was bolted to the floor. He grabbed it with both hands and pulled himself toward the fixture with every ounce of strength in him. T-shirts, books, mugs, games, and every other possible kind of gift was flying past him and over his head in the wind tunnel created by the blown-out windows. To his right, Marcus saw another terrorist coming around the corner. But before the man realized the danger, he, too, was blown out of the building.

Scrambling to the leeward side of the shelf, Marcus stayed low and took a moment to catch his breath. He had lost track of how many terrorists were down. All he knew was that there had to be more and all he had left was the Sig Sauer in his shoulder holster. He had his earpiece in, but it didn't matter.

He couldn't hear a thing. There was no sign of his partners, nor could he communicate with them. He had to get to the east side of the Skydeck and neutralize any of the terrorists still alive before they could fire another rocket at the stadium.

Still on his stomach, Marcus army-crawled through the gift shop until he reached one of the massive round pillars. Ten feet away, he spotted one of the terrorists he had killed, lying facedown in a pool of blood. There was a Glock 9mm pistol lying beside him for the taking. It would be better to have two weapons than one, he decided. Marcus got up and was about to make a dash for the Glock when a hail of gunfire erupted from his right. He pulled back behind the pillar as rounds of ammo blew off chunks of concrete all around him. He had no doubt whoever was shooting at him was going to rush him the moment he realized Marcus was not shooting back.

Drawing his Sig Sauer, Marcus carefully rose to his feet and pivoted around the pillar. Sure enough, two gunmen were coming straight at him. He double-tapped one to the head, then shifted and fired three rounds into the other man's chest. Both were dead before they hit the floor.

Marcus began to wheel around to check his six but took a right jab square in the jaw. The sucker punch blindsided him and sent him reeling. Before he knew what was happening, his attacker had picked up the Sig Sauer and was standing over Marcus, aiming his own gun at him. He was shouting something, though Marcus couldn't hear a word. He did, however, recognize the face. He was staring into the eyes of Tariq Youssef, one of the Troika.

Marcus froze. He had no other pistol. No knife. And no time. Youssef was bent over, leaning forward, and straining to stay on his feet in the gusting wind. He raised the Sig Sauer a bit higher, squinted, and tilted his head slightly to the left.

Suddenly Marcus heard an explosion. Then another. Yet Marcus felt nothing. He'd seen no flash. There was no smoke coming out of the barrel. And yet . . .

Blood began to trickle out of Youssef's mouth. Then his eyes rolled up in his head. Then the Kairos operative collapsed to the ground. Standing behind him, no more than ten feet away, was Pete, an M4 in his hands.

It took a moment for Marcus to process how close he had come to dying, that Pete had just saved his life. Then Jenny came rushing to their side. Together, she and Pete pulled Marcus to his feet and into a nearby stairwell. Here, behind the shut door, it was quieter, though only slightly so. But they could talk to one another, even if they had to shout.

Pete went first. He had news and it wasn't good.

"Dell just radioed," Pete shouted. *"You didn't respond."*

"Couldn't hear," Marcus shouted back. *"Did you tell her the shooters are down?"*

"Yeah, yeah, but listen to me," Pete said. *"When the shooting started, Roseboro shut down all air traffic in- and outbound to O'Hare and Midway."*

"Finally."

"But there's still a plane on approach. It's not responding to any radio traffic, and it's heading toward us."

"What do you mean, us?"

"The stadium," Pete screamed.

"Now?"

"Yes."

"What kind of plane?" Jenny shouted.

"It's a 737—a cargo plane, DHL."

"From where?" Marcus asked.

"Grand Rapids."

"How far out?"

"Six minutes—no more—and the Patriot system was destroyed."

A chill went down Marcus's spine.

He shot out of the stairwell and back onto the Skydeck. Moving to the east end, keeping away from the dead bodies and the blown-out windows, Marcus looked out over Lake Michigan. But despite clear blue skies and very few clouds over the lake, Marcus didn't see a 737. He saw no planes of any kind. Of course, he'd pleaded with Hernandez and Roseboro to shut down all the airspace in the area until the event was over. He'd been overruled, and now . . .

No. Marcus wouldn't let himself go down that road. There was no time for recriminations. Moving to one of the high-powered viewing machines, he suddenly realized he had no change on him. Neither did Jenny. Nor Pete. There was no way to power up the tourist telescopes.

Marcus tasked Pete with retrieving both rocket launchers and Jenny with getting whatever rockets had not been fired. As they did so, Marcus continued scanning the skies to the northeast. Dozens of questions flooded his mind. Was the plane really a threat? Or just having radio problems? And if it was a threat, how in the world had Kairos operatives seized it?

Out of the stairwell and thus deafened again by the roaring winds, Marcus needed a way to communicate with his team and commanders. Still seeing nothing in the eastern sky, he created a group text with Dell, Roseboro, Annie, Jenny, and Pete. The moment he did and explained his situation, data began streaming in.

The plane was forty-three miles out.

It was moving at 564 miles an hour.

9.4 miles per minute.

That gave him barely four minutes to spot the plane and take it out.

Marcus asked where the F-22s were.

Roseboro replied that they had been scrambled but might not make it in time.

How could the fighters not already be in the air? Marcus asked himself, furious, but chose not to respond. There wasn't time, and it hardly mattered now.

Marcus looked up from his phone and strained to see anything in the distance. The visibility was perfect. He ought to be able to see up to fifty miles away. But so far, Marcus still saw nothing.

Are you absolutely certain it's a threat? he wrote.

Yes, Dell replied. **Michigan State Police just found the pilots and ground crew.**

A moment later: **Murdered.**

Then: **IDs missing. Security tapes show four men. Leader appears to be Zaid Farooq.**

Was that possible? Was Abu Nakba's chief of intelligence flying this plane?

Another text came in.

26 miles out.

Can't see it, he texted back.

Annie texted that the plane should be at Marcus's nine o'clock, if he was looking northeast. That surprised him. Grand Rapids was northeast of Chicago. Thus, the plane should be right in front of him. Maybe it had headed west for a while to throw off air traffic controllers before banking and heading for the stadium.

Marcus looked up again. This time he saw it. It was only a glowing speck in the sky as the sun reflected off the fuselage. It was right where they said it would be, but now it appeared to be heading east to approach the stadium from over the lake to the north.

Pete and Jenny rushed up behind him. Pete had found only one rocket launcher. The other, Pete motioned, had been sucked out of the building. Jenny had two rockets, which she carried in her arms like babies. They all knew the risks. They were handling radioactive devices. But cancer wouldn't kill them for years. This 737 could kill everyone left in the stadium in less than three minutes.

Pete loaded the SA-7. Jenny took the other rocket back into the stairwell, the safest place she could think of from the hole they were about to blast in the side of the building. Marcus smashed the glass of a fire control box next to the stairwell. From it, he pulled a fire hose, wrapped it several times around his waist, then double-checked and triple-checked to make sure the hose was properly screwed into the pipe running through the pillar. Then he took the rocket launcher from Pete, ordered his two friends back into the stairwell, and moved toward the northeast windows.

His hands were trembling, but this was it.

There was no time to practice.

He was out of time.

It was now or never.

Marcus hoisted the Russian SA-7 launcher on his shoulder.

He'd been trained in the Marines and the Secret Service on several American versions of MANPADS—man-portable air defense systems—though it had been years since he'd seen one, much less used one. Fortunately, the Russian version wasn't significantly different.

Taking aim, he could see the 737 clearly.

Too clearly.

It was barely ten miles out, losing altitude, and screaming toward the city.

At this range, he had less than a minute, and he worried his first shot might not work. If that was the case, would he even have time for a second?

Ten feet back from the window, Marcus powered up the weapon, set his stance to brace against the wicked recoil he knew was coming, and activated the automatic target lock. Then he took a deep breath, exhaled, and pulled the trigger. The five-foot, twenty-pound rocket erupted out of the tube and streaked across the Skydeck at twice the speed of sound, filling the hall with fire and toxic smoke and shattering the window almost instantly. The problem, as he had feared, was that the rocket's infrared sensor was destroyed upon impact with the superthick tempered glass window, driving the rocket far off course and into Lake Michigan.

Marcus ran back to the stairwell, struggling to maintain his balance now that fresh sixty-mile-per-hour winds were surging through the gaping new hole in the side of the building. Pete and Jenny quickly loaded the second rocket into the launching tube.

Moving back into position, Marcus again tried to stabilize himself, but the howling winds made that nearly impossible. He took aim again at the yellow-and-red 737 as best he could. Marcus couldn't hear the tone indicating he'd locked on to the jet. But there was no time to make adjustments. He could actually see Zaid Farooq in the cockpit and another jihadist at his side. It was only a matter of seconds before this 125,000-pound ballistic missile barreled into Soldier Field, killing upwards of 100,000 people, his mother and friends included.

Marcus pulled the trigger. Once again the rocket exploded out of the tube. Marcus held his breath as the missile streaked through the smashed-out window, then sliced across the sky and scored a direct hit, driving right through the windshield of the plane.

The explosion killed the terrorist piloting the plane instantly. But to Marcus's shock, the jet was not fully destroyed. Whatever was left of it had been knocked off course for sure. It was losing altitude fast. It was no longer headed for Soldier Field.

But an instant later the destroyed aircraft smashed headlong into the side of the Willis Tower, no more than five or maybe ten floors below them.

The building rocked violently on impact. Every window on the Skydeck was immediately blown out. Then came the massive fireball as five thousand gallons of aviation fuel set the iconic building ablaze. The combination of no windows, sixty-mile-an-hour winds, and a roaring fire threatened to suck Marcus right out of the building. His feet were already off the ground, and but for the fire hose tied around his waist, he would have been gone already.

Struggling to breathe amid the billowing smoke, Marcus used the hose to reel himself back in, but it was a losing battle. He felt his arms losing strength. Suddenly Pete and Jenny threw open the door to the stairwell. Pete grabbed hold of Marcus while Jenny held on to Pete. Straining against the surging winds, they were in danger of getting blown out of the building themselves. But eventually they were able to drag Marcus back into the stairwell. Pulling the door shut against the tempest was not an option. So they hauled Marcus down nearly a full flight of stairs until the hose wouldn't go any farther.

The problem now was that it was impossible to untie the hose as it had been pulled so tightly around Marcus's waist. Finally giving up on that option, both Pete and Jenny drew their utility knives and hacked away until Marcus was free.

Drenched with sweat from the heat of the flames and with no time to catch their breath, the two yanked the badly shaken Marcus to his feet and began hustling him down the stairs. They only descended three levels, though, before the heat became so intense that they could not proceed any farther. They could hear the raging fire below and the stairwell was filling with smoke.

Barely able to hear each other, they knew there was only one direction to move now.

Up.

Annie stood paralyzed as the 737 plowed into the tower, erupting in a fireball.

For several minutes, she just stared in horror at the video monitors.

She waited to hear Marcus's voice.

Or Jenny's. Or Pete's.

But all she heard was static.

Then, all at once, she snapped out of the daze and bolted from the command center. She prayed that Marcus and his team had survived. But there was nothing she could do for them. As for his mom and her friends, that might be a different story.

Sprinting across several parking lots, Annie had to make a wide berth around the roaring fires of the destroyed Patriot battery. Navigating past what was left of the makeshift field hospital took even more time. What's more, thousands of panicked people were rushing out of the stadium as she tried to force her way up a one-way street against traffic.

Marcus was desperate to get to the roof.

Only there, outside the concrete stairwell, would their satellite phones work. Only then, Marcus knew, could he call Roseboro and get a helicopter to pick them up and take them to safety. As Marcus ascended, however, he remembered that none of the employees who worked on floors above the Skydeck had been evacuated.

Coughing violently, he grabbed Pete and Jenny and pointed to the doorway to the 104th floor. Using hand gestures, he did his best to explain that he was going to round up anyone on the floor and send them to the roof. He motioned for them to clear the next two floors and meet him at the top. They instantly took his cue and raced to their assigned floors.

Marcus burst onto the 104th and found a mass of people terrified and huddled in the vestibule, away from the shattered windows. He tried shouting instructions to them, but no one could hear a thing. So he pointed to the roof. As they filed into the stairwell, Marcus moved from office to office, looking to see if anyone was still there. When he found two women hiding under a conference table, clutching one another, he pulled them out, led them to the stairwell, and again pointed to the roof. Then he made one last sweep around the floor to make sure no one else was left.

Back in the stairwell, Marcus was barely able to see because of the amount of smoke now pouring up from below. He knew Pete and Jenny were clearing the 105th and 106th floors, so he burst onto the 107th. It looked empty. He hoped people from the lower floors had already alerted them and sent them to the roof. Still, he could not bear the thought of anyone being left behind. Moving office to office, restroom to restroom, kitchen area to maintenance closet, Marcus finally confirmed that the floor was, in fact, clear.

He found Pete and Jenny back in the stairwell, and they all spread out on the final floor—the 108th—then raced up to the roof. Now that they were out of the wind tunnel created by the building's crosscurrents, the wind—though still strong—had lost some of its force.

Smoke was rising from the north, east, and west sides of the building. Still, the air was marginally more breathable than what they'd been experiencing for the last several minutes.

Jenny took a head count and found that there were only forty-two people total. Marcus had no idea how many people had been in the building at the time of impact, but he took some comfort in the fact that it wouldn't be twenty-five thousand. Still, he feared many others had come to watch the event at the stadium from the unique vantage point of their offices.

Annie finally pushed her way into the north entrance to the stadium.

She couldn't hear a thing over her earpiece due to all the screaming.

She called the command center on her satellite phone. Not wanting to bother Roseboro, whose hands were more than full, she asked for a deputy watch officer she'd met with. When he came on the line, she explained her location. *"I'm under the jumbotron. Pull up the seating chart."*

"All right—wait one," the deputy said.

Not only had DSS and the Secret Service required every person to have an assigned seat, they had also required attendees to upload their photo IDs to a special app a full week before the event so their names and images could be run against the terrorist watch list.

"Okay, I've got it," the deputy finally replied.

"I'm looking for a woman by the name of Marjorie Ryker," Annie shouted over the din. *"Last name: Romeo. Yankee. Kilo. Echo. Romeo."*

"Got it—Ryker, Marjorie—she was in the United Club skybox."

"Where's that?"

"East side—second floor—box 204."

Marcus pulled out his satphone and was about to call Roseboro.

Then something stopped him dead in his tracks.

The antennas.

There were two of them—white, thick, and towering another thirty or forty feet into the air, at least. In addition, there was a phalanx of smaller antennae, satellite dishes, HVAC equipment, and other mechanical gear. What there was not was any place for a helicopter to land.

Marcus had to fight the instinct to panic. For most of his life, fear had been foreign to him. Even now, he did not fear for his own life. But he could see the terror in the eyes of the people that he and his team had just led to the roof. They all could see the flames licking up the north and east sides of the tower. They all knew what had happened to the World Trade Center towers. On 9/11, the searing heat caused by the raging fires feeding on thousands of gallons of aviation fuel had melted the steel structure of the upper floors. Once the upper floors began to collapse, the crushing weight was simply too much for the lower floors to bear. That was why both of the towers in Manhattan had collapsed after only about thirty minutes, killing nearly everyone remaining in the buildings and the first responders attempting to rescue them.

Marcus told Jenny to direct everyone to sit down, stay calm, and if they were religious, pray. Meanwhile, he would call the DSS command center and figure out a plan. He asked Pete to care for anyone with immediate medical issues. Then Marcus ran to the south end of the roof and called the command center.

On speaker with Roseboro, Dell, and the senior watch commander, he summarized their situation. "I realize we can't land any choppers up here," he conceded, "but would it be possible for helicopters to hover and lower stretchers?"

"Impossible," Roseboro responded. "With the antennae, the choppers wouldn't be able to get close enough. And even if they could, I'm not certain we could get forty-five people off that roof in time."

In that instant Marcus realized that Roseboro—and probably Annie and the others—believed the tower was going down. And Marcus feared they might be right.

Air Force One streaked down O'Hare's runway 22R at full throttle.

The moment the Boeing 747-200B lifted off and began gaining altitude, its pilots fired the plane's unique rocket-like engines. This caused the plane—the newest craft in the fleet—to shoot nearly straight up into the sky, quickly reaching nearly the speed of sound. Flanked by an escort of four fully armed F-22 fighters, the jumbo jet banked to the southeast, far from the site of the crime, heading back toward Washington.

On board, the head of the Secret Service detail administered oxygen and heart medication to President Hernandez and the First Lady in their suite in the front of the plane while the chief of the White House medical unit and Commander Gianetti focused on the pontiff in the surgical suite in the back of the plane.

The pope had suffered a minor heart attack the moment DSS agents had put him in the presidential limousine and was now unconscious.

“Annie, are you there?” Marcus asked.

“No, she’s not,” Roseboro said.

Marcus was confused. “Get her, Carl—put her on the line.”

“I can’t,” Carl said. “She’s not here.”

“Why? Where is she?”

“In the stadium.”

“What for?” Marcus asked.

“She went in with the first responders. I think she’s looking for your mom.”

Marcus feared for all their lives: Annie’s, his mom’s, Maya’s, the Garcias’. But as there wasn’t a thing he could do for them, he knew he had to stay focused on those around him.

“Carl, are the fire-suppression systems in the building working?” he asked, abruptly shifting gears.

“On the floors impacted by the plane?” Roseboro asked.

“Right.”

“No, they’re not.”

"Then how are we going to put out this fire?"

"I've got planes and helicopters rushing to the scene with foam."

"Is that going to be enough?" Marcus asked.

It was a scenario they hadn't even discussed, much less war-gamed.

"I don't know. I hope so."

"Carl, I need to get these people off this building—*now*."

"We're working on it. Give me a few minutes."

"We don't have a few minutes."

"Hang in there, Marcus. We're going to figure this out. Believe me. I'll call you right back."

The line went dead.

The problem was that Marcus didn't believe Roseboro. He knew his friend wasn't purposefully lying to him. The man simply had his hands full with a far bigger rescue operation in the stadium. Looking eastward, Marcus could see the chaos unfolding on the ground. Roseboro and the rest of the Joint Task Force were in the throes of trying to evacuate a hundred thousand people from the stadium and doing so amid fires and radioactive material.

Marcus closed his eyes and said a prayer.

He needed wisdom and he needed it now, or they were all going to die.

When he opened his eyes again, he found himself looking at one of six pieces of robotic window-washing machinery. It was far from ideal. It wasn't going to be fast. But it just might work. More importantly, it was the best chance they had. Actually, Marcus realized, it was the only chance they had.

He dialed Roseboro again but got a busy signal. He called back four more times but didn't get through. The three direct numbers to the command post that he knew by heart were likewise dead ends. Marcus speed-dialed Annie but couldn't reach her either. Maybe that was for the best. By his count, the tower had been burning for twelve minutes. That gave him less then eighteen—at best—to get these people off the roof.

As Marcus was putting his phone back in his pocket, it rang. It was the deputy director of security for Willis Tower. Roseboro had told him to give Marcus anything he needed.

"Get me your boss," Marcus ordered.

"I can't," the deputy said.

"Why not?"

"He's dead, sir."

"Dead?"

"Everyone in our operations center was murdered," the man replied. "I would have been too, but they sent me for coffee. When I got back, the door was locked. Someone was in there but wouldn't let me in. A SWAT team eventually broke in and shot the guy dead."

Marcus was floored. But that certainly explained why there had been no rapid response to the slayings on the Skydeck until he and his team had arrived on scene.

"I'm sorry to hear that," Marcus said. "But I need the head of maintenance and I need him fast."

"All right, sir; hold on."

But two minutes went by, and he couldn't be found. Apologizing profusely, the man explained that cell towers and landlines were overwhelmed. And with fires raging between the 82nd and 91st floors, the building's internal communications system had shut down.

"Forget it," Marcus said. "I need to know how to operate the window-washing machines. I've got forty-five people up here, and I'm going to send them down the sides of the building. So walk me through it yourself."

"That's not my area, sir."

"I don't care," Marcus said. "You've seen it done, right?"

"Of course, but . . ."

"Listen, I don't have time for excuses—I'm counting six window-washing machines, right?"

"Right."

"Are there more?"

"No, just six."

"And how many people can fit on each one?"

"They're robotic, sir. They're not designed for anyone to ride down on them."

"I'm looking at one right now," Marcus said. "It's got a narrow section behind the washing unit itself. There's a place to stand. And there are places to clip in carabiners. That has to be for maintenance crews, right?"

"Sure, but again, they're not really built for—"

"Where are the safety harnesses and carabiners kept?"

"Well, uh, there's a mechanical room in the middle of the tower."

Marcus turned back, caught Jenny's eye, and waved her toward him. As she approached, he shouted for her to open the door to the mechanical room.

"It's locked," she shouted back.

Marcus took a deep breath to steady himself.

"Where are the keys?" Marcus asked the deputy.

"My boss had a pair. So do I. And the maintenance guys all have—"

"Is there a spare set up here?"

"No, no, I don't think so."

"Padlock?" he shouted to Jenny.

"Right."

"Shoot it off."

Marcus watched Jenny fire her Sig Sauer at the door.

With the padlock blown off, Marcus shouted at her to bring every safety harness she could find and get them to him quickly.

Speaking again into his phone, he asked the man how to power up the cranes that moved the window-washing units into position. The security chief walked him through each step as best as he could remember. Soon, all six units were firmly and securely attached to the edge of the south side of the building, the only side where there were no flames or smoke. Not yet, anyway.

When Jenny brought over the vests, he ordered her to race back to the group.

"Start sending people over here in groups of six—women first—go," he said.

Then he pressed the phone back to his ear and addressed the chief of security.

"How much weight can each of these machines bear?"

"I don't know."

"Do you have the manual there? Look it up."

"No."

"Where is it?"

"The chief of operations has it."

"Where?"

"In his office, I suppose."

"Get it."

"I would but—"

The line went dead. Marcus looked at his phone. The battery had just died. He glanced back at his watch. Sixteen minutes had gone by. There was a real likelihood that none of them were going to make it. Still, he refused to give up and shouted for Jenny and Pete to move faster.

The first batch of six people were approaching. But as Marcus looked down at his feet, he found only six safety harnesses.

"Put these on," he ordered them.

"You've got to be kidding," one woman protested.

"Fine—go without one or stay up here and die," Marcus said. "There's no time for a discussion."

He motioned for Pete and Jenny to keep all the others back for the moment. Then he explained what was about to happen to the six people in front of him and helped them into their harnesses. Attaching each carabiner to the window-washing unit, he helped each person—drenched in sweat yet shivering with fear—over the ledge and onto the narrow platform. There was no point telling them to stay close together. It was obvious the platform was not made for six. But Marcus assured them the device could sustain their weight and prayed that was true.

When everyone was in, he showed the woman closest to him the control panel, just as the security chief had explained to him. He showed her how to set the system into manual override so they would not automatically stop at every floor. He also showed her how to go at the fastest speed. Then before she could respond, he hit the green button and sent them hurtling downward. There was no time to tell them more.

Now he shouted for Pete and Jenny to bring the next group.

Quickly and in a tone that projected confidence he didn't actually have, Marcus explained how little time they had and that this was the only way down. He also explained that there had only been six safety harnesses and that he had given them all to the women in the first wave. Then he ordered the next six women to get in. Only two of them could do it. So Marcus brought four more from the next group and told them to get in. At the same time, he told Pete and Jenny to load the remaining four machines.

Shouting at the top of his lungs, Marcus walked everyone through the process. Then one by one, he and his colleagues hit the green Go buttons, and the next five machines began their rapid descent down the south side of the tower.

A total of thirty-six people had been evacuated. There were only nine more, including Marcus, Jenny, and Pete. But where were the machines? Why weren't they coming back up? How long would it take? Marcus had no idea. Glancing at his watch, he found that twenty-nine minutes had already passed. Marcus could feel the building rocking beneath them. He could see the fear growing in everyone around him.

Marcus ordered everyone to hit the deck, lying facedown. Tanker planes were approaching from the northeast. Seconds later, the first plane roared overhead and released its flame-suppressing foam. Marcus and the others were not hit directly, but much of the rest of the roof was, and the wind pushed some of it onto them. The next three planes did better, hitting their marks directly, or almost so, as did the three tankers after that.

Marcus checked his watch.

Thirty-two minutes had passed.

Then thirty-three.

Thirty-four.

Thirty-five.

Finally Marcus heard one of the window-washing units arrive back at the roof. It was the first one they'd used, so the safety harnesses came with it. Marcus and his colleagues scrambled to their feet, put the remaining six employees in the vests, and clipped them into the machine. Marcus did not waste time explaining the procedures again. He simply hit Go and heard them scream as they dropped from the sky.

Annie finally reached the United Club.

The place was on fire and filling with smoke. It was also empty.

No one was around.

Bursting into box 204, Annie found the windows shattered, the ceiling partially collapsed, wires sparking, and pieces of charred shrapnel all around. Mrs. Ryker and Maya Emerson were covered in blood. So were Mr. Garcia and his wife. Mrs. Garcia was unconscious, and her husband was giving her mouth to mouth.

"Annie," Marjorie shouted. *"What are you doing here?"*

"I came for you guys," she said, rushing to her side. "Where are you hurt?"

The woman had cuts and contusions all over her body, but she wouldn't accept help. Nor would Maya. Louisa Garcia had just suffered a heart attack, and knowing Annie had first aid training, Marjorie begged her for help.

"Do you know CPR?" Javier Garcia asked, his hands trembling, his face covered in blood and tears. "I don't. I'm just trying to—"

"Yes, yes," Annie said, asking him to move aside.

She bent down and listened for a heartbeat. Finding none, she told everyone to back up, then slammed the woman's chest with her fists as hard she could. Then again. Then a third time. And a fourth.

It worked. She felt a beat, though it was erratic.

Annie pinched the woman's nose, tilted her head back, and blew a lungful of air into her mouth. Then she began compressing the woman's chest cavity, desperate to get and keep her heart pumping again.

Mr. Garcia dissolved into tears, begging Annie to save his wife as Marjorie and Maya laid their hands on his back and prayed aloud in the name of Jesus for the Lord to work a miracle and do it fast.

They were now at thirty-nine minutes.

If this tower was going down, it was going down soon. Marcus couldn't believe it hadn't gone down already.

At the forty-two-minute mark, another machine reached them.

"After you," he shouted to Jenny.

But all the color drained from her face as she looked over the edge.

"No, you first," she replied, her knees beginning to buckle under her.

This was a strong woman. One of the strongest Marcus had ever met. She had taken a bullet for him in Moscow. She'd saved his life numerous times. This was the most afraid he had ever seen her. But Pete did not wait. Climbing over the edge, holding on for dear life as the fierce winds along the side of the skyscraper threatened to blow him away, Pete got into the second machine, crouching down somewhat to balance himself.

"We're out of time, Jenny—if we're going, we have to go now," Marcus shouted, just as scared as she was but knowing there was literally no other option.

Holding her under the arms as tightly as he possibly could, making it difficult for her to even breathe, he helped Jenny over the edge. Pete reached up and grabbed her around the waist, holding her just as tightly until she dropped down into the machine and collapsed to her knees. Pete told her to put her head down between her legs to battle the nausea.

And then it was Marcus's turn.

And there was no one to help him climb over the edge.

Staring down 109 floors, Marcus wasn't sure he could do it. For almost a minute, he became fixated on the height and the whipping winds and the perspiration on his hands and the surging flames. Pete and Jenny were screaming at him to get in. He'd said it himself. They had to go now, or they might not have another chance. But the fear overtaking him was unlike anything he had ever experienced in combat or even in captivity.

But it really was now or never.

Gripping the metal railing as tightly as he possibly could, his hands shaking as much as his legs, Marcus turned himself around so he was facing the roof. Slowly he lifted his right leg over the edge and stepped onto the top of the machine. Just as slowly, he swung his left leg over the edge and did the same. But as he did, he slipped. His right foot hit the Go button and with a jolt, the machine started down.

Jenny gasped. Marcus gripped the railing for dear life but had only a split second to decide. Pull himself back up. Or let go and hope he landed squarely on the platform, narrow though it was.

There was no time to think.

No time to hesitate.

Marcus let go.

Jenny screamed.

Only Marcus's right leg had landed inside the machine. His left knee hit the outer edge, sending a searing pain up his leg. He was losing his balance and leaning too far to the left. His right hand grabbed for something, anything, but found nothing. Marcus began to hurtle over the edge when Pete and Jenny lunged for him, grabbed hold of his shirt and belt, and with everything they had, yanked him back. They collapsed on top of one another, grasping for any part of the machinery they could and trying to steady themselves as the platform plunged toward street level.

None of them spoke. For thirty or forty floors, they dared not move. About halfway down the 1,400-foot drop, though, they tried to shift their weight and get a bit more comfortable. But the machine began to sway back and forth. Gears started scraping against the side of building and Marcus feared the whole thing might detach.

All three of them froze and remained still for the next terrifying minutes.

Marcus closed his eyes. He couldn't bear to watch. Wind surged through his hair. He was having trouble breathing. But finally, six terrifying minutes later, the computerized tracking system slowed them to a smooth, almost-gentle stop two feet above the plaza around the tower. Marcus opened his eyes, his stomach in his mouth. He pulled himself to his feet, legs shaking beneath him, and climbed over the edge and jumped to the pavement. Pete helped Jenny do the same. Then Pete jumped down as well.

Marcus steadied them both, made sure they were okay, then turned away and vomited all over the sidewalk.

First responders raced to them. Police officers and FBI agents surrounded them and held back the crowd of bystanders and news crews that had been watching the terrifying ordeal unfold. Finally a team of paramedics helped Marcus into the back of an ambulance, put an oxygen mask over his face, and started taking vital signs. An EMT gave him a shot of something to calm his nerves. Marcus had no idea what. He could tell one of the medics was saying something but could not make out the words.

The oxygen helped.

So did the Valium or whatever it was.

Almost immediately, Marcus felt his heart slow as he sat in the back of the ambulance and scanned the chaos all around him. Pete and Jenny were gone. They'd been right beside him, he told a paramedic, but now he'd lost them.

The young woman, seeing him searching, told him his friends had been rushed to the hospital—a precautionary measure, she thought, though she wasn't actually sure.

"You should go as well, sir," she told him.

"No, I need to get to the stadium," Marcus replied, taking off the oxygen mask.

"That's not possible, sir. It's bedlam over there."

But Marcus wasn't going to take no for an answer. He flashed his badge, then spotted an FBI agent and waved him over.

"My name is Ryker," he said, still trying to catch his breath. "I'm with DSS."

"I know who you are," the agent said.

"Then get me to the stadium—*now*."

Marcus called Annie, but she didn't answer.

He called the command center lines but got busy signals.

By the time the DSS van he was riding in reached the west parking lot of the stadium, the place was filled with fire trucks, ambulances, and hazmat units. To their left, two Coast Guard MH-60 Jayhawk helicopters were landing side by side. That drew his eye, and as he looked in that direction, Marcus spotted paramedics rushing two stretchers over to the choppers. Then he spotted Annie, Maya, and Mr. Garcia. Fearing the worst, he ordered the driver to head that way. He jumped out of the van before it stopped and reached the first chopper in time to see Mrs. Garcia, drenched in blood, being loaded inside.

"Marcus," Annie shouted over the roar of the rotors. "Thank God you're safe," she said, wrapping her arms around him.

He held her tightly, grateful she, too, was alive. Then he saw his mom being loaded into the second chopper. He raced to her side, but she told him she was fine. Cut up, but fine.

"Go with Louisa," she insisted. "Maya will come with me, and we'll see you there."

Marcus was going to protest, but Javier grabbed him.

"Marcus, please come with us."

Marcus nodded and followed the older man and Annie into the first chopper with two paramedics. They lifted off and headed south.

Minutes later they were landing on the roof of the University of Chicago's level-one trauma center. A team of doctors was waiting for them. Mrs. Garcia was rushed inside while Annie, holding her hand, did her best to answer their many questions.

Marcus helped his former father-in-law into a wheelchair and then into an exam room. Javier was pleading to stay with his wife, and the nurse promised she would take him to her soon. First, however, she needed to treat him.

"I'm fine," he protested. "It's my wife who needs help."

"And she's getting the best care in the city," the young woman replied. "But right now, Mr. Garcia, I need you to lie down. I'm going to give you oxygen, and I need to take your blood pressure."

He continued to protest until Marcus took his hand, looked him in the eye, and told him everything was going to be fine.

Finally Javier lay back on the examining table as a doctor and a second nurse entered the room.

"Agent Ryker, I'd like you to lie down as well," the doctor said.

"No, really, I'm fine," he protested. "I just—"

"Agent Ryker, you're not fine," the doctor said calmly. "You've lost quite a bit of blood, and you've got third-degree burns on your hands and forearms."

Marcus just stared at the man.

"How do you know who I am?" he asked.

The doctor said nothing but nodded toward a television mounted on the wall. It was tuned to one of the local TV stations, replaying the events of the past hour, including footage from far away of Marcus firing the rocket at the 737 and helping people off the roof of the Willis Tower.

Glancing from the TV set to the doctor's name badge, Marcus realized that this man was the head of the trauma center, and he was still insisting that Marcus lie down. Marcus looked down at his shirt. It was soaked in blood. He looked at his hands and arms. They really were burned. In the surge of adrenaline back in the tower, he hadn't realized he'd been shot. He hadn't felt the effect of the rocket exhaust or the rest of the flames. Now, as the adrenaline wore off, he did.

Obeying the doctor, Marcus climbed onto an examining table as a nurse helped him lie back. And the last thing he remembered was hearing Mr. Garcia say, "Please, Doctor, take good care of this boy. He's a son to me."

Marcus awoke in a private room.

He had no idea how long he'd been under. But when a nurse came in to check on him, she informed him that he'd undergone surgery and been given several blood transfusions and that it had been Annie—type O—who'd donated it.

"That girl—" she smiled—"she's a keeper, she is. Your wife?"

Marcus didn't have the energy to tell the woman they weren't married, and after checking his vitals, she was gone anyway. Soon, however, his mom stepped into the room. She had bandages on her face and arms but quickly assured him that she was fine and would be as good as new before long.

"I'm sorry, Mom."

"My goodness, for what?"

"Not calling you back. For being so busy."

"Well, you lived—and saved all our lives—so I guess I'll forgive you this time." She smiled. "But don't let it happen again, young man."

"How's Mrs. Garcia?" he asked.

"Better than you."

"Really?"

"Really—Annie saved her life."

"Are you serious?"

"Louisa wouldn't have made it without that girl."

"I'm not sure I would have either."

For once, his mom didn't comment. Instead, she kissed him on the forehead, told him to rest, and said she'd check back on him in a few hours.

When she left, the door didn't close entirely. Marcus could see a DSS agent standing in the hallway. He could also hear voices and realized they belonged to Javier, Maya, and Annie.

"I don't know how I can ever repay you, Miss Stewart," he heard Mr. Garcia say. "My Louisa would never have made it without you. I cannot thank you enough."

"I'm so glad she's making such a fast recovery, Mr. Garcia," he heard Annie reply. "And you too. How are you feeling?"

"Still a little shaky. But I'll be fine."

"Good. And your girls? Are they here yet?"

"Soon."

Marcus heard a phone ring. He knew that ring. It was Annie's satphone.

"Excuse me, Mr. Garcia. It's the White House. I need to take this."

"Do what you have to do, young lady. I just wanted to come over and say thank you."

"You're most welcome, sir. God bless you."

"And you, Miss Stewart."

It was quiet for a bit. Marcus tried to sit up but was in too much pain. He strained to hear more over the hum of the emergency wing and the still-incoming ambulances. Pulling back the sheet covering him, he could now see all the gauze and bandages and medical tape covering the right side of his stomach near his hip. He realized, too, that he was hooked up to an IV and to a range of monitors.

Laying his head back on the pillow, he now heard Mr. Garcia's voice again. "Maya, who is that exactly?"

"Who, honey?" Maya asked in her distinctive Southern drawl.

"Miss Stewart."

"Annie? Why she's the new deputy director of the CIA, not to mention one of my dearest friends."

"But how does she know Marcus?" he asked. "They seem, I don't know, close."

Marcus tensed.

"You really don't know?" Maya asked.

"Know what?"

"Marj hasn't told you?"

"Told me what?"

"Maybe we should talk about this later."

"No, tell me now," Mr. Garcia insisted.

"Well, Javier, it's like this," Maya said. "Yes, they're close. That young lady is dating Marcus."

There was a long, uncomfortable pause.

"Dating him?"

"Yep. I didn't know you weren't aware."

"No," he said, almost inaudibly. "No one told me."

Then it was quiet again, until Mr. Garcia walked into the room.

"Marcus, is it true?" he asked.

"Is what true, Mr. Garcia?" Marcus asked, trying to buy some time as he had no idea how best to respond.

This was, after all, a man who hadn't spoken with him in years. Had banned his family from all contact with Marcus after the deaths of Elena and Lars. And now . . .

"Are you and Miss Stewart . . . ?" he asked, his voice trailing off. "Are you . . . seeing each other?"

"Yes, sir."

There was another awkward silence.

"Just recently," Marcus added. "But yes, sir. We are."

The man stood still in the center of the room. He turned and looked out the window. Then turned back and looked Marcus in the eye.

"That's good," he said, tears welling up in bloodshot eyes. "She's remarkable. And . . . and I want you to be happy."

The man was fighting to control his emotions.

"You deserve to be happy, Marcus. You're a good man. And it was not your fault. It was not your fault. . . ."

The man's hands shot to his face as he dissolved into tears. Then he left the room as quickly as he came.

Marcus lay in silence for several minutes. It *wasn't* his fault. It wasn't. He'd done everything to protect the man's daughter and his only grandson. Now Mr. Garcia knew it too. He really knew. And Marcus could finally rest.

EPILOGUE

COROLLA, NORTH CAROLINA

Marcus looked out over the Atlantic and the children playing on the shore.

From behind a pair of Ray-Bans, he was enjoying the monotony of the waves lapping on the shore. And watching an old couple feeding the seagulls. And a young couple strolling down the beach, hand in hand, splashing their feet in the surf.

Nearly three weeks had passed since the events in Chicago. Now here he was, recovering at Annie's beach house, sitting on her porch in an Adirondack chair, wearing shorts and a polo shirt, sipping a freshly brewed cup of coffee. His hands and arms were still wrapped in gauze. So was his left knee, which had been more badly damaged than he'd first realized. And his stomach, of course. The stitches were still in. He still found himself wincing in pain when he got up or sat down. But he was finally on the mend and enjoying the company of his nurse.

The team had called twice to check in on him. The president had called once. Commander Gianetti had even called to express his gratitude and that of his boss. The pope was recovering nicely, and the public had never even been told about the heart attack. "Why give Abu Nakba, wherever he is, the satisfaction?" the pope had quipped. And though it had hurt to do so, Marcus had laughed, enjoying the man's courage under fire and overall joie de vivre.

Beyond this, however—and a few calls with his mom and sisters—Annie had shielded him from the deluge of calls and emails and from the news and from the congressional investigations into how Chicago had happened, as well as from coverage of the confirmation hearings for the country's new vice president, secretary of state, and director of the CIA.

She had certainly shielded Marcus from the ongoing hunt for Abu Nakba. The founder of Kairos had once again vanished into thin air. The last known sighting of him had been in the mountains of Kandahar. After that, the trail had once again gone cold.

And yet, what really was left of Kairos? Every member of the Troika was dead. Three cells of the group's most senior and experienced operatives were dead. The Kremlin was actively helping hunt down and uproot the terrorist network, the price Hernandez had imposed on Petrovsky for not exposing the fact that the SA-7s had carried radioactive material that had come, originally, from Moscow.

The damage in Chicago had been extensive. But by the grace of God, the death toll had not. The stadium and its surrounding areas were not a nuclear hot zone. The warheads had not contained as much uranium as originally feared. And the Willis Tower was still standing. It would remain empty for many months to come. But air crews had extinguished the fire rather quickly, and given that the plane had been a 737 and not a 757 or 767—and had been mostly destroyed by the SA-7 and thus hadn't plunged into the tower intact—the attack hadn't proven anywhere near as devastating as 9/11.

There was much to be thankful for. But the truth was Marcus had not had the time or energy to focus on almost any of these matters. Not in any depth, anyway. For the two weeks he had spent in the hospital under the watchful eye of a dozen federal agents—including Pete, Jenny, Geoff, and Donny Callaghan—he had mostly been sedated. After his release, Annie had asked that they be flown to her home in South Carolina. Then somehow she had persuaded Hernandez and Dell that she and Marcus wouldn't need armed protection any longer. She was going to take him to a "secure and undisclosed location" to rest and recover. Far from Kairos. Far from the Iranians. Far from Washington. And his friends. And even his family.

And for this Marcus was most grateful.

"Hey, sleepyhead," Annie said as she stepped out onto the porch in a sundress, kissed him, and sat down next to him with a cup of tea. "How are you feeling today?"

"Happy," he said, taking off his sunglasses. "Really happy. And I haven't been this happy in a long, long time."

"I'm glad," she said with that beautiful smile and those emerald eyes. "So am I."

"Thank you," he said.

"For what?" she asked. "Saving your mom? Your friends? Whisking you away to paradise? That pretty darn good French roast I just made?"

He laughed, though it hurt.

"For waiting for me till I was ready," he said, more serious than she'd expected.

"I was starting to think you'd never come around."

"Well, I'm not the sharpest knife in the drawer," he conceded. "But I'm in love with you, Annie Stewart. Utterly, completely, head over heels in love with you. And even though there's no way I can get down on my knees right now, I'd really like to ask you: would you marry me?"

The question completely blindsided her.

As did the diamond ring he produced from his pocket.

She could barely speak.

"What? How? But where . . . ?"

"I bought it after our second date," he confessed. "That's when I knew. Last week, just before I was discharged, when Mr. Garcia came by to see me, you stepped out to take a call. I told him about it and asked him to have it sent from my house. And he did. He told me if I had any brains at all, I would propose to you the first chance I had. And then he said he hoped we would invite him and his family to our wedding."

Annie's eyes filled with tears.

"So please say yes, Annie—it's already been a week, and Mr. Garcia is waiting for an answer."

"Then yes, Marcus Johannes Ryker, I can't think of anything I'd like more than to be your wife, crippled or not," she replied. "I love you so much."

"I know," Marcus said, slipping the ring on her finger. "And I couldn't be more grateful."

As he was nearly immobile, Annie got up out of her seat, wiped her eyes, and knelt beside him. Then she put her arms around his neck and kissed him until he could barely breathe.

ACKNOWLEDGMENTS

Someone once said, "The two most important dates in a man's life are the day he is born and the day he realizes *why* he was born."

For reasons beyond my understanding, I was born to be a storyteller. It took me a while to understand that, but the day I did changed everything.

I couldn't love this calling more, but I couldn't do it without an amazing team for whom I am deeply and forever grateful.

Scott Miller remains my rock-star literary agent and dear friend from the first days of my career as an author—he and the Trident Media Group are fantastic.

Tyndale House remains my rock-star publishing team for all but my first two novels and they are equally fantastic—Mark Taylor, Jeff Johnson, Ron Beers, Karen Watson, Jeremy Taylor, Jan Stob, Andrea Garcia, Maria Eriksen, the entire sales force, and all the remarkable professionals who make Tyndale an industry leader. Thanks to copy editor Erin Smith. And yet again my deepest gratitude to Jeremy Taylor, without question the best editor in the business, and to Dean Renninger, who keeps designing one amazing book cover after another.

Nancy Pierce remains my rock-star executive assistant after all these many years. She takes care of all my logistical needs, from scheduling and correspondence to flights and finances and so much more—always with good cheer, grace, and faithful prayer. God bless you and thank you, Nancy!

My parents, Len and Mary Jo Rosenberg, are a Rock of Gibraltar for me, as are all of my extended family and Lynn's. Year after year, they love me, pray for me, encourage me, keep my feet firmly planted, and truly make me laugh!

Our sons and their wives are a treasure to me: Caleb and his lovely wife, Rachel; Jacob; Jonah and his lovely bride, Cassandra; and Noah.

And my wife, Lynn, is a saint to me—the wellspring of joy in my life and such a gifted teacher and storyteller in her own right. I love you so much, sweetheart! Thank you, thank you, thank you for loving me.

ABOUT THE AUTHOR

Joel C. Rosenberg is a *New York Times* bestselling author of seventeen novels and five nonfiction books with nearly 5 million copies in print.

Rosenberg's career as a political thriller writer was born out of his filmmaking studies at Syracuse University, where he graduated with a BFA in film drama in 1989. He also studied for nearly six months at Tel Aviv University during his junior year. Following graduation from Syracuse, he moved to Washington, D.C., where he worked for a range of U.S. and Israeli leaders and nonprofit organizations, serving variously as a policy analyst and communications strategist.

He has been profiled by the *New York Times*, the *Washington Times*, and the *Jerusalem Post* and has appeared on hundreds of radio and TV programs in the U.S., Canada, and around the world. As a sought-after speaker, he has addressed audiences at the White House, the Pentagon, the U.S. Capitol, the Israeli president's residence, the European Union parliament in Brussels, and business and faith conferences in North America and around the world.

The grandson of Orthodox Jews who escaped out of czarist Russia in the early 1900s, Rosenberg comes from a Jewish background on his father's side and a Gentile background on his mother's side.

Rosenberg is the founder and chairman of The Joshua Fund, a nonprofit educational and humanitarian relief organization. He is also the founder and editor in chief of All Israel News (allisrael.com) and All Arab News (allarab.news).

He and his wife, Lynn, are dual U.S.-Israeli citizens. They made aliyah in

2014 and live in Jerusalem, Israel. They have four sons, Caleb, Jacob, Jonah, and Noah.

For more information, visit joelrosenberg.com and follow Joel on Twitter (@joelcrosenberg) and Facebook (facebook.com/JoelCRosenberg).

FROM *NEW YORK TIMES* BESTSELLING AUTHOR

JOEL C. ROSENBERG

"IF THERE WERE A *FORBES* 400 LIST OF GREAT CURRENT NOVELISTS, JOEL ROSENBERG WOULD BE AMONG THE TOP TEN. HIS NOVELS ARE UN-PUT-DOWNABLE."

STEVE FORBES, EDITOR IN CHIEF, *FORBES* MAGAZINE

FICTION

J. B. COLLINS NOVELS

THE THIRD TARGET

THE FIRST HOSTAGE

WITHOUT WARNING

DAVID SHIRAZI NOVELS

THE TWELFTH IMAM

THE TEHRAN INITIATIVE

DAMASCUS COUNTDOWN

JON BENNETT NOVELS

THE LAST JIHAD

THE LAST DAYS

THE EZEKIEL OPTION

THE COPPER SCROLL

DEAD HEAT

THE AUSCHWITZ ESCAPE

MARCUS RYKER NOVELS

THE KREMLIN CONSPIRACY

THE PERSIAN GAMBLE

THE JERUSALEM ASSASSIN

THE BEIRUT PROTOCOL

THE LIBYAN DIVERSION

NONFICTION

ENEMIES AND ALLIES

ISRAEL AT WAR

IMPLOSION

THE INVESTED LIFE

EPICENTER